ARTHUR

Arthur is the third and fi.... ....or of the Pendragon cycle: a magnificent epic set against the backcloth of Roman Britain and the legends of Arthur and lost Atlantis.

'Arthur is no fit king. Merlin's pawn, he is lowborn and a fool. He is wanton and petty and cruel — a sullen, ignorant brute.

All these things and more men say of Arthur. Let them.

When all the words are spoken and the arguments fall exhausted into silence, this single fact remains: we would follow Arthur to the very gates of Hell and beyond if he asked it. Show me another who can claim such loyalty.

"Cymbrogi," he calls us: companions of the heart.

Cymbrogi! We are his strong arm, his shield and spear, his blade and helm.

Cymbrogi! We are earth and sky to him. And Arthur is all these things to us and more.

Ponder this. Think long on it. Only then, perhaps, will you begin to understand the tale I shall tell you . . . '

STEPHEN LAWHEAD has established his name among the front ranks of contemporary fantasy authors. His novels bear the hallmarks of a master storyteller— compelling narrative, gripping suspense and awesome climax. Among his dozen or more novels the *Pendragon* cycle and the three books which make up his *Song of Albion* trilogy are the most recent and the most outstanding.

Research for his Celtic-based novels led Lawhead, an American, to Oxford, where he now lives and works with his wife, writer Alice Slaikeu Lawhead, and their two sons, Ross and Drake.

ARTHUR

BOOK III OF THE PENDRAGON CYCLE

STEPHEN LAWHEAD

A LION BOOK

Copyright © 1989 Stephen Lawhead

Published by
Lion Publishing plc
Sandy Lane West, Oxford, England
ISBN 0 7459 1311 3

First published by Crossway Books
Published by arrangement with Good News Publishers

First UK edition 1989
20 19 18 17 16 15 14 13 12 11

All rights reserved

A catalogue record for this book is available
from the British Library

Printed and bound in Great Britain
by Caledonian International Book Manufacturing, Glasgow

**FOR ALICE
WHOSE LABOUR AND LOVE WAS
NO LESS THAN MY OWN**

PRONUNCIATION GUIDE

While many of the old British names may look odd to modern readers, they are not as difficult to pronounce as they seem at first glance. A little effort, and the following guide, will help you enjoy the sound of these ancient words.

Consonants — as in English, but with a few exceptions:
c: hard, as in *c*at (never soft as in *c*entury)
ch: hard, as in Scottish Lo*ch*, or Ba*ch* (never soft, as in *ch*urch)
dd: th as in *th*en (never as in *th*istle)
f: v, as in o*f*
ff: f, as in o*ff*
g: hard, as in *g*irl (never *g*em)
ll: a Welsh distinctive, sounded as 'tl' or 'hl' on the sides of the tongue
r: trilled, lightly
rh: as if hr, heavy on the 'h' sound
s: always as in *s*ir (never hi*s*)
th: as in *th*istle (never *th*en)

Vowels — as in English, but with the general lightness of short vowel sounds:
a: as in f*a*ther
e: as in m*e*t (when long, as in l*a*te)
i: as in p*i*n (long, as in *e*at)
o: as in n*o*t
u: as in p*i*n (long as in *e*at)
w: a 'double-u,' as in vac*uu*m, or t*oo*l; but becomes a consonant before vowels, as in the name G*w*en
y: as in p*i*n; or sometimes as 'u' in b*u*t (long as in *e*at)

(As you can see, there is not much difference in i, u, and y — they are virtually identical to the beginner.)

Accent — normally is on the next to last syllable, as in Di-gán-hwy

Dipthongs — each vowel is pronounced individually, so Taliesin = Tallyéssin

Atlantean — Ch=kh, so Charis is Khár-iss

*Ten rings there are, and nine torcs
on the battlechiefs of old
Eight princely virtues, and seven sins
for which a soul is sold
Six is the sum of earth and sky,
of all things meek and bold;
Five is the number of ships that sailed
from Atlantis lost and cold
Four kings of the Westerlands were saved,
three kingdoms now behold;
Two came together in love and fear,
in Llyonesse stronghold;
One world there is, one God, and one birth
the Druid stars foretold*

SRL

PROLOGUE

Vortipor! Foremost in corruption, supreme in spite! A pig with its snout sunk in the entrails of its rival is not swifter than you to suck down iniquity. Your wickedness flows from your smoke-filled hall and inundates the land in a vile flood of wrongdoing.

You call yourself noble. You call yourself king. You call yourself exalted. Exalted in sin, perhaps. You have wreathed your head with laurel, but this is not deserved — unless men now bestow the laurel crown for immorality, at which you are a champion among men!

Urien Rheged! Your name is a reproach. Fornicator! Adulterer! Chief Despoiler! Pillar of Impurity! The lowest vermin in your refuse pit is not lower than you.

Chief Drunkard! Chief Glutton! Defiling all you touch. To you is given the depravity of ten, the iniquity of a hundred, the perversion of a thousand! Your chancrous body is bloated with your corruption. You are dead and do not know it, but the stench of your corpse rises to heaven!

Maelgwn! Great Hound of Gwynedd! How far have you fallen from your father's high position. Maelgwn the Tall earned his stature through righteousness and virtue; you steal it from his memory. Is it possible that you have forgotten all that you once knew?

You have seized the kingship by murder and rapine. For this you call yourself Chief Dragon of the Island of the Mighty. You think to wrap yourself in another man's glory, but it has become a shroud of infamy to you. Pendragon! May eternal shame devour you for your presumption.

Yet, there was once a king worthy of that name. That king was Arthur.

11

It is the paramount disgrace of this evil generation that the name of that great king is no longer spoken aloud except in derision. Arthur! He was the fairest flower of our race, Cymry's most noble son, Lord of the Summer Realm, Pendragon of Britain. He wore God's favour like a purple robe.

Hear then, if you will, the tale of a true king.

BOOK
ONE

PELLEAS

ONE

Arthur is no fit king. Uther's bastard, Merlin's pawn, he is lowborn and a fool. He is wanton and petty and cruel. A glutton and a drunkard, he lacks all civilized graces. In short, he is a sullen, ignorant brute.

All these things and more men say of Arthur. Let them.

When all the words are spoken and the arguments fall exhausted into silence, this single fact remains: we would follow Arthur to the very gates of Hell and beyond if he asked it. And that is the solitary truth.

Show me another who can claim such loyalty.

'*Cymbrogi*,' he calls us: companions of the heart, fellow-countrymen.

Cymbrogi! We are his strong arm, his shield and spear, his blade and helm. We are the blood in his veins, the hard sinew of his flesh, the bone beneath the skin. We are the breath in his lungs, the clear light in his eyes, and the song rising to his lips. We are the meat and drink at his board.

Cymbrogi! We are earth and sky to him. And Arthur is all these things to us — and more.

Ponder this. Think long on it. Only then, perhaps, will you begin to understand the tale I shall tell you.

How not? Who, besides the Emrys himself, knows as much as I? Though I am no bard, I am worthy. For I know Arthur as few others do; we are much alike, after all. We are both sons of uncertain birth, both princes unacknowledged by our fathers, both forced to live our lives apart from clan and kin.

My father was Belyn, Lord of Llyonesse. My mother was a serving woman in the king's house. I learned early that

I would receive nothing from my father's hand and must make my own way in the world.

I was little more than a boy when Myrddin agreed to make me his steward, but I have regretted not one day. Even through those long years of his madness, when I searched the hidden ways of wide Celyddon alone, I desired nothing but to be once more what I had been: servant and companion to Myrddin Emrys, Chief Bard in the Island of the Mighty.

I, Pelleas, prince of Llyonesse, will tell all as I have seen it. . . And I have seen much indeed.

'Are you certain, Myrddin?' Arthur whispers, anxiously. 'Everyone is watching. What if it will not work?'

'It will, as you say, "work". Just do as I have told you.'

Arthur nods grimly, and steps up to the great keystone where the sword stands, its naked blade stuck fast in the heart of the stone.

The yard is mostly empty now. Those going in to Urbanus' mass have done so. It is cold, the day dwindling towards dusk. A few small snowflakes drift out of the darkening sky, to fall on the flagged stone pavement at our feet. Our breath hangs in clouds above our heads.

It is the eve of the Christ Mass, and the lords of Britain have come to Londinium to hold council — as they do nearly every year — to essay who among them might become High King.

Fifteen years have come and gone since the sword was first placed there. Now the once-fine steel is rusted, the stone weathered and stained. But the eagle-carved amethyst in the hilt still glows, its imperial fire undiminished.

Macsen Wledig's sword it is. The Sword of Britain. Emperor Maximus once owned the sword — and Constantine, Constans, Aurelius, and Uther after him, each in his turn High King of Britain.

Yes, fifteen years have come and gone since that first council. Fifteen years of darkness and unceasing strife, of dissent, disappointment and defeat. Fifteen years in which the Saecsens have grown strong once more. Fifteen years for a boy to grow to manhood.

A young man now, he stands grim-faced gazing at the sword thrust deep into the stone. . . hesitant, uncertain.

'Take it, Arthur,' Merlin tells him. 'It is your right.'

Arthur reaches slowly for the bronze hilt. His hand shakes. Cold? Fear? A little of both, perhaps.

He grasps the hilt and glances at Merlin, who nods silently. He drops his eyes and draws a breath, taking courage, steeling himself for whatever will happen.

Arthur's fingers tighten on the silver-braided hilt: see how naturally it fits his hand! He pulls.

The Sword of Britain slides from its stone sheath. The ease with which this is accomplished shines in the wonder in Arthur's eyes. He truly cannot believe what he has done. Nor can he comprehend what it means.

'Well done, Arthur.' Merlin steps to the stone beside him, and Arthur, without thinking, offers the sword to him. 'No, son,' he says gently, 'truly, it is yours.'

'What should I do?' Arthur's voice is unsteady, rising. 'Myrddin, you must tell me what to do! Else I am lost.'

Merlin places a calming hand on Arthur's shoulder. 'Why do you fear, my son? I have ever been with you. God willing, it will always be so.' They turn together and walk into the church.

Yes, we have ever been with him, it is true. I cannot remember a day when we were not. Even so, it is difficult. . . difficult to believe that the young man standing on the threshold of the church has not simply stepped full-grown from out of a hollow hill, or an enchanted pool in Celyddon Forest.

That Arthur has not always existed seems odd to me. Like the wind on the moors and the wild winter stars, surely he has always lived. . . and always will.

Arthur, with his keen blue eyes and hair of burnished gold, his ready smile and guileless countenance. Wide and heavy of shoulder, long of limb, he towers above other men and, though he does not yet know the power of his stature, he is aware that smaller men become uneasy near him. He is handsomely knit in all; fair to look upon.

The native brashness of the northern hills clings to him still. He is like an untamed colt brought into the company of humankind: curious, wary, eager to discover the source of the strange delights that rouse his senses. He is green and untried, but ripe with the promise of greatness.

When he enters a hall the eye travels naturally to him. Those who hunt with him find themselves contesting who shall ride at his right hand. Already, he draws men to him; that is his birthright.

'Go on, Arthur,' Merlin urges, as Arthur hesitates on the threshold. 'It is time.'

I do not possess a prophet's vision; I cannot see what will be. But, at my master's words, I see once more all that has gone before this moment. . . see now Arthur as I first saw him.

A near-naked babe, wearing nothing but a short, dirty sark, his long yellow locks well tangled with leaves and bits of straw, he stumbled forth on legs like little stumps, blue eyes merry with infant mischief. In each chubby fist he grasped a half-grown cat.

A mere babe, but he clutched those two grey cats by their necks in his grip and held them dangling above the ground. Hissing, spitting, writhing mad, they scratched at his arms — and Arthur laughed. We stared in wonder at the sight. The mite endured their claws and laughed for all his tiny soul was worth.

It is said that from the mould of the child, the man is cast.

Well, my master and I sat astride our horses, looking on, and this is what we saw: wild young Arthur, alight with life and laughter, indifferent to pain, already master of an impressive strength — and a more impressive will.

Merlin smiled and raised his hand in declamation, saying, 'Behold, the Bear of Britain!'

Then he shook his head and sighed. 'A wayward cub, look at him. Still, he must be taught, like any young beast. Our work is before us, Pelleas.'

Oh, what a work it was!

TWO

The interior of the church blazed with the light of hundreds of candles. Kings and lords knelt on the bare stone floors before the huge altar, heads bowed, while Bishop Urbanus read out the sacred text in a loud, droning voice. Kneeling, those haughty lords appeared the image of humility and reverence. Indeed, that they knelt at all was no small thing.

We entered in silence, Arthur holding the sword in his hand as if it were a live thing that might squirm and bite him; as if it were an offering, and he the penitent, dutifully bringing it to the altar.

Eyes gleaming in the shimmering light, he licked dry lips and advanced to the centre, turned and, with a last look over his shoulder at Merlin, started down the long, pillared aisle to the altar.

As Arthur approached, Urbanus glanced up, saw the young man advancing steadily towards him, and frowned with annoyance. Then he recognized the sword, and froze.

Bowed heads lifted as the bishop stopped reading. The lords beheld the priest's face, then turned as one to see what halted him.

Arthur was simply there in their midst, the sword in his hand.

Their faces! I could almost read their thoughts as their eyes started from their heads: What? The sword! Who is this upstart? Where has he come from? Look at him! A north country savage! Who is he?

See it now: astonishment gives way to anger. Their eyes quicken to rage.

They are on their feet, the mass forgotten. No one speaks. There is only the dry rustle of leather shoes on stone.

It is the silence before the lowering storm.

19

All at once, the violence breaks: thunder after the lightning's sharp flash.

Voices: questioning, demanding, angry. Hands: grasping, making fists, reaching for knives. Bodies: thrusting forward, crowding in, threatening.

Wonder of wonders, Arthur does not flinch! He grimly holds his ground as the lords of Britain close in around him. I can see his head and shoulders above the rest. He is more perplexed than concerned or frightened.

They are shouting: 'Usurper!' They are demanding his name and lineage. Trickery! they cry. Perfidy! Deceit! They scream like scalded pigs. The holy sanctuary has become a vortex of spite and fear. Arthur stands silent in its centre, unmoved and unmoving. He is an effigy carved in stone, and the noblemen are writhing dancers.

The hate! The hate is like the heat from an oven. It is the thrust of a spear, the blow of a closed fist. It is the venom of a spitting viper.

I struggle towards Arthur. I do not know how to help him, but I must stand with him. The throng around him is a solid wall. I cannot reach him.

Arthur stands alone in the fury his appearance has created.

Swords are thrust in the air; knives glint. I am certain they will kill the boy. They will see his head on a spike before they bow the knee to him. It was a dreadful mistake to bring him here.

Urbanus, arms above his head, hands waving, shoves close. His face white as death, he is calling for peace, for order. No one hears him. They do not want to hear him. A hand snakes out, and blood spurts from the bishop's nose. Urbanus falls back with a muffled cry.

The crowd closes. 'Kill him! Kill the usurper!' It is a death chant.

Arthur's eyes go grey and hard. His brow lowers. His grip tightens on the hilt of the sword in his hand. It is no longer an offering, it is a weapon once more, and he will use it.

Kill him! . . . Kill him! . . . Kill him!

The din is horrific. The mob presses closer.

My sword is ready. Where is Merlin?

Father God! It is all a dreadful mistake. We are dead men.

And then, just as I begin to raise my sword to cleave a path to Arthur's side, there comes a sound like a tempest wind — the blast of a mighty sea gale. Men fall back, suddenly afraid. They cover their heads with their arms and peer into the darkness above. What is it? Is the roof falling? The sky?

The strange sound subsides and they glance at one another in fear and awe. Merlin is there. The Emrys is standing calmly beside Arthur. His hands are empty and upraised, his face stern in the unnatural silence he has created. . .

It did not end there. In truth, it had not even begun.

'Enough!' Merlin declared, a father speaking to disobedient children. 'There will be no life-taking this holy night.'

The noblemen murmured fearfully, eyeing Merlin with contempt and suspicion. He made them feel small and afraid, and they did not love him for it.

'*You* have done this!' someone shouted. King Morcant of Belgarum pushed his way through the throng. 'I know you. This is a trick of yours, Enchanter.'

Merlin turned to face the king. The years had done nothing to sweeten Morcant's soul. The hunger for the High Kingship burned in his belly as fiercely as ever. Morcant it was — together with his friends Dunaut and Coledac — who gave Aurelius and Uther such trouble. Dunaut was safely in his grave, his realm ruled by Idris, a young kinsman. Coledac now ruled the rich Iceni lands reclaimed for him from the Saecsens by Aurelius. In consequence, Coledac was of a mind to view Arthur in a kindly light.

But Morcant, more powerful than ever, was still dagger keen for the High Kingship. He did not intend letting it go without a battle. And his son, Cerdic, had learned the lust from his father. Cut of the same cloth, the boy, no older than Arthur, already saw himself adorning the throne.

'I recognize you, Morcant,' Merlin replied, 'and I know you for what you are.'

'Trickster!' Morcant sneered. 'It will take more than your enchantments to make this whore's whelp a king.'

Merlin smiled, but his eyes grew cold. 'I will not make

him king, Morcant. These lords gathered in this place will do that — and of their own will.'

'Never!' Morcant laughed bitterly. 'On my life, that will not happen.' He turned to those gathered around him, seeking approval for his words. Some gave it outright; others were more uncertain but on the whole agreed with Morcant.

Emboldened by this support, Morcant moved to the attack. 'We do not know this boy; he is no king. Look at him! It is doubtful he is even of noble birth.' He indicated the sword with a scornful flick of his hand. 'Do you expect us to believe that the blade in his hand is the true Sword of Britain?'

'That,' Merlin told him calmly, 'can easily be shown. We have but to step into the churchyard to see the empty stone from which the sword was drawn.'

Morcant was of no disposition to agree with Merlin. But, having pressed the matter, he could not now back down. 'Very well,' he said, 'let us see if this is the true sword or not.'

Pushing, jostling, the crowd, noblemen and all shouting at one another, fought their way out of the church and into the darkened yard, where even in the fitful glow of flickering torchlight everyone could plainly see that the great stone was indeed empty.

This convinced a few, but Morcant was not one of them. 'I would see him take it for myself,' he declared, firm in the belief that it was plainly impossible for Arthur to have drawn it in the first place, and that he would in no wise be able to repeat this miracle. 'Let him put it back,' Morcant challenged, 'and raise it again if he is able.'

'Let him put it back!' cried someone from the crowd, and others shouted, too: 'Put it back! Let him put the sword back!'

At Merlin's nod, Arthur advanced to the stone and replaced the sword, let it stand for a moment, then drew it out again as easily as before.

'Ha!' crowed Morcant, 'that is no true test. Once the spell has been broken, anyone may draw the blade!'

'Very well,' said Merlin flatly. He turned to Arthur. 'Replace the sword.' Arthur did so and stepped aside.

Grinning wickedly, Morcant seized the sword with both hands and pulled. The great king grunted and strained. His face darkened and his muscles knotted with the effort. But the sword was stuck as fast as ever it was before. There was no moving it. He fell back, defeated.

'What enchantment is this?' Morcant snarled, rubbing his hands.

'If it is enchantment,' Merlin told him, 'it is God's enchantment and none of mine.'

'Liar!' screamed Morcant.

Others crowded in around the stone and tried to draw the sword. But, as ever before, the Sword of Britain remained firm-fixed to the keystone. No one among the greatest in the Island of the Mighty could pull it out, save Arthur alone.

When all had tried and failed, King Morcant raged: 'This proves nothing! I will not be tricked by night. Let him lift the sword in the bright daylight, I say! Then we will know that all is as it should be.'

Morcant believed no such thing, of course. He merely wished to put off the test a little longer, in the vain hope that he might yet discover a way to win the sword.

Merlin was of a mind to challenge Morcant in this, but Urbanus came forth, with the holy cross upraised, and appealed to all gathered there in the name of the Christ to put off the test until the morning.

'Tomorrow is the Christ Mass,' the bishop said. 'Come inside the church and pray to the Holy King of all men, that in his great mercy he will show some miracle by which we will know beyond all doubt who shall be High King.'

To some, this sounded like wisdom itself. I could see what Merlin thought of the scheme. I could almost hear his scornful retort: *As I stand before God, we have already had our miracle! How many more will you require before you believe?*

But, to my surprise, Merlin politely acquiesced. 'So be it,' he replied. 'Tomorrow let us assemble here once more and see what God will do.'

With that he turned and started away. Arthur and I followed, leaving the torchlit crowd gaping after us.

'Myrddin, why?' asked Arthur, as soon as we were away from the churchyard. The narrow street was dark and wet with melted snow. 'I could do it again — I am certain of it. Please, Myrddin, let me.'

Merlin stopped in the street and turned to Arthur. 'I know perfectly well that you could. In truth, you could draw the sword fifty times, or five hundred — yet it still would not be enough for them. But this way we give them something to think about. Let them worry with it through the night, and perhaps tomorrow they will see things differently.'

'But tomorrow Lord Morcant might — ' began Arthur.

'Morcant has had fifteen years to find a way to defeat the sword, or find a way round it,' Merlin explained. 'One more night will make no difference.'

We started walking again. Our lodgings were not far from the church, and we soon arrived. Arthur was silent until we reached the doorstep. 'Myrddin, why did you bring me here like this?'

'I have told you, boy. It is time to see what you will become.'

'That is no answer. You knew what would happen. You knew there would be trouble tonight.'

'Come in, Arthur. It is cold.'

'No,' Arthur refused flatly. 'Not until you tell me.'

Merlin sighed. 'Oh, very well. I will tell you. Now, let us go in. Gradlon has a fire. We will drink some of his wine, and I will tell you all that can be told.'

We entered the house where, as Merlin had said, Gradlon the wine merchant had prepared a fire. In the elegant style of old Londinium, there were chairs drawn up to the fire, a small long-legged table bearing a tray with cups of silver, and a fine glass jar filled with ruby-red wine.

Gradlon himself was nowhere to be seen, nor did it appear that any of his servants were about.

'I will see if anyone is here,' I said, and went to look. The rooms of the ground floor were empty. The upper floor contained two rooms — one of them Gradlon's private chamber. The other he kept as a small storeroom and a place to make his accounting. Gradlon was in neither room. The house was empty.

I returned to the hearthroom. Merlin and Arthur were settled before the fire. Three cups stood on the hearthstone, warming.

'There is no one in the house, lord,' I reported.

Merlin nodded. 'Yet he prepared our welcome. No doubt he was called away and will appear shortly.'

Arthur slumped in his chair, his large hands clasped over his chest. 'I thought they would have my head,' he muttered. 'They would have, too, if you had not stopped them. But why, Myrddin? Why were they so angry? And where is Meurig? And Ectorius and Cai — where are they? And Custennin and Bedwyr? They should all be here to support me.'

'They should,' Merlin agreed. 'But they have been delayed. Perhaps they will arrive tomorrow. Perhaps not.'

'What? Do you not care what happens?' Arthur's voice rose shrilly.

Patiently, Merlin replied. 'Do you doubt me? I only say what is: either they will come tomorrow, or they will not. But whether they come or no, there is little I can do about it.'

Arthur glared darkly, but said nothing. I moved to the hearthstone and poured wine into the warmed cups, handing one first to Merlin, then one to Arthur.

'Fret not, Arthur,' I told him. 'All is as it should be — as it was ordained to be. Meurig and Custennin know well the Christ Mass Council. They know and will come.'

He accepted this with the wine, gulped down a mouthful. 'You said you would tell me everything. You agreed. Well? I am ready to hear it now.'

Merlin appraised him carefully for a moment. 'Are you? Are you ready to hear it all? I wonder.'

The crackle of the flames on the hearth filled the room. I felt my master weighing out the words carefully in his heart and mind, trying each one as a man might try a grain bag before committing to it the wealth of his harvest.

'Arthur,' Merlin said at last, 'If I have hidden anything from you, forgive me. It appears that the time for hidden things is over. Knowledge must lead you now where I cannot. But I ask you to remember that, what I did, I did as I have ever done — for one purpose and one purpose only: the better to serve you.'

The young man accepted this readily. 'Because you knew I would be a king one day?'

'Precisely. Because I knew you would be king one day.'

'By the sword? But I thought — '

'And I let you think it, Arthur. Believe me, it was not for lack of trust in you, but for mistrust of others.' Merlin paused, considered, sipped from his cup, and said, 'Tonight was a test, yes — but not the test you thought it was. You were not merely showing yourself worthy to become a king — '

'No?'

'You were showing yourself *already* a king, Arthur. The High King.'

Arthur's brow furrowed as his mind raced ahead. I could see him working on it, struggling to take it all in. Still, Arthur did not question that this could be true; his own heart answered for him that it was so.

The boy sat dazed, but only for a moment. Then he leapt to his feet. '*That* is why they were so angry! Myrddin! They hated me for succeeding where they had failed. The prize was far greater than I knew.'

The young man grinned, as if this were the solution to his woes. In truth, he had already forgiven the small kings their treachery. He was happy once more.

As he paced before the fire, his face fairly shone with joy. 'The High King — oh, Myrddin, it is true. I know it is. I am the High King.'

This joy was short-lived, however. For, even as the idea shaped itself in his mind, Arthur recognized the implications of his new-found nobility. 'But that means. . .'

His face fell; his shoulders slumped. From the height of happiness, he now appeared utterly downcast and forlorn.

'Oh, sit down, Arthur.'

'Who am I? Myrddin, tell me! Who am I that I should be High King? For reason tells me that I am no kin to Ectorius — or Meurig, or Custennin either.'

Myrddin gently shook his head. 'No, you are not of Custennin's lineage, nor Meurig's, nor even Ectorius'.' He rose and came to stand before Arthur, putting both hands on the boy's shoulders. 'It has been a long time, Arthur. The Island of the Mighty has been without a High King for far too long.'

'Who am I, Myrddin?' whispered Arthur. 'Tell me! Am I the Pendragon's son?'

'No, not Uther's. Your father was Aurelius,' Merlin told him simply.

'Aurelius?'

'Yes, and Ygerna was your mother.'

'Uther's wife!' His eyes went wide.

'It was not like that,' explained Merlin gently, 'Ygerna was Aurelius' queen before she was Uther's. You are Aurelius' true son, Arthur. You have no cause for shame.'

This was too much for the boy to comprehend. 'If there is no shame in it, why has it all been kept secret? And do not say it was to *serve* me better!'

'To protect you, Arthur.'

'From Morcant?'

'From Morcant, yes, and others like him. You saw how it was tonight. I wanted to tell you when your mother died, but you were too young. It is difficult enough now; you would have understood it even less then.'

Arthur bristled. 'I am not liking this, Myrddin. I tell you plainly, I am not liking this at all! If Ygerna was my mother, why — ' He guessed, even before he could finish asking the question. 'Uther.'

Merlin sighed. 'I asked you to remember that, what I did, I did to serve you, Arthur. There was no other way. . . No, there might have been another way; I will not say there was not. But, if there was, it was not revealed to me. I have acted by the light I was given, Arthur. No man can do more.' He reached a hand towards the boy. 'I do not ask you to approve, lad — only to understand.'

Young Arthur nodded, but said nothing.

Merlin picked up Arthur's cup and handed it to him. The boy took it and held it between his hands, staring into its depths. 'Drink your wine,' my master told him. 'Then go you to your bed. Let there be no more words; we have said enough tonight.'

Arthur drained his cup in a gulp, then made his way to his sleeping-place. I moved to attend him, but he put out his hand and bade me stay. He wished to be alone.

When he had gone, I said, 'He is right to be angry.'

Merlin agreed. 'We have lived with this moment in our

minds for years — hoping, praying that it would come. But Arthur knew nothing of all this until now. We should not wonder that it takes him by surprise. Nevertheless, give him time and he will rise to it. You will see, Pelleas.'

I refilled our cups and Merlin drank his down, refusing more. 'No, enough. Go to bed, Pelleas. I mean to sit here a little longer,' he said, and turned his chair to the low-burning fire. 'Perhaps Gradlon will return. I would speak with him.'

I left him staring into the red-gold embers, searching the myriad paths of the Otherworld for that which would bring him wisdom and courage.

We would have much need of both in the days to come.

THREE

The morning dawned raw and cold. Snow sifted sullenly from a sky of hammered lead. We awoke and breakfasted by rushlight in Gradlon's house. Our host bustled around us, ordering his servants, fussing over each small detail, full of the excitement of great events.

'Eat!' he urged, directing porridge into our bowls and steaming mulled wine into our cups. 'It is a long day you are facing. You will need your strength — and your wits. A man cannot think if he is hungry. Eat!'

In his long life the canny merchant had many opportunities to be close to momentous affairs. Indeed, truth be known, Gradlon's had been the hand unseen behind many transactions and negotiations of power.

Governors, kings, lords might come and go, but always to Gradlon's profit. Though he held to no one and nothing but himself and his purse, his ability to sense the prevailing side of any contest — often long before the battle lines were clearly drawn, or the combatants engaged — made him an invaluable ally.

Gradlon simply understood the fickle ways of power — though unlike most men had no desire of it for himself. He much preferred his own life of trade and barter, of gamble, risk, and speculation. With Arthur in his house, Gradlon was in his glory.

'You can be sure Morcant is eating hearty this morning,' he said, directing his servants to greater industry. 'That man never missed a mouthful in his life!'

'Sit,' Merlin ordered. 'I would hear of your discussion with Governor Melatus. You were late returning last night.'

Gradlon rolled his eyes and puffed out his cheeks. 'Melatus is impossible, of course — a spine like a willow wand, and a

29

mind like a sieve.'

This brought a chuckle from Arthur, who alone among us possessed an appetite. The boy heeded Gradlon's advice and ate with zeal. If it were to be his last meal, I reflected, at least it would be a good one.

'The problem, of course,' Gradlon continued, breaking the hard bread and dipping the crust in his porridge, 'is that the governor is of no certain opinion about the matter. He has no opinion because he is living in the past. Tch! Melatus and his cronies believe the emperor will come in the spring with four cohorts.' The merchant withdrew the crust from his mouth. 'Four cohorts! Why not a hundred? A thousand!'

Merlin shook his head. Gradlon laughed, '*Which* emperor, I asked him? Oh, he is a fool, I tell you. Gaul is finished. The empire is a memory. Eat! You have not touched your food.'

'He will not side with us?' asked Merlin.

'No more than he would side with the Saecsens. God's mercy, the man thinks *you* are Saecsens! Melatus believes that anyone not born behind the crumbling walls of Londinium is a barbarian or worse.'

'Then at least he will not side with the others,' I ventured.

'Do not be over certain of that, my friend,' Gradlon answered. 'Melatus is a fool, and practices a fool's wisdom. He may side with the others simply to confound you. Also, Morcant styles himself an emperor and that looms large with Melatus.'

'Then it seems we cannot ignore him,' Merlin replied. 'This is going to more difficult than I thought.'

'Leave Melatus to me!' declared Gradlon. 'I will deal with him.'

Arthur finished his porridge and pushed his bowl away. He took up his cup and sipped the spiced wine. The steam rose from the rim as he drank. Gradlon's glance lingered on him for a moment, then he said, 'Aurelius' son — who would have thought it, eh? Hail, Artorius! I salute you.' Gradlon raised his palm in an informal but genuine salute.

Arthur grinned. 'I am not king yet.'

'Not yet,' Merlin agreed. 'But perhaps by the end of the day we will all say otherwise.'

Still, despite Merlin's hopeful words, it was not to be.

Arthur had little stomach for appeasement, or for the schemes of men like Morcant. Given a choice, I think he would have preferred settling the matter with the edge of his sword. Better the short, sharp heat of open battle than the cold poison of intrigue.

Merlin sympathized but knew there was no other way. 'You were born to contention, boy,' he said. 'What is a little strife to you? Bear it lightly; it will pass.'

'I do not mind that they hate me,' replied Arthur. I believe he meant it, too. 'But it angers me that they refuse me my birthright.'

'I will tell you something, shall I? They treated Aurelius no better,' Merlin confided, 'and him they loved. Think on that.'

Arthur turned his eyes to the throng gathered in the churchyard. 'Do *they* hate me as well?'

'They have not decided yet.'

'Where are Ectorius and Cai? I do not see them.' Ectorius and his son, Cai, had arrived in Londinium and found us as we were making our way to the churchyard.

'I told them to find Morcant and stand with him.'

'With *him?*'

'Perhaps he will not rail quite so loudly if his own is the only voice he hears.'

Arthur smiled darkly. 'I do not fear Morcant.'

'This is not about fear, Arthur, but about power,' Merlin said seriously. 'And Morcant holds the very thing you need.'

'I do not need his approval.'

'His acquiescence.'

'It is the same thing,' snapped Arthur.

'Perhaps,' allowed Merlin. 'Perhaps.'

'I would have liked to have talked to Cai.'

'Later.'

'Why are we waiting? Let us get on with it.'

'We will wait a little longer — let Morcant and his crowd stew in their juices.'

'I am the one stewing, Myrddin! Let us do it and be

done.'

'Shh, patience.'

Despite the cold, people continued to crowd into the yard. Arthur, Merlin and I stood out of sight inside the archway of the church, waiting while the kings and lords gathered to witness once more the miracle they would neither accept nor acknowledge. But they came anyway. What else could they do?

I scanned the crowd, too, wishing in my heart that Meurig and Custennin had arrived, and wondering why Lot was not here. What could have detained them? I could not help feeling that their presence would make a difference somehow — even though I knew this hope was futile.

In any event, Merlin had already decided the way the thing would go.

Urbanus, bald and jowly, bustled up, his sandals slapping the wet stone at our feet. 'All is ready,' he said, slightly out of breath. 'All is ordered as you have asked.'

Arthur turned to regard the bishop. 'What is ready?' The question was for Merlin.

'I have asked Urbanus to prepare us a place where we may sit and talk like civilized men. I do not propose to haggle in the churchyard like horse traders in a market. This is too important, Arthur. When men sit down together they are like to be more reasonable.'

'Yes,' replied Urbanus. 'So, when you are ready. . . ?'

'I will give you a sign,' answered Merlin.

'Very well. I will take my place.' Urbanus pressed his hands together and hurried off, his breath puffing in the icy air.

Arthur stamped his feet. The restless crowds shifted in the cold. Some of the lords gathered round the keystone were talking loudly and looking around pointedly. In a few moments the shout would go up for Arthur to appear. If he did not, there would be a riot.

Arthur felt the tension in the throng and sensed it shifting like a tide against him. He turned to Merlin and implored, 'Please, can we get on with it?'

In the same instant, the crowd began to shout.

'See? They are tired of waiting, and so am I.'

This, I think, was why Merlin had been waiting. He

wanted the emotions of the people, and Arthur's too, to be prickly sharp; he wanted them alert and uncomfortable.

'Yes,' agreed Merlin. 'I think we have kept them waiting long enough. Let us go. Remember what I told you. And, whatever happens, see that you do not release that sword to anyone.'

Arthur nodded once, curtly. He understood without being told.

Merlin pushed towards the keystone and was recognized at once. 'The Emrys! Make way for the Emrys! Make way!' And a path opened before him.

We came to stand before the keystone. As if to thwart and defy us, Morcant and his friends stood directly opposite, haughty sneers and scowls on their faces. Their enmity seethed within them, escaping in the steam from mouths and nostrils. The day seemed to have grown darker.

The stone, with its thin dusting of snow, appeared immense and white and cold. . . so cold. And the great sword of Macsen Wledig, the Sword of Britain, stood plunged to its hilt, solid as the keystone that held it; the two were for ever joined, there would be no separating them.

Had I only dreamed that he had drawn it?

In the starved light of that bleak day, all that had gone before seemed as remote and confused as a faded dream. The stone had defeated all who set hand to the sword. On this drear day it would conquer Arthur, too. And Britain would go down into the darkness at last.

Merlin raised his hands in the attitude of declamation, although the throng had stilled already. He waited and, when every eye was on him, said, 'The sword has already been drawn from the stone, as many here will testify. Yet it will be drawn again by daylight, in full view of all gathered here, that no one may claim deception or sorcery.'

He paused to allow these words to take hold. The wind stirred and snow began to fall in earnest — huge, powdery flakes, like bits of fleece riding the shifting wind.

'Is there a man among you who would try the stone? Let him try it now.' The steel in Merlin's voice spoke a challenge cold and hard as the stone itself.

Of course, there were some who would try, knowing what they already knew in their hearts — that they would be

33

defeated as they had been defeated before. But, like ignorance and folly, they would not be denied their opportunity to fail yet once more.

The first lord to try was the young viper Cerdic, Morcant's insolent son. Lips curled in a sneer, the fool thrust his way to the stone, reached out and grabbed the hilt as if laying claim to another's wealth. He pulled with all the arrogance in him — and it was no small measure. The crowd urged him on with cries of encouragement, but he fell back a moment later, red-faced with exertion and defeat.

Maglos of Dumnonia, Morganwg's son, came next — more out of curiosity than hope. He touched the hilt diffidently, as if the thing might burn him. He was defeated before he pulled, and gave in good-naturedly.

Coledac shoved his way forward. He glared at the sword — as if it were beneath him to touch it — wrapped his hand around the hilt and pulled, releasing it almost at once. He turned and pushed back into the crowd.

Owen Vinddu, the Cerniw chieftain, stood next at the stone, gazing earnestly. And, placing both hands on the hilt, gripped it with such strength his knuckles went white as he pulled. With a mighty groan he fell back, vanquished.

Others crowded in: Ceredigawn of Gwynedd and Ogryvan, his neighbour king; Morganwg, following his son's example, and faring no better; old Antonius of the Cantii, stiff with age, but game to the end. . . and others — lords, kings, chieftains, each and every one, and their sons as well.

All who had a mind to rule tried that day, and all went down in defeat to the stone until Arthur only was left. The cheering, jeering throng fell silent as they turned to him.

Arthur stood tall and grim, his eyes the colour of the lowering sky, his shoulders straight, lips pressed to a thin, bloodless line. The hardness in him surprised me, and others saw it, too. Yes, he would be a match for the stone — he looked as if made of the very stuff.

He put forth his hand and grasped the hilt as if retrieving it from the gut of an enemy. There came the cold rasp of steel on stone as he pulled, and the gasp of the crowd as he lofted the great weapon and brandished it in the air for all to see.

A few, to their everlasting credit, bent the knee at once, recognizing their king. Most did not. They could not believe what they had seen. Men had waited long years for this sight and then failed to acknowledge it.

What did they expect? An angel in shining raiment? An Otherworld god?

'Trickery!' The voice was one of Morcant's chieftains who had no doubt been instructed to start the uproar. 'Usurper!' Others salted through the crowd did likewise, trying to raise the rabble against Arthur. But Merlin was ready.

Before the thing could come to blows, he nodded to Urbanus, who stepped up beside Arthur and spread his arms in a gesture of conciliation. 'Silence!' he cried. 'Why do you persist in doubting what you have seen with your own eyes? On this day of Christ Mass let there be no dissension among us. Rather let us enter the church and pray God's guidance as Christian men ought. Then let us sit together and take counsel with one another, and so determine what is best to do.'

This was unexpected. The dissenting lords had thought only of rebellion and bloodshed, and were unprepared to answer the calm reason of Urbanus' suggestion. Ectorius was quick to ratify the plan. 'Well said!' he shouted. 'We are reasonable and temperate men. Where is the harm in sitting down together? And what better place than this holy church?'

The dissenters were hard-pressed to answer. If they refused, the people would know them for the traitors they were, and would proclaim Arthur. Yet conceding to Urbanus' suggestion admitted Arthur's claim as genuine. They were neatly trapped.

Urbanus saw their hesitation and knew its cause. 'Come,' he said reasonably. 'Put aside strife and vain contention. On this high and holy day let there be peace among us. Come into the church.'

The people murmured their approval, and the small kings realized that this particular battle was lost. 'Very well,' said Morcant, rallying his forces, 'let us take counsel and decide what is best. I invoke the Council of Kings.' He hoped with this to imply that the matter was far from settled, and that he was in authority. So saying, he turned and led the way into the church.

If he hoped to benefit by taking the seat of honour for himself, that hope died stillborn in his breast. Merlin had instructed Urbanus to arrange the kings' chairs in a large circle inside the sanctuary — as had been done in Aurelius' and Uther's time, but never since.

Thus seated, no king stood above his brothers; therefore, no lord's opinion counted for more than another's. This lessened Morcant's hold on the lords below him.

Morcant did not like it, but there was nothing he could do. He stalked to his chair, turned, and sat down with as much superiority as he could command. Others took chairs on either side of him as they chose, their advisers and counsellors ranged around them, and the more curious of Londinium's citizens filled in behind. Within moments the vast room, alight with hundreds of candles and fragrant with the haze of incense, buzzed like a hornet's hive. Urbanus could not have imagined a larger gathering for Christ Mass.

Consequently, he could not allow the opportunity to go unmarked. So he began the council with an admonitory prayer — both in Latin and in the British tongue, so that no one would fail to understand what he said. And he said it at some length.

'All Wise Father,' he concluded, 'Great Giver and Guide, lead us in wisdom and righteousness to the king you have chosen, and grant us peace in the choosing. Bless our counsel with the light of your presence, and let each man among us please you in thought and word and deed.'

His prayer finished at last, Urbanus rose and turned to the assembly: 'It is many years since this body has gathered in accord; many years since a High King ruled in Britain — much to our hurt, I declare.' He paused and allowed his gaze to sweep across the entire throng before continuing. 'Therefore, I charge you: let not this council depart hence without redressing this wrong by establishing the High Kingship once more.'

The people liked the sound of that and chorused their approval. Urbanus then turned to Merlin. 'I stand ready to serve in any way you deem useful.'

'Thank you, Bishop Urbanus,' Merlin said, dismissing

him. He addressed Morcant at once. 'As you have called this council, Morcant,' he began, 'perhaps you should tell us why you will not accept the sign by which we all agreed the next High King of Britain should be recognized. For, unless you have discovered some compelling reason why we should disregard the thing we have seen with our own eyes, I tell you all that the High King stands before you this day with the Sword of Britain in his hand.'

Morcant frowned. 'There is every reason to disregard what we have seen. This is, as we all know, an evil age; there is much sorcery in the land round about. How do we know that what we have seen with our own eyes,' he mocked the phrase, 'was not accomplished by enchantment?'

'How by enchantment, Morcant?' demanded Merlin. 'Make plain your objection: do you accuse Arthur of sorcery?'

Morcant's frown deepened. To imply sorcery was far simpler than proving it. He had no proof and knew it. 'Am I a sorcerer that I know such things?' he fumed.

'*You* were the one to name the sin among us. I put it to you, Morcant, is Arthur a sorcerer?'

His face twisted with rage, Morcant nevertheless held his temper and answered reasonably. 'I have no proof save the sword in his hand. If it was not gained by sorcery, I demand to know by what power it was obtained.'

'By the power of virtue and true nobility,' Merlin declared. 'The same power given to all who will choose it.'

The people cheered at this, and Morcant realized he was losing ground to Merlin's wit and logic. Yet he could not help himself. Spreading his arms to the assembly, he demanded, 'Do you malign the nobility of the good men here assembled? Do you impugn their virtue?'

'The words are yours, Morcant. I merely uphold the virtue and nobility of the one standing before us,' Merlin lifted a hand to Arthur standing rigid beside him. 'If you feel maligned and impugned in his presence,' he said, 'no doubt it is the truth working in you.'

'Are you God that you presume to know the truth?' sneered Morcant.

'And are you such a stranger to the truth that you no longer recognize it?' Merlin made a dismissing gesture with his hands. 'Stop this foolishness, Morcant. If you have objections, speak them out.' He included the others in his challenge. 'If anyone knows just reason why Arthur should not receive the High Kingship he has won by right, I command you to speak now!'

The silence in the great chamber was such that I might have heard the snowflakes alighting in the yard outside. No one, Morcant included, held a single legitimate reason why Arthur should not be High King — save for his own ambitious pride.

Merlin's golden eyes gazed over the assembly and the gathered crowd. The time had come to force the issue. He rose slowly and stepped to the centre of the ring. 'So,' he said softly, 'it is as I thought. No one can speak against Arthur. Now then, I ask you, who will speak for him?'

The first to answer was Ectorius, who leapt to his feet. 'I speak for him. And I own him king!'

'I also own him king.' It was Bedegran.

'I own him king,' said Madoc, rising with him.

Those who had already bent the knee now proclaimed Arthur once again. The throng cheered at this, but the acclamation died in their throats. For no one else recognized Arthur or held him king. The Council of Kings remained divided, and not enough supported Arthur to allow him to claim the throne in spite of the dissenters.

Morcant wasted not a moment. 'We will not accept him as king over us,' he crowed. 'Someone else must be chosen.'

'He holds the sword!' shouted Merlin. 'And that has not changed. Whoever would be king must first take the sword from Arthur's hand. For I tell you truly, none among you will be king without it!'

Morcant's fists balled in his anger. As carefully as he tried to steer the issue around that fact, Merlin managed to guide it back.

'Arthur, come here,' summoned Merlin. The young man joined the Emrys in the circle.

'Here he is,' said Merlin, stepping away. 'Who among you will be first to try?'

Arthur stood alone in the centre of the ring of kings. In the flickering light of the Christ Mass candles, holding the sword easily by the hilt, alert, resolute, unafraid, he appeared an avenging angel, eyes alight with the bright fire of righteousness.

Clearly, anyone wishing to take the sword by force would have a fight on his hands. Fools they were, perhaps, but not fool enough to risk single combat with this unknown young warrior. Merlin's challenge stood.

Even so, Arthur could not demand the High Kingship outright. He had no lands, no wealth, no warband; and his supporters were too few. The issue remained in deadlock. Nothing had changed since the night before.

But Merlin was not finished.

FOUR

All that winter's day and far into the night the kings
twisted and squirmed, but Merlin held them in his iron
grasp and would not let go. He became first a rock, and
then a mountain in Arthur's defence. Arthur stood equally
unmoved. No power on earth could have prevailed against
them. . .

. . . just as no power on earth can make a man honour
another who does not himself desire it.

In truth, the petty kings did not desire to honour Arthur.
He would have to earn their honour and their loyalty.
Merlin's great care was to make that possible.

This he accomplished through reviving the title *Dux
Britanniarum*, Duke of Britain — Uther's old title from the
time when he was war leader for Aurelius — and conferring
it upon Arthur.

The council agreed to this in the end, for it saved them
from having to make Arthur king outright. But once he
obtained this compromise, then did Merlin sow his scheme:
a warband supported by all the kings equally, for the benefit
of all. A free-roving force dedicated to keeping the lands of
Britain secure. Beholden to no king, supported equally by
all, this roaming warband could strike wherever and whenever needed — without regard for the restrictive pacts and
alliances of the petty kings.

Since, it was reasoned, Britain faced a common enemy we
would field a common warband, led by a war leader owing
allegiance to no one, but serving all equally as need arose.

This, of course, was far less readily agreed upon, for it
meant that kings like Morcant and Coledac would have to
give up their warring ways — else they would find themselves facing Arthur and the warband they themselves

helped to support.

Thus, making Arthur Duke of Britain enforced the peace. This was the beauty of Merlin's plan, and also its greatest weakness. For, in truth, the kings who had no intention of swearing fealty to Arthur would not support him to their own hurt.

Other kings saw a different menace: a free-roving warband they could not rule was scarcely less dangerous than the Saecsen raiders this selfsame warband was supposed to hold at bay.

Yet, as they had already conceded Arthur's title, there was nothing they could do in the end. A War Leader implied a force to command. And no one could deny the need. Arthur would be the War Leader, and the warband would be raised from the pledged support of the council.

True, it was not the High Kingship. But Merlin's scheme gave Arthur what he needed: leave to act to win the kingship. And he did.

When Arthur left the church that night — cold and bright it was, and windy, the black ice shining in the white moonlight — his long legs striding, hastening him away, the Sword of Britain on his hip for good, he was no longer the young man who had entered that morning. The malice of the petty kings, their narrow spites, their biting rancour and jealousy had hardened him. But the All-Wise Spirit moves in mysterious ways: Arthur now knew them for what they were.

In this he had the better of them, for they knew him not at all.

Arthur has always learned quickly. When as a boy in Ectorius' house he laboured at his Latin and numbers with Melumpus, the Gaulish tutor from the abbey at nearby Abercurny, Arthur needed only to be told a thing once and he understood it, twice and it was his for ever.

As often as not, when I came for the boys in the afternoons, to ride or take weapons practice, there would be Arthur patiently explaining a word or sum to Cai while Melumpus dozed in the sun, his hands folded over his paunch. Arthur could teach as well as learn, though he always preferred doing to thinking.

If a thing could be done, Arthur wanted to do it. If it could not be done, better still — *that* was the thing he wanted most to do.

Nothing comes so vividly to mind in this regard as when we journeyed to Gwynedd on our way to Caer Myrddin to visit Tewdrig. Ectorius and Cai were with us, and Merlin of course, along with a small escort.

It was the summer of Arthur's eleventh year, I believe, and there had been reports of renewed Irish raiding along the western coasts. Merlin wanted to discuss the situation with Tewdrig and Meurig, and see for himself how things stood. He had planned to go quietly, alone. But, once Arthur heard of it, he quickly included himself and Cai, and there was no gainsaying him. Since we could in no wise risk travelling with Arthur unprotected, it was decided that we would all make the journey together.

All went well until we reached Yr Widdfa. Upon seeing those great cold looming mounds of slate, Arthur nearly fell off his horse in astonishment. 'Look at that one! Have you ever seen a higher mountain? There is snow still on it!'

'It is a sight indeed,' agreed Merlin.

'Does it have a name? What is it?'

'It does. All this is Yr Widdfa, Region of Snows.' Merlin pointed to the highest peak. 'The one you are gawking at is Eryri.'

'It is. . . ' he searched for words, ' . . . enormous! Enormous and beautiful.' He gazed in wonder at it, filling his eyes with the sight. 'Has anyone ever climbed it?'

The question caught Merlin off guard. 'I do not believe so,' he answered. 'I do not think it possible.'

That was the wrong thing to say, certainly. 'Good! Then I will be the first,' Arthur declared. He meant it, too. And he meant to begin at once. With a lash of the reins, he rode towards the mountain.

Merlin made to call him back. But Cai intervened. 'Please, Lord Emrys, I would like to climb it, too.'

'You, Cai?' Merlin turned and looked into the ruddy face. The clear blue eyes held all the hope any one human creature can bear. To dash it would have been unthinkable.

And Merlin saw that, much as Arthur wanted to climb the mountain, Cai wanted it more, but for a far different reason.

'Now, Caius, you cannot — ' began Ectorius.

Merlin cut him short with a gesture. 'Of course,' Merlin told him, 'I think it is time this mountain was conquered. And you two are just the men to do it. Well, hurry or you will be left behind.' He waved Cai away, and the boy rode after Arthur.

'Do you think it wise?' asked Ectorius, watching his son with some apprehension. Long had he protected his son's lame leg — the result of an accident and a poorly set bone when Cai was first learning to ride.

'No,' replied Merlin, 'it is foolishness itself to let them go.'

'Then why — ?'

Merlin smiled, lifting a hand to the mountain. 'Because if we prevented them now they would never again risk the impossible with a whole and open heart.'

'Is that so important?'

'For ordinary men, no.' Merlin shook his head, watching the boys ride away. 'But, Ector, we are not about making ordinary men.'

'They could get themselves killed!'

'Then they will die in glorious defeat,' Merlin declared. Ectorius opened his mouth to protest, but my master stopped him, saying, 'Ector, they will die one day in any event and we cannot prevent that. Do you not see it?'

'No, I do not. This is needless hazard.' Ectorius showed his contempt for such an idea.

'The dead are so long dead,' Merlin said. 'Better to have lived while alive, yes? Besides, if they achieve this they will have conquered a giant; they will be invincible!'

'If they do not?'

'Then they will learn something about the limitations of men.'

'A costly lesson, it seems to me,' muttered Ectorius.

'Then it will be valued all the more. Come, be of good cheer, my friend,' coaxed Merlin, 'If God and his angels stand ready to uphold them, can we do less?'

Ectorius lapsed into a sullen silence, and we turned our horses to follow the boys, catching them up some time later in one of the high meadows beneath the looming slopes, as they stood discussing the best way to begin.

'Well? What is it to be?' asked Merlin.

'This appears to be the best way,' answered Arthur at once. 'The others are too steep. On this side we can walk a fair way up.'

'Then get on with it,' Merlin told them, casting an eye towards the sun. 'The best of the day is yours. We will make camp and await you here.'

'He is right,' said Arthur to Cai, setting his jaw. 'Let us begin.' Taking only a waterskin apiece and a couple of barley loaves, they bade us farewell and began their assault on Eryri. We, in turn, began making camp and settled down to wait.

Ectorius and some of his men went off hunting just after midday, and returned at dusk with a dozen hares and as many pheasants. The larger game they had let go, since we could neither eat it nor take it with us.

While the men cleaned the game and made our supper, Ectorius described the wealth of game they had seen — casting his eyes now and again at the slopes of the mountain above us. At last, he said, 'Will they stay up there all night, do you think?'

'I expect so,' I answered. 'It is too far to come down, and they cannot have reached the top yet.'

'I do not like to think of them climbing up there in the dark.'

'They are sensible enough,' I assured him. 'They will stop and rest for the night.'

'It is not their rest I am worried about.' Ectorius turned abruptly and went about his chores.

I wondered at Merlin, for he seemed not at all concerned about the enterprise. Usually, he exercised the utmost care where Arthur's safety was concerned. A little later, as the hares and pheasants were roasting on spits over the fire, I sought him at the streamside where he was filling waterskins and watering horses. I asked him about this and he simply replied, 'Be at ease, Pelleas. I see no hurt in this place.'

'What have you seen?'

He stopped and stood, turning his eyes back to the mountain, whose top was aflame with sunset's crimson afterglow. He was silent for a moment, his eyes alight with the strange fire from the heights. 'I have seen a mountain wearing a man's name and that name is *Arthur*.'

We waited all through the next day, and Ectorius held his peace. But, as night came on and a chill crept into the air, he stalked over to Merlin, hands on hips. 'They have not returned.'

'No, they have not,' agreed Merlin.

'Something has happened.' He glanced uneasily up at the darkening mountainside, as if to see the boys clinging there. His mouth worked silently for a moment, then he burst forth: 'Cai's leg! Why the boy can hardly walk as it is — I should never have allowed them to go.'

'Peace, Ector. You have no cause for worry. They will return when they have done what they can do.'

'When they have broken their necks, you mean.'

'I do not think that likely.'

'More like than not!' Ectorius grumbled. But he said no more about it that night.

The next morning the boys had still not returned and I began to feel Ectorius' misgiving. Might Merlin be mistaken?

By midday Ectorius' thin patience had worn through. He stormed silently around the camp, muttering under his breath. He respected Merlin enough not to insult him openly by insisting on going after the boys. But it was on his mind — and for all his great respect he would not wait another night.

Merlin pretended not to notice Ectorius' acute discomfort. He occupied himself walking the valley and gathering those herbs that could not be found further north.

Finally, as the sun disappeared behind the rim of mountains surrounding Eryri, Ectorius decided to take matters into his own hands. He ordered four of his men to saddle their horses, and made ready to begin the search.

'Think what you are doing,' Merlin told him equably.

'I have thought of nothing else all day!' Ectorius snapped.

'Let be, Ector. If you go after them now you will steal

their glory; they will know you did not trust them to succeed.'

'What if their broken bodies lie bleeding in a crevice up there? They could be dying.'

'Then let them die like the men you hoped they would one day become!' Merlin replied. 'Ector,' he soothed, 'trust me just a little longer.'

'I have trusted you altogether too long!' Ectorius cried. As deep as his love, so deep was his pain. I believe he held himself to blame for his son's infirmity — the horse had been his own.

'If you cannot trust me, then trust the Good God. Patience, brother. You have borne your misgiving this long, bear it but a little longer.'

'It is a hard thing you are asking.'

'If they have not rejoined us by dawn, you need not lead the search, Ector; *I* will lead it.'

Ectorius shook his head and swore, but he accepted Merlin's reassurance and stalked off to rescind the orders to his men.

Dusk came on apace. I think night always comes first to the high places of the world. There were stars already winking in heaven's firmament, though the sky still held the day's light, when we sat down to our supper. The men talked loudly of hunting, trying to distract their lord from his unhappy thoughts.

Merlin heard the shout first. In truth, I believe he had been listening for it most of the day and was beginning to wonder why he had not heard it.

He stood, holding out his hand for silence, his head cocked to one side. Neither I nor anyone else heard anything but the thin, trilling call of mountain larks, as they winged to their nests for the night.

Though I knew better than to doubt him, it seemed he was mistaken. The men grew restless.

'It was only — ' began Ectorius.

Merlin rose and held up a silencing hand. He stood rock still for a long moment and then turned towards the mountain. A slow smile spread across his face. 'Behold!' he said. 'The conquerors return!'

Ectorius jumped up. 'Where? I do not see them!'

'They are coming.'

Ector ran forward a few steps. 'I do not see them!'

Then the shout came again. I heard it: the high, wavering 'halloo' one uses in the mountains. The others were on their feet now, too — all of us straining eyes and ears into the gathering gloom.

'It is them!' cried Ectorius. 'They are coming back!'

We did not see them until they were very close indeed, for in the dusk their clothing did not show against the darkening mountainside. When they shouted again, I made out the two forms hastening towards us.

'Cai! Arthur!' cried Ectorius.

In a moment they appeared, and I shall never forget the expression on their faces. For I had never seen such triumph and exultation in a human countenance before — and have seen it only once since. They were bone weary, dishevelled, but ablaze with the light of victory. They were heroes. They were gods.

They staggered to the camp fire and collapsed on the ground. Even in the firelight I could see their sunburnt cheeks and noses; Arthur's fair skin was peeling and Cai's neck and brow were as red as his hair! Their clothes were dirty — torn and ragged at knees and elbows. Their hands were raw, and there were bruises, scrapes and scratches on their arms and legs. They appeared to have passed through walls of hawthorn and thickets of thistle along the way.

'Get them something to drink!' ordered Ectorius, and someone hurried off to fetch the beer. The lord of Caer Edyn stared at his son, pride swelling his chest till he looked like a strutting grouse.

I gathered food from our supper and gave it to them. Arthur took the bread and stuffed half the loaf into his mouth; Cai, too tired to eat, simply held it in his hand and stared at it.

'Here,' said Merlin, handing them a waterskin, 'drink this.'

Cai drank, swallowing great mouthfuls at a time, and then handed the skin to Arthur, who gulped the cool stream water down in noisy draughts.

Ectorius could contain himself no longer. 'Well, how did you fare, son? Did you reach the top?'

'The top,' replied Cai reverently. 'We reached the top, we did.' He turned his face to Arthur and his eyes held the look of a man who has learned a profound and life-changing truth. 'I would never have made it but for Arthur.'

Arthur lowered the waterskin. 'Never say it, brother. We climbed it together — you and I *together*.' He turned to the rest of us standing over him. 'It was wonderful! Glorious! You should have been there, Merlin — Pelleas! — you should have come with us. You can see from one end of the world to the other! It was — it was. . . wonderful.' He lapsed into silence, at a loss for words.

'You said it was impossible,' Cai reminded Merlin. 'You said no one had ever done it. Well, we did it! We climbed it all the way to the top!' He paused and added softly, turning once more to Arthur, ' . . . He all but carried me.'

I have seen a mountain wearing a man's name and that name is Arthur, Merlin had said.

I was not to discover the full meaning of these words until many years later when bards learned of Arthur's youthful exploits and began referring to the mountain as The Great Tomb — by which they meant he had conquered and slain the snow-topped giant.

Well, the day he strode from the Council of Kings with the Sword of Britain on his hip, he had another mountain to conquer, and another giant to entomb. That mountain was forging the unity of Britain — the vaunting pride of the small kings was the giant.

These two together made Eryri and its forbidding heights appear but a mound in a maiden's turnip patch.

I have bethought myself many times what was accomplished that dreary day — what was lost, and what the gain.

We lost a High King certainly. We gained a *Dux Britanniarum*, a war leader — if in title only. There were no legions to command, no auxiliaries, there was no fleet, no mounted *ala*. Arthur had no warband — he did not even own a horse! And so the grand Roman title meant nothing and everyone knew it.

Everyone except Arthur. 'I will be their Duke,' he vowed. 'And I will lead the battles so well and rightly they will be forced to make me High King!'

Still, there was no force to lead. There was only Bedwyr, and Cai, the two pledged to Arthur and one another since childhood. Mind, taken together, the three were a power to be esteemed. Any king would have given the champion's place to any one of them, simply to have such a warrior in his keep.

Arthur's first trial would be to gather a warband. Implicit in this was the support and maintenance of the warriors. It was one thing to raise the men, and quite another to provide sustenance for them: arms, horses, food, clothing, shelter — that took an endless supply of wealth.

Wealth derives from land. The ants in the dust possessed more of that than Arthur.

This lack, however, was soon addressed, for upon returning to Gradlon's house that night we found Meurig arrived from Caer Myrddin with three of his chieftains, all of them exhausted and near frozen to their saddles.

'I am sorry, Lord Emrys; I beg your forgiveness,' Meurig said, upon settling himself before the hearth with a warming cup in his hand. And hastily turning to Arthur, added, ' — and yours, Lord Arthur. I am heartily sorry to have missed the council. My father desired so badly to come, but the weather — '

'You missed nothing,' Arthur replied. 'It does not matter.'

'I understand your displeasure,' Meurig began. 'But — '

'What he means,' interrupted Merlin, 'is that your presence, welcome as it is, would not have helped matters.'

'But if I had been here. . .'

'No.' Merlin shook his head gently. 'As it is, you have had a long, cold ride for nothing. Still, since you are here I would have you hail the Duke of Britain, and drink his health. I give you Arthur, *Dux Britanniarum*!'

'What happened?' Meurig had expected to find Arthur made king.

'In a word,' muttered Ectorius, 'Morcant.'

Meurig gestured rudely at the name. 'I need not have asked. I should have known that old deceiver would put down Arthur's claim. He was not alone?'

True, Meurig had expected to find Arthur made king — it was to his father, Tewdrig, King of Dyfed, that Merlin

49

brought the infant Arthur for protection, the first years of his life. Consequently, Meurig had long since discovered Arthur's identity. Yet even Meurig, close as he was, did not fully appreciate the strength of Arthur's claim to the throne of Britain.

In fairness, few men did in those days. Aurelius' son he might be, well and good; but it took more than that to make a man High King. It took the support of all the kings. Or at very least as many as would silence the dissenters — which, in practical terms, amounted to almost the same thing.

No one fully believed that a youth of fifteen, a mere boy, could accede to the High Kingship, nor would they abet him.

'Morcant had all the help he needed,' replied Merlin sourly.

'I would gladly flay those wattled jowls,' swore Cai, 'if it would do any good.'

'I should have been here,' Meurig repeated. 'My father is not well, or he would have made the journey with us. We were prevented by the weather. As it is, we lost two horses.' He turned to Arthur. 'I am sorry, lad.'

'It does not matter, Lord Meurig,' said Arthur, belying his true feelings, which anyone could see on his face. The unhappy group fell silent.

'Duke of Britain, eh? That is a beginning anyway.' Meurig, feeling responsible, forced a jovial mood. 'What will you do now?'

Arthur had his answer ready. 'Raise a warband — that is first. It will be the greatest warband ever seen in the Island of the Mighty. Only the finest warriors will ride with me.'

'Then you will need lands — to raise horses, grain, meat,' announced Meurig grandly. Arthur frowned, feeling his poverty. 'Therefore, my father and I are agreed that you shall have the lands south of Dyfed.'

'Siluria? But those lands are yours!' objected Arthur.

'*Were* mine,' Meurig corrected him. 'My father is old and will rule no longer. I am to rule in Dyfed now. Therefore we need a strong hand in the south and, as I have no heir to follow me, I can think of none better to hold the land than you. Yes?'

Arthur's frown turned to incredulity.

'Now then,' Meurig hurried on, 'there is an old hill fort lying between the Taff and Ebbw rivers, with a port on Mor Hafren — Caer Melyn is its name. It would take a deal of work, but you could make it a serviceable stronghold. The land is good; with care, it will provide.' Meurig beamed his pleasure in making the gift. 'How now? Nothing to say, young Arthur?'

'I scarce know what to say.'

The young Duke appeared so disconcerted by this news that Ectorius clapped him on the back, shouting, 'Be of good cheer, my son. You will just have to accept your good fortune and get on with life as best you can.'

'Lands *and* a sword!' called Cai. 'What next? A wife and squalling bairns, no doubt.'

Arthur grimaced at Cai's gibe, and turned to Meurig. 'I am in your debt, my lord. I will do my best to hold the land and rule it as you would yourself.'

'I do not doubt it. You will be to us a wall of steel, behind which the people of Dyfed will grow fat and lazy.' Meurig laughed, and the shadows which had dogged our every move during our stay in Londinium rolled back.

I poured mead from the jar. We drank to the fortune of the Duke of Britain, and then began to talk of establishing Arthur's warband. Ectorius and Cai, it was decided, should return to Caer Edyn as soon as the weather would allow, to begin raising a force that could join Arthur in the south.

Naturally, Arthur could not wait to see his lands. He had visited there as a boy, of course, but had not been in Dyfed for a very long time. Winter lay full upon the land, but Arthur did not care. He would have it that next morning we should ride at once to Caer Melyn to inspect it.

'Wait at least until the snow has melted,' urged Merlin. 'Meurig says that winter has been hard in the southlands this year.'

'What is a little snow?'

'Have a care, Arthur. It is cold!'

'Then we will wear two cloaks! I mean to see my lands, Myrddin. What sort of lord would I be if I neglected my holdings?'

'It is hardly neglect to wait until the roads are passable.'

'You sound like a merchant,' he scoffed, and proceeded with his plans just the same.

I believe he had it all worked out before ever we left Londinium: how he would raise his warband, how he would support it, how he would build his kingdom, using Caer Melyn and the rich southlands given him as his strong foundation. He saw it so clearly that doubters were forced to join with him or stand aside. In this, as in so many things with Arthur, there could be no middle ground.

So we left Londinium the next morning and hastened west. Upon arriving at the Ebbw river — after more freezing nights along the track than I care to remember — Arthur rode at once to the hill fort. Like all the others in the region it was built on the crown of the highest hill in the vicinity, and offered a long view in every direction. Caer Melyn stood surrounded by a ring of smaller strongholds, a dozen in all, guarding the entrances to the valleys and the river inlets along the nearby coast.

Directly east lay another interlocking ring of hill forts, with Caer Legionis at its centre. The Fort of the Legions stood in ruins, deserted now, worthless. But Meurig had established a stronghold on a high hill a little to the north, above the ruined Roman fortress, and this, like Caer Melyn, was also surrounded by its ring of smaller hill forts.

The whole region was thus protected by these interlinked rings, making all of Dyfed and Siluria secure. Meurig, however, had never lived at Caer Melyn. Indeed, it had been many years since the Irish Sea Wolves had dared essay the vigilance of the southwestern British kings. Consequently the hill forts had been allowed to become overgrown and derelict from disuse. Certainly, Caer Melyn stood in need of repair: gates must be rehung, ramparts rebanked, ditches redug, wall sections replaced, stores replenished. . .

As Meurig had said, it would take a deal of work to make the place habitable. But, to Arthur, it was already a fortress invincible and a palace without peer.

Caer Melyn, the Golden Fortress. It was so called for the yellow sulphur springs nearby, but Arthur saw another kind of gold shining here. He saw it as it *would be*, imagining himself lord of the realm.

Nevertheless, we were forced to sleep in what was — a

forlorn hilltop open to the ice-bright stars and deep winter's bone-rattling blasts. Arthur did not care. The place was his and he was master of it; he insisted on spending his first night in his own lands in his own fortress.

We banked the fire high and slept close to it, wrapped in our furs and cloaks. Before we slept, Arthur prevailed upon Merlin to sing a tale to mark the occasion. 'As this is the first tale sung in my hall' — there was no hall — 'it is fitting that it be sung by the Chief Bard of the Island of the Mighty.'

Merlin chose *The Dream of Macsen Wledig*, changing it just a little to include Arthur. This pleased the young Duke enormously. 'Here will I make my home,' he declared expansively. 'And from this day forth let Caer Melyn be known as the foremost court of all Britain.'

'Of all courts past, present, and yet to come,' Merlin replied, 'this will be chief among them. It will be remembered as long as memory endures.'

Mind, it would be some time before the ruin could be called a caer, let alone a court. On that raw wintry morn when we arose to the frost and blow, beating our arms across our chests to warm ourselves, Arthur had not so much as a hearthstone to his name.

All he had, in fact, was Merlin's shining promise.

That day we rode to several of the surrounding hill forts to further Arthur's inspection of his realm. He seemed not to mind that the places were fit more for wolf and raven than for men. It was clear that Meurig's gift would exact a price of its own, but Arthur would pay, and with a song on his lips.

As the sun started on its downward arc in the low winter sky, we turned towards Caer Myrddin to join Meurig there. We reached the stronghold as the pale green-tinted light faded from the hills. The horses' noses were covered with frost and their withers steamed as we trotted up the track to the timber-walled enclosure.

Nothing now remained of the old villa that had stood there in the days, now long past, when young Merlin had ruled here as king with Lord Maelwys, Meurig's grandfather. Maridunum it had been in those days. Now it was Caer Myrddin — after its most famous ruler, though he was not a king any more and had not lived there in many, many years.

Torches already burned in the gate sconces — yellow flame in the deep blue shadows on the hard, frost-covered ground — but the gates were still open. We were expected.

Horses stood unattended in the yard. I wondered at this, and turned to point it out to Merlin who rode beside me. But Arthur had already seen them and knew in his heart what this meant.

'Yah!' he slapped the leather reins across his mount's flanks and galloped into the yard, hardly touching ground as he raced for the hall. Those within must have heard his cry, for as Arthur flung himself from the saddle, the door to Meurig's hall opened and a knot of men burst into the yard.

'Arthur!'

One of the men emerged from the throng and ran to meet him, caught Arthur up in a great bear hug. The two stood there in the pale golden torchlight from the hall, locked in a wrestler's embrace, then drew back, gripping one another's arms in the ancient greeting of kinsmen.

'Bedwyr! You *are* here.'

'Where should I be when my brother needs me?' Bedwyr grinned, shaking his head. 'Look at you. . . Duke of Britain, indeed!'

'What is wrong with that?'

'Arthur, the sight of you is earth and sky to me,' replied Bedwyr dryly. 'But if I had been there you would be a king now.'

'How so, brother? Are you Emperor of the West, so that you can play at king-making?'

Both laughed heartily at this exchange and they fell upon one another once more. Then Bedwyr saw us. 'Myrddin! Pelleas!' He hurried to us and hugged us both. 'You have come as well. I had not thought to find you all here. Happy I am to see you. Bright Spirits bear witness, God is wise and good!'

'Hail, Bedwyr! You look a very prince of Rheged,' I told him. It was true. Bedwyr's dark locks were gathered in a thick braid; richly enamelled gold bands glinted at his wrists and arms; his woollen cloak was bright yellow and black, woven in the cunning checked pattern of the north; his soft leather boots painted with serpentine designs reached to his knees. In all, he appeared a Celt of old.

'Pelleas, God be good to you, I have missed you. It has been a long time.' Indeed it had; eight years, in fact.

'How did you come here?' asked Arthur. 'We thought you would wait until the thaw to set out.'

'We have enjoyed the mildest of winters in the north,' Bedwyr replied. 'In consequence, we were forced to stay longer than we might have: Sea Wolves troubled us late into the season, or we might have come in the autumn.' He laughed quickly. 'But I see we have surprised even Myrddin, and that makes the wait worth while!'

'Unexpected, perhaps' Merlin allowed. 'But I count it no surprise to greet one whose company we have so often desired. It is joy itself to see you, Bedwyr.'

Meurig, who had been looking on, approached with torch in hand, beaming his good fortune. 'Let my hall be filled! We will have a feast of friends this glad night.'

And so we did. Of food there was no end, and drink flowed in a ceaseless stream from jar and skin. The hall blazed with pine knot and rushlight, and the hearthfire crackled merrily, casting its ruddy glow all around. Meurig had acquired a harper of some skill, so we did not lack for music. We held forth in song and danced the old steps.

The next days were full: hunting, eating and drinking, singing, talking, laughing. Bishop Gwythelyn came from the nearby abbey at Llandaff to bless the merriment and to consecrate Arthur in his new position as protector of Britain. This was done in fine style. I see before me still the image of Arthur kneeling before the good bishop, holding the hem of Gwythelyn's undyed cloak to his lips, while the bishop lays holy hands on him.

It was like that: one moment Arthur was the Duke of Britain, wearing the full honour and responsibility of that title, the next he was the Cymry prince, light-hearted, his laughter easy and free. It was a feast for the soul just to watch him, to be near him.

Sweet Jesu, I cannot remember a happier time. No one enjoyed it more than did Arthur and Bedwyr, who sat together at the board laughing and talking the whole night through. And when the last lights were put out, they still sat head to head, pledging to one another their hopes and dreams for the years ahead.

Each had so much to say to the other, so much lost time to redeem. Arthur and Bedwyr had known one another almost from birth, for Merlin and I had brought Arthur to Tewdrig's stronghold in Dyfed when Arthur was still a babe. Arthur's first years had been spent at Caer Myrddin with King Bleddyn's youngest son, Bedwyr: a slim, graceful boy, as dark as Arthur was fair. Bold shadow to Arthur's bright sun.

The two had become constant friends: golden mead and dark wine poured into the same cup. Every day of those early years they spent together — until separated at the age of seven by the strict necessity of fosterage in different royal houses. Bedwyr had gone to live with King Ennion, his kinsman in Rheged, and Arthur to Ectorius at Caer Edyn. And except for all-too-brief occasions such as Gatherings, or the infrequent royal assembly, they had rarely seen one another. Their friendship had endured long privation, but it had endured.

No one thought ill when the two of them rode out to inspect Arthur's lands one morning and were gone three days. Upon their return Arthur announced that the eastern portion of his lands — these included many deep, hidden valleys — would be given to the breeding of horses, and would be placed under Bedwyr's rule.

They were already thinking far, far ahead, to the day when each horse they could provide would mean one more warrior for Britain.

So, early in that spring the course was set which, for better or worse, would steer the Island of the Mighty through the gathering gale of war. Directly after Pentecost, work began at Caer Melyn. Seven days after Beltane, Cai arrived with the first of Arthur's warband: twenty well-trained young men chosen by Ectorius as the best north of the Wall.

And six days after Lugnasadh, King Morcant decided to test the young Duke's mettle.

FIVE

Word came to Caer Melyn that Morcant was gathering his warband to ride against Bedegran and Madoc in but the latest clash of that long-standing blood feud. Arthur had only twenty men; counting himself, Cai and Bedwyr there were twenty-three. Hardly a match for Morcant's hundreds.

Nevertheless, Arthur determined that if he allowed Morcant to succeed in cowing him through strength of superior numbers, he might as well give the Sword of Britain to the old scoundrel — and the High Kingship into the bargain.

I was prepared to ride with him, but Merlin counselled against it. 'Stay, Pelleas. There will be other battles where we will be needed more. Let them win this first one on their own. A victory will give them courage and earn them a measure of renown in the land. Besides, I would have Morcant and his like know that Arthur is his own man.'

That this test should come so early was not fortuitous, but Arthur was undaunted. Indeed, he welcomed it. 'That toothless old lion has roared once too often, I tell you,' he said. 'We will go and shear him for a sheep, aye?'

With no more concern, and scarcely more preparation, the warriors rode at once to Morcant's stronghold.

The Belgae are an old, old people whose tribal seat is at Venta Belgarum. Owing to an early peace with Rome, the Belgae established themselves pre-eminent in the region and Uintan Caestir became an important *civitas*. The Belgae and their city prospered and grew powerful serving the Legions.

When the Legions left, the city shrank in upon itself — as all cities did — and the Belgae returned to the land and their former ways. But bits of the city still remained, and it was here that Morcant held his power.

Caer Uintan had once possessed a public forum and a basilica. These had long ago been taken over by the lords of the Belgae for private use: the forum became a palace, the basilica a hall. For all his British blood, Lord Morcant styled himself a ruler of the Roman stamp.

To walk into his palace was to enter again another time, now long past. A time more and more recalled — by those who had never seen it — with impossible grandeur and glory, a great golden age of order, prosperity, peace and learning.

Certainly, Morcant revelled in such belief. He lived surrounded by objects of the past, attended by ranks of servants who maintained for him the semblance of that faded era. He lived like an emperor. . . but an emperor in exile from his beloved empire.

Like Londinium, Caer Uintan boasted a rampart of stone around its perimeter. In recent years a deep ditch had been dug below the wall to make it higher still. However much it had declined from its former glory, Caer Uintan was still the fortress of a powerful king.

But its king was not there.

Morcant was with his warband, harrying the settlements on Madoc's borders a small distance away. By the time the rapacious lord heard about Arthur's intervention and returned to his palace, the young Duke and his few men were already manning the ramparts of Morcant's stronghold against him.

In this Arthur showed the first glimmer of that martial genius he was to exhibit time and time again in the years to come. The manoeuvre took Morcant completely by surprise. Well, did he really expect Arthur to meet him on the field?

Morcant's forces outnumbered Arthur's fifteen men to one. The young Duke's forces could not have withstood Morcant's in pitched combat. Though keen and determined, and lacking nothing in courage, they were green and unseasoned. And Arthur had no experience leading untried men. Indeed, young Arthur had little enough experience leading a warband of any size or description.

Morcant hoped, I think, to belittle Arthur and defame him. He knew Arthur could not ignore the challenge, so the old lion should have expected Arthur to use what few weapons he possessed. But Morcant was the fool, truth to tell; and his foolishness had already cost the lives of more than a few good men. That folly had to be put down once for all.

This is the way of it:

Arthur made for Caer Uintan and found it, as he expected, virtually unprotected — such was Morcant's arrogance, he did not deem it a danger to leave his stronghold unguarded when he raided.

'Oh, we had no trouble getting in,' Cai told me, delighting in every detail of the events he described. 'We simply rode up as if we were expected, and "What is that you say? Morcant not here? Is this any way to greet the Duke of Britain? Why, yes, go and fetch your lord. We will wait for him inside."

'Once inside we gather everyone — it's mostly women and children anyway — and bring them to the hall. And Bedwyr tells them it is an offence to Morcant's good name if they do not receive the Duke with a feast. This throws them all in a fluster, so they scurry around preparing a feast for us. It is such confusion that no one even notices Arthur has sealed the gates.'

Cai chuckled, savouring his tale. 'When Morcant learns that Arthur has come, back he storms to his fortress. But it is too late. The gates are secured, and the walls manned against him. He rages for the better part of a day, but the Duke will not speak to him.

'He would scream. Oh, how he could scream! And that son of his, Cerdic, has a mouth on him as well. But Arthur would not answer them. Instead, my lord bade me deal with them. So, I called down to him from his own walls:

'"Hail, Morcant! Hail, Cerdic! How is it that we come to you and find no one to receive us?" I ask him. "As it is, we have had to prepare our own feast of welcome."

'And the roaring old lion answers me, he says, "By whose authority do you overrun my palace and stronghold?"

'"By authority of the Duke of Britain," I answer, "the very same who now sits in your chair at meat." Oh, he does not like this; he does not. He calls me no end of names to prove it, and he has even more for Arthur. But I pretend to ignore him.

'"Tell me, great king," I say to him, "explain to me if you can, how it is that you have come to be locked outside your own gates at your own feast? This is a wonder I would hear told throughout all Lloegres." Well, this makes him even angrier. Up he puffs, just like an adder about to strike — but there is nothing to bite. So he begins shouting some more.

'Cerdic is beside himself. "Come out and fight!" he cries. "Cowards! Thieves! Let us settle this with swords!" It is all he knows, you see. But again I make no reply.

'Well, this goes on until sunset. I go to Arthur and ask if he means this to continue all night. "Yes," he tells me, "we have ridden hard and need our rest. Tell Morcant we are going to sleep now, and not to make so much noise,"' Cai chortled at the audacity of it.

'So back to the rampart I go and tell Morcant what the Duke has said. Does this make him happy, Pelleas? No, it does not. He screams like a pig when the knife goes in. He is all a-lather, and his men are beginning to laugh — which only makes it worse for him, you see.

'But what does Morcant expect? So, we leave him there for the night and next morning I go to see what he is about. There he is, red-eyed and temper-twisted; I believe he spent the night in the saddle cursing! "You have given me no choice," he cries, "I have laid siege to my own stronghold." And, indeed, his men are ranged without the walls as if to keep us from escaping.

'He thinks he is being clever with this, but when I tell Arthur what Morcant has done, Arthur only laughs and calls for someone to bring him a torch. Out into the yard we march and there the Duke sets fire to one of the storehouses. Do you believe it? Pelleas, it is God's truth I am telling!

'And when the flames are set, says Arthur, "Now let us go and see if Morcant will speak more civilly to his servant, or whether his sharp tongue will cost him his fine palace." So that is what we do.

'On the wall, up speaks Arthur, "Greetings, my king, I hear that you have been calling for me. Forgive me, but I have had many things on my mind, what with one thing and another." This he says as sweet as you please — the right innocent is Arthur.

"'Do not think you can escape punishment, boy!" So bellows Morcant. "Aurelius' bastard or no, I mean to have your head on a spike where you stand."

'The old fool is foaming mad, and I am beginning to think we have made a grave mistake. Some of the men are clasping their swords and muttering to one another — they can be forgiven, because they do not know Arthur. Still, it is a tight place and no mistake.

"'Is this the hospitality you are so widely renowned for?" asks Arthur. Ha! It is and well he knows it!' Cai crowed. Then, rubbing his hands in glee, he continued, 'Well, by now smoke is starting to rise in plumes from the yard behind. Morcant sees it, and sees the torch in Arthur's hand — Arthur is still holding it, you see — and "What have you done?" the king demands. "What is burning?"

"'Someone appears to have been rather careless with this torch," says Arthur. "A shame, too, for now I do not know where I shall sleep tonight," he tells him — for all it is barely daylight! You should have seen Morcant's face — a rare sight, I tell you.

"'My palace!" screams Morcant. His face is blue-black with venom now; he is bloated with it. "You are burning my palace!" His eyes bulge as he stares at the smoke.

"'Yes," says Arthur, in a voice hard as cold steel, "I am burning your palace. There is but one way to save it: end your war with Madoc and Bedegran, and pay me tribute."

"'The Devil take you!" cries Morcant. "No one dictates terms to me!"

'Arthur turns and hands the torch to Bedwyr and says, "Take this to the stables and stores. See if they leap as quick to the flame as Morcant's hall." So, Bedwyr obliges,' laughed Cai. 'He is only too eager to please.

'Morcant hears this, of course. And he cannot believe his ears. "No! No!" he screams, just like that, losing all command.

'But Arthur heeds him not.' Cai shook his head in admiration. 'He is fearless, Arthur is.'

'What happened next?' I asked, relishing his story immensely.

'Well,' Cai took a long draught of his beer, 'Morcant orders his men to attack. Cerdic leads them. But what can they do? They beat on the gates with the pommels of their swords. Some of them have cut down a small tree and they try with that to break in. But their hearts are not in it.

'Arthur knows this, so he tells us not to stone them. "Let be," he says. "Our sword brothers are confused. Do not hurt them."

'The smoke is rolling thick and black now. Bedwyr has not actually set fire to the stores, but has dumped a quantity of grains into the yard and is burning that, you see, so it makes a deal of smoke. They have put a wagon or two full of hay into it as well, I think, *and*,' Cai broke off to laugh, 'he has brought some horses to stand nearby. The horses are afraid of the fire, of course, and they start raising a fearful din.

'Morcant hears this — how can he help it? "Stop! Stop!" he cries. "I will do as you ask. Name your tribute," he roars; he can hardly spit out the words he is so raged. Cerdic howls like a dog gone mad.

'"Thirty of your warriors," Arthur tells him.

'"Never!" King Morcant bellows.

'"Fifty then," the Duke replies.

'"Go you to hell, whore spawn!" is Morcant's answer.

'"Cai, I do not think Lord Morcant believes that we are in earnest. Take you a torch to his chambers and treasury," Arthur orders. He gazes down upon the writhing snake below and says, "Fortunately, we find no end of things to burn."

'And I make ready to do as I am bid. Well, Morcant is hearing this with his mouth open. He cannot believe what his ears are telling him. Still, he does not say anything, so I am beginning to think that he is stubborn enough to let it all go up in flames, just to spite Arthur.

'But, just as I leave the wall, I hear him shouting again. "Stop! Stop!" he cries. "I will do it!"

'I know better than to trust Morcant. I imagine him letting us think we are safe away and then turning on us the moment we show our backs. But Arthur has already thought of this, you see. So he says to Morcant, "Very well, you had better come in and tend to this fire before your palace is a heap of ashes." And he orders a gate to be opened.'

'How did he keep Morcant from overwhelming you all when they came in?' I asked, thinking that this was precisely what Morcant would do.

Cai threw back his head and laughed. 'We let them in but one at a time and took their arms as they came through,' Cai replied. 'Oh, he was canny, was Arthur. He took sword and spear, and issued jug and jar — to fight the fire, you see. By the time Morcant gains entrance, his men are busy fighting the flames and their weapons lie in a heap in the yard.

'Morcant was mad enough to bite the heads off snakes, but even he saw the futility of attacking Arthur alone. He boiled about like a cauldron left on the hearth too long, but he did not raise blade against us. I think he hoped to catch us in a mistake later on.' Cai's voice lowered to a tone approaching reverence. 'But Arthur was Morcant's master long before Caer Uintan's flames sprouted.'

'How did you get out alive?' I wondered. 'It was a dangerous game Arthur played.'

'Oh, it is a marvel indeed,' Cai agreed. 'In the end we simply rode out the way we rode in — but there were more of us by fifty, mind. For the Duke took his tribute from Morcant's best warriors.

'"Cai," he says to me, "you and Bedwyr choose out the best from among them. But mark you well: take only young men who have no kinsmen among those we leave behind." And this we did.'

I too marvelled at the shrewdness of it, as incisive as it was brazen. It took courage, yes, but it also took a rare and ready wit. Fifteen years old and well along to becoming a tactician the likes of the legendary Macsen Wledig. Arthur had ridden out with twenty-two and returned with seventy-two. He had increased the size of his warband threefold and more — and not a drop of blood spilled!

'See, by taking only the younger men — men with no ties of kinship to any of Morcant's,' Cai explained, 'the Duke gained men he could command as his alone. They would not be looking to return to Morcant, and would not hesitate to fight against Morcant if pressed to it at need.' He paused and added, 'Though, truth be told, Arthur could have had them all. Any man among them would have followed him without so much as a backward glance. I am telling you, the warriors did not love Morcant.'

All this Cai related upon their triumphant return. And the same tale was told Merlin in turn. 'Well done,' said Merlin. 'Oh, very well done, indeed. Mark me, Pelleas, Arthur has won more than renown with this deed. With this he has won as many men as have ears to hear it!'

Perhaps. But, for the present, Arthur had a problem housing and feeding the men he already had. Whatever else, tripling his warband was a costly manoeuvre. In summer they could hunt, of course, but during the long winter — when there was nothing to be done but repair weapons and wait for spring — the food would simply vanish. Little wonder we wasted not a moment sending out demands for tribute to the kings who had promised to support us.

That summer was heady and hectic: a hall to raise, stores and granaries to erect, enclosures to build for cattle and horses, walls and earthworks to secure, food and supplies to collect. Fortunate indeed that Arthur had so many men; there was so much to be done that every hand was busy from dawn's crack to dusk's last light, and still much went undone.

As summer faded to autumn we waited for the wagons bearing the tribute. For with each passing day our need grew more acute and we knew that we could not last the winter without the promised supplies. We had cattle pens, yes, and we had storehouses — but nothing to put in them. We had a hall, but not enough skins to sleep on, nor cloaks enough to keep us all warm.

As I say, all the kings had pledged tribute for the maintenance of Britain's warband. But when the first wagons began arriving — half-empty most of them, and the little they carried hardly worth transporting in the first place — we saw where the next battle would be fought.

'Why are they doing this?' Arthur gestured hopelessly at the meagre cargo being unloaded and trundled into the stores.

'Keep the *Dux* needy and they can control him. Control him and they can rule him,' Merlin answered. 'Men do not follow whom they rule.'

'Curse them!' Arthur grew instantly livid. 'I could take by force what was promised me.'

'That would avail nothing,' Merlin soothed.

'Then are we to starve because of them?'

'No one will starve. Custennin and Meurig will see us through the winter, never fear.'

'And after that? It will be long before we can get crops sown and harvested.'

'Please!' cried Merlin. 'One worry at a time, Arthur. Do not borrow tomorrow's troubles today.'

'We have to think about these things.'

'Agreed, which is why I have already decided what to do.'

Arthur kicked at the dirt with his boot. 'Then why do you let me take on so? Do you enjoy watching me work myself into a sweat?'

'If you will stop raving for a moment, I will tell you what is to be done.'

Which is how I came to find myself aboard a ship, sailing across the sea called Muir Nicht, on my way to Armorica.

SIX

I had never been on a ship before, and discovered sea travel most unnerving and disagreeable. Though the sea remained calm, the ceaseless motion — rising, falling, rolling side to side — made me feel as if I were wine drunk and riding an unbroken colt. The crossing took the whole of one day and most of another, and never was a man more happy to espy those dust-brown hills of Armorica than I.

Gleaming darkly in the ruddy dusk, bold red-grey banks of clouds towered high above and twilight stars already showed overhead. I saw those hills and I felt as if I had spent all my life on that cramped boat and knew land only as a rumoured thing contrived by seafarers. The miracle — Great Light, the relief! — of that landfall brought the mist to my eyes, I tell you.

Merlin bore the journey without difficulty. He talked to the ship's pilot and crew, gleaning all he could from them. In this way he learned how affairs stood in Armorica, so that we should not be surprised at our reception there.

Upon making landfall, Merlin hired a messenger to take word of our arrival to the lord of the realm — a land called Benowyc. We stayed the night in the seaside settlement favoured by the ship's men. The people of this port were friendly and well disposed to serving the needs of travellers. Hence we were well provided with good food and better wine than I had tasted before. They talked freely of the events of Gaul, though considered themselves apart from it — more a part of Britain, as the likeness of our shared tongue confirmed.

I slept well that night — despite the sensation of phantom waves heaving beneath me. As we broke fast next morning, the messenger returned with a token from the lord and a message urging us to come to him at once and receive a proper welcome.

King Ban of Benowyc was kinsman to Hoel, the king who had sheltered Aurelius and Uther from Vortigern when they were young. Hoel it was who had sent a warband to aid Aurelius against the Saecsen war leader Hengist. Thus the name of Merlin was well known to Ban, and to many others.

We mounted our horses — I vowed never to complain of the saddle again — and proceeded at once to Benowyc, where Ban was awaiting us with all eagerness. It was no great distance, and we soon reached our destination: Caer Kadarn, a large, well-kept stronghold on a hill overlooking the sea to the north and west.

'Hail, Merlin Embries!' he called from horseback as he rode out to greet us. 'Long have I desired to meet you.' He leaned from his saddle and gripped my master by the arms in the manner of kinsmen. 'Greetings and glad welcome to you. My hearth is yours for as long as you will stay — and I pray that stay be long.'

My master accepted this greeting graciously. 'Hail, Lord Ban! We have heard of the hospitality and courtesy of the kings of Armorica. Surely you must stand foremost among them to welcome strangers this way.'

This reply pleased Ban enormously. Indeed, the Armoricans enjoyed praise and ever sought means to elicit flattering words. 'But you are not strangers, my lord,' Ban said. 'The name of the great Embries is a name of renown and respect among us. You are merely a friend we have not owned the pleasure of meeting until now.'

As I say, the Armoricans were ever mindful of our good opinion, and eager to secure it. This they accomplished adroitly and without undue effort, so adept were their skills.

We were conducted to Ban's hall, where he had prepared a small meal of welcome: seeded bread, cheese, and a kind of heavy sweet wine. We tasted of these and listened as Ban described the events of the summer, and how he and his brother, Bors, the battlechief of Benowyc, had fought three battles against the Angli and Jutes in Gaul.

'I would like to meet your brother,' Merlin said.

To which Ban replied, 'Fortunate men bring their fortune with them I find. For, indeed, Bors is expected to return here the next day but one. He will want to greet you, too.'

We spent the day talking and riding, for Ban was keen to show us his realm, and to hear us praise it. As it happened, this was no burden to us for Benowyc was a fine and fair place, good to look upon, blessed with wide fields, forests of tall timber, and long, lush hunting runs second to none. Therefore was Ban a wealthy king.

Like many rich men, Ban proved overproud of his possessions, and took pleasure — perhaps too much — in showing them, speaking about them, lauding them and hearing them lauded.

Still, he had the respect of his people, who knew him to be a calm and steady ruler, and generous in his dealings. And whatever else might be said, he had not allowed his fondness for wealth to corrupt his good judgement. He was not one to make another feel abused or cheated.

Bors, on the other hand, was head to heel the warrior: hasty, intemperate, easily incited to arms and action, as fond of boasting as of drinking — and he was a champion of the cups, I can tell you! Nevertheless, he was superbly skilled in battle and in leading men, a ferocious fighter, possessing both the strength and temperament of a charging boar.

But the brothers shared the same love of life and hatred of the barbarian. Ban and Bors could be counted on to aid any who warred against the enemies of order and right. And, with their wealth, this aid could be considerable.

This was why Merlin had come, of course: to tell them of Arthur, and secure their good will and support. As their kinsman Hoel had aided Aurelius, Merlin hoped Ban would aid Arthur.

But there was another reason. It was something Merlin had glimpsed in the black oak water of the Seeing Bowl — an ancient druid object he sometimes employed to search out the tangled pathways of time. He would not say what he had seen, but it disturbed him and he wanted to discover its source.

The second day we were with Ban, the warband returned. A lavish meal — put on as much for our benefit as for the warband's, I believe — had been laid in the hall and we supped well. Bors, expansive in his pleasure at being home, turned to Merlin with a jar of beer in his hand. 'What is this I hear about you, Merlin? They tell me you are a bard. Is this so?'

Bors meant no disrespect, so Merlin suffered his ignorance with good grace. 'My lord,' he replied modestly, 'I have been known to stroke the harp now and then. Some find the noise agreeable, I believe.'

Bors grinned and slapped the board with the flat of his hand. 'By Lud, that is a fine thing! The harp, you say? Well, I am your man, Lord Embries.'

'Pledge me no pledges until you have heard me play,' Merlin told him. 'Armorican ears may not find favour in what they hear.'

Bors laughed loudly at this. 'Play then, I say, that I may judge the value of British noise.'

At my master's bidding, I fetched the harp, ready tuned, and brought it to him. And, as was the custom in that land, the women, who had taken their meal elsewhere, now entered the hall to hear the tales sung. They came into the hall and found places at the board with the men, or near the hearth.

As it happened, Ban had a harper in his court, a young man named Rhydderch, whom everyone simply called Rhys: a thin, long-boned youth, unremarkable in aspect except for his eyes, which were large and wonderfully expressive, the colour of wood smoke. We had heard him play the night before.

At the sight of Merlin's harp, Rhys rose from his place at one of the further tables and made his way to the king's board. There he stood a little removed, watching intently as Merlin came to stand before the assembly.

'What would you hear, my lord?' asked my master.

Ban thought for a moment, then replied, 'As this is a friendly gathering, let us hear a tale of friendship and honour.'

Merlin nodded and began strumming the harp. The first notes leapt into the hushed hall, shimmering like silver coins flung from an Otherworldly purse, as Merlin's fingers wove the melody for his words.

The tale Merlin offered was *Pwyll, Lord of Annwfn*, as

fine a tale of honour among friends as any that exist. It was especially fitting that night in Ban's hall, for through it Merlin was claiming friendship on behalf of Arthur, just as Arawn claimed it of Pwyll in the tale.

When he finished, the hall sat rapt, unwilling to desecrate the blessed silence following Merlin's inspired song. Then, as the last notes faded back into Oran Mor, the Great Music, as waves fall back into the gifting sea, we heard a crash. Bors was on his feet, his bench thrown over.

The battlechief climbed upon the board, where he stood gazing down at Merlin in awe and wonder. Bors raised his hands into the air and declared to all gathered in the hall, 'My people, hear me now! May I fall dead upon these stones at once if ever a man has heard such song beneath this roof. I say this noble service shall be rewarded. . . ' he grinned expansively and added, 'yes, even to the half of my kingdom.'

So saying, Bors jumped to the floor before Merlin and gathered my master in a fierce embrace. He then removed one of his golden armbands and placed it on Merlin's arm, to the delighted approval of all gathered there.

The people cheered and Ban banged his cup on the board, calling for more. But Merlin refused, begging pardon and promising to sing again before leaving. It was not his custom to flaunt his gifts.

After it became clear that there would be no more singing that night, the warriors and their women began drifting off to their various sleeping-places. Ban and Bors bade us good night and left us to our rest.

Upon reaching our chamber, however, we discovered someone waiting for us — Rhys, the young harper. His first words went straight to the matter on his heart. 'Does your lord have many fine harpers?'

'Good night to you, Rhys,' replied Merlin. 'Leave subtlety to the wind and waves, is that it?'

Rhys coloured at his own presumption, but did not back down. 'Forgive the impudence, lord. I speak only as one harper to another. And I would have your answer.'

The arrogance! He considered himself an equal to Merlin!

'Speak your mind, lad,' Merlin told him. 'Such reticence has no place among friends.'

Rhys blinked back witlessly and looked to me for help.

'You are being reminded of your manners,' I told him.

The young man blushed still brighter, but blundered on. 'Guile is most distasteful to me, my lord, I assure you. If that is what you mean.'

'Your directness is refreshing, Rhys. I stand admonished,' Merlin laughed. 'How may I serve you?'

'But I have already said.' He spread his hands helplessly.

'Then hear my answer,' replied Merlin. 'The lord I serve owns merely the cloak on his back and the sword at his side. He is gathering his warband and retinue now, it is true, but there is not a harper among them. It is a luxury he can ill afford.'

Rhys nodded, as if making up his mind. 'Then your Lord Arthur will require someone to sing his victories before the hearth.' The harp in Merlin's hands might have been an oar for all he noticed.

'I trust you will allow my Lord Arthur to content himself with first getting a hearth.'

'All the more reason,' declared Rhys triumphantly. 'How else will his renown increase sufficiently that men will esteem and follow him? Besides, I can wield a sword as well as I play the harp, and I am the best in all Benowyc at that. Ask who you will.'

'Then I invite you to come with us, if nothing prevents you,' my master told the young harper. 'However, I think your lord will have a word or two to say in the matter. Indeed, from what I have seen, Bors is himself a lord worthy of his renown. No doubt your art would be far better rewarded here.'

'Lord Bors is indeed a worthy chieftain,' agreed Rhys readily. 'But he has *four* harpers to sing his praise, and. . . ' here was the source of his complaint to be sure, 'I am the least among them — in rank, mind, not in skill. They are jealous, and for this reason take no account of me.'

'I see,' Merlin allowed, pulling on his chin. 'Yes, that is a problem. And you think that with Arthur you might fare better. Is that it?'

'For a truth, it is,' Rhys agreed seriously. 'At least, I do not think I could fare much worse.'

'Then, if you are not afraid to ply the sword as well

as the harp, I believe you might account yourself well received.'

We left the matter there for the night, and thought no more about it until the next day when, as we took our midday meal, Bors approached. 'God be good to you, my friends,' he called. 'I hope you are finding our simple fare to your liking.'

'You and your brother are most kind and generous. And, yes, the food is to our taste.'

'Good!' cried Bors, as if he had been waiting all day to hear it. 'That is very good.' He settled on the bench beside Merlin and helped himself to the bread and meat in the bowls before us.

'Now then,' he said, tearing the bread between his hands, 'what is this I am hearing about you stealing one of my bards?'

'Rhydderch told you about his plan, did he?'

'Will you take him?' Bors asked amiably.

'It is not for me to say,' Merlin explained. 'The decision will be yours and Arthur's — as I told the boy. Will you let him go?'

Bors chewed thoughtfully for a moment before answering. 'Although I am loath to lose a good harper, I am honour-bound to grant you your reward — '

'I have asked no reward,' protested Merlin quickly.

' — grant your reward for last night's song,' Bors continued. 'Why, half the realm heard the promise from my own mouth!'

'Please, you owe me nothing. I gave as I have been given.'

'Would you have it whispered about that Bors of Benowyc's word is worth less than the air it takes to speak it?' Bors shook his head gravely, but his eyes were merry. 'That would never do.'

'True. . . ' Merlin agreed slowly.

'So, you shall have Rhys, my Lord Embries,' said Bors, and added shrewdly: 'But I would be less than prudent if I let him go alone.'

'True again. What do you propose?'

'I propose to go with him. To make certain that the boy does not come to harm, you understand.'

'I see,' my master replied. 'By all means, please continue.'

72

'Of course,' said Bors, as he tossed a bit of meat into his mouth and licked his fingers, 'I could not go alone. As I am a friendly man, I would need my companions with me lest I become lonely.'

'To be sure, sojourning far from home often makes a man lonely.'

'A hundred of my best should suffice, I think. With weapons and horses for all, I should not be lonely then.'

Merlin laughed heartily and commended Bors' thoughtfulness. Bors enjoyed his jest, but held up his hands, saying, 'You praise me too highly. I assure you, I am only looking to my own comfort in the matter.'

Ban and Bors had guessed why Merlin had come, and were not willing to see him demean himself by begging support which they were only too happy to provide. So, to save him the embarrassment — little did they know my master if they weened he would shrink from any deed in the advancement of Arthur! — the brothers made the offer of men and horses in this way. Nor did Merlin fail to recognize the gesture for what it was. He also acknowledged their prudence: every battle fought against the Saecsens in Britain was one less to fight on their own soil.

'I tell you, Pelleas,' he said later, 'these men are first in hospitality and honour. Would that Britain's kings were as well disposed to aiding Arthur.'

One purpose of our journey had been accomplished, and far more quickly than we could have hoped. Of the other purpose Merlin still had said nothing. The next day Ban conducted Merlin on a circuit of his realm, visiting the places deemed most likely to impress a stranger. I stayed behind to hunt with Bors, and we enjoyed long rides and evenings in the hall, good food and better wine, and the best of song.

The curious custom of the women — eating apart and joining the men in the hall for the entertainment — was observed on these occasions. So it was not until the third night that I saw her: a peerless maid, possessed of a rare and exquisite beauty.

She entered with the other women and found a place

near the hearth. From the moment that I saw her sitting there — leaning forward slightly to hear the song, hands folded in her lap, eyes bright with joy and anticipation, lips framing a smile that spoke pure delight and a soul in love with life. . .

Bors saw my lingering glance, laughed, and said, 'Yes, she is beautiful, is she not? Her name is Elaine.'

Elaine! The name stirred within me such feeling that I lost all power of speech.

Elaine. . .

From the depths of my mind, the memory surfaced: of Avallach's four ships to escape the cataclysm that destroyed Atlantis, only three had reached Britain. The last, the fourth, had been lost. . .

Avallach had lost his son, Kian; and Belyn, my father, had lost his wife and queen: her name had been Elaine. Although my father never spoke about her, I had heard the story of the missing ship many times in his court.

I did not require further confirmation. By her stature, grace and bearing alone, I knew in my heart that the lady before me was of my race. I sat gazing at her, the realization making my head swim: Fair Folk in Armorica!

Could it be?

Bors mistook my stare for fascination, saying, 'You would not be the first man to succumb to the charm of a Faery maid.'

'How came this woman to be in your court?' I asked, my voice harsh in my ears.

'That is no mystery. My father's father, King Banw, married one of their kind. Though beautiful, the woman was frail and died without giving him an heir. He took another wife, of course, but always said his heart belonged to his Faery queen. Since Banw's time there have been Faery with us. Elaine is of their race. They are aloof and haughty, it is true, but they are a peaceable folk for all their strangeness, and keep to themselves.'

'Where do they abide?'

'In the forest Broceliande — a goodly distance to the east.' Bors observed me closely, as if regarding me for the first time. He leaned close, as if offering a confidence. 'I have heard it said that Lord Embries is of the Faery. Is this so?'

'So it is said.'

Bors nodded as if that explained much. 'And you?'

'Yes.'

'I thought as much. I mentioned it to Ban, but my brother said it was nonsense.'

'People make more of it than there is,' I assured him. 'The Fair Folk are not so different as many believe.'

He accepted this with a ready laugh. 'There is no end of things people believe. I have heard it said that your people can change shape as you will — become wolves or stags or owls, or whatever.'

Our talk turned gradually to other things, but I thought to myself, Fair Folk *here*, here in Armorica! Merlin must hear of this!

SEVEN

Broceliande lay two days' ride from the coastland into the wide low hills of Armorica. The land across the Narrow Sea is not as wet, not as given to mists and fogs and rain as Ynys Prydein. And at the height of summer it can be hot; the heat rises from the earth to dance in shimmering waves along the hilltops and ridges, and the dust puffs up beneath the horses' hooves.

It is a fair land. Streams and rivers, lakes and springs and pools there are in number. Trees grow tall, and the woodlands abound with all manner of game for the table. A lord would call himself blessed to hold such a realm; indeed, many I know hold far less of far worse and think themselves fortunate.

Thus it is something of a mystery to me that there are not more settlements in that region. Although we did pass through two new holdings on our way, these were being cleared and settled by Britons who, like others from the eastern and southern regions of Britain, had begun crossing the sea to escape the raiding Saecsen. A forlorn and slender hope. The Saecsen left Armorica alone for the most part because Britain was the more ripe for plunder.

If Britain fell, or if it rallied and discouraged raiding altogether, the barbarian would look to Armorica soon enough, and where would civilized men escape to then?

The thought that fellow countrymen — our own kinsmen! — were deserting our land discouraged Merlin. He did not like to see it, nor did I. But I understood and forgave them their fear, whereas Merlin felt betrayed.

'Do they think to escape the Darkness simply by crossing a little water?' he asked, eyeing the rude settlement sadly. 'I tell you the truth, Pelleas: when the sun goes down, the

76

light fails for everyone, and all men will curse the night as one.'

He sighed and shook his head slowly. 'And there will be no bringing back the light once it has gone.'

So it was not altogether a light-hearted journey for us. But upon arriving at the edge of the forest we encountered a small holding — not more than a handful of mud-daubed huts and a briar cattle enclosure. The people living there were kindly and eager for news of the wider world. When we asked after the Fair Folk settlement, they were pleased to tell us where and how to find it, and would have sent someone to conduct us there if we had allowed it. The Fair Folk, they said, were solitary and did not welcome strangers. Nevertheless, they possessed the knowledge of many extraordinary secrets and helped the settlement from time to time as need arose.

In all, we found Broceliande to be very like Celyddon, and the Fair Folk settlement almost identical to Custennin's. The forest, dark and deep grown, hid the settlement from the world as surely as any enchantment.

The holding was built of timber on the steep rock banks of a broad forest lake — as at Goddeu in Celyddon they had chosen to build near a secluded lake. The forest had not been entirely cleared; the dwellings and storehouses were scattered among the standing trees. This aided the illusion of secrecy, to be sure; but it also gave the place an air of brooding and sombre silence.

'This is a cheerless place,' said Merlin when he saw it. We had followed the narrow pathway into the forest for a fair distance, and ridden up a slow rise, pausing on the crest to look down at the settlement below. There did not appear to be anyone about, nor signs that anyone marked our arrival. 'Well, let us go and make ourselves known to them.'

We urged our horses forward slowly, watching the settlement for any sign of life as we came nearer.

Sitting our horses before the foremost dwelling — a timber hall with a high-pitched roof of thatch — we waited, and a feeling of eerie foreboding crept over us. Merlin, frowning now, gazed intently at the dwelling as if to discover what had happened to its inhabitants. For neither of us weened anyone alive in the whole place.

'They are not here,' said Merlin at length, and made to dismount. 'Let us go inside and see if we may discover what has happened to them, or where they have gone.'

The hall smelled of decay. The rushes on the floor were spotted with mould, and webs hung from the beams and torch sconces. Platters of food stood on the board — untouched, but by mice. The ashes on the hearth were cold and damp.

Clearly, no one had entered the hall for some time. And those last there had left it hurriedly.

'It will be the same elsewhere,' Merlin said. 'They are gone from this place — and in great distress, I believe.'

'Let us search the other dwellings. Perhaps we will find something to tell us where they have gone, or when.'

So we set about inspecting the other dwellings in the settlement. Everywhere there were signs of a hasty departure: food prepared, but not eaten; hearthfires allowed to burn untended; useful objects and utensils gathered, then discarded in haphazard heaps. In one dwelling a rushlight had been lit and set on the board where it smouldered a long while, leaving a thin black scorch mark in the wood before guttering out. And in another an earthen pot set on the hearth to warm had broken from the heat, and its stew spilled out to char in the flames.

'How strange,' I said. 'It is as if they expected to leave, but did not know when. See?' I swept the near-empty dwelling with my open hand. 'There are no weapons or clothing, no treasure or objects of value left behind. Yet there are no signs of destruction or pillage — I do not think they were attacked.'

'Yet they *were* attacked,' replied Merlin, his eyes narrowed as he gazed around the interior of what surely must have been the lord's chambers. A candle tree stood by the bedplace, the tapers wasted into lumps of hardened wax on the dusty floor. 'But not by Saecsens or any of their kind.'

'Who then?'

He simply shook his head and said, 'Let us go from here.' He turned and led the way outside. As we emerged from the dwelling, I caught a flash of motion at the edge of my vision. I looked, but there was nothing. A moment later, my master and I heard a splash in the nearby lake — as if someone had thrown in a very large rock.

Merlin stopped and glanced toward the lake. Without a word, we turned and walked past the horses and down a path to the lakeshore. The surface was smooth and untroubled, but at the water's edge we saw the indentations in the coarse-pebbled shingle. Merlin knelt and pressed his palm into one of the marks. 'These were made by many feet,' he said. The sorrow in his voice made it husky and thick.

I followed the tracks to the water's edge where they disappeared.

'Why?' I asked, my voice a whisper. I strained to see below the lake surface, thinking, I suppose, to see the tangled bodies floating there.

'*This* is what I saw in the Seeing Bowl,' Merlin murmured. 'And I have come too late.' He glanced sharply at me. 'Why? As soon ask the wind — it knows far more than I.' He stood and looked long at the smooth, glimmering water, calm in the deep solitude of the forest.

'But I can tell you this,' Merlin said quietly, 'the scent of death is in this place. . . it lingers. . . like the stench of rotting meat in the ground. . . like a killing fog over the fen. Death is here. . . '

All at once he squeezed his eyes tight and pressed his palms flat against his temples. His mouth opened in a tremendous cry of anguish. 'AHHH!' Merlin's voice echoed over the water and was swallowed by the close-grown forest round about.

I took him by the arm to steady him. He opened his eyes slowly, the bright golden gleam now darkened with pain and sorrow. 'Morgian!' he uttered, his voice strangled with grief. 'It was Morgian. . . '

He turned at once and began climbing back up the trail to the horses. I stood for a moment longer, gazing into the clear water. The lake, cold and deep and dark, revealed nothing. But, as I made to move away, the glint of metal caught my eye and I glanced down at my feet. A small silver brooch lay on the shingle where it had fallen.

I picked it up and held it in my hand. A simple shell-shaped disc with a hole through which to gather the cloth, and a long silver pin to hold the garment. The ornament was bent — trodden on, I thought.

As I turned it over, I saw a tatter of bright blue cloth still firmly held by the pin. It came into my mind that the brooch had been wrenched from the garment by force; torn from the body of the person who had worn it, and thrown down to be trampled underfoot. I looked once more at the unruffled surface of the lake, and at the marks made by many feet on the shore. Cold dread stole over me where I stood.

I tucked the brooch under my belt and hurried up the track to where Merlin waited. I swung into the saddle and wheeled my horse onto the trail, well ready to be gone from this melancholy place.

We started back at once, wending through the shadows and gloom in silence, sensing with every plodding step the dull horror of the deserted settlement and wondering what atrocity had been committed there.

I led the way along the path and Broceliande became even more forbidding than when we had entered. Neither of us spoke; Merlin kept his own counsel, and when I looked behind me I saw him wrapped in his cloak although the air was warm.

We stopped beside a clear, dish-shaped pool to make our camp for the night. The pool lay in an airy, open glade within the forest which ringed the glade like a tall, dark wall. A small stand of beech trees grew near the forest wall, and around the pool a few small willows and elder bushes.

I watered the animals, unsaddled and tethered them — allowing an extra length of rope, so that they could graze as widely as possible among the trees. Then I set about making camp. Merlin sat a little apart, watching absently, lost in thought.

As daylight began to fail, I walked the short distance to the beech copse to gather dead wood for our fire. I fetched a sizeable load in no time, and began making my way back to the pool. Halfway between the copse and the pool I stopped —

What is that? I wondered, listening.

Was it the breeze in the grass and barren branches that

made the slight singing sound? I continued on my way. But the sound grew louder as I approached the pool.

I saw her in the same instant that she saw me. A maid with golden hair, dressed all in green — mantle, shift and shawl — and carrying a leather bucket in her hand. Her skin was lightly freckled, hinting at various labours in the sun. She was finely formed and graceful; her eyes were large and dark as polished jet. Her free hand went to her mouth and she stifled a cry when she saw me.

'Peace, lady,' I told her. 'You have nothing to fear.'

She lowered her hand, but still held the bucket as if to throw it at me. 'Who are you?' her voice was low, and rich as cream.

'I am a traveller,' I told her, 'and the steward of a nobleman who waits for me at the pool.' I indicated the willows ahead.

She glanced at the bucket in her hand and, as if offering it to me as proof of her words, replied uncertainly, 'I have come for water.'

'And you shall have it,' I said. I started once more towards the pool. She hesitated. 'Come, there is no harm.'

Reluctantly she followed, two paces behind me. We came to where Merlin waited, resting, his back against one of the willows. Merlin opened his eyes when we came near, saw the girl, and stood.

'She has come for water,' I explained, dropping the firewood to the ground.

'I give you good day, lady,' Merlin said by way of greeting. 'You must live very near. Yet we have seen no settlements hereabouts.'

'Oh, there are none, my lord,' the maid replied. 'My father and I — we live alone,' she turned to point vaguely behind her, 'just there.'

'Perhaps we should go and pay our respects to your father,' Merlin said. 'As it seems we are passing through his lands.'

The girl bit her lip, her brow furrowed in concern. I did not like to see her in such distress. I reached a hand towards her and touched her gently on the arm. Her flesh was warm and soft. 'You need have no fear of us,' I told her. 'We are honourable men.'

She smiled, and lowered her eyes. 'I meant no disrespect, my lord. It is just that. . . my father has gone hunting and I am alone.' As she said this, she raised her head and looked directly into Merlin's eyes.

'What is your name, girl?' he asked.

'Nimue, my lord,' she replied softly.

'Your father's?'

'Lord Meleagant,' she answered hesitantly.

'Are you often left alone, Nimue?'

'Often enough. But never for long, my lord,' she added quickly. 'Hunting is difficult in this place, and my father must range far for our meat.' She smiled, becoming more at ease. 'Thus I am often alone, but I do not mind. I have become accustomed to it.'

'Are you never afraid to be alone, Nimue?' said Merlin, speaking my thoughts precisely.

She tossed her golden locks. 'How should I be afraid? No one comes here, and there are no wild beasts to beset me. My father is not long away; I am well cared for. This,' she indicated the land with an upraised palm, 'is not like other places; there is never any trouble here.'

'Neither will we trouble you,' Merlin replied, turning away, 'save for a night's rest beside your pool.'

She held him with the silky insinuation of her voice. 'Oh, but you need not sleep beside this pool, my lord — not as long as I have a roof to cover you, and a hearth to warm you. You are clearly a man of renown; it is beneath you to sleep on the cold ground.'

'Your offer is kind,' said Merlin. 'But as your father is away, we would not think to intrude upon you.' He made to dismiss her, but again she challenged him.

'Whether my father is here or away, the hospitality of our house is mine to extend to whoever I will. And as I believe you to be upright men,' she glanced at me and smiled prettily, 'I would deem it an honour for you to accept my humble offer — ' her eyes sparkled with good humour, 'and an offence if you do not.'

Strangely, the maid spoke like a woman of high birth: forthrightly, and with courtesy. I found myself admiring her and wondering how she came to be living in this wilderness.

Merlin laughed. 'Never let it be said that we have given offence where it might be prevented.' He turned to me. 'Pelleas, we will accompany this maid to her dwelling.'

I gathered up our few belongings and turned to the horses. 'It is not far,' Nimue said. 'The beasts will fare well here.'

'We can leave them,' Merlin told me.

'But — ' I opened my mouth in protest.

'It will be well,' insisted Merlin. 'Leave them.'

I did not like to leave them unattended, but as the house was nearby, and there was no danger, I did as I was bade. Tucking our weapons under my arm, I fell into step behind Nimue as she led the way.

Indeed, the house was not far. I do not see how we could have missed coming upon it, for if we had ridden but a few dozen paces further we would have seen it. Perhaps the pool held our attention, or the willows obscured it. . .

It was a solid house, built all of stone. A small yard lay before it, clean and carefully tended. To one side was a sheep enclosure, but I saw no sheep within. Inside, the floor was flagged with stone, and the walls were limed. In all it was neat and well-cared-for. Clearly, Nimue and her father lived well and took pride in their small holding.

A fire was burning in the hearth, and there was meat on the spit: three good-sized fowl of some kind. A black pot of porridge bubbled next to the flames. A great table of the sort often found in a king's hall occupied much of the single room. An enormous white ox-hide concealed an alcove next to the hearth which served as a bedplace. Another white hide hung across the further part of the room.

Behind this, Nimue disappeared upon entering the house, only to emerge a moment later bearing a wineskin and silver cups on a tray of polished wood.

She poured the wine into the cups and, after dashing a few drops over the rim in honour of the household god, offered the first to Merlin. 'The guest cup, my lord. Health and long life be yours.'

She waited until he drained his cup before offering the next to me. I raised the cup to my mouth, but as the ruby liquid touched my lips I was overwhelmed by the urge to sneeze. I sneezed once, violently, and then again.

When I regained my composure, I once more lifted the cup

to my mouth — only to sneeze yet again. Nimue glanced at me furtively. Was it concern? Or was it fear I saw in her eyes?

Seeking to reassure her, I apologized, saying, 'Wine sometimes has an unfortunate effect on me. Think no ill of it, but I will decline.' So saying, I replaced my cup on the board.

The evening passed pleasantly. We dined on the roast fowl and porridge, and talked of the affairs of the realm. Nimue was most interested in the news we brought, and asked many questions — questions which revealed a lively intellect and a wide knowledge of the world beyond her door. Certainly, we were not the first travellers to have sheltered beneath her father's roof.

After we had eaten and talked, it came into my mind to return to the horses. I was still a little anxious for them, and considered that it would do no harm to see them settled for the night. I stood up to take my leave, and Nimue came to me. Taking my hands, she said, 'Do not go, my lord. It is dark and you might fall into the pool.'

'I can swim,' I replied with a laugh, and stepped outside.

It was a clear night, the moon bright overhead. I could see my way with ease, and began walking along the path. The pool shimmered in the moonlight, glowing like an earthbound star. The horses stood flank to flank, heads down. They whickered softly as I approached. I stroked their necks gently and spoke to them. Then I examined the tether ropes, satisfied myself that they were secure, and started back.

I suppose I must have lost direction in the moonlight, for, after walking a fair way, I did not reach the house.

It is possible to become lost in unfamiliar places, especially in the dark. Yet I had no difficulty finding my way back to the pool. Then, as I sought to retrace my steps to the house, I heard singing — the same lilting voice I had heard before encountering Nimue — though I could see no one.

I continued on and inexplicably returned to the pool a short time later. I struck off once more along the path — certain that it was the correct path and not some other, for I was more careful to mind my way. Nevertheless, I soon found myself lost amidst a growth of elder bushes. And again I heard the eerie singing. I called out, but there was no answer. I waited and called again. The singing stopped.

Turning my steps once more to the pool, I marked that it took longer to regain it this time. The way had become confused and altered subtly.

At last I reached the pool, approaching now it from a different direction. This puzzled me, but instead of starting off once more, I sat down for a moment to think it out clearly.

The house was nearby — not more than a few hundred paces from the pool in any event. It did not seem possible that I could walk and miss the place: the moon was high and bright, the way easily marked.

Yet, thrice I had lost my way. Drawing a deep breath, I set off once more, careful to keep the pool at my back, ignoring the path and trusting my own quickly diminishing sense of direction.

I walked for a short while — much further than I remembered — and was about to turn back when I saw it. Directly ahead, shimmering in the moonlight, stood the house; the light from the hearthfire faintly glowing in the doorway. Smoke seeped slowly through the roof-thatch, silvery in the moonglow, rising like the vapours from a fetid fen.

I moved towards the light, and upon reaching the door I heard singing: soft, lilting, sweet; and yet I shivered to hear it. For, more than anything else, the sound possessed the haunting melancholy quality of a chill autumn wind through bare willow branches.

I paused on the threshold of the house and listened, but the last few notes trailed away into silence and the song was finished.

'The horses are set — ' I began, then froze, staring.

Merlin lay on the floor near the hearth, his head in Nimue's lap. She held Merlin's knife in her hand. At my intrusion, her face turned towards me, and — I cannot be certain — but in the flickering firelight it seemed her features contorted in an expression of unutterable rage and contempt. And I felt as if a spear pierced my belly and twisted in my entrails.

Nimue smiled invitingly. Placing a long finger to her lips, she whispered, 'Your master is asleep.' She smoothed his hair and bent to kiss him.

My reaction was sharp and quick. Anger blazed through

me like lightning. 'No! You cannot — ' I leapt forward, but she held up a hand and I halted.

'Shh! You will wake him!' Then, more softly, 'I was singing and he fell asleep. . . he was so tired.'

As quickly as it had erupted, the heat of my fury melted away and I stood looking on, feeling foolish and contrite. 'I am sorry,' I mumbled, 'I thought. . . '

Nimue smiled. 'Say no more. I understand.' She turned and, as if forgetting me, began stroking Merlin's head once more, then bent and kissed him chastely on the forehead, and replaced the knife in his belt. She murmured something over him and then carefully lowered his head and shoulders to the hearth.

She rose and came to me, smiling, and put her hands on my chest. 'Forgive me,' she whispered, putting her face close to mine. I caught the scent of apple blossoms on her breath. 'He looked so peaceful, I could not resist. . . '

Her lips parted, and her eyelids closed. She pressed her mouth against mine and I tasted the sweet warmth of her lips. I felt her fingers on my wrist, guiding my hand to her breast, and in that moment I wanted her as I have desired no other woman.

Nimue held her body next to mine, pressing her loins against my thigh. I felt her firm warm flesh beneath my hands and I ached for her.

The next thing I knew she was standing before the fire and her mantle was slipping to the floor.

Her body was exquisitely formed, flawless, its curved symmetry revealed by the shadows and light from the hearthfire. She turned, cupping her breasts with her hands, and walked slowly towards me, as if offering me the ripeness of her body.

I reached out a hand to touch her, to take her.

Into my mind sprang the image of two people coupled in the act of love, limbs intertwined, bodies straining. And it seemed to me that something hideous was happening. The image shifted slightly and I saw that the body of the woman was a rotting corpse. . .

All desire vanished in that instant, replaced by an unspeakable repulsion. Sickened, I turned away.

'Pelleas. . . ' her breath was hot on the back of my neck,

her voice a moan of desire. 'Take me, Pelleas, I want to love you.'

'No!' The shout tore unbidden from my throat. 'No!'

Her hands were on me, encircling my waist, caressing me. 'Love me, Pelleas. I want you.'

'Leave me!' I screamed again and whirled towards her, my hand poised to strike.

Nimue stood defiant, a look of haughty triumph on her beautiful face. 'Do it,' she urged, 'strike me!'

With an effort of will, I lowered my hand. The desire to strike her remained strong, yet I resisted. 'I will not.'

Her seduction failed, she nevertheless could not resist gloating. 'I despise weakness,' she hissed. 'Show me you are not weak.' She stepped towards me, her hands stroking her thighs.

'Get away from me, whore!' I said, forcing out each word. 'In the name of Jesu, stay back!'

She halted, her lips twisting in revulsion. 'You will live to regret this, Pelleas ap Belyn!' she rasped, as if she had been struck a blow in the stomach. Then she whirled away, scooped up her clothing, and fled from the house.

As soon as Nimue vanished, a great weariness came over me. The room grew dark, and wavered in my sight like a reflection in a pool. I felt drunk — yet I had touched no wine. On unsteady, unfeeling legs I stumbled to the bedplace; it was all I could do to keep from falling over. I tumbled headlong onto the straw pallet. . .

I awoke to sunlight streaming into my eyes, and the sound of a horse nickering softly. I raised myself up and saw that I lay in the grass beside the pool. My horse grazed nearby on its tether. Merlin was nowhere to be seen.

All at once, memory of what had happened the night before came rushing back to me and I jumped to my feet. My head pounded with a dull throb, my eyes ached and my limbs were sore, but I was unharmed. I ran up the path towards the house.

The dwelling was not there!

I searched until I panted for breath, but could not find it. The solid stone structure was nowhere to be seen. The house was gone — and Merlin with it.

I realized what had taken place. But it was too late. Too late. I cursed my blindness, and the ease with which I had succumbed to the enchantment.

And then I remembered Nimue and the threat uttered in her rage: You will live to regret this, *Pelleas ap Belyn*. . .

She had called me by name! A wave of sick dread convulsed me. The bile rose to my gorge and I retched —

— Morgian!

EIGHT

Fear came swimming out of the very air. What if Morgian should return to claim her prize?

Blessed Jesu, help me! Where is Merlin?

I ran. Searching blindly. Stumbling, falling, picking myself up and running on, I searched for the house — but I could not find it, or Merlin. I called his name, but there was no answer. . . no answer.

In the end, I returned to the pool and forced myself to kneel down and drink. Somewhat refreshed, I washed my sweating face and then set about saddling the horses.

I was resolved in my soul to find my master, or die trying. Though Morgian returned. . . though all the powers of hell raged against me. . . I determined to find him and free him from the sorcery that bound him.

With this vow in my heart, I went down on my knees and prayed for the leading of the Guiding Hand and the protection of angels and archangels. Then I rose and swung into the saddle, and thus began my search anew.

Perhaps prayer is so rarely heard in that wilderness that it is answered all the more readily. Or perhaps wherever the Adversary flaunts his power, the Most High quickly grants the plea of any anguished heart that seeks him.

However it was, my urgent prayers soon turned to shouts of praise, for I had ridden but half-way round the pool when I saw my master. He was lying face down beneath an elder bush, his legs and feet in the water.

I vaulted from the saddle and ran to him, hauled him from the pool and rolled him on his back. Pressing my ear to his chest, I listened. He lived. His heart beat slowly, but rhythmically. He slept — a deathlike, leaden sleep: no movement, breath light and shallow.

Cradling him in my arms, I began chafing his hands and shaking his shoulders in an effort to rouse him. But I could not.

I rose to my feet, contemplating what next to do. Clearly, we could not stay in the forest. We needed help. There was nothing for it but to ride for Benowyc, but I could not leave Merlin.

'Forgive me, Master, there is no other way.' So saying, I raised him up to sitting position and, bending low, took his weight on my shoulders and lifted him.

Slowly, and with immense difficulty, I eased my master onto his horse. Then, though it hurt me to do it, I drew his hands together around his mount's neck and bound them — all the while praying his forgiveness for the pain I knew it would cause him.

At last, satisfied that he would not topple from the saddle, I took his mount's reins and tied them to the cantles of my saddle. Without a backward glance I started for Benowyc.

'Whatever is required will be done,' Ban repeated earnestly. 'You have but to name it.'

I could think of nothing save bearing Merlin away to Ynys Avallach as soon as possible. For I had made up my mind that if my master were to be healed anywhere on this earth it would be at the Shrine of the Saviour God near the Fisher King's palace. And if anyone in this worlds-realm could heal him, it would be Charis, the Lady of the Lake.

'Again I thank you, Lord Ban,' I told him. 'The use of your fastest ship will avail us much. It is all that we need now.'

'I will come with you.'

'It is not necessary.'

'Allow me to send a physician in any case. I will summon one from the abbey.'

'I dare not delay even a day longer. There are physicians at Ynys Avallach who will know how to free my master from this sorcery.'

Ban frowned. 'Very well, you shall leave at once. I will accompany you to the ship and instruct the pilot and crew myself. Also, I will send a man to help you.'

We left Caer Kadarn as soon as a litter could be prepared for Merlin. The tide was flowing when we reached the port; the ship was manned and ready. We boarded as soon as the horses were safely picketed, whereupon Ban delivered his orders to the boatmen. But a few moments later, I felt the ship surge away from the quay and turned to call farewell to Lord Ban.

'Whatever happens,' he replied, 'we will come to you in the spring. Also the supplies you have asked for will be sent as soon as the harvest is gathered in. I will not forget my promise of aid! '

In truth, I had forgotten all about Arthur and our reason for coming to Benowyc in the first place.

All that can be said of the sea journey is that it was mercifully short. Favourable winds carried us swiftly over the sea and into Mor Hafren. We made landfall late in the third day, along the Briw river, having sailed inland as far as the river would allow. From there we rode, following the river directly to the lake surrounding King Avallach's Isle.

We came upon the Tor at dawn, glowing red-gold in the new day's misty light. We had ridden through the night, stopping neither for food nor sleep. The horses were near exhaustion, as I was myself.

'We are home, Master,' I said to the body lying deathly still on the litter beside me. 'Help is at hand.'

I started along the lakeshore and struck the causeway joining the Tor to Shrine Hill and the lands beyond, leading Ban's steward and Merlin. We crossed the causeway, and then began slowly climbing the winding track to the summit — all the while keeping my eyes on the palace lest, like Morgian's enchanted dwelling, it should vanish in the mist.

The Fisher King's palace is a strange and wonderful place. It somewhat resembles my father's palace in Llyonesse, but Avallach's realm is the sun to Belyn's black night. Surrounded by its lakes and salt marshes, with groves of apple trees rising on its lower slopes, Ynys Avallach is a true island — a landlocked island, yes, but cut off from the main as completely as any seabound crag.

Out of necessity, the Fair Folk adapted the open, light-filled structures of their lost homeland to the bleaker clime of Ynys Prydein. But they still sought the noble, uplifting line, and the illusion of light — much needed in this often melancholy corner of the world.

Fair Folk. . .Faery: the adopted name of the orphan remnant of Atlantis' lost children who settled here. Fair we are, by comparison; for we are taller, stronger, and more agile than the Britons; by nature more comely, possessing higher gifts. Also, our lives are measured differently.

Little wonder that we are often looked upon as very gods by the easily mystified inhabitants of this island realm. The simple people esteem us unnecessarily, the backward revere us without cause, and the superstitious worship us.

It is folly, of course — the more to be believed, apparently. We are a separate race; that is all. And a dying one.

I know full well that I am the last of my line. There shall be no more after me. As God wills, so be it. I am content.

Merlin is different, though. How different is not easy to tell. He is fully as much a mystery, in his own way, as his father.

I never knew Taliesin. But I have talked with those who did know him — including Charis, who shared his life however briefly. 'In truth,' she told me once, 'Taliesin is more a wonder to me now than ever — and it deepens with each passing year.

'You ask me who he was, and I tell you plainly: I do not know.' She shook her head slowly, gazing into that vivid past where she and Taliesin still walked together as one. 'We were happy, that is all I know. He opened my heart to love, and hence to God, and my gratitude, like my love for him, will endure for ever.'

Seeing the Tor at first light brought these things to mind, and in my fatigue I wrapped myself in reverie as I made my slow way up the twisting path to the Tor.

It was early yet, and the gates were still closed. So I roused the gatesman, who hugged me like a brother and then ran to the palace, calling at the top of his voice. 'Pelleas has come home! Pelleas is here!'

Weary to the bone, I had not the strength to call after

him. It was all I could do to stand upright in the empty yard.

'Pelleas, welcome!' I knew Avallach's voice when I heard it, and raised my eyes to see the Fisher King advancing towards me. He saw Merlin stretched upon the litter and his greeting died with the smile on his lips. 'Is he. . . ?'

I had no time to answer. 'Pelleas!' Charis appeared, dressed in her night clothes, and hurried barefoot across the yard, hope and terror mingling in her expression. She glanced behind me to where Ban's steward waited, head bent as if in sorrow. 'What has happened? Oh, Pelleas, does he live?'

'He lives,' I assured her, my voice the croak of a crow. 'But he sleeps the sleep of death.'

'What do you mean?' Her green eyes searched my face for comfort, but there was none to be found.

'I cannot rouse him,' I told her. 'It was. . . ' How could I say the words? 'It is sorcery.'

Charis' long experience treating the sick and dying served her well. She turned to the gatesman lingering near and said, 'Go to the abbey and bring the abbot at once.' Her voice was calm, but I sensed the urgency as if she had shouted.

Avallach bent over Merlin's body. 'Help me, we must get him inside.' Together Ban's steward and Avallach raised Merlin from the litter; the Fisher King gathered him up and carried him into the hall.

Dizzy with exhaustion, I swayed on my feet. Charis put her arms around me to support me. 'Oh, Pelleas. . . I am sorry, I did not — '

'There is no need, my lady — ' I began, but she did not hear.

'You are weary. Come, let me help you.'

'I can walk.' I took a step and the ground seemed to shift under my feet. But for Charis I would have collapsed in the yard. Somehow we reached the hall and crossed it to the chamber prepared for me.

'Rest you now, Pelleas,' Charis told me, placing a coverlet over me. 'You have done your part; I will care for my son now.'

It was late when I awakened. The sky was golden in the west as the sun slipped down to touch the hill-line. Desperately hungry, I rose, washed myself, then made my way back to the hall. Charis was waiting for me, her head bowed, praying. A tray of meat, bread and cheese, lay next to her on the board. Cups stood nearby, and a jar of beer.

She rose and came to me when she saw me, smiled, and said, 'You look more like the Pelleas I remember. Are you hungry?'

'Famished,' I admitted. 'But I can wait a little. Is there any change?'

She shook her head slowly. 'There is not. I have been considering what to do — I have spent the day with my books, seeking a remedy. But. . . ' She let the words go unsaid. 'You must break your fast now,' she instructed, guiding me to the board and seating me, 'and regain your strength.'

'We will bring him back,' I said boldly, more from encouragement than confidence.

Charis put her hands on my shoulders, leaned near and kissed me on the cheek. 'You serve him well, Pelleas. More than a servant, you are his truest friend. He is fortunate; any man would be blessed to have such a companion. I am glad he has chosen you to go with him.' She seated herself beside me and poured drink into the cups.

'My lady, I chose him.' I reminded her. 'And I will never forsake him.' I glanced out of one of the high windows. The light was fading outside. Was it fading for Merlin as well?

I ate nearly all that was before me. How many days had it been since I had eaten? I more than made up for it, I think. Satisfied at last, I pushed the tray away and took up the cup.

'The man with you,' Charis said when I had finished, 'he told Avallach he was from Armorica, a realm called Benowyc. Is that where Merlin was. . . was stricken?'

'It is,' I replied, and began to explain the aim of our journey. 'The trouble here in the south — Morcant's stupid war, strife in a dozen different places — it is only just beginning. Now more than ever we need a High King, but Arthur's claim was not upheld.'

I told her of the council and of Arthur's becoming War

94

Leader, and of our journey to Ban in Benowyc to secure aid. I described finding Fair Folk in Ban's court. . . and then I told her of Broceliande.

Charis became earnest. 'Pelleas, if I am to help, I must know — what happened to the people in Broceliande?'

'I cannot say for certain, but I think it was Morgian's doing.'

'Morgian!' Charis' hand flew up as if to ward off a blow.

'It is so, my lady.'

'When you said it was sorcery, I did not think. . . ' her voice trailed off. Presently she nodded — as if forcing down bitter herbs. 'Tell me what happened to my son,' she said. 'I will bear it.'

Slowly, each word weighted with dread and sorrow, I told Charis of our encounter with Nimue. The Lady of the Lake listened calmly, holding her head erect. But her eyes bespoke the torment in her soul. 'It *was* Morgian,' she whispered, when I finished.

'I fear it was,' I said. 'I do not know how it is, but she anticipated us. In truth, I believe she lured us there to our destruction.'

'But you were not destroyed.'

'No,' I said. 'God is good; we were spared.'

'My heart wishes to tell me that you are wrong, that there must be some other explanation. But my spirit tells me you are right: this is Morgian's doing. I feel it.'

'When I found him, and saw that he still lived, my only thought was to bring him here. If Merlin is to be saved, it will be here.' I spoke with far more certainty than I felt at that moment.

'Your faith is admirable, Pelleas. But I know nothing of sorcery. As it is, I have not been able to discover how the spell may be broken or how Merlin may be released from it.' Charis sighed, and I heard heartbreak in the sound.

The room was bright with candlelight. As if to banish the dark thing stealing her son, Charis had ordered the chamber to be filled with burning tapers. Together we entered a room warm with the scent of beeswax.

Merlin lay on his back, his arms at his sides. Abbot Elfodd

sat beside him on the bed, his ear close to Merlin's mouth, listening to the sleeping man's breathing. His face was calm, but his eyes were grave.

'Nothing has changed,' Elfodd said softly, as he came to the bed. They had shared this same sickbed vigil too many times to be counted; no greeting was necessary between them.

'The spell is Morgian's,' Charis said, naming her worst fear.

'Ah, . . . ' The good abbot passed a hand before his eyes. 'God help us.'

We fell silent, gazing at Merlin, wondering what, if anything, could be done to save him. Could *anything* be done to save him?

Elfodd was the first to shake off his dismay. 'This!' he declared, throwing a hand to the room. 'Do you feel it? This fear, this dread is part of the spell. It is meant to discourage us. To defeat us before we have even begun to fight against it.'

'You are right,' Charis agreed quickly.

'Well,' Elfodd declared, 'I know something stronger than fear.' And at once he began to recite a psalm in a bold voice: 'The Lord is my rock, my fortress and my deliverer; my God is my rock, in whom I take refuge. He is my shield and the sword of my salvation, my stronghold. I call to the Lord, who is worthy to be praised, and I am saved from my enemies!'

Instantly, the atmosphere in the room seemed lighter; the heavy dread receded.

Turning to me, the abbot said, 'Now then, Pelleas, I would hear you tell me what you know of this spell — but not here. We will go into the hall. Excuse us, lady,' he said to Charis, 'we will return directly.'

I told him all, as I had told Charis. The good abbot listened, a frown on his face, nodding occasionally as he followed my woeful recitation. 'Undoubtedly,' he said when he had heard, 'it is as we suspect: a most powerful enchantment. The weapons we will need to fight it must be equally powerful.'

'What is in your mind, Elfodd?'

'You will see very soon. Now then, bring a little oil,

Pelleas. And the cross that Dafyd gave to Avallach — bring that as well. I will return to Merlin now.'

So saying, the abbot hurried away and I turned to my errand. I fetched the oil in a vial, and sought Avallach for the cross. I had seen it once, a long time ago, but did not know where it was kept. I found Avallach alone in his chamber. The pain of his long-standing ailment was on him once more and he was lying on his couch.

'I would not disturb you, lord,' I said when he bade me enter. 'We have need of the cross given you by Dafyd.'

The king raised himself slowly on an elbow. 'Dafyd's cross?' His eyes went to the vial in my hand. 'No change?'

'None,' I told him. 'Elfodd is with him now.'

'The cross is there.' He indicated a small casket on the table beside his couch. 'Take it. I will come along — ' He tried to rise, but the pain prevented him. 'Ah!' He slumped back, then struggled up once more, his teeth clenched.

'Please,' I said quickly, 'stay here and support us with your prayers. We have need of them just now.'

'Very well,' he agreed, falling back once more. 'I will do as you say. But come and tell me as soon as there is any word.'

I left Avallach with my promise and returned to Merlin's room with the cross and oil. Dafyd's cross, as Avallach called it, was a small crucifix of rough-carved oak, smoothed and polished by years of frequent handling.

Elfodd kissed the cross when I handed it to him, and then, holding his palm above the vial, said a prayer of consecration over the amber liquid.

He went to the bedside and sat down opposite Charis, poured some of the oil into his left hand and, touching the fingertips of his right hand to the sanctified oil, began anointing Merlin.

When he lowered his hand, Merlin's forehead glimmered softly in the candlelight with the sign of the cross.

Then, taking up the cross, he held it above Merlin's head, and said, 'Great of Might, Protector, Defender of all who call upon your name, shelter your servant beneath your strong hand. He sleeps, Father, an unnatural sleep, for an enemy has snared and bound him in a strong enchantment.

'His spirit has been poisoned, Father, by sorcery great and

foul. Raise and restore our brother, we pray you. Beloved of Heaven, go to him, walk beside him where he is, and lead him back to us.

'Living God, show yourself mighty in the defence of your own. Great Giver, give us cause to sing your praise from the hilltops. This we ask, in the name of your most holy and compassionate son, Jesu, who is the Christ.'

The prayer finished, Elfodd lowered the cross and placed it gently on Merlin's breast.

Charis forced a tight smile. 'Thank you, Elfodd.'

The abbot folded his hands and gazed at Merlin. 'We have done what we can do,' he said.

'It is enough,' Charis replied. 'Pray God it is enough.'

'I will watch with him through the night,' Elfodd volunteered. He stepped round the low bed, took Charis by the hands and raised her to her feet. 'Go now. Take some rest. I will send for you if there is any need.'

Charis hesitated. Her eyes did not leave Merlin's face. 'No. . . I will stay. I would have no rest apart from him.'

'It is better that you go,' Elfodd insisted. His voice had lost none of its gentleness, but was now most firm.

'If you think — ' began Charis, glancing away from her son for the first time.

'Trust me. I will summon you if you are needed.'

Reluctantly, Charis agreed, saying, 'Stay with the abbot, Pelleas. He may need you.'

'As you wish, my lady.'

She left then, closing the door silently behind her.

'It is hard for her,' Elfodd sighed, 'but believe me this is for the best. She wants to help him so badly, but her anxiety — so natural in a mother — can only make things worse. The Enemy will use it, you see. Doubt, fear, dread — it all feeds the curse.'

The abbot drew the chair close to the bed and settled himself for his vigil. 'Go now, Pelleas. Leave him to me; I will look after him.'

'I will stay,' I replied, 'as I have promised to do.'

'I honour the intent of your promise, but you will help your master the more by looking to your own health just now. Go to your rest. I will wake you if I need you.'

Though the sky still held light in the west, I went to my

chamber and stretched myself on my pallet. I thought that I would not be able to sleep, but, closing my eyes, I felt the tide-pull overwhelm me and I knew no more.

In my sleep I entered that state where a human being stands closest to the Otherworld. The veil that separates the two worlds grew thin and I could sense the seething darkness that had enveloped the Tor. Deep, impenetrable, black as death, it was the shadow of a great ravening beast — a ghastly thing with wings and coils like a serpent, with which it bound the Tor and palace.

I could not see the unholy creature, but I could feel the bone-aching chill of its presence, and I heard the howl of its mindless hate. I quailed to think of the power that had called it into being and loosed it on the world.

But as darkly powerful as the hell-thing was, something held it at bay — something stronger still — though I could not see what it was.

Further I drifted in sleep, haze dimmed my inner sight, but my senses remained sharp — sharper than in waking life. I slept, but did not sleep. My soul-self remained alert within me and alive to the danger round about me.

Danger there was. Very great danger.

It seemed to me then as if I took wings and flew — for I sensed the earth rushing by beneath me: rock crags and broken hills, blurred to sight by the speed of my flight and the vaporous darkness. On and on, over this menacing landscape I flew, hastening onward, but not arriving.

Yet, when it seemed as if I must journey on this way for ever, I sensed a lightening in the strange obscurity around me. Light, faint and faded, tinted the black to grey.

Feeling the light on my eyes, I turned towards it and the grey cloudlike mist separated — darkness below, and light, thin but perceptible, above.

At the same moment, I became heavier; my limbs grew wooden and stiff. I began to fall back, plummeting down towards that sharp rockscape somewhere far below me. And, though I knew myself to be dreaming, it came into my mind that if I allowed myself to fall onto the cruel rocks, I would surely be crushed and killed.

I fought against the downward pull, flinging my arms and kicking my legs as if in swimming. I sank more quickly. The thought of the terrible rocks rushing up to meet me roused me to fury. I fought on, with all the strength I had.

I fell faster. My limbs began to ache with the effort and I knew I would not be able to continue much longer, but set my teeth, vowing to go on swimming and swimming until my muscles knotted up and I could no longer move.

On and on I went, struggling, striving, falling back and back. After what seemed an eternity I came at last to the end of my strength. . .

But, instead of falling, I felt myself rising.

I looked and saw that while I struggled the light had become brighter. Indeed, it was as if my feeble efforts had increased the light somehow. Inexplicably, I was being drawn upward by the light I had helped to magnify; the selfsame light that I helped generate was now saving me.

Very soon I came to a place where the light shone bright and unhindered. It was dazzling white, like the radiance of the morning sun on fresh snow. And, shielding my eyes with my hands, I looked back the way I had come and saw that I had not flown at all, nor struggled half so much as it seemed. For the light revealed a smooth, unbroken pathway along which I had been led. . . step by careful step.

And it came to me that this is how the spirit travels towards God: beginning its journey in darkness, setting off in danger and confusion, and struggling upward into the ever present light which draws it and upholds it always. . .

NINE

I awoke to a stream of sunlight in my room. I rose instantly. How long had I slept? It was daylight already!

But, even as the thought came into my head, the light faded, pearling to dawn. It was early yet.

I rose and hurried to Merlin's room, where I found Elfodd dozing lightly in his chair beside the bed. He started when I entered the room; he had not been asleep after all, merely bowed in prayer.

'How is he?' I asked.

'The same,' the abbot told me. 'There has been no change.'

'I am here,' I said. 'I will watch with him now.'

He hesitated, reaching over to touch Merlin's hand. 'I will remain a little longer.'

'You have done your part, Elfodd,' I insisted gently. 'I am ready to do mine.'

The good abbot yawned and rose stiffly from the chair, pressing his hands to the small of his back. 'Very well, I will sleep a little,' he said as he moved away, 'that I may serve him the better.'

Charis appeared but a moment after Elfodd had gone. 'Oh,' she said softly, the glint of hope dying in her eyes as she beheld her son, 'I had hoped to see him awake.'

'So had I, my lady,' I replied. 'I had hoped to see the enchantment broken.'

Without another word, we began our vigil together.

For three days Merlin lay asleep under the wicked spell. We prayed, we read psalms to him, we invoked the protection of the Most High, we bathed him, anointed him, we spoke to him, filling his heart and ours with words of encouragement.

All the time he hung between life and death in that trance-like stupor. Whatever our fears, we did not allow them in the room with him, but put them off upon entering into his presence. In this way, he was surrounded always with hope and healing prayers.

On the evening of the third day, Elfodd returned from the abbey, where he had retired at daybreak, and brought with him twelve of his dearest, most blessed and holy brothers. They were men of solid faith, bold in belief, and wise to the wiles of the enemy. They had come from chapels, abbeys and monasteries both near and far — for word had gone out that Merlin had fallen under an enchantment and lay near death.

Avallach, pale and grim, received them solemnly in his hall and gave them bread, meat and wine to restore their strength for the work ahead.

Then Elfodd led them to Merlin's chamber where Charis waited. She saw the holy men and, thinking they had come to perform the rites for the dying, buried her face in her hands.

'Peace, sister,' Elfodd said, 'think not the worst. Rather take hope. For these men have come to help us. We contend not with flesh and blood. As our adversary is mighty, we must be mighty, too.

'It is three days, Charis, and we have not been able to loosen the evil enchantment's hold. Therefore I have summoned these good brothers to lend their aid to our struggle.'

Tears in her eyes, Charis nodded.

'Go you now,' Elfodd said, 'rest a little. Return when you have refreshed yourself.' The abbot motioned for me to accompany her.

'I will go with you, my lady,' I offered. 'Come.'

Taking her arm, I led her unresisting from the room. I saw her to her chamber and then went to the kitchens to request food to be brought to her. I returned to sit with her while she ate, and to see that she slept.

When the food arrived she glanced at the bowl and pushed it aside. I pushed it back before her, saying, 'You must eat something.' It hurt me to see her suffering so. 'It will not help him to weaken yourself — eat.'

Reluctantly, she picked up the wooden bowl and began stirring the stew with her spoon, then lifted the spoon to her mouth, chewed and swallowed. I do not think she tasted a bite, but that did not matter. One spoonful led to another, and another, and soon she replaced the bowl, empty.

Charis rose and smiled thinly. 'I feel a little better. Thank you, Pelleas. I will sleep now.' She turned to her bed.

'I will leave you to your rest,' I said, moving to the door, 'and I will look in on you after a little.'

'Please, take no heed of me. I would have you stay with Merlin.'

I returned at once to Merlin's chamber, where the holy brothers knelt side by side as Abbot Elfodd moved from one to the other with a chalice of wine and blessed bread, offering each man the sacrament of holy communion. When the last had been served, he came to me. I knelt down and received the bread and wine from his hand.

Then the twelve rose and went to Merlin's bed, which they lifted and moved to the centre of the room. Each man took up a candle from one of the many Charis kept burning in the room, and Elfodd passed among them, giving each one a censer to be lit from the candle. Candle in one hand and censer in the other, the brothers took up places around the bed, forming a ring. They knelt and bowed their heads, some moved their lips silently. Smoke from the sweet incense now filled the room, rising up in curling tendrils in the still air. I took up a place by the door, ready should the good brothers require anything.

After a few moments, Abbot Elfodd began speaking a prayer in Latin, and one by one the other holy men joined him. I know the scholar's tongue not at all well, but I gleaned from a phrase or two here and there that it was a strong petition for the All Mighty to show his power in the saving of his servant.

As I listened, it became clear that the prayer was actually a plea of sacrifice: each man offering to take Merlin's place, if Merlin could be freed from his sleep of death.

I marvelled at their faith. Every man among them was prepared to lay down his life for Merlin. Moved by their love, I sank to my knees by the door and, stretching myself out on the floor, began repeating the essence of their prayer in my heart: *Great Light, I give myself to you for the sake of my brother. Restore him, I pray; and if it is that a life for a life is required, please take mine.*

This I prayed over and over again until it became a litany, flowing up from the depths of my soul to spread like a fragrant balm before the throne of Jesu.

I do not know how long I lay like this. I was not aware of the passage of time, or of anything else. It was as if the world of men had ceased to exist, and I felt the innumerable ties that bind the soul loosen and fall away until I was completely free. There remained only the voices of the monks, the sweetness of the incense, and the prayer in my heart.

Gradually, I sensed a subtle shifting in the light around me. I smelled hot wax and thought that the candles must be burning out. I raised my head and, at the same time, heard a sound like that of a harp when it sings of itself — as when the wind brings forth mysterious music.

The air stirred softly, as with the light stirring of feathered wings. I felt it cool on my face, and tasted honey on my tongue. I inhaled a fragrance surpassing in sweetness any I have ever known.

In the same moment, there appeared a maiden dressed in a flowing white garment. Tall and most wonderfully fair, with hair the colour of pure sunlight, and skin pale as milk. Her eyes were like finest jade, deep and green, and her lips were the colour of ripe berries. On her high and noble brow she wore a circlet of gold discs which shone each one like a golden sun. Around her slender waist she wore a girdle of bright golden discs.

I do not remember whether the door opened to admit her — it must have — and yet, it seems to me that she just appeared in our midst.

In her hands this wondrous vision held a silver tray which bore a vessel covered with a cloth of white silk, thin and light as a cloud. And from beneath the silken cover, this vessel shone with a clear and steady light.

Without word or glance, the maiden approached the place where Merlin lay. The good brothers and Abbot Elfodd fell back amazed; some crossed themselves with the holy sign, others knelt down and bowed their heads low.

I lay as one struck a stunning blow, staring at the maiden: to take my sight from her would have been to pluck the very eyes from my head. I could not breathe for feeling such awe and wonder. I thought my heart must burst. Sweet Jesu, I have never felt anything so fine and terrible in all my life!

She stood at the bedside, looking down upon the sleeping, dying Merlin with a look of infinite compassion. And then softly she spoke — her words were the hush of snowflakes falling to earth.

She said, 'Merlin, your sleep is ended. Wake you now, fair friend, your work is not yet finished.'

At these words, the maiden lifted her hand and withdrew the cloth from the vessel on the tray. Instantly, the vessel shone forth with the brightness of the noontide sun, casting a dazzling light all around. I could not bear it, and threw my hands over my eyes.

When I dared look again, the light had gone; the vessel was covered once more. The lady smiled and touched Merlin lightly on the forehead with her hand. 'Arise,' she told him, 'you are restored.'

In that selfsame moment there came a great uproar from outside the palace — the commotion of the driven wind when the storm passes. The palace was buffeted; somewhere a door slammed to sunder its hinges. And, above the wind, I heard a wailing cry like that of a wounded beast when the hunter's lance is driven into its breast; but thin and high and bloodless — it was no earth-spawned thing.

Merlin, pale and gaunt in his bed, opened his eyes and lifted his shoulders.

Free from the evil enchantment that bound him, my master gazed at those gathered around him in uncomprehending surprise. Then, as understanding grew, he lowered his face into his hands and wept.

TEN

With a shout of joy we all rushed to him. *Merlin is restored! The spell is broken! Glory to our Great Redeemer! Merlin is alive!* Our praise rang from the rooftrees, and echoed through the corridors of the Fisher King's palace.

And suddenly Charis appeared in the doorway, her face anxious and alarmed. But dismay quickly gave way to delight as she saw her son rising up from his deathbed.

She rushed to him and gathered him in her arms. Merlin wept still and she wept with him, holding him, rocking him gently back and forth as if he were her babe once more. I stood near enough to hear him murmuring, 'I am unworthy. . . unworthy. . . Great Light, why was I born so blind!'

A strange thing to say. Merlin born blind? But he wept like a man broken by grief, as if his heart lay riven in his breast, as if nothing could ever heal the rent in the gaping wound of his soul. I do not think I have ever seen or heard a man so forlorn and inconsolable.

His misery was complete.

I see them there still. I see it all: Charis holding her son, the two of them swaying gently back and forth; the monks encircling, uncertain, caught between joy and distress; candles bright, the room hazy with heavy light; the heave and shift of Merlin's shoulders as the sobs break from his wounded heart.

And the woman — the Bright Bearer who released Merlin from his enchanted sleep — where is she?

She is gone. Vanished as quietly, as mysteriously as she appeared. She is gone, and the marvellous Grail with her.

Yes, and I feel again the numb despair stealing over me. . . the howling emptiness of futility. . . the staggering desolation of defeat, of knowing the battle is yet to be joined, and that the battle will be lost.

Merlin understood this at once. He was a true prophet; he saw it all. In the dazzling light of his release, he saw the cold, sodden ashes of his failure.

Small wonder that he wept.

He could speak not a mote of this for some time. Later, when he could fit words to it, I began to understand why he wept.

'It was arrogance!' he told me. 'It was pride. I was blind and stupid with it, Pelleas. Do not think to say me otherwise! Vanity! You should have let me die.'

I made to soften his reproach, but there was no stopping him.

'I went to Broceliande searching for a sign. I am given no end of signs, yet I heed them not! You see how ignorant I have been? How foolish? The Queen of Air and Darkness traps me with a child's trick! Such a splendid idiocy! Do you not love me for it, Pelleas?'

'Surely, master — '

'I wonder that you still call me master. I am unworthy of it, Pelleas. Trust that I am telling you the truth. No man was ever more unworthy.'

'But you did not *know*.'

'Did not know? It is my duty to know! I belittled her power. I ignored the danger.'

He began to pace the hall restlessly. 'How could I be so close to her and not realize it? How is it possible that she could disguise herself so completely?'

'Nimue?'

'Oh, it was more than a new name, Pelleas. She was innocence itself. How is it possible that such an immense, corrupting evil can cloak itself in such beauty and purity?'

It was, could *only* be, he concluded, a measure of Morgian's power. That she could so disguise herself — both in form and nature — was indeed a dire wonder.

'Oh, great Merlin!' he jeered in self-mockery. 'He is so wise and powerful. Merlin is invincible! Do you not see it, Pelleas? Morgian can act openly, and with arrogance, and we are powerless against her. There is nothing to stop her now.'

I was becoming frightened. I had never seen him in such a state. 'There is the Grail,' I said, grasping for any aid I could lay hand to.

Merlin stopped stalking. He turned and gazed at me with the light in his golden eyes.

'Yes,' he replied slowly, placing a finger to his lips. 'There is the Grail. I must not forget that.' Then he looked at me sharply. 'I saw it once, you know. I have never told that to anyone. I think Avallach has seen it, too. And now you, and Elfodd and the others.'

'Yes, but what is it exactly?' I wondered. No one had yet explained it to me.

'It is,' replied Merlin slowly, choosing his words, 'the cup Jesu used at his last supper, brought here by the tin merchant, Joseph of Arimathea — the same who founded the first shrine on Shrine Hill and established the teaching of the Christ in the Island of the Mighty.

'The very cup Jesu blessed, saying, "This is my blood which is shed for your sins." The cup was passed hand to hand among the Twelve on the night he was betrayed. Our Lord drank from it.

'Joseph it was who paid for the room, and for the supper that night. After the Christ's death and resurrection, when his followers were sent out to tell the Gospel, Joseph came here. And he brought the cup.'

I had never heard the story before, and said so.

'No?' Merlin replied. 'Well, I suppose not. It is an old story and not something voiced freely about. Those who see the cup are most reluctant to speak of it. There is a mystery and a power at work here — '

'That is not the half of it!'

'Be that as it may, the Grail is possessed of a high holiness, and one does not speak lightly of such things.'

Indeed, Merlin would speak no more about it.

The next day, having prayed for him and blessed him, the monks departed. Merlin thanked them for their help and devotion, and gave them presents to take back to their homes with them. Elfodd was last to leave; having seen the others on their way, he lingered to speak to Merlin.

'I will not ask how such an enchantment came upon you,' the abbot said. 'But it is clear that there are great and terrible forces working in the world. I would rest the better to know where you stand on this matter of sorcery.'

Merlin cocked his head to one side. 'Why, Elfodd, do you think I caused this hurt to myself with some obscure dabbling?'

Elfodd frowned. 'I do not reproach you, my friend. But we have seen much in the way of evil spirits and such at the Shrine. It is almost as if we are under siege here.' The abbot's frown deepened. 'We hear many rumours of the druids.'

'And since I am a bard, you think — '

'Do you deny receiving the druid learning?'

'I deny nothing! And for the sake of our friendship, Abbot Elfodd, I will forget at once what you have just said.'

'It is out of friendship that I *tell* you!'

Merlin paused and drew a long breath. 'You are right. Forgive me.'

Elfodd waved aside the apology. 'I take no offence at your words. Do not take offence at mine.'

'I forget that the Learned Brotherhood is not what it once was,' Merlin admitted sadly.

'No, it is not.' The abbot clasped his hands earnestly. 'It grieves me to see you troubled like this. You must understand that you cannot fight the enemy with the enemy's weapons — even for good.'

'I understand, Elfodd.' Merlin sighed. 'Never doubt it.'

'Sorcery is an abomination — '

'And never doubt my loyalty,' Merlin added. Though he spoke softly, I heard the steel in his voice. 'I will do what I have to do.'

The abbot gazed at Merlin for a moment, nodded, and turned to leave. 'Farewell, Merlin.' he called. 'Come to the Shrine for a blessing before you leave.'

'Farewell, Elfodd.' Merlin watched until Elfodd had crossed the yard and disappeared beyond the gate, then turned to me. 'He thinks I practise sorcery — they all think that. For the love of God, are they insane? Why do they doubt me?'

'They doubt because they do not know you,' I said, although no reply was expected.

'Have I lived this long in the service of the Truth only to be reviled? They believe me a traitor, Pelleas.'

'They are confused. They do not know.'

'Then they do not *think*!' he growled.

It was no use talking to him; I could only make matters worse trying to reason with him. He would hear nothing I said.

Anyway, I did not know myself what answer to make. My heart agreed with Merlin: that of all men the faithful should have more faith in him. His every thought was for the Truth, and for Britain and the good of its people. As some have said: Merlin *is* the Soul of Britain.

He had power, yes. Very great power.

But I tell you the truth, Merlin never used his power for his own gain. All Heaven bear witness! If he had so chosen, he could have been High King. He could have been emperor!

Downcast and discouraged, Merlin sought solace in his time of need. He walked along the lake, and among the apples hanging golden and ripe for the harvest, letting the peace of the Glass Isle spread its healing into his soul. Left to himself, I think he would happily have stayed at Ynys Avallach for ever.

But the days turned grey and the wind blew a chill reminder of the winter to come, and Merlin heeded the warning. 'Time is fleeting, and we are needed elsewhere,' he said, one rainy morning. 'Arthur will be wondering what has become of us.'

By this I knew that the Glass Isle had completed its work in him and he was ready to face the world of men once more. Avallach and Charis were sorry to see us leave so soon, but accepted Merlin's decision with all good grace. I spent the day assembling the necessary provisions for the journey, and Merlin rode to the Shrine to pray, and to take his leave of Elfodd as he had promised.

I finished late in the afternoon, but Merlin had not returned. I waited. Charis came into the hall, then, and we talked of this and that, but I noticed that her eyes kept stealing to the doorway and the yard beyond. She too was anxious about Merlin's return.

As the last light of afternoon faded from the sky to the east, she said, 'Something has happened to him. We should go down there.'

I agreed. We rode the steep and narrow trail down to the causeway below the Tor, across the marsh and around the lake to the little abbey that stands at the foot of the Shrine.

We were met by several monks, who indicated that Merlin had indeed gone up to the Shrine and had asked to be left alone. No one had seen him since. No one had dared disturb him.

Charis thanked the brothers and we continued on our way, climbing the path leading to the Shrine.

Shrine Hill is a small hump of earth lying hard by the Tor. It is an ancient and holy place, for it is here that word of the Blessed Christ first reached the Island of the Mighty. And here the worship of the True God first began in this land.

The Shrine itself is a small, round building of wattle and mud, washed white with lime. The bare earth floor is swept every day, and the thatched roof is continually renewed, so that the tiny chapel always appears new-made.

In recent years, an abbey was constructed nearby at the foot of the hill, so that the Shrine will never lack for care. The abbey itself has become a place of healing — due largely to the ministrations of Charis. The Lady of the Lake, as she is called by the humble folk, is known to be a skilled and compassionate healer.

We mounted the hill and walked to the Shrine. No sound came from within. The air was dead; nothing moved, no bird sang the evensong. We listened for a moment, then stepped through the low doorway. Inside the shadows deepened to dusk.

At first we did not see anything but a dark heap before the altar — as if a careless monk had left a tangle of clothing there. We approached and Charis knelt down.

'Merlin?' She reached out a hand and the heap moved at her touch. There was a rustle of cloth and Merlin rolled over.

'Merlin?'

'Oh — Mother. . . ' His face shone pale in the fading light. 'I — I must have fallen asleep.'

'Come,' said Charis, bending over him, 'we will take you home now.'

'Mother,' said Merlin, getting to his knees and unwinding the altar cloth from around him. He appeared haggard and gaunt — as if he had been battling demons in his sleep. 'I am sorry. I meant to have this day with you, and I — '

'It is well,' Charis replied quickly. 'Come, we will go home now.'

Merlin rose slowly. I picked up the altar cloth, shook it out, and placed it back on the altar. As I turned to follow Merlin and Charis out, I noticed a dark place on the ground. . . Sweat? Tears?

The earth was damp where Merlin had lain his head.

ELEVEN

We departed the Glass Isle the next day as we had planned, much to Charis' misgiving. It was not a happy farewell. We all knew too much of the evil stalking the land, and the havoc Morgian could wreak with her power. Our thoughts were heavy with foreboding.

The world, with the change of season, had become a colder, wilder place. Summer had fled like a hart through the brake, and an early winter stood poised for the chase.

The land brooded doom. Menacing, sinister — as if desolation lurked behind every tree and destruction behind every hill. Wickedness inhabited each wilderness, and iniquity streamed from every lonely place.

I do not recall ever passing through a land so gravid with apprehension. The way became strange; familiar pathways seemed malignant with peril. Every plodding step was laboured and slow.

Merlin, wrapped in his cloak, journeyed with his head down, hands folded on the pommel of his saddle. A passer-by might have mistaken his attitude for that of prayerful meditation. It was not. It was the posture of a defeated chieftain returning in humiliation and disgrace.

One grey afternoon, as we rode through Morganwg's lands, we encountered a band of Iceni fifty strong — old men, women, and children mostly — leading a few head of cattle and some sheep. Four wagons creaked slowly along behind them. Aside from the lowing of the cattle, and the creak of the wagon wheels, they made no sound as they trudged through the gathering mist.

Merlin hailed them and they halted to give us the sorry news: their settlement and many others like it had been destroyed by a Saecsen raid three days before.

'That is bitter to hear,' replied Merlin in all sympathy.

'There is no cheer in the telling,' spat the group's leader, a man with an axe wound in his side. 'The shore forts fell at once. There was no defence at all.'

'What of Coledac?' wondered Merlin.

'Killed with the warband. Every man of them dead. No one escaped, and the Sea Wolves left none alive. When the strongholds fell, the barbarians turned to the farms. We fled when we saw the smoke in the east.'

'Our settlement was small — the others were attacked first. . . and destroyed,' lamented the haggard woman who stood beside him.

'That is so,' agreed the man unhappily. 'I fear the other holdings had the worst of it. From what we are hearing, it was much worse in the south along the Saecsen Shore.'

Commending them to God, we rode on.

That night Merlin gazed into the flames of our desultory camp fire searching for a sign. There was little hope in what he saw, little light to hold against the gathering darkness. In all it was a drear and cheerless journey, and a sorry return.

We arrived at Caer Melyn in driving rain. Soaked to the skin, shivering with cold, we stood before the fire in Arthur's new-finished hall, feeling the life seep back into our stiff limbs. Arthur brought spiced wine to us and served us from his own hand.

'Myrddin! Pelleas! It is a fine and happy sight I am seeing! Welcome, welcome!' Arthur called in greeting. His smile was as immense as it was genuine. 'How did you fare in the south, my friends?'

Merlin did not have it in him to soften his reply. 'Disaster threatens, boy,' he said, 'and darkness must soon overtake us.'

Arthur, the smile still on his broad happy face, glanced from one to the other of us, as if unwilling to believe. Indeed, the hall was warm, the fire bright — despairing words held little meaning. 'How so?'

'There is a power in this land that will not be appeased until all are in subjection to it.'

'Well, that is a worry for another day. Tonight, I am with my friends and the wine is good.' He lifted his cup. 'To our enemies' enemies! And to your safe return!'

It was Arthur's welcome alone, I believe, which turned the tide of misery for Merlin.

For I saw my master behold the young Duke in all his youthful zeal, the light of life burning so brightly in him, that he determined for Arthur's sake to put the gloom and depression that had dogged our journey behind him. I saw the line of Merlin's shoulders lift; I saw his chin rise. And though the smile with which he returned Arthur's welcome was forced, it was a smile nonetheless, and the greeting with it true.

Thus, soon after our arrival at Caer Melyn the pall which hung over Merlin's spirit began to lift. This was Arthur's doing, as I have said. For even then he was beginning to display that rarest of qualities: a joy inspired by hardship, deepened by adversity, and exalted by tragedy.

Arthur could find the golden beam of hope in defeat, the single glimmer of blue in the storm-fretted sky. It was this that made him such a winning leader — the kind of man for whom other men gladly lay down their lives. Arthur's enthusiasm and assurance were the flint and steel to the dry tinder of men's hearts. Once he learned to strike the spark, he could set the flame any time he chose. And that was a sight to see, I tell you.

That night, as we stood together before the hearth, my master found reason to hope against all evidence to the contrary. He began, I think, to sense the shape of our salvation: it was larger, grander, higher, purer and far more potent than he had ever imagined.

'Of course,' he would say later, 'it had to be like this. There was no other way!'

That would come in time. All in good time. And not for a long, long time. But it would come.

That night of homecoming, however, it was only young Arthur lifting our hearts with his boundless joy at our return. Oh, how he loved Merlin!

'Tell me about your journey,' Arthur said, as the board was being readied for supper. 'Did Ban receive you? Will he help? Is he sending aid? When will it — '

'Arthur, please!' cried Merlin, holding up his hand to stay the flood of Arthur's curiosity. 'One question at a time.'

'Answer any one you like, only tell me something!'

115

'I will tell you everything,' Merlin promised. 'Only let us sit down and discuss it in a civilized manner. We have ridden far today and I am hungry.' We took our places at the board to await the stew.

'There,' said Arthur when we had our cups in hand. 'Now sing, bard. I am waiting.'

'Yes, Ban received us. Yes, he is sending aid. Supplies will arrive as soon as the harvest is gathered — '

'Well done!' Arthur slapped the board, making our cups jump. 'Well done, Myrddin! I knew you would succeed.'

' — men will arrive in the spring with Bors.' To Arthur's look of amazement, he added. 'Yes, in addition to supplies, Ban is sending his warband and his brother Bors to lead them. They are yours to command.'

'Better and better!' cried Arthur, leaping up. 'Cai! Bedwyr!' he called across the hall as the door opened to a group of men just entering. 'Come here!'

Shaking rain from their cloaks, the two came to stand at the board, dripping water over us. 'Greetings, Myrddin. . . Pelleas,' said Bedwyr. 'What news do you bring us?'

'Is Ban with us?' asked Cai. Apparently, the king of Benowyc's disposition was much on everyone's mind.

'Men and supplies!' Arthur fairly shouted. 'Bors is bringing his warband.'

'Horses, too?' asked Bedwyr.

'A hundred warriors, and horses for all. Supplies enough for them and us, too. That is the bargain.'

Bedwyr and Cai grinned at one another, and at Arthur. Bedwyr clapped Merlin on the back, saying, 'Truly, you are a wonder worker, Myrddin!'

'Cups!' called Cai. 'Bring us something to drink! We must celebrate our good fortune.'

'They are not coming until the spring,' Merlin told him.

'We will celebrate then, too,' laughed Bedwyr. 'You would not deny us the first good news we have heard since you left.'

'Why? What has happened while we were away?'

Bedwyr glanced at Arthur, who said, 'We have heard that Morcant has made an alliance with Coledac and Idris against me.'

'Owen Vinddu has pledged men and horses to them,'

muttered Cai. 'This, when he told us he could not spare an oat or he would starve this winter. Curse the lot of them!'

'By summer they hope to field a war host a thousand strong against us,' added Bedwyr. 'More if they can get other lords to throw in with them.'

The hurt in their voices was real enough, the sense of betrayal strong. Merlin nodded in sympathy. 'Well,' he offered, 'it may not come to that. One of them, at least, will be in no position to make war against you in the spring.'

'Why? What do you know?' asked Arthur.

'Coledac is dead,' Merlin said, 'and most of his warband with him.'

'Ha!' barked Cai mirthlessly. 'Treachery repaid.'

'What happened?' asked Bedwyr.

'Sea Wolves have taken the Saecsen Shore.' Merlin let the significance of this news grow in them.

Arthur was first to speak. 'How bad was it?'

'The strongholds seized and the settlements burned — the small holdings as well. Coledac was killed in the first onslaught and the warband routed. No one escaped. After that there was no defence.'

Arthur, eyes narrowed, weighing the danger in his mind, gripped the brass cup between his hands, bending the metal. 'How far inland have they come?'

'It is not certain,' Merlin replied. 'From what we were told, the main attack appears to have taken place further south.'

Thus was it a sombre group that assembled to celebrate our return. The next days, the dire news was repeated once and again, as straggling groups of homeless came to the caer seeking shelter on their way to the west.

Gradually, from many confused and conflicting stories, the truth emerged: Saecsens under a war leader named Aelle had overrun several of the old fortresses on the south-east coast between the Wash and the Thamesis. The main attack, however, was concentrated a little further south between the Thamesis and the Afon, the old lands of the Cantii. This assault was led by a king named Colgrim, with the aid of another — Octa, the son of Hengist now grown, and returned to avenge his father's death.

This south-eastern region is the Saecsen Shore, so called by the Romans for the linked system of beacons and out-posts erected along the coast to protect against raiding Sea Wolves.

It was along this same stretch of southern coast that Vortigern settled Hengist and Horsa and their tribes, in the vain hope of ending the incessant raiding that was slowly bleeding Britain dry. And it was from this coast that the barbarians spilled out to flood the surrounding land, until Aurelius contained, defeated and banished them.

Now they were back, taking once more the land Hengist had overrun. The Saecsen Shore — its name would remain, but henceforth for a different reason. These invaders meant to stay.

We worried at this through the long winter. The thought of Saecsens seizing British lands burned in Arthur like a banked fire, but there was nothing to be done save endure the ignominy of it. Indeed, we had no other choice. We had to await Bors' arrival in the spring with the needed men. And then, Morcant must be brought to heel before we could even consider facing the Saecsens.

In all, it was a sorry winter for us. Despite Ban's generous gift of provisions, food began running low just before mid-winter. We had grain enough, thanks to Ban, but no meat. The eve of the Christ Mass found us riding the hunting runs, clutching our spears in stiff, frozen hands, hoping to sight a deer, or pig, or hare — anything that would put meat on the board.

Merlin sang often in the hall, doing what he could to keep our spirits up. But spring found our courage at lowest ebb nonetheless, anxiously awaiting the arrival of Bors with Ban's men. With each day that passed, Arthur's resent-ment of the small kings hardened and his anger against them grew.

Spring saw no improvement. The weather stayed cold, the sky grey. Day upon day, icy rain whipped the southern hills. The wild wind howled through long chill nights; and it seemed the earth would never warm beneath the sun, nor know any milder clime again.

Then, one day, the weather broke. The clouds parted and the sun shone brightly in the high, blue sky. Light returned to the land. And with it came the news that we had feared all winter.

The messenger's feet had hardly touched the ground when the cry went up: Morcant rides against us!

'Where?' asked Arthur.

The messenger wiped sweat from his forehead. 'They are coming along the coast. They will have crossed the Ebbw by now.'

Arthur nodded sharply. The Ebbw river formed the eastern border of Arthur's realm. By riding along the Mor Hafren coast a force could move much faster than one having to thread the winding glens. It was speed Morcant wanted.

'How many?'

'Three hundred.'

'What!' Cai demanded. He had hastened to Arthur's side at the arrival of the rider. 'How did the old lion raise so many?'

'There is time yet before we meet them.' With the coming of spring, Arthur had ordered the ring of smaller hill forts to be manned with watchers — especially those along the coast, where he hoped for word of Ban's ships arriving any day. It was the watchman at Penygaer who saw Morcant's forces crossing the Ebbw estuary along the coast.

'Artos,' said Cai calmly, 'how do you propose to meet them? It is seventy against three hundred.'

'I admit the fight is not even,' Arthur's grin was lopsided and reckless, 'but Morcant will just have to survive as best he can.' He turned to me. 'Pelleas, fetch Bedwyr and Myrddin. We will gather in my chambers.'

'At once, lord.'

He and Cai strode off across the yard as the hunting horn sounded the alarm. I found Merlin and Bedwyr together at one of the granaries, examining our dwindling supply of barley.

'Hail, Pelleas,' called Bedwyr as I dashed towards them. He saw my face and his smile of welcome faded. 'What is it? What is wrong?'

'Morcant is riding against us. He is on his way here now with three hundred.'

'We cannot meet them,' observed Bedwyr. 'There are just too many. Even with Meurig's warband, they would still outman us three to one.'

'Where are they?' Merlin asked. His tone showed no surprise or concern.

'They have crossed the Ebbw river at the coast to take us from the south.'

'Yes,' mused Merlin, 'that is what I would do.'

'There is no time to ride to Caer Myrddin anyway.'

'We are to meet Arthur in his chambers at once,' I told them.

Arthur and Cai sat over the long board in Arthur's chambers, at one end of the hall. 'It is not possible,' Cai was saying as we entered, 'and even if it were, the risk is terrible.'

Arthur smiled and reached across the board to ruffle Cai's red curls. 'Trust Cai to count the risk.'

'God's honour! That is the truth. I do heed the risk. *Someone* must.' Cai folded his arms across his chest, glowering out from beneath his copper-coloured brows.

'What impossible thing is he proposing this time?' Bedwyr laughed as he sat down on the bench. I settled beside him; Merlin remained standing.

Cai, a pained expression pinching his ruddy features, put up his hands. 'Do not ask me to repeat it. I will not.'

Arthur gazed placidly at Cai and then shrugged. 'Perhaps he is right — it cannot be done.' He turned to Bedwyr and Merlin. 'Well, wise advisers? Advise me wisely, or Morcant will.'

We all looked at one another, silently calculating our chances of surviving this day.

'Well,' said Merlin after a moment, 'perhaps it is a day for impossible feats. Who knows?'

'It seems we have no other choice,' muttered Cai.

'Are we to know this impossible plan of yours?' demanded Bedwyr. 'Speak it out.'

'I was only thinking,' began Arthur slowly, 'you know how these hills catch the echoes. . . '

120

The sun stood directly overhead and there was still no sign of Morcant's war host. Scouts had been dispatched and had returned with confirmation that indeed a force of three hundred or more were approaching along the coast. They had crossed the Ebbw and were making for Glyn Rominw — the vale of the Rominw river.

The deep glen circled Caer Melyn, describing a half-moon arc to the east before curving away to meet Mor Hafren just to the south. Any attacking army would find it a natural roadway straight into the heart of Arthur's realm.

The young Duke knew the vale for what it was, and knew his enemies would regard it a weakness. But part of Arthur's genius lay in his remarkable ability to read the land.

He had only to see a place once to know it — each hill and hollow, every freshet and stream, every dingle and dell, rock cliff and standing stone. He knew where it was safe to ford, where the ground cover was thickest, where the hidden trails met and where they led. He knew all the ancient tracks and ridgeways, where men might safely ride without being seen, how the fields of the various realms were laid, which height would afford protection, which lowland a hiding-place, where natural defences could be found, where the land favoured attack, or retreat, or ambush. . .

All these things and more Arthur could read in the fold and crease of the earth. The land spoke to him, readily revealing its secrets to his quick eyes.

This is how I came to be squatting on a hillside overlooking a ford on the Rominw, holding a blackthorn bush before me, surrounded by a company of warriors, each similarly hidden. Across the glen, Cai, with another company, lay hidden behind a low, grassy rise. And to the north another company; to the south another, and so on all along the vale.

Time passed. I sat watching cloud shadows on the hillside opposite me or gazing south along the curving length of the river, listening for the sound of the approaching warband and wondering what detained them — thinking that perhaps they had not chosen Glyn Rominw after all.

The wind had shifted to the north, making the sound of Morcant's approach more difficult to hear — if indeed he had entered the vale. What was taking the old lion so long?

Perhaps he had continued on along the coast to come at

us out of the west. Perhaps he had forded the Rominw and crossed back to the east to come inland along one of the smaller streams. Perhaps he had — the thought never finished itself, for at that moment I heard it: the quick, rolling drum of horses hooves upon the earth.

I craned my neck to the south and peered through the branches of my blackthorn bush. A moment later I saw them, Morcant's forces moving through the glen. They came on in a loose pack; there were no orderly ranks, no coherent divisions of any sort. They spread across the valley floor in a ragged swarm. More a mob than a force of disciplined men.

That was the pith of it! So arrogant was Morcant, so smug and self-assured, so confident in his superior numbers, he made no attempt at order in his ranks. He meant to overwhelm Arthur's warband — like a wave on the shore, to simply wash over us and crush us with its all-engulfing weight.

I watched the unruly throng stream into the valley below, and anger leapt up, a hot red flame within me. Fool! Morcant esteemed Arthur not at all. So lacking in respect he did not even deem it wisdom to order his ranks. Oh, the insolence was blinding, the pride deafening.

I saw it all and did not care that we were only seventy against three hundred. Blessed Jesu, if we die today, let it be as true warriors with honour.

The first foemen had reached the ford. Some splashed through the stream, others stopped to drink — the ignorant louts. Careless and stupid in their arrogance. My anger burned more fiercely in me.

As soon as the main body of the warband reached the opposite bank, a mighty shout went up, an all-encompassing shout, a shout to shake the roots of the world. 'ALLELUIA!'

I looked and saw Merlin standing alone on the hilltop, arms raised over his head, his cloak loose and blowing. At the very same instant there came an answer from across the glen. 'A-l-l-e-l-u-i-a!'

The echoes rang. 'Alleluia! . . . Alleluia!'

I joined in the gladdening cry, and the warriors with me on the hillside shouted too. 'Alleluia!'

The shouts were coming from all along the glen now, the echoes pealing like bells, ringing on and on. Alleluia! Alleluia! Alleluia!

The effect was immediate and dramatic. At that first enormous shout, the enemy had halted. The cries of alleluia assailed them from every side. They scanned the hillside for the foe, but saw no one. Now the echoes encircled them, pelting down upon them. . . Alleluia! Alleluia! Alleluia! Alleluia!

Morcant's host scattered. The main body drove back across the stream into those still straggling behind. Seeing the ford hopelessly blocked, others turned to the hills. A group of twenty broke off, riding straight towards us.

We let them come. Nearer. . . nearer. . .

With a mighty shout we threw off the blackthorn branches that hid us. 'Alleluia!'

Up we leapt, sword in hand, striking, pulling the startled riders from their saddles. We struck them to the ground and sent their terrified horses back down the hill into the confused host. I looked across the glen. The same thing was happening on the opposite hillside, as astonished warriors disappeared behind the grassy rise where Cai's men waited.

Shouting, raving, screaming, the vale throbbed with the unearthly and unnerving sound. Morcant's war host, confronted by this invisible, seemingly invincible foe, bolted in chaotic retreat back down the valley.

Seeing this, we ran for our horses, tethered behind the crest of the hill. But a few heartbeats later we were hurtling down the face of the hill and into the retreating war host. Morcant and Cerdic stood at the ford, their warriors fleeing away like a flood parting around them. They raged at the men, screaming for them to turn and fight.

And then there was Arthur in their midst with his eleven. They had simply appeared, it seemed — sprung to life from the rocks at their very feet, horses and all.

It was too much. Cerdic wheeled his horse and fled after his men. Morcant was too crazy with rage to heed his own danger. He lifted his sword and rode at Arthur. The two met. There was a quick flash of steel and Morcant fell. His body rolled into the stream and the king lay still.

The fight did not end there. We escaped death that day, nothing more.

Though we were all grateful to walk the land of the living, as the sun faded behind the western hills and we returned to the caer we knew that only a battle had been won. We suffered no losses, and only two men wounded. Cerdic had fled with his warband almost intact; he would nurse the injury to his pride for a season and then he would return to avenge his father. Others who thought to gain from the strife would rally to him, and the war would go on.

While we Britons fought among ourselves, the ships would come; the settlements would burn. More and still more land would fall beneath the shadow. And the Saecsen kind would grow strong in Britain once more.

TWELVE

'This is insane!' Arthur spat. 'I hate this, Myrddin. I hate it worse than anything I have known.'

'So did your father,' Merlin replied calmly. 'And despite what they say of Uther, your uncle had no stomach for it, either. But they endured it, and so will you.'

'As if we did not all have better things to do than carve up one another in this senseless slaughter. I have lost sixteen Cymbrogi this month. Sixteen! Do you hear?'

'The whole world hears you, Arthur.'

'This is Urbanus' doing. If I had that meddling bishop here before me now, I would — I would. . . ' Arthur sputtered, reaching for words to express his frustration.

'Hand him his head on a platter?' Cai suggested hopefully.

'Even that is too good for him,' muttered Bedwyr.

We were at table with Arthur in his tent. The tent flaps were open, but it was hot — the tail end of a sultry, frustrating day. We were all tired, and hungry still, though the meal was long since finished. The humour of the group had soured a good time before talk turned to Urbanus.

Very likely, Arthur was right. Urbanus' efforts at peacemaking had only succeeded in making matters far worse than they might otherwise have been. The ambitious cleric had no talent for diplomacy, and less understanding. He knew nothing of the forces involved in the struggle.

To Urbanus it was utterly simple: choose a High King acceptable to all. If Arthur was not accepted, the rule of Britain must fall to someone else.

He did not see how this undercut Arthur's claim and authority. He did not see how his constant peacemongering prolonged the fight.

For, if the church had backed Arthur solidly, the dissenters would have had no support for their position. What is more, they would have found themselves fighting against the church in order to continue their ruinous rebellion. As it was, the rebellious lords took hope from Urbanus' equivocation. And the war continued.

It had started the spring Morcant was killed — four years before. Four years. . . it might just as well have been a hundred for all the nearer we were to ending it.

Cerdic, seeking vengeance for the death of his father, and the lean and hungry Idris, hoping to increase the lands left him by his kinsman Dunaut, formed the foundation of the alliance of lords who stood in open revolt against Arthur.

Rebellion pure and simple, under the guise of protesting what they termed Arthur's abuse of the war chest: the supplies and money he collected from the lords to maintain the warband of Britain. 'He takes too much!' they cried. 'He has no right! If we do not pay, his men punish us. He is worse than any Saecsen!'

Lies, all lies. But it gave them an excuse to unite against Arthur. It justified their treachery. And by it they even succeeded in luring men like Owen Vinddu, Ogryvan and Rhain into their wicked scheme. Others, petty lordlings all, seized the chance to join in, hoping to improve their meagre holdings with pillaged gold and plundered honour.

Of Arthur's friends, only Custennin, Meurig, and Ban committed men and supplies to his support. Shamefully, even his would-be allies — Madoc, Bedegran, Morganwg and others like them — stood aside until the war decided the issue one way or another. Still, between Arthur's fearless extortion and the generosity of his allies, we scraped by.

That first year was hard enough. Bors arrived with his men in time to forestall our outright slaughter. By autumn of the second year we were battle-seasoned warriors, each and every one of us. The third year we succeeded in moving the fight from Arthur's realm to Cerdic's.

Now, late in our fourth summer, we were fighting a battle nearly every other day. Winning most of them, it is true; but fighting nonetheless, on little rest and poor food — and this is hard on warriors.

If not for Bors, I do not know what we would have done.

He and his men sustained us, upheld us, strengthened us while we learned the craft of war. Together Bors and Arthur led Britain's only hope into the fray and saved it from certain ruin. Not once only, but time and time and time again.

We did not know how long we could continue. But each day we drew strength from the previous day's victory, and somehow we fought on.

'We have been pressing them all summer,' said Arthur. 'They must give in.' The anger of the moment had passed. He had returned to his other preoccupation: trying to discern when the kings would capitulate. 'It cannot last another year.'

'It can easily last another year,' Bedwyr observed. 'It is harvest time soon. They will have to go home to gather in the crops. And it is expected that you will do the same. There will be a truce through the winter, as there always is.'

'Well, let them go back to their lands for the harvest. I will grant them no truce — ' he paused thoughtfully. All of us sitting round the table with him saw the light come up like sunrise in his clear blue eyes.

'What is it?' asked Bedwyr. 'What have I said?'

'We will take the war to them in their own fields,' replied Arthur.

'I do not see how that will sol — ' began Cai, but Bedwyr was already far beyond him.

Bedwyr was seeing what Arthur had seen. 'We could ride ahead!'

'Burn the crops where they stand!'

'Let *them* go hungry this winter, as we will. Why not starve together?'

Bors slapped the board with his hands. 'I like it!'

Cai shook his head. 'I do not see how this is helping at all.'

Arthur draped an arm over Cai's wide shoulders. 'Losing their precious grain will make them think twice about continuing the war next year,' he explained. 'They will either have to give in or buy grain from Gaul.'

'And that will be expensive,' said Bedwyr. 'Only Cerdic can afford that.'

'And him none too well after this year,' put in Bors. He laughed and pounded on the table until the cups and supper dishes rattled. 'Let Cerdic chew on that all through the winter, and he will not be so keen to fight next spring.'

'Well said!' Arthur slapped his knee approvingly.

'But I still do not see the use of us starving along with them,' insisted Cai stubbornly. 'We would not have to.'

'Oh? Have you a better plan?' asked Bedwyr carelessly.

Cai frowned. 'Do not be burning it. Let us harvest it instead.'

'We are not farmers!' protested Bedwyr.

'Beat our swords into sickles?' Bors jeered. 'Ha!'

Cai's frown deepened. His green eyes darkened, as they always did whenever he suspected people of making fun of him, or failing to take him seriously.

'Cai is right.' Merlin's soft tone stopped them dead. 'We are hungry. Burning it would be a sin. Besides, it would not wound any of you to be seen with a scythe in your hand.'

'But we cannot — ' Bedwyr's protest died in Arthur's wild whoop of joy.

'It is perfect!' Arthur leapt to his feet. 'It is beautiful in its simplicity! This is salvation sweet and sure!' He pounded Cai on the back and the frown altered to a dubious grin.

'We will harvest their grain for them — ' Arthur began.

'And they just let us carry it off?' Bedwyr shook his head. 'Not as long as a man among them can still hold sword and spear.'

'We will harvest their grain, because they will be too busy dealing with this annoying Bors here and his disagreeable Armoricans.' Arthur stalked round the table with long, sure steps, his hands waving in the air, his mind already speeding on, ahead of us all. 'Then, when they are hungrily eyeing their dogs and horses next winter, we offer to sell it back to them.' He paused for emphasis, his voice going hard as iron. 'The price will be full allegiance.'

Merlin smiled grimly. He banged the butt of his staff on the ground three times. 'Well done, Arthur! Well done!' He raised his hand to Cai. 'And well done, Cai. You kept your head and followed the wiser course.' His words praised, but his tone mocked.

'You agree, Myrddin? It is the wisest course? It is a good plan, yes?'

'Oh, a very good plan, Arthur. But even the best plans can fail.'

'Do you think it will fail?' asked Bedwyr.

'It matters little what I think,' replied Merlin diffidently. 'I am not the one to convince. It is for your warriors to decide.'

'As to that,' stated Arthur, 'I do not know a single man among them who would not welcome the chance to lay down his sword for a day or two.'

'Even if he knew it was only to take up the sickle and flail?' Bors grimaced with distaste.

'Never worry, Lord Bors,' Arthur soothed, 'you will not have to touch that dread implement. You will lead your men on harassment forays, diversions — anything you like, so long as you keep those hounds occupied while we steal their grain.'

'That I will do! By the God who made me, that I will do.'

They fell at once to making plans for keeping the rebel kings occupied, and for transporting the grain once they had it. Merlin left them to their plans, moving silently from the tent and out into the early twilight.

I followed him and joined him as he stood gazing up at the lingering blush of red in the western sky. I stood with him for a moment, and then said, 'What is it?'

Merlin did not answer, but continued looking at the sky, and at a flock of crows winging to their roosts in a hilltop wood nearby.

'Is it the grain raid? Will it fail?'

'In truth, I do not know. . . '

'What is it, then? What have you seen?'

He was long in answering, but when he spoke at last his words were, 'Ships, Pelleas, and smoke. I have seen the sharp prows dividing the foam, and many feet splashing onto the shore. I have seen smoke, heavy and black, flattening on the wind.'

'Saecsens?'

Merlin nodded, but did not take his eyes from the sky. 'In the north. . . I think Eboracum has fallen.'

Eboracum fallen to the Saecsens? We had heard nothing of this. I did not doubt my master, however; his word would prove true.

'What is to be done?'

'What is to be done?' He turned to me, golden eyes dark with sudden anger. 'End this senseless rebellion. The waste, the waste! We tear at one another and the Saecsen brazenly seize the land. It must end. There must be an end.'

He turned and started down the hill towards the stream. After a few paces he paused and glanced back over his shoulder. 'Will the grain raid succeed?' he called, then answered. 'Pray, Pelleas! Pray with everything in you that it does succeed. For the time is here and now gone when we can suffer the Saecsen kind to take root among us.'

The men of the settlement stood mute and angry as they watched Arthur's warriors heave the last sack of grain onto the overloaded wain. When the driver came with the goad to turn the oxen onto the trail, an old man — one of the farmers who had been watching the grain disappear — stepped forward to stand before Cai.

'It is not right that you take everything,' the farmer accused. 'You should leave us something.'

'If you have a grievance, take it to your lord,' Cai told him flatly. 'This is Cerdic's doing.'

'We will go hungry this winter. If you leave us nothing we will die.'

'Then die!' Cai shouted, vaulting to his mount. From the saddle he challenged them. 'I tell you the truth: we would not be stealing your grain if Cerdic had not broken his sworn oath to support Arthur. As it is, we take only what has been promised to us.' With that, he wheeled his horse and trotted off to take his place behind the wain.

As at the other settlements, no one lifted a hand to stop us. Not that it would have made a difference if they had. The silent accusation in their eyes was enough. We all felt like barbarians and worse for our part in the scheme.

'Bear it but a little longer,' Arthur told us all repeatedly. 'It is soon over and the war will end.'

Only Arthur's assurance, solid and unfailing, kept us at it. At one holding after another, three and four at a time, we hastily gathered the year's crops of barley and corn, and cattle and sheep in fair numbers also. All the while,

130

Bors occupied the massed war host of the rebel lords with cunning little raids and forays designed both to annoy and to keep them far away from us.

It worked, yes. Perhaps too well. We succeeded too easily. This should have been a warning.

But, when Cerdic and the rebel lords finally discovered what we were doing, the grain was safely behind Caer Melyn's walls. In fact, we could not keep it all — our stores would not hold it. We sent a good portion to Meurig, and what he could not take we piled on the ground in the yard and covered with hides.

The weather broke early that year. Indeed, the autumn rains started as the last wagons began their ascent of the hill to the caer. As the warriors rode ahead to get in out of the rain, Arthur stood at the gate and welcomed them.

'Well, that is that,' he said, as the last wain trundled into the yard a little while later. He stood looking out across the hills and made no move when Bedwyr joined him. 'That is the last of it,' Arthur said.

'I hope so.' Bedwyr shook his head slowly.

Arthur cocked an eye at him. 'Then why do you frown so?'

'I tell you the truth, Artos, I am ashamed.'

'Would you rather be dead?' Arthur snapped. 'Cerdic will oblige you.'

'Na, na,' Bedwyr replied soothingly. 'I agree it is necessary. For the love of God, Artos, I know it is. But that does not mean I have to like it. And I will rest easier over this when Bors has returned.'

'He is late, that is all.' Arthur made a dismissing motion with his hand, and moved away to where the wains were being unloaded. One of the wet grain sacks slipped and fell, landing on the ground before Arthur, where it burst and poured forth a golden flood over his feet.

He glared at the spilled grain for a moment, the colour rising to his face. 'Clean it up!' Arthur shouted angrily. The men stopped their work to stare at him. 'Clean it up at once, do you hear? For I will not allow a single kernel to be wasted.' He shook the grain from his boots and stalked off.

Yes, Bors was late. It was on everyone's mind. He should

have returned days ago, but there had been no word or sign and we feared that something had happened to him.

Days passed and Arthur grew more edgy and short-tempered, as did we all. Rhys, Bors' harper, sang in the hall each night, doing what he could to lift our spirits. Unfortunately, playing to an ill-tempered and unappreciative audience, he could do very little.

'I am going after him,' Arthur declared one night. 'Jesu knows, we cannot sit here like this all winter.'

The morning came dark and damp with a thick curling mist. Arthur chose twenty warriors to ride with him. As they were saddling their mounts, we heard a cry from the gates. 'Open! Let Tegal in!'

Immediately, the gates swung open and the rider — a watchman at one of the border watchtowers — reined up and slid from the saddle. At once a knot of people gathered round the rider.

'What is it?' demanded Arthur, pushing his way through the throng.

'My lord, a war host approaches.'

'How many?'

'Five hundred.'

'Cerdic.' Arthur's voice was flat and sharp-edged as his sword. 'Very well, today we will settle it once and for all.' He turned to his warriors. 'Arm yourselves! We ride to meet them.'

The caer was thrown into instant chaos as men ran to don arms and saddle horses. But we did not ride out that day. In fact, we did not even leave the caer.

For, as we assembled in the yard — in this we followed the Roman generals, readying ourselves in orderly ranks before riding into battle — there came a messenger from Cerdic, riding under the sign of safe conduct: a willow branch raised in his right hand.

'Let him enter,' Arthur commanded. 'We will hear what he has to say.'

The gate was opened and the rider entered. Arthur came to stand before him. 'Do not bother to dismount,' he told the messenger. 'Deliver your charge. What has Cerdic to say to us?'

The rider's brows rose slightly in surprise that we should

know his mission already. 'Lord Cerdic asks that he may draw near your stronghold.'

'To what purpose?'

'He would speak with you.'

Arthur glanced at Cai and Bedwyr before answering. Neither made any objection, so he said, 'Go and tell Cerdic that I grant him leave to approach. He may bring three advisers with him — but no more than three.'

The messenger inclined his head and, wheeling his horse, rode back the way he had come.

We waited for Cerdic on the ramparts, the mist beading up on our cloaks and hair. And, but a short while later, we saw the war host of Cerdic and the rebel kings crest the far-off hill and begin their traverse of the long valley that stood before Caer Melyn.

'He has brought them all,' breathed Cai. 'Every motherless one of them.'

'Good,' said Arthur. 'Let there be an end.'

Merlin, too, stood on the rampart watching. But he said nothing.

When the war host reached the foot of the hill they stopped. We watched, then, as four riders came apart from the rest and continued on up the hill. Closer, we could see Cerdic flanked by two of his allies — Idris and Maglos, who rode a little behind him. Between Idris and Maglos rode a third man.

It took a few moments to discern the identity of the third, but when we did all became clear.

'Bors!' cried Cai. 'In God's name, they have Bors with them.'

Alas, it was true, Bors rode between Idris and Maglos, his hands and arms bound behind him. The warriors murmured darkly at this, but Arthur silenced them with a quick cut of his hand.

The four rode to the gates and stopped. 'Hail, Arthur! I give you good greeting,' called Cerdic insolently. 'What? Is this how you receive your masters — quaking behind closed gates with your sword in your hand?'

'I agreed to listen to you,' Arthur replied coolly. 'Content yourself with that. You will receive no welcome cup from my hand.'

133

Cerdic barked a mocking laugh. 'Do you think me in the habit of accepting the hospitality of a thieving whorespawn of a Duke?'

'I will kill him for that,' muttered Cai under his breath.

Arthur ignored the taunt. 'If you have something to say, Cerdic, speak out. I am waiting.'

'I have come to make a bargain with you — ' began Cerdic.

'Arthur, no! Do not do it!' shouted Bors, for which he was rudely silenced with the back of Maglos' hand across his mouth. Blood spurted from his split lip.

'Lay hand to him again,' warned Arthur ominously, 'and you will lose that hand, Maglos.'

'Save your threats, Duke Arthur,' Cerdic sneered, 'you are not in authority here. The bargain is this: the grain you have stolen from each of us, for the life of your minion, Bors. I make this offer once, and once only. What do you say? I will wait while you confer with your advisers. But I warn you, do not keep me waiting long.'

'Since you are so impatient, I give you my answer at once. Hear me now: kill Bors and his warband if that is what you intend. For I have vowed that none of you will ever so much as see a kernel of that grain except under one condition.'

The smile left Cerdic's face. He turned and spoke a few hasty words to his allies. 'What is this condition of yours?' asked Cerdic.

'Swear fealty to me, and renew your pledge of support. Then, when you have paid the tribute that you owe into the war chest of Britain, I will give you back your grain.'

'Never!' spat Cerdic. 'I will never swear fealty to you!'

'Then you will not have the grain.'

'I will kill him!' screamed Cerdic, thrusting a finger at Bors.

'Do what you will with him. I will not trade the grain for anything except the fealty and tribute promised me.'

'You value the grain more than his life?' demanded Idris incredulously.

'I value the life of my friend no less than I value my own. But I value Britain above all. This war between us will be ended.' Arthur spoke boldly and with supreme assurance.

'The grain stays here until you swear the oath of fealty to me.'

'May it rot in your mouths!' cried Cerdic. 'I will burn this fortress to the ground.'

'And then what will you tell your people when the winter hunger gnaws at their bellies? What will you tell them when their children starve?' replied Arthur in a voice as cold as the tomb.

Idris and Maglos winced; it was not in them to support Cerdic to the hurt of their people. Indeed, I believe they had grown weary of supporting him and wanted to make an end.

'Well, Cerdic? I am waiting. What is it to be?'

Cerdic writhed with indecision.

'You have lost, Cerdic,' said Bors through bloodied lips. 'Give in with honour.'

'No! I can still fight. We will fight you and take back what is ours.'

'We have fought all summer, Cerdic, as we have each summer for four years. I tell you there will be an end to this war between us.'

'Not while I have breath to curse you, bastard!'

The day had grown cold and the mist had turned to a light rain. Idris and Maglos glanced at one another uneasily. They were cold and dispirited. They had reached the end of their patience and endurance, and wanted nothing more than to be done with it.

'Lord,' began Idris, 'we have no choice but to do as he says.'

'He is right,' Maglos added. 'Let us end it here and now.'

'Do you desert me, too? Be gone, then. Take your men. I will fight him alone.' Cerdic's eyes flashed with hatred — and the sudden light of desperate inspiration. 'What say you, Bastard of Britain? Will you fight me for it? Or are you the coward men say you are?'

'I am not afraid to fight you, Cerdic.'

'Then come out from behind your walls and we will fight.'

'No, Artos,' said Cai. 'Allow me to fight in your place.'

'Peace, brother,' replied Arthur. 'It will be well.'

'You are not going to fight him,' Bedwyr said. 'He is

already beaten. Idris and Maglos are deserting him. He has lost.'

Arthur shook his head sharply. 'He does not know it. And I will not suffer him to leave this place to continue his treason against me. Those who support Cerdic must know that they have failed at last. I tell you the truth, I will have the fealty of all, or the fealty of none.'

So saying, the Duke turned back to Cerdic. 'I will fight you, Cerdic. If you win, you can take back the grain. But if I win, you will make an oath of fealty to me. Do you agree?'

'I agree,' answered Cerdic hastily. 'Let us begin.'

At Arthur's command the gates of Caer Melyn were opened and Cerdic, Idris, Maglos and Bors entered. 'Unbind him,' Arthur told them. Idris drew his knife and cut the thongs at Bors' wrists.

Then Arthur mounted his horse and, taking up his sword and shield, called out to all of us gathered around him. 'Hear me now, Cymbrogi! If I am killed, let no one lift a hand against Cerdic. I am not to be avenged. Let all men among you avow it.'

The warriors answered in a single voice. 'Let it be as you say!'

With this, Arthur gathered up the reins and turned to meet Cerdic, who had taken his place across the yard.

Bedwyr turned to my master. 'Myrddin, stop this. Nothing good can come of it.'

'Oh, a very great good can come of it. For, if Arthur wins he will have won Britain. That is worth the risk, I think.'

Bedwyr appealed to me, but I knew better than to try persuading Merlin once he had spoken his mind — as soon persuade a mountain to uproot, or a stream to reverse its course. 'Let be, Bedwyr,' I told him. 'Have faith.'

'I have faith in Arthur,' he replied. 'But I trust Cerdic not at all.'

The two combatants turned to face one another. We formed a hollow ring around them. The rain came down and we stood there silently, waiting for the deadly contest to begin.

Here is the way of it:

Cerdic urges his horse forward and begins trotting around the perimeter of the ring, slowly at first, but gathering pace as he goes. Arthur does likewise, and they circle one another, around and around, circling, circling, taking the measure of one another.

Suddenly Cerdic turns his mount and drives to the centre of the ring. Arthur is not caught, for in the same instant he throws his reins to the side and flies to meet Cerdic head on.

The clash of their meeting rings sharp in our ears. The shock of the blow shakes the ground beneath our feet. Cerdic is thrown back in his saddle. The horses leap away at once. Cerdic circles again. His face is set, intense.

As before, they chase one another round the ring and then turn and fly towards one another at full gallop.

The air is rent with the force of their collision. Swords flash. Arthur sways in the saddle. Cerdic's horse stumbles to its knees and the king topples to the ground.

The Cymbrogi shout with loud acclaim. They think that he has won. But Cerdic is on his feet, his sword before him, his shield ready. His face is grim. Arthur is stronger than he knew.

There is hatred in his eyes still, but now there is also fear.

Arthur quits the saddle and slides lightly to the ground. He advances on Cerdic.

As they close, Cerdic looses a wild cry and throws himself forward, hewing with his sword. Striking, striking, again and again, with the fury of madness. Arthur thrusts his shield before him and is beaten back.

Each blow of Cerdic's sword bites deep into Arthur's shield. The wood splinters, the metal is rent. Now the boss is cleft, and now the rim. Pieces of it fall away.

Arthur!

With a mighty effort Cerdic heaves his sword over his head and slashes down. Arthur's broken shield is split asunder. Cerdic raises his sword once more. It hovers in the air — and falls.

Arthur flings the remains of his shield away. His arm is bloody where Cerdic's sword has bitten through. Cerdic's sword slices the air as it slashes towards Arthur's unprotected chest.

137

Watch out!

But Arthur is quicker than Cerdic kens. The Sword of Britain flicks out and up, meeting Cerdic's stroke in the air. The sound is that of the hammer striking the anvil.

Cerdic's arm shudders with the force of the blow, and the point of his sword wavers. Arthur leaps upon his foe, beating him down. Cerdic falls back, throwing his sword above his head to ward off the withering blows raining upon him.

'Yield, Cerdic!' cries Arthur, raising Sword of Macsen above his head.

'Never!' shouts Cerdic defiantly. And slashing carelessly with his blade, he catches Arthur on the hip.

With a tremendous groan Arthur brings his weapon down. It falls like lightning from the grey sky. And like lightning it divides the air. Cerdic throws the shield over his head to save his skull. Arthur's blade catches the shield boss squarely in the centre and Cerdic's arm collapses. The shield's iron rim strikes Cerdic on the forehead and he drops like a dead man.

The fight is over.

But there is no cheering. No great cry of acclaim celebrates Arthur's victory. Silence steals over the throng. For we have all seen what Arthur himself does not yet see.

Arthur turns and raises his sword in triumph. And then he sees: the Sword of Britain is shattered.

THIRTEEN

Arthur brooded over the loss of Macsen's sword. True, he had won Britain — at Cerdic's defeat the rebel lords quickly abandoned the rebellion and made their peace — but that offered less consolation than it might have done. The reason for his distress was simple enough: by losing the Sword of Britain, he felt that he had lost his rightful claim to the throne. This was nonsense, and Merlin told him so. But Arthur heeded him not.

So it was a long winter for him. And for us all.

'This cannot be allowed to continue,' Merlin said in exasperation one day. 'Look at him! He sits there moping like a hound banished from the hearth. If this keeps up, his sour mood will poison the whole realm.'

It was nearing mid-winter and the time of the Christ Mass was close at hand. I pointed this out, and said, 'Perhaps a feast to celebrate the holy day would cheer him.'

'He needs another sword, not a feast.'

'Well, let us get him one then.'

Merlin made to reply, but thought better of it. He paused, holding his head to one side, then all at once burst out, 'Yes! That is exactly what we will do. Bless you, Pelleas. In years to come all Britain will sing your praises!'

All well and good. But two days later I wished I had never opened my mouth.

Freezing mist clung to the hillsides and hung above us as we made our way through the long, meandering glens. The wind remained light out of the north, thankfully, but that little went straight to the bone and stayed there. The horses plodded through the snow in the valleys, blowing clouds of vapour from their nostrils. I tucked my hands beneath the saddle pad to keep them warm against the steaming horse-flesh. Arthur and Merlin rode ahead, wrapped chin to knee in long, heavy winter cloaks, stiff with cold.

Our only glimpse of daylight the whole miserable day came just before dusk when, as we crested a steep, heathered hill, the clouds parted in the west and we saw the deep red blush of the dying sun.

It was the fourth day and we had travelled little more than half the expected distance. Our spirits were low. But with the light came hope. For in the last rays of the sun we glimpsed a settlement in the valley below. At least we would not be forced to sleep on the ground.

'We will seek shelter there for the night,' said Merlin. 'It is long since I was forced to sing for my supper. This night, of all nights, I hope we do not go hungry.'

I was not worried. I had never known a song of Merlin's to disappoint. 'We will not starve,' I assured him grimly. 'If all else fails, *I* will sing!'

Arthur laughed and it was the first lifting of our hearts all day.

The clouds closed in again, darkening the glen. The wind stirred, biting cold. We urged our horses to a trot and made for the settlement.

Upon reaching the cluster of stone houses beside the clear-running stream, we were met by a large, black, barking dog. We reined up and waited for the animal's yelps to summon someone and, presently, a brown-braided young girl appeared.

No more than six or seven summers, she threw her arms around the dog's neck and chided it. 'Tyrannos! Be quiet!'

The beast subsided under the child's insistence, and Merlin, leaning low in the saddle, addressed the girl, saying, 'I give you good day, my child.'

'Who are you?' she asked frankly, eyeing the harp-shaped hump under the leather wrap behind Merlin's saddle. Curious how children always saw that first.

'We are travellers. And we are cold and hungry. Is there room at your hearth this night?'

She did not answer, but spun on her heel and dashed back to the house. I caught her shout as she disappeared behind the ox-hide hanging in the doorway. 'The Emrys! The Emrys is here!'

Merlin shook his head in astonishment. 'Has it come to this?' he wondered. 'Even small children know me by sight.'

'There are not so many harpers hereabouts,' Arthur suggested, indicating the telltale bulge behind Merlin's saddle. 'And there is only one Emrys, after all.'

'Be that as it may, I would rather the whole of the island did not know our every move.'

'Be at peace, Worrier,' replied Arthur good-naturedly. 'It is a harmless thing.' He stretched in the saddle, and eyed the rapidly darkening sky. The rising wind whined on the hilltops — a cold, forlorn sound. 'I wish *someone* would take an interest in us.'

He had his wish. A moment later, the flint-chip yard was full of people. We were greeted by a man named Bervach, who welcomed us warmly. 'It is not a day for travelling, my lords. Come in by the fire and we will chase the cold from your bones. There is meat on the spit and drink in the skin.'

'We accept your hospitality,' replied Merlin, climbing down from the saddle. 'Your kindness will be repaid.'

The man grinned happily, showing a wide gap between his front teeth. 'Never say it! The Emrys does not pay to sleep beneath the roof of Bervach ap Gevayr.' Despite his words, the man could not help himself; his eyes stole to the bundle behind the saddle and his grin widened.

'Nevertheless, you shall have a reward,' promised Merlin. He winked at me, and I loosened the harp from the saddle and cradled it under my arm as the horses were led away to fodder.

'It is not a day for travelling,' repeated Bervach, as we stooped to enter the low-beamed house. 'The wind on the hills can chill the marrow. Come in, friends, and be welcome.'

Arthur strode to a wide, deep hearth that occupied the whole of one wall. He stood before the hearth and held out his hands, sighing with pleasure as the warmth seeped in.

Bervach watched Arthur for a moment, curiosity glinting in his eyes. 'I feel I should know this one with you,' he

141

said to Merlin, by way of coaxing a name from him. When Merlin did not rise to the bait, he added, 'Yet, I have never set eyes to him before now.'

I saw the quick clash between pride and prudence mirrored in Merlin's glance. He desired to keep Arthur's identity hidden — we were not in our own lands and Arthur still had enemies. And yet Merlin wanted men to know and esteem Arthur, for their respect and devotion would one day be required.

The contest was brief. Pride won.

'Since you ask,' replied Merlin, 'I will tell you who it is that stands before your fire: Arthur ap Aurelius, Duke of Britain.'

Bervach's eyebrows lifted at this knowledge. 'I owned him a lord the moment I saw him.' He nodded slowly, then with a shrug dismissed Arthur, saying, 'I have heard of this Duke Arthur, though I did not think to see one so young. But come, I stand here between you and the fire. Go now. I will fetch a warming draught.' It was clear who counted with Bervach.

We joined Arthur at the hearth. A rosy fire crackled smartly beneath a long spit, bending beneath the weight of the great haunch roasting there. The aroma of venison filled the single large room. Smoke hung thick, sifting its way out slowly through the heavy reed thatch of the roof. Barley loaves baked in neat rows in a corner of the hearthstone.

In all it was a close and comfortable dwelling, now filling with other families of the settlement, all talking excitedly in hushed voices. As Bervach produced horn cups, the people of the holding continued to crowd in, until the small house could hold no more. And still they came: man, woman, and child; thirty souls in all — the entire settlement.

Women bustled about, bearing vessels of wood and pottery, whispering, working efficiently. They were assembling an impromptu feast in our honour. Clearly, the visit of the Emrys was an event not to be missed. And none, apparently, would.

Bervach ap Gevayr was, for this night at least, the equal of any lord in the Island of the Mighty, for tonight the Emrys slept beneath his roof. What happened this night would be remembered and discussed, and all events following would date from it for years to come. Future generations would be told that on this night the Emrys passed by, and he stayed in this house, ate our food and drank our mead, and slept on this very hearth.

And he sang! Oh, yes, he sang. . .

Merlin was well aware of the expectations his presence created. Although tired, and desiring nothing but food and sleep, he would please his hosts.

So, after the meal — and it proved as good and satisfying a meal as any we had enjoyed in far richer houses — Merlin motioned to me for his harp. I had tuned it, of course, and brought it out to squeals of delight and sighs of pleasure.

'Were I a king,' declared Merlin loudly, so that all could hear, 'I could not have obtained a better supper. But since I am no king, I must do what I can to reward you.'

'Please, you are our guests. Do not feel you must repay us,' said Bervach, seriously. 'But,' he paused, flashing his gap-toothed smile suddenly, 'if it would please you to ease the hardship of the road in this way, we will bear it for your sake.'

Merlin laughed heartily. 'Once again, I am in your debt. Still, it would please me if you would endure a song — for my sake.'

'Very well, since you insist. But a short song only — nothing of length. We would not want you to tax yourself overmuch on our account.'

Merlin sang *The Children of Llyr*, a very long and intricate tale of great and haunting beauty. I had heard it twice before — once in Aurelius' war camp, and once in Ban's hall — but never have I heard it sung as Merlin sang it.

The harp spun its shining silver melodies in the still air, and Merlin's voice followed, weaving among them a melody of its own, reciting again the age-old words. The words! Each word, every note and breath sprang to life new-born: bright and fresh as creation, whole, untainted, innocent.

To hear him sing. . . Oh, to hear him was to witness the birthing of a living thing. The song was alive!

Those crowded beneath Bervach's roof that night heard the work of a true bard, as few ever would. And they were blessed by it, as few are ever blessed in this sorry age.

When the song was finished, and Merlin laid the still-quivering harp aside at last, it was late indeed. But it seemed that the evening had passed in a blink, the little space of time between one heartbeat and the next; it seemed — and I believe in some way it did happen — that while Merlin sang we who heard him were lost to time, having passed through it and beyond to that place where time no longer touches us.

For the duration of the song we breathed the air of a different world wherein is lived a different kind of life, richer, higher, and more complete in every way.

Merlin possessed the gift; it was, I imagine, much like his father's.

'Now I know what men heard when Taliesin sang,' I told him later, when we had a word alone together.

He shook his head firmly, the corners of his mouth bending in a frown. 'Taliesin's gift was as high above mine as the sighted man's vision above that of the wretch born blind. The two are not to be compared.'

Early the next morning, a little before dawn, we took our leave of Bervach and the rest of the holding who had gathered in the yard to watch us away. As we mounted our horses, some of the mothers stepped forward and lifted their small children to Merlin to receive the Emrys' blessing. He gave it with good grace, but it disturbed him.

We made our way through the valley in silence, and on into the lowlands beyond. It was not until we stopped at midday to rest and water the horses and take a small meal ourselves that Merlin would voice what was on his heart.

'This should not be,' he muttered. 'I am no holy man that babes should receive blessing from my hand.'

'Where is the harm?' I asked. 'The people need someone they can look to.'

'Let them look to the High King!' The words were out before he knew it. Arthur winced as if pricked by a thrown knife.

'No. . . no,' Merlin said quickly, 'I did not mean it. I am sorry, Arthur. It is nothing to do with you.'

'I understand,' said Arthur, but the pain lingered in his pinched expression. 'I am no king, after all.'

Merlin shook his head sadly. 'Oh, the Enemy has set a

most subtle trap. There is danger here and we must tread lightly.'

The unhappy spirit of this exchange reigned over the rest of the journey like the dark, wet clouds that hung above our heads — and continued until reaching Ynys Avallach.

Coming in sight of the Glass Isle lifted our hearts. There was food and drink and warmth, blessed warmth, awaiting us in the Fisher King's hall. And, though the cold wind lashed our frozen flesh and stung our eyes, we slapped leather to our horses and fairly flew down the hillside towards the lake. Arthur shouted at the top of his lungs, glad to arrive at last.

The lake and salt marshes remained open, and ducks of all kinds had gathered to winter there. We raised flocks of them as we galloped along the lakeside.

Even though the groves were empty, the trees bare and lifeless, the pall of white snow on the ground made the isle appear as if made of glass indeed. The sudden flaring of the afternoon sun, as it burned through the clouds, lit the Tor with a shattering light: a beacon against the gathering storm.

But, as we came to the causeway leading to the Tor, Merlin halted and said, 'We will seek shelter at the abbey tonight.'

I stared at him in disbelief. Why spend the night in a monk's cell when all the comforts of the Fisher King's palace lay just across the lake? We could be there in less time than it takes to tell it!

Before I could voice my astonishment at Merlin's suggestion, he turned to Arthur, 'The sword you are to have is near. You will spend the night in the Shrine of the Saviour God, praying and preparing yourself to receive it.'

Arthur accepted this without question, however, and we turned off the track and made our way round the lake to the abbey below Shrine Hill. Abbot Elfodd gave us good greeting and bade us warm ourselves by the hearth. He offered a blessing for Arthur, whom he knew by sight though they had never met.

'You are welcome here, of course,' the abbot said, pressing cups of mulled wine into our hands, 'but Charis and Avallach will be expecting you.'

'They do not know of our journey,' replied Merlin.

'Oh?'

'We will see them soon but we have a purpose to accomplish first.'

'I see.'

'Arthur has come to consecrate himself to the saving of Britain.'

Elfodd raised his eyebrows. 'Is this so?' He regarded Arthur with renewed interest.

'It is,' Arthur answered evenly.

'We thought to hold vigil in the Shrine,' explained Merlin.

'As you wish. So be it. I have no objection — save that it is cold, as there is no place for a fire.'

'It will serve.'

Merlin and the abbot talked briefly of the affairs of the realm, and Arthur joined in from time to time, but I noticed the Duke glancing towards the door as if eager to be away. Finally, Merlin rose. 'Thank you for the wine and the warmth, Elfodd. We would stay, but we must be about our business.'

'Please, as you see fit. We will not hinder you.'

So saying, we took our leave and returned to the yard. The sky was nearly dark, the setting sun all but obscured by the clouds which had moved in once more. 'There is the Shrine,' Merlin said, indicating the small white chapel on top of the nearby hill. 'Go now and begin your vigil.'

'Will you join me?'

Merlin shook his head slightly. 'Not now. Later, perhaps.'

Arthur nodded solemnly, turned, and began climbing the hill to the Shrine. It came to me that Merlin's words — about a vigil of prayer and preparation, of consecration to the task of saving Britain — had begun to work in Arthur, answering the brooding in his soul manifest since losing Macsen's sword.

'This is well and good, Pelleas,' Merlin said quietly, watching Arthur walk away. 'You will stay here with him tonight, and I will return at daybreak tomorrow.'

The horses were nearby and he swung up into the saddle and started away. I walked a few paces after him. 'Where are you going?'

'To arrange for Arthur to get his sword,' he called over his shoulder, as he galloped away.

We spent a long, cold night together, Arthur and I. I slept somewhat, huddled in my cloak. Arthur knelt before the altar of the little round building, head bowed down, hands crossed over his chest.

Once I stirred, thinking it was morning, and awakened to a sight I shall never forget. The sky outside had cleared, and a bright mid-winter moon had risen and was shining full through the narrow, cross-shaped window above the altar.

Arthur was kneeling in the pool of light — in the same attitude I had seen him before — head down, arms folded. I thought he had certainly fallen asleep. But, as I watched, the Duke of Britain raised his head and slowly turned his face to the light, at the same time lifting his arms as if to embrace it.

He stayed like that the longest time. Head up, arms open wide in acceptance and supplication — all the while bathed in the soft, silvery light. And I heard the quiet murmur of his whispered prayer.

As I listened, the chapel filled with such peace and tranquillity, I knew it to be a high and holy sign. I had no doubt that Arthur had entered the presence of Jesu, whose kindly light shone upon him in benediction. My heart swelled to bursting with the wonder of it, for I knew myself to be favoured among men to witness this sign.

But a little while later, I heard a low whistle outside. I rose and went out to meet Merlin leading the horses. 'It is time,' he said. 'Fetch Arthur.'

I looked and the sun was rising in the east. The moon, so bright only moments before, now waned as the sky lightened. Crisp and sharp, the cold dawn air pricked me fully awake, and I went back into the Shrine to summon Arthur. At the sound of his name, he rose and came forth.

We mounted and silently made our way along the lakeside path leading to the causeway. The world seemed new made, delicate, yet invincible in its beauty: the pale white snow underfoot and deepest blue night above. . . the smooth black water of the reed-fringed lake. . . the red-gold of the rising sun flaming the eastern sky.

I first thought we would go to the Tor directly, but Merlin led us along the causeway and continued on around the lake, stopping at a clump of leafless willow-trees. Here we stopped and dismounted. Merlin faced the placid, dawn-smooth lake and pointed to the bank of reeds before us.

'There is a boat,' he told Arthur. 'Get into it and pole yourself across the lake to the island. There you will meet a woman. Heed her well. She will give you the sword.'

Arthur said nothing; there was no need. His face shone with all the hope and glory of the rising sun. He walked calmly to the reeds and stepped into the boat — which I recognized as Avallach's fishing-boat. Taking up the pole, Arthur pushed away from the bank. The reeds rasped and rustled as he passed, and then he was gliding out onto the dark water.

Merlin sensed the questions whirling inside me. 'Charis will meet him and give him the sword,' he told me. 'She is waiting for him in the grove.'

'Why?' I asked, for I found this elaborate diversion most confusing. Why not simply ride to the Tor and give Arthur the sword outright. 'It is just a sword, is it not?'

'Not to Arthur,' Merlin replied, watching the Duke raise and lower the dripping pole. 'It will be his life from this day forth, until the Island is rid of the Saecsen.'

He turned to me. 'Besides, it is a good sword. There is not another like it in all the world.'

'Whose sword is it?'

'Arthur's.'

'But — '

'It is the one Charis had made for Avallach. I wore it for a time, you will remember. But it was never mine. It was, I think, made for Arthur. He alone will truly possess it.'

I looked across the lake and saw that Arthur had reached the island. He jumped from the boat, and walked up the slope to the grove. The trees all stood bare, their leafless branches dark under a thin coating of snow.

In a moment, I saw Charis step lightly from among the trees. He saw her and stopped. She raised her right hand in greeting, and I saw that she clasped the naked blade in the left. Then she lifted the sword and placed it across her palms and offered it to him.

Arthur approached, his face solemn, his tread purposeful and slow. Charis offered the sword, but the Duke did not take it. He knelt before her and raised his hands. She spoke to him and then placed the sword across his upraised palms.

Then did Arthur rise, lofting the sword. New sunlight dazzled along its tapered length in a keen flash of gold. He waved the blade in the air, and an expression of awe slowly transformed his features.

'Come,' said Merlin, turning again to the horses. 'We will join them now.'

We rode back to the causeway, crossed it, and turned towards the grove, leading Arthur's horse behind us. Charis greeted her son with a kiss, and me as well.

'Have you seen it, Myrddin?' cried Arthur, holding the sword reverently, his face alight with the singular beauty of the weapon. For indeed it was a thing of dire beauty: long and slender, cold, deadly. Two crested serpents, their red-gold bodies entwined, jewelled eyes winking, formed the hilt. Forged long ago of an art far surpassing any now known, it was, as Merlin said, the weapon of a dream, made for the hand of a god.

'Oh, yes,' replied Merlin, touching the blade with his finger-tips, 'I have seen it once or twice. What will you call it?' He did not say that he himself had once worn it.

'Call it?'

'A weapon like this must have a name.'

'Has it a name, my lady?' Arthur asked Charis.

'No name that I know,' she replied.

'The Lady of the Lake has told me that the blade is made of steel far stronger than any in Britain,' said Arthur.

'Call it Caliburnus,' suggested Merlin.

Arthur's brow wrinkled. 'Latin — meaning?'

'Caledvwlch, the Cymry would say.'

'Cut Steel!' declared Arthur, lofting the weapon once more. 'Very well, as I am a Roman Celt, I will call it Caledvwlch.'

Arthur was well pleased with his new weapon. He lightly held the sword in his hands and fingered the strange markings on the blade near the hilt. 'These figures,' he said, turning once more to Charis, 'I cannot read them. What do they mean?'

'It is Atlantean script,' she explained. 'It says here, *Take Me Up*,' she turned the blade over, 'and here: *Cast Me Aside*.'

Arthur frowned over this. 'I will never cast it aside,' he vowed and, raising his eyes to hers, said, 'I am in your debt, my lady. Whatever you ask of me, if it is in my power, I will do.'

Charis smiled. 'The sword is a gift — obtained for one king and given to another. I ask nothing in return.'

'Yet,' Arthur replied, letting his glance slide once more along the flawless length of the sword, 'I would deem it an honour to repay you in any way I can.'

'Come,' said Merlin, placing a hand on Arthur's shoulder. 'Let us go into the hall and break fast. Have you forgotten what day it is? It is the day of the Christ Mass. Let us begin the celebration at once.'

With that, we began threading our way up the narrow track to the Fisher King's palace. Arthur gazed out, as the landscape fell away below, watching the radiant fingers of sunlight sweep the hills and hollows round about. By the time he stepped through the great arched gates and into the palace yard, he was firmly captured by the natural enchantment of the place.

We did not wait to be greeted, but hurried in to the hall to warm ourselves. Avallach was there, and upon seeing us he came forth to greet us with glad welcome on his lips. His hand, however, was pressed to his side, as it always was when his wound distressed him.

'God be good to you!' he called, his voice a low thunder in the hall. 'Merlin! Pelleas! How often I have thought of you these last days and longed for your company. Come, sit by the hearth. Have you travelled far?'

'Merlin came to us last night, but you were in your chambers and we did not like to disturb you,' Charis explained, linking her arm through her son's.

'Grandfather,' said Merlin, holding his hand out to Arthur, 'I present to you Arthur ap Aurelius, Duke of Britain.'

King Avallach looked long on the young duke, holding

him in his gaze that became at once sharp and formidable. Arthur endured this scrutiny with good grace; he did not flinch, nor did he counter it by growing haughty, as I have seen men do. Arthur stood square-shouldered, head erect, eyes level, motionless, letting the other make of him what he would.

In all the years I had known him, I had never seen Avallach react this way with anyone — certainly not with a guest in his house. Charis opened her mouth to intercede, but Merlin urgently pressed her hand and she subsided.

His appraisal finished, the Fisher King raised his palm shoulder high, saying, 'Hail, Arthur, Duke of the Britons, I greet you. Long have we awaited your coming.' Avallach then stepped forward and enwrapped Arthur in a great embrace. A simple enough gesture, but more than that somehow.

Merlin looked on, with narrowed eyes. The significance of this act stirred him, and his senses quickened. He was, I knew, seeing far more in Avallach's welcoming embrace than Charis or I.

'It is the union of forces, Pelleas,' Merlin explained later. 'Do you not see it? Do you know what this means?' Before I could protest that I did not understand, he rushed on. 'It is true! All that we have hoped for Arthur, all that we have worked for — the years, Pelleas, the years we have worked! — it is coming to fruition! Arthur *is* the Summer Lord! His reign will establish the Kingdom of Summer.'

'Because Avallach greeted him?'

'Because Avallach recognized him.'

'But we have always known it would begin with Arthur.'

Merlin raised a forefinger. 'We have always *hoped* Arthur would be the Summer Lord. There is a difference.'

I still did not see how Avallach's greeting changed anything, or why Merlin thought that it did. But I believe that Avallach had grown increasingly sympathetic to the subtle promptings and presences of the spirit. Over the years he had grown in wisdom and holiness — through his discipline of prayer and meditations on the holy writings Bishop Elfodd brought him — so perhaps he saw something in Arthur that moved him.

But it did not matter what I thought. Merlin, for whatever

reason, had seen something in the welcome Avallach gave Arthur that kindled the certainty of the Summer Realm within him. And that was enough.

After breaking fast, we rode down to the abbey to attend the Mass of Christ. Merlin again presented Arthur to Abbot Elfodd, who prayed for him and commended him for ending the rebellion at last. The Christ Mass was read, and hymns were sung by the monks, who afterwards passed among us with the peace of Christ on their lips.

As we were leaving, Avallach bade Elfodd to join us at eventide to share our meal. In all, it was a fine and happy time, though I could not help remembering the festive and joyous celebrations I had seen in old Pendaran's and Maelwys' court; nor could I help recalling the masses led by saintly Dafyd.

Oh, but those were times long past now, and I did not think I would ever see their like again.

That night, as we gathered before the hearth after our evening meal, Merlin produced his harp and began playing. We listened for a while, whereupon he stopped.

'When I was a child,' he said, 'on nights like this my mother would tell me of the vision my father, Taliesin, had entrusted to her. As you know, it has ever been my work to advance this vision and establish it in this worlds-realm.

'But Arthur, I have never spoken the vision to you as it was spoken to me. And, though you know of it, you have not heard it as I heard it. Tonight you shall, but not from my lips. I would have you hear it from the one who has ever guarded it in her heart.' And, looking to his mother, he said, 'Speak to us of the Kingdom of Summer.'

Charis observed her son for a moment, then rose to stand before us, erect. Her hands clasped before her, she closed her eyes and began to recite.

And this is what she said:

'I have seen a land shining with goodness, where each man protects his brother's dignity as readily as his own, where war and want have ceased and all races live under the same law of love and honour.

'I have seen a land bright with truth, where a man's word is his pledge and falsehood is banished, where children sleep safe in their mother's arms and never know fear or pain.

'I have seen a land where kings extend their hands in justice rather than reach for the sword; where mercy, kindness, and compassion flow like deep water over the land, and men revere virtue, revere truth, revere beauty, above comfort, pleasure, or selfish gain. A land where peace reigns in the hearts of men; where faith blazes like a beacon from every hill, and love like a fire from every hearth; where the True God is worshipped and his ways acclaimed by all.'

Charis opened her eyes, glistening from a mist of tears. 'These are the words of Taliesin. Hear and remember,' she said, and, looking down at her feet saw Arthur kneeling there, holding the sword she had given him across his palms. No one had seen him leave his place.

Merlin was on his feet, his face glowing in the light of the fire. Excitement drew his features taut. 'Arthur?'

Charis raised a hand to Merlin and stopped him. She touched Arthur lightly on the cheek, and he raised his head. His eyes were shining, too — not from tears or the fireglow, but from the glory of the vision awakened by Charis' words.

'What is it, Arthur?' she asked.

'You have given me the sword,' he said, in a voice stiff with emotion. 'And now you have given me the vision with which to use it. Now I know the reason for my birth: I will be the Summer Lord. With the help of God and his angels, I will do it. I will establish the Kingdom of Summer.'

'What is it you wish of me?'

'Consecrate me, my lady, to the task for which I was born.'

'But I — ' began Charis, glancing at Abbot Elfodd for help. The abbot came to stand beside her and, putting his hand into his sleeve, withdrew a small vial of oil. This he pressed into Charis' hands, encouraging her to do as Arthur bade.

She accepted this and, laying her hands on Arthur's head, began to speak in a voice tender and low, saying 'As a servant of the Saviour God, I commend you to this noble task, Arthur ap Aurelius. In the name of Jesu, who is the Christ, I anoint you with this oil as a symbol of his authority and abiding presence.' She touched her finger-tips to the vial and made the sign of the cross on his brow.

153

'Be upheld in his power; be filled with his wisdom; be strong in his love; be just and merciful in his grace. Rise, Arthur, follow the vision that Our Lord Jesu has given and called you to obey.'

Arthur took Charis' hand and pressed it to his lips. Then he rose up, and I beheld him with new eyes. For he was not the same Arthur any more; he had changed.

His hands gripped Caledvwlch with solemn purpose; his clear blue eyes radiated peace and joy. Yes, and the light streaming from his countenance blazed with a high and holy fire.

Merlin came to stand before him with upraised hands, in the manner of a declaiming druid. With a solemn and mighty voice he began to speak. And this is what he said:

'Behold a king of stature in ring-forged mail, helmed with majesty and light! Behold a bright warrior, who strives against the pagan with the cross of Christ upon his shoulder! Behold a lord in whom other lords find their substance and worth!

'See his court! Justice erected it, stone by stone. See his hall! Honour raised its high-peaked roof. See his lands! Mercy nurtures root and branch. See his people! Truth reigns in their unselfish hearts.

'Behold a kingdom of peace! Behold a kingdom of right! Behold a king ruling with wisdom and compassion as his stalwart counsellors!

'Behold Arthur, of whom it is said: His days were like the Beltane fire leaping from hilltop to hilltop; the soft wind from the south laden with fragrant airs; the sweet rain of spring on the red-heathered hills; autumn's full harvest bringing wealth and plenty to every hearth and holding; the rich blessing of heaven from the Gifting God to his contrite people!

'Behold the Kingdom of Summer!'

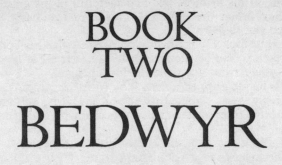

BOOK
TWO

BEDWYR

ONE

I Bedwyr, a prince of Rheged, write this. My father was Bleddyn ap Cynfal, Lord of Caer Tryfan in the north, kinsman to Tewdrig ap Teithfallt and the lords of Dyfed in the south.

Though the Devil take me, I will always remember meeting Arthur for the first time. It was at Caer Myrddin in Dyfed. Myrddin had brought Arthur there to hide him from his enemies, and my father had come to deliver me to Tewdrig's court, where I would receive my first fosterage. Arthur was but a squally babe.

Not that I was so very much older myself — all of five summers, perhaps, but old enough to think myself already a warrior of vast renown. I stalked the rampart of Tewdrig's stronghold, gripping the shaft of a short wooden spear my father had made for me.

While the kings held council concerning affairs of the realm, I marched around the caer pretending that I was its lord and chief. My only thought was that one day I would become a warrior like my father, a respected battlechief, and I would kill Saecsens and make my people proud of me.

To be a warrior! It was sun and stars to me. I could not sleep unless I held my wooden spear in my hand. The life of a warrior held great allure for me then; it was all I knew. Oh, but I was very young.

Caer Myrddin — Maridunum of old — fairly blazed under a hot summer sun. Everywhere men were busy and working; hard metal glimmered and gleamed from every corner, and the sound of a hammer on steel rang in the shimmering air like sounding iron, or church bell. The caer was a good deal larger than our own at Penllyn. It bespoke the power and wealth of the king, as was fitting.

And Tewdrig had a smith — which we did not have. The hall was larger, too; timber and thatch, with a great planked door bound in iron. The walls were timber, topping steep earthen ramparts.

I stood on the bank above the ditch, imagining I alone defended the gates and that victory depended upon me. Absorbed in my dreams of future glory, I felt a touch on the haft of my spear and glanced round. The infant Arthur was clutching the end of my spear in his chubby hands and grinning toothlessly at me.

I jerked the spear angrily. But he held on. I jerked again, and still he did not let go. Such a grip! Well, of course I was forced to show him that I was his better, so I stepped close and shoved the spear against his chest. His unsteady stumps buckled and he toppled backwards into the dust. I laughed at him and gloated in my superior strength.

He did not cry out as I expected him to, nor did the smile disappear from his round face. He simply gazed merrily at me with not so much as a mild reproach in his wide blue eyes.

Anger and shame battled within me. Shame won. Glancing around guiltily — lest anyone should see what I had done — I quickly stooped and took his fat little arm in my hand and pulled Arthur to his feet.

We were friends from that moment, I believe. Little Arthur became my shadow, and I the sun that rose in the sky for him. Few were the days that we did not spend in one another's company. We broke the same bread, drank from the same cup, breathed the same air. And later, when he joined me in the boys' house, we became closer than brothers.

When men think of Arthur now, they think of the emperor and his lands and palace. Or they think of the glorious battlechief, whose victories stretch behind him like a gem-crusted strand. They think of the invincible Pendragon who holds all Britain in sure, strong hands.

God's truth, I believe they consider him an Otherworld being, sprung up in their midst from the dust under their feet, or called down by Myrddin Emrys from the mists of high Yr Widdfa. Certainly, no one thinks of him as a man — with a birth and boyhood like any other man. Nor do bards tell of it.

Stories abound in the land in these days; they grow thick, like moss on a fallen branch. Some few have a mote of truth in them, but far too many do not. It is natural, perhaps, the desire to make more of things — a tale does often grow greater in the telling.

But it is not needful. Purest gold needs no gilding, after all.

It is Arthur the War Leader that I speak of, mind. *Artorius Rex*, he was not. All through that long season of strife he remained unacknowledged by the small kings. Small dogs, more like. Though they begrudged him even the title of *Dux* — and that was a travesty! — he wore it proudly, and fought the wars for them.

The wars. . . each glorious and hideous, each different from all the others, yet each one exactly alike in the end.

There were twelve in all. The first took place the very next summer after Arthur bested Cerdic in single combat and ended the rebellion against him. Arthur had spent the winter at Ynys Avallach and returned in the spring, bearing his new sword, and burning with his new vision of the Kingdom of Summer.

I had gone to the breeding runs — the sheltered glens east of Caer Melyn, where we wintered our horses and maintained the breeding stock — to see what we could count on for the coming year. It was foaling season, so I stayed on to help midwife a few colts into the world.

Winter had lingered long and I was glad to be free of the caer for a few days. I have always disliked close places, preferring wide hills and a lofty sky to the walls and peaked roof of a hall. Though cold at night, I was glad to stay with the herders in their hut, and ride with them during the day as they tended the animals.

One gusty morning, I was leading four swell-bellied mares down the valley to the enclosure near the hut where they could be delivered more easily. Feeling the fresh wind on my face, my spirit rose within me and I began to sing — loudly and with vigour — or I might have heard the rider calling me.

Indeed, I did not hear him until he was all but on top of me. 'Bedwyr! Hail, Bedwyr! Wait!'

I turned to see one of the younger warriors galloping towards me. I greeted him as he reined up and fell in beside me. 'Greetings, Drusus, what do you here?'

'Lord Cai has sent me to bring you. Arthur has returned and would have you with him. We are riding out in three days' time.'

'Riding where?' I knew nothing of any trouble anywhere.

'I cannot say; Cai did not tell me. Will you come?'

'I will see these horses settled first. Rest yourself while you wait, and we will return together.'

I continued on down the valley and gave the mares over to the care of a herdsman. I gathered my cloak and weapons from the hut, and rode back to the caer at once. All the while, I bethought me what could be happening. I could get nothing more from Drusus, so contented myself with flying over the windswept hills as fast as my horse could run. God's truth, I would have made all speed anyway, I was that anxious to see Arthur.

He was standing in the centre of a tumult of urgent bustle, talking to Cai, when I rode in. I threw myself from the saddle, and ran to meet Arthur. 'Jesu be praised! The wanderer has returned!' I cried.

'Hail, Bedwyr!' he called, a great grin appearing instantly on his face. 'Have we a herd?'

'We have a herd. Fifteen foals already, and twenty more perhaps before the season is done. It is blood and breath to see you, Artos.'

I stepped close and we gripped one another by the arms like brothers, and he wrapped me in his rib-cracking bear hug. 'You have weathered well, I see.' He thumped me soundly on the back. 'Was the winter to your liking?'

'A little long,' I admitted, 'but not too cold.'

'Cai has told me you drove Rhys nearly mad with your complaining. He is only a bard, Bedwyr. Would you have him change the weather with a song?'

'A fresh tale to pass the time would suffice. But look at you, Bear — you seem to have fallen in with the Fair Folk.'

His smile became mysterious and he drew his sword for

me to admire. 'This is Caledvwlch,' he told me. 'It was given me by the Lady of the Lake.'

I had never seen a weapon like it, and told him so. 'A man could win a kingdom with this,' I observed, feeling its quick weight fill my hand. The blade seemed instantly a part of me, more a bright extension of my arm than a measured length of cold steel.

'Well said,' Arthur replied, 'and that kingdom has a name.'

That is all he said, and he would speak no more about it then. 'Come to me in my chambers. I will summon Myrddin.' He walked away across the yard.

I glanced at Cai, who shrugged, as puzzled by the change in Arthur as I was myself. For our friend *had* changed.

Or perhaps, because of his long absence, I was only seeing a different side to Arthur from any I had seen before. But no, we were brothers! I knew him well enough to know that something had happened to him at Ynys Avallach. I determined to find out from Myrddin.

'I hear we are to ride in three days,' I said, as Cai and I moved off towards the hall. 'Any idea where we are going?'

'To the Saecsen Shore.'

I stopped walking and turned him round by the arm. 'Is this one of your tasteless jests?'

'It is no jest.' For once the green eyes in his ruddy face were serious. 'That is what he told me — although he said no more than that. And now you know as much about it as I do.'

'Did you notice how he grinned at me?' I said, as we continued to the hall. 'I have seen a smile like that only twice in my life till now: the first time was on the face of a slow-witted youth who stole a pig from my father's sty and was caught trying to sell it in the market, and the second was when old Gerontius died at his prayers.'

Cai laughed out loud. 'I do not think Arthur has been stealing pigs, but that is always a possibility.'

'It is the truth I am telling, Caius; I do not like this. Mark me well, nothing good will come of this.'

'Come of what?'

'This. . . this! You know what I mean.'

He laughed again and slapped me on the back. 'You think

161

too much, Bedwyr. You should have been a druid. Let be; all will be well.'

We walked through the hall to Arthur's chamber at the far end and waited. Presently, Pelleas entered and greeted us warmly — after his peculiar fashion.

The Fair Folk always astonish me. They are not like us in the least. They are a lofty race, for ever holding themselves apart from the life around them. Wondrous fair to look upon, they are nonetheless shy, and by nature do not display their emotions. I think it is pride.

Myrddin is less like this. But then, he is only half Fair Folk. . . although, what the other half is no one knows.

'Any news from Ynys Avallach, Pelleas?' I asked. I had never been to the Fisher King's palace, but I had heard Myrddin talk about it often enough to know the place.

'We passed a most agreeable winter, Prince Bedwyr,' he replied. This was meant, I suppose, to be a most detailed account of their activities. I had known Pelleas since I was a twig, and this was how he talked to me.

'Is it true that it never snows on the Glass Isle?' Cai put the question to him seriously, but I saw the edges of his mouth twitch in mirth.

'Of course it snows, you young genius!' The voice was that of the Emrys, who entered at that moment with Arthur behind him. 'Greetings, Cai and Bedwyr.'

'Myrddin!' I turned and was swept into his embrace.

'Winter starved and spring hungry, eh?' he said, gripping my arms and peering into my eyes as if searching my soul for the answer. He always did that. Some people find it most unnerving, I am told.

'God's truth, I am!' I declared. 'But you look as if you have lived on roast duck and honey cakes all winter. Jesu be good to you, look at you now!'

Indeed, he appeared as fit as I have ever seen him — not that he ever changed all that much.

'Sit down, all of you,' said Arthur, indicating the benches at his council table. 'We must talk.' He drew up his chair — it was Uther's old camp chair. I never learned where or how he had come by it, unless Tewdrig had somehow got it for him.

Spreading his hands across the board, Arthur studied his

fingers, as if trying to decide which of the ten pleased him most. 'It is my intention to ride to the Saecsen Shore in three days' time.'

I glanced round at the others. No one showed a flicker of surprise. *Perhaps I have misheard him*, I thought; *perhaps he said, 'It is my intention to have mutton for supper.'*

But, as no one else responded, I said, 'Forgive me, brother, did I understand you to say that we were to attack the Saecsen Shore in three days?'

Arthur smiled his fishy smile again, and shook his head. 'No, there will be no attack. I am going to offer them terms for peace.'

'Peace?' I stared dumbfounded. 'Now I know you have straw for brains, Artos. Leaving aside the fact that you have not the authority, what makes you think they will honour a treaty of peace made with you?'

'I am the Duke of Britain, the war leader. Who else has the right to grant peace if I do not?'

'But, the *Saecsens*! Have you forgotten the slaughter of four years ago?'

'I have not forgotten, Bedwyr. But I stand ready to forgive them, if they will hold peace with us.'

'And if not?'

'Then we will do what we have to do,' he said, sounding a little more like the Arthur I knew. 'But we would be less than Christians if we did not offer peace before taking up the sword.'

'I see. And what will prevent them from cleaving your head from your shoulders before your tongue has finished flapping? They are Saecsens!'

'And they are men, as we are. No more will I make war on any man — be he Saecsen or Briton — unless I have first offered peace.' The conviction with which he spoke was unassailable.

'Is that the way of it?'

'That is the way of it.' Arthur might have been a standing stone for all he would be moved. Once he had an idea in his head, there was no shaking it from him. Arthur was not the Bear of Britain for nothing.

'I am sending messengers to bid any king who will to ride with us,' Arthur continued. 'I pray that some will. But whether they ride with me or not, we leave Caer Melyn in three days.'

'And may God go with us,' I said.

We fell to talking about readying the warband to ride — moving so many men is always a chore. Nothing more was said about Arthur's crack-brained peacemongering scheme. When we finished, Arthur called for beer to be brought and we drank. Then we went about our various tasks.

So it was not until we returned to the hall for our supper that I found opportunity to speak to Myrddin.

'Tell me, Wise Emrys,' I said, as I sidled up to him, 'what has become of our beloved Duke?'

He regarded me closely with those golden eyes of his. 'He is coming into his power.'

'That is no answer. What power? How has it come to him? Who conferred it? Where has it come from? And why does it make him soft-headed?'

'It is not his head that has changed, Bedwyr, but his heart.'

'Head, heart — I hardly recognize him!'

Myrddin smiled understandingly. 'Give it time. He will come back to himself.'

'I welcome your assurance. Unfortunately, we will all be dead. Saecsens do not want our peace, they want our land and cattle.'

'Arthur has learned a greater truth. His kingdom will be established on justice and mercy towards all men who shelter in this island.'

'Including the Saecsen?'

'Yes, Bedwyr, including the Saecsen. It must be this way.'

'That is not truth, that is madness.'

'If any man has reason to hate the Saecsen, it is me,' Myrddin replied gently. 'Do you know what my friend Hafgan used to tell me?'

Hafgan, I knew, was Myrddin's druid teacher. He was now remembered as the last of the Three True Bards of the Island of the Mighty. 'No, Wise Emrys, enlighten me. What did Hafgan tell you?'

'He said that once some men were digging a well and

164

came upon a great flat stone. It was, they discovered, the foundation stone of this worlds-realm, so they decided to lift it up and see what lay beneath it. This they did. And do you know what they found?'

'I cannot say. What did they find?'

'Love,' replied Myrddin simply.

'Love. That is all?' I resented myself for being cozened by Myrddin's children's tale.

'There is nothing else, Bedwyr. Love lies beneath all that is and upholds it. Arthur has seen that this is so. His kingdom will be built upon the only enduring foundation.'

I went away, shaking my head. It was not that I did not believe. For the love of God, if faith alone lent men rank, I would be Pope! But I know a thing or two about Saecsens, I *will* say. And it is a difficult thing to preach the love of Christ to a man with his axe in your skull!

Wonderfully benevolent Arthur's plan might be, and wonderfully foolish as well.

Yet, if Myrddin was with him in this, there was nothing to be done. Bors might have been counted on to argue against Arthur's peace scheme, but he had not returned from Benowyc, and would not until the spring seas calmed. It was no good trying to enlist Cai's aid. Cai would never hear a word against Arthur, God love him. His devotion knew no hindrance, his loyalty no restraint. He gave all to Arthur without stint. Right or wrong — it was all the same to Cai, where Arthur came into it.

This was due, I believe, to something that had happened between them years ago. I once heard the tale from Pelleas — how the two of them had climbed a mountain together. With Cai's crooked leg, this could have been no easy task. Be that as it may, when the deed was done Arthur had inspired in Cai the kind of devotion few men ever know: zealous, deep, unselfish, stronger and more steadfast than death.

So, since that was the way of it, I decided to say my prayers and sharpen my sword.

TWO

A Saecsen camp is not a pleasant sight. They are barbarians, after all.

But, after thirteen days in the saddle, I would have thought even a hole in the ground a palace if it kept the rain off my head at night. Thirteen days of rain! Why, it is enough to make misery seem good company. We were well past misery.

I think the Saecsens were unhappy, too, and looking for a diversion. Or perhaps the rain had softened them. However it was, we found them in a most rare temper: docile.

That is to say, they did not kill us upon first sight.

We had left Caer Melyn three days after Arthur's return, and had slowly made our way east to the Ouse River on the old Iceni border where we camped. We knew that Aelle, who was battlechief of the Saecsen hordes there, would already have detected our movements. We wanted him to know that we were not trying to attack outright. So we settled down in the mud and waited.

And, yes, two days later we awakened to the horns and drums of a Saecsen war host across the river. Arthur rose and ordered three horses to be saddled: his, mine and Cai's. Myrddin protested that he should go along, but the Duke would not hear it. He said, 'If anything happens to me, at least the Soul of Britain will still be alive.'

To Cai and me he said, 'Leave your weapons. If all goes well you will not need them.'

'And if it fails?' I asked.

'They will be no help.'

Reluctantly, we obeyed — although this was going several paces too far, even for Cai's loyalty.

'Help or no, I would ride easier with my sword to hand,'

he grumbled, as we mounted our horses and rode out of camp.

'Things might be worse,' I told him. 'At least it is not raining. I would hate being killed in the rain.'

The Ouse is deep-set and good fording-places few. We had camped near enough to one of the best — the site of numerous battles in the past — and made our way to it now, each of us holding green willow branches in our hands. The Saecsen used this sign themselves: they recognized it when it suited them. I prayed it might do so now.

At our approach, the war host raised their ear-splitting shriek. This went on for a good while, but when they saw it was just three men with willow branches, they quieted and waited to see what we would do.

Arthur rode to the centre of the river ford and halted, Cai and I on either side. 'Now,' he said, 'we will see what sort of men they are.'

I could have told him what sort of men they were!

'Aelle!' called Arthur. 'Come, Aelle! I would speak to you!'

I surveyed the host arrayed against us — there were a thousand if there were ten, and none of them with glad welcome on their lips. They remained silent, and in a moment a single warrior stepped away from a throng gathered round one of their hideous skull-and-horsetail standards. He was a huge brute, with hair the colour of new thatch hanging in two long braids, and he walked with such arrogance, such insolence in his gait, I knew him to be Aelle in the flesh.

He came down to the water's edge, his great war axe in his hand. 'I am Aelle,' he said, not bothering to conceal his conceit. 'What do you want?'

Oh, yes, he spoke our tongue. This is not as surprising as you might think, for many of the Saecsen had lived longer on *our* shores than ever they stayed on their own. Britain was the only home they knew.

'Peace,' replied Arthur, just like that.

I nearly fell off my horse. It is foolish enough to try making a treaty with the Saecsen, but you must be cunning about it. They respect nothing but the sharp edge of a sword and the strength behind it. Everything else is weakness to them, and is despised. We were lost.

'Arthur! Think what you are doing!' I whispered harshly.

'I know what I am doing!' he replied.

Aelle stood at the river's edge blinking. Then it started to rain.

The Saecsen battlechief glared at Arthur with one eye, and at the rain clouds with the other, and decided that neither was going to go away very soon. Under the circumstances, he could at least escape the one by talking to the other.

'Come,' he called across the water, 'I will talk to you.'

With that, Arthur lifted his reins and his horse moved forward. Cai and I followed, and together we three crossed over into Saecsen-held land.

Upon reaching the far shore we were immediately surrounded by Aelle's house carles — twenty enormous hulking savages, chosen for their size and courage to protect their leader to the death. I could read nothing but loathing in their cold blue eyes.

'Who are you — *Wealas*?' sneered Aelle. He had been about to say something rude, and I swear he would have got a boot in the face for his insolence. But he showed at least that much sense.

'I am Arthur, War Leader of Britain. I have come to offer peace to you and your people.'

Aelle considered this as he scanned our camp across the river. We were less than two hundred, for aside from Meurig none of the British kings deigned to ride with us. Aelle did not fail to grasp this fact, and it did not argue well for us.

'Are you so powerful?' It was a strange question. And it came to me that Aelle was genuinely confused. He did not know what to make of Arthur.

I began to see the matter through his eyes. Here was a British lord who rode to meet a host many times larger with only a small force, unarmed, and offering peace — it was madness, surely. Unless the lord before him was a very, very powerful man indeed — a man so powerful that he had no need of a larger force, no need of the support of the other British lords. But who possessed such might?

'I am as you see me,' replied Arthur. This confused the Saecsen even more. What did *that* mean?

The rain fell, running down our faces in rivulets. The barbarians seemed not to notice it.

'Come, let us go where it is dry and we can talk.'

Aelle gazed at Arthur for a long moment, making up his mind. Then, with a sharp nod, he turned to his men and barked a harsh command in their repulsive tongue. The carles turned as one and hastened away. In a moment, the whole war host began moving back, retreating from the river.

'We will go to my camp,' Aelle said, and began leading the way.

The Saecsen camp lay but a short distance away — just a valley and a hill east of the Ouse. We passed through the charred ruins of a small settlement on the way, and that was hard. Cai did not look at the fire-blackened remains, nor did Arthur. But I saw his hands tighten on the reins.

As I say, a Saecsen camp is a wretched place. They despoil everything they touch — including the earth where they squat. A few crude skin tents and huts made of grass and branches formed a loose circle, in the centre of which burned a fire. The hacked carcasses of butchered cattle and sheep lay on the ground near the fire ring, among the scattered bones of others. The place stank of excrement and refuse.

The foremost dwelling belonged to Aelle, and he entered it. We dismounted outside, and followed him in. It was a dark, damp, filthy, fetid hole, but it kept the rain off. We sat on the bare earth — Aelle sat on an ox-hide — and waited while a slave fixed torches to the tent poles on either side of Aelle. The slave, I noticed, was Gaulish, but I did not doubt there were Britons among the slaves in Aelle's camp.

'What have you to say to me?' asked Aelle.

This is how it began. The Saecsen leader did not deem it necessary to include any advisers in the proceedings. Except for their omen readers, by which they set great store, Saecsen rulers rarely consulted their minions.

'I have this to say to you, Aelle,' said Arthur, speaking with an easy authority. 'These lands you now hold do not belong to you. They are British lands. You have killed our people and burned our settlements to get them.'

Aelle frowned defiantly at this, and opened his mouth to speak. But Arthur held up a hand and continued.

'I could demand your life and the lives of all your people

in repayment for the wrong you have done us. I could raise the entire war host of Britain and attack you, and we would win. You would be killed.'

Aelle's frown deepened to a scowl. 'Others have tried. I am not so easy to kill, I think. Maybe I will kill you.'

'Perhaps. Perhaps we would both be killed, and all our warriors with us. And then what? Other lords and battlechiefs would rise up against you. The war would continue until there was no one left to fight it.'

'We are ready to fight,' muttered Aelle stubbornly.

'But we do not have to fight,' Arthur said. 'There can be peace between us, and between our people. The bloodshed can end now, and you can keep the land you have taken from us.'

'How can this be?' asked the Saecsen warily.

'I will grant it,' replied Arthur. 'I will give the land to you in return for your promise.'

'What is this promise?'

'Your word, your vow never to make war against my people again. That is first,' said Arthur, making a stroke with his finger in the dirt before him. 'Then you must agree to stay on this side of the Ouse water.' He drew another mark, and Aelle watched him.

'And then?'

Arthur made a third mark, saying, 'And then you must give back those of my people you have taken as slaves.'

Aelle stared suspiciously at the three marks in the dirt — as if they were a ruse by which Arthur meant to trick him somehow.

'What if I do not agree?' he said at last.

'Then you will be dead before Beltane.'

The Saecsen bristled at this. 'I am not afraid.'

'I am the War Leader of Britain,' Arthur reminded him, 'and I have conquered all who rose against me. I will see this land at peace, Aelle. I offer peace freely from my hand today. . . tomorrow I will win it with my sword.'

This was said with such certainty that Aelle accepted it without question. He turned his face and gazed out at the rain for a moment, then rose and went out.

'We will have our answer soon,' Arthur said. Cai and I looked uncertainly at one another, neither one knowing what to say. The rain pattered down outside, filling the footprints in the mud with water. Our horses stood sodden and forlorn, heads down, manes streaming water.

'Patience, Brother,' Arthur said. I turned and found him looking at me. 'Have faith. It is God's work we are doing here; he will not see us fail.'

I nodded, tried to smile, and gave up with a shrug.

'I wonder if it will rain all day?' muttered Cai.

'Why should this day be any different from the others?' I said.

'Take heart,' Arthur told us, 'the rain aids our purpose most excellently. No man likes to fight in the rain, least of all a Saecsen.'

'That is true,' allowed Cai doubtfully.

We sat for some time in the tent, and I began to believe that Aelle had forgotten about us. But just as I was about to get up and stretch my legs, there came a commotion from outside the tent. Someone shouted and a crowd gathered. The shout was answered by a low, spitting threat in the barbarian tongue. The clash of steel rang sharp and quick.

I made to rise, but Arthur pulled me back down. 'Stay. It is not for us to intrude.'

No, but we craned our necks and peered out through the tent slit. I saw nothing but the backs of the throng gathered round the fire ring. But from the grunts of the combatants and the shattering chime of steel on steel, it was clear to us that a fight was in progress.

It ended as quickly as it began. And, with much murmuring and muttering — although of approval or disdain, I could not tell — the throng dispersed.

A moment later Aelle entered the tent once more. He was wet and muddy, and breathing hard. Blood trickled from a vicious-looking scrape on his chest, but he smiled as he settled himself once more on his ox-hide. He gazed at Arthur, and the faintest trace of emotion flickered across his broad features. What it was, I could not tell. Pride? Remorse? Gratitude?

'It will be as you say,' Aelle said at last.

'You will not regret this, Aelle,' said Arthur. 'Hold faith with me and I will see that your people suffer no wrong.'

Just then the tent flap opened and a Saecsen entered with

171

a round shield in his hands. Balanced on the shield were two long horn cups of the kind the barbarians prize. The shield was placed between Arthur and Aelle, and the servant left — only to return a moment later with a haunch of roast meat which he placed beside the cups.

Aelle lifted a cup and handed it to Arthur. 'Was Hael!' he said. And, taking up his own cup, he dashed down its contents in a single gulp. Arthur drank and then handed the cup to me. I sipped the sour brew and passed the cup to Cai, who forced down the rest.

Aelle watched this, and grunted. Then he took up his knife and attacked the haunch with vigour, ripping off a great chunk of meat which he gave to Arthur. He carved a second hunk for himself and began to eat, tearing at the meat with his teeth.

Arthur ate a few bites and passed the meat to me. I did as Arthur had done and then passed the meat to Cai.

As before, Aelle watched us closely and grunted his approval when we had finished. This was, I understood, some sort of ritual. And, now that it was completed, Aelle seemed to soften towards us. He motioned to the cups on the shield, and the servant gathered them and left the tent.

'We have shared meat and drink together,' Aelle said. 'I will speak the oath you ask.'

Arthur shook his head. 'I ask no oath of you — only say me this: that you will hold to the peace we have spoken between us.'

'I will hold to it,' replied Aelle, 'and all my people who are with me.'

'Good,' said Arthur with a smile. 'The peace is begun. Let him be damned who breaks it.'

The Saecsen battlechief appeared puzzled at this. He shook his head slowly. 'What gage will you have?'

'I ask no gage or pledge. But I give you my trust that you will do all to keep the peace we have made this day.'

Aelle considered this for a moment, then shook his head. He rose and beckoned us to follow. We stepped outside and saw a young woman standing in the rain, a sodden pelt wrapped around her slender shoulders. This, we were given to know, was the daughter of Aelle's sister; his nearest kin, and, by Saecsen reckoning, the person he was most beholden to for care and protection.

'She is Behrta,' said Aelle, summoning the maid to him. 'I give her to you. If I break the peace I have made this day, you will kill her.'

Arthur shook his head slowly. 'By this I know that you value your pledge. There is no need to give me a hostage.'

But the Saecsen leader remained adamant. 'It is not for me, *Wealas*; it is for my people.' He indicated the host looking on expectantly. '*They* must know the value I have placed on this peace.'

I understood then what he was saying. The maid was of noble Saecsen blood; she would likely be a queen among her kind one day. By giving her to Arthur, the canny chief was doing what he could to seal the pledge he had made to Arthur.

Arthur turned to Cai, 'Bring her with us. Put her on my horse.' Cai stepped forward and took the maid by the arm, but gently, and led her to Arthur's mount.

'Will you come with me to Octa?' said Arthur, turning back to Aelle. 'I seek peace with him as well, under the same terms as I have granted you.'

Aelle gave his assent. 'I will come to you tomorrow.'

We climbed onto our horses and turned back upon the path to the river. As we passed from the camp, I saw the naked body of the man Aelle had killed in the short dispute outside the tent. The arm-ring on his right arm marked him for a chieftain. Blood still oozed from the ragged gape in his chest.

Myrddin stood on the far side of the river, watching for our return. When he saw us crest the hill, he dashed forward into the water and ran to meet us as we came to the ford.

Arthur threw himself from the saddle with a whoop and caught Myrddin up in a great hug.

'I have prayed for you every moment until now,' Myrddin told him. Glancing at the maid, he said, 'I need not ask how it went with you — I can see you did well.'

'She was Aelle's idea,' Arthur said. 'I did not want a hostage, but he would have it no other way. He said it was for his people to know the value of the peace.'

Myrddin pursed his lips. 'Very shrewd. Yes, I see. And if

anything happens to her in your care, he will have cause to break faith with you. His sword cuts both ways.'

They turned and made to cross the ford. Half-way across, they began to laugh, and the echoes of their laughter set the valley ringing. Oh, they had planned this very carefully, the two of them.

I watched Arthur and Myrddin, their arms round each other's shoulders, splashing their way across the river and I felt the same giddy relief wash over me. I laughed out loud. Cai stared at me and then he began laughing, too!

We had done it! We had walked into the lion's den and returned with his beard in our hands. Had anything like this ever happened before?

More, could it happen again?

THREE

Aelle and his carles came to our camp at dawn the next morning, and we departed, moving south along the Ouse. We travelled slowly because the Saecsens walked. They do not like horses and fear them. This made the journey tedious to begin with, and it was made more so by Arthur's decision to stay well away from Londinium.

But the weather cleared and held good for the while. As before, we camped at the ford of a river — the Stur, this time — and waited for Octa to come to us, which he did in exactly the same way as Aelle had done.

Octa came with Colgrim, his kinsman, and we met them at the ford — Aelle with us. This caused some distress on the far side of the Stur where Octa and Colgrim stood with their massed warbands. I could see them working on it: what did it mean? Had Aelle joined the enemy? Had they conquered him? But where was the British host?

Arthur let them take it in and then, as before, rode to the centre of the river and called to them. 'Octa! Colgrim! I want to speak to you!'

Colgrim conferred with Octa, who answered, 'Why have you come to us like this?' His eyes never left Aelle, who stood with his weapons at his side.

'I have come to make peace with you.'

Colgrim and Octa exchanged a puzzled glance. Again, it was Octa who answered, pointing to Aelle, 'Let Aelle go, and we will talk with you.'

'Aelle is free to come and go as he will.' Arthur lifted a hand to the Saecsen leader, who strode forth across the water to join his kinsmen on the other side. The three stood together, talking for a moment — with much gesturing and pointing in our direction.

Then Aelle turned and beckoned us to come forward. Arthur dismounted as soon as he set foot on the opposite shore, throwing his reins to Cai. The Saecsens regarded him with keen suspicion — as if this impressive show might somehow suddenly turn into a fatal ambush. Yet the sight of a British battlechief striding purposefully towards them, alone and unarmed, intrigued them. What was this madman doing?

'I am Arthur,' he told them — just as he had told Aelle. 'I am War Leader of Britain, and I have come to offer peace to you and your people.'

Colgrim and Octa stared at him, and then at Aelle. They muttered something to Aelle in the Saecsen tongue. Aelle answered them and put a hand on Arthur's shoulder, smiling.

Then, before any of us could think or move, Aelle's hand darted to his belt and a knife flashed out. Instantly, the knife was at Arthur's throat.

A trap! Arthur was helpless. Colgrim's hand went to the knife in his belt. Octa hefted up his axe and made to signal the war host.

But before Octa could cry out — indeed, before Cai or I could lift our hands to lash our horses forward to Arthur's defence — Aelle took the knife and, turning it in his hand, placed the handle in Arthur's hand. Then he raised the knife which Arthur now held and placed the blade over his own heart.

Naked amazement distorted the faces of the Saecsens. Colgrim and Octa stared as if they had just witnessed a miracle of the highest order. Perhaps they had.

Then, next thing I knew, the Saecsens were all chattering together at once and they were touching Arthur and pounding him on the back. Apparently, Aelle had accomplished more in that simple act — harrowing though it was — than whole days of coaxing and convincing could have achieved.

'I thought we were orphans,' I muttered to Cai, wiping my brow. Cai only grunted and rolled his eyes.

We did sit down and talk to them then. As before, Colgrim and Octa accepted the peace which Arthur offered and then called for food and drink to be brought, whereupon we ate and drank with them — which is how the Saecsen kind like to show peaceful intentions.

When we had done this, Colgrim rose up and declared — mostly through Octa, who showed some small skill with our tongue — that he would feast the British in honour of the new peace treaty. I could imagine nothing I would enjoy less. Feast with a Saecsen! It could not be done.

Nevertheless, we did it. Arthur insisted, and Myrddin agreed. 'We must honour the good that they intend,' Myrddin said. 'Sitting next to a Saecsen at the board will not harm you overmuch.'

'All the same,' grumbled Cai ominously, 'I am bringing my sword.'

Arthur allowed us our knives, but no swords, lances, or shields. 'It would not look right,' he said.

Well, I will say that it was not as bad as I feared. . . It was a good deal worse.

Think of it! For a start, the Saecsen idea of a feast is simply to heap mounds of badly-cooked meat onto the board and gorge on it until sated, whereupon you are supposed to drink whole butts of their sour beer. And, when everyone is falling-down drunk, they begin wrestling with one another. The two biggest among them pair off and all the others gather round and begin shouting at them, urging them on. The point of it seems to be for one to maim the other for life. They grunt and sweat and yell — all for the privilege of throwing one another into the fire.

When this display palls, they all fall exhausted onto the ground and one of their bards — or *scops*, as they are called — comes and begins raising the most horrible din. The Saecsen beat their fists on the ground in ecstasy over their scop's small accomplishments. The howling which greets his every word is enough to deafen a stump.

In short, a Saecsen feast is ghastly beyond belief. But they are barbarians, after all.

I thought that we would return to Caer Melyn. Having achieved a summer's respite from Saecsen raiding — which is how long I reckoned Arthur's peace would last — I expected Arthur to inform the small kings and await their

177

replies. God's truth, I thought all hell would be loosed upon our heads when the British lords found out what Arthur had done.

Make peace with the Saecsens? The reason he had been made War Duke was so that he could rid us of them. And what does he do? He embraces them at first opportunity and *gives* them the land they stole from us.

So I thought we would go back to Caer Melyn to await the breaking of the storm. But I was wrong. We rode instead for Londinium and boarded a ship bound north for the Orcades. That is, Arthur, Myrddin and I. Pelleas and Cai took the warband back to Caer Melyn to await Bors' return.

Since we had days aboard ship, and little else to do, I managed to get out of Arthur exactly what he thought he was doing offering peace to Britain's enemies.

'We have been at war with the Saecsen, Pict, Scot and Irish for three hundred years and more. Think of it, Bedwyr! There has never been a generation to know peace on this island,' Arthur said, as we stood on deck watching the coastline rise and fall with the waves.

'There has never been a generation to know peace anywhere on this earth, God love you!'

'That may be true,' he allowed, 'but that does not mean it is not possible. I believe it can happen. But someone has to make a start.'

'You have made a start, Bear. But do not expect the small kings to shower gifts of gold upon your head. Gifts of steel, perhaps.'

'The killing must stop. If I must endure the hurt, so be it. I will endure it gladly, and more besides — but the fighting must end.' He smiled thoughtfully. 'It is no less than Our Lord the Christ did for men.'

I shook my head and looked out across the grey-waved sea, listening to the keen of the gulls following our wake. What Arthur said made a certain sense. But I knew Arthur — *knew* him, Blessed Saviour! — and I could not believe he was so innocent, so guileless and trusting about this.

'Do you not believe me?' asked Arthur, after a moment.

I took my time answering. 'I believe you, Bear. And I

pray God you are right, I swear it. But this is not like you.'
I turned to find his clear blue eyes gazing at me, mirth drawing up the corners of his mouth. 'You think this is funny? I do not. I tell you it chills me to the marrow.

'Yes, it does! We have given land to our most deadly enemies — something even Vortigern in all his glory never contemplated. Yet we have done this, and asked for nothing but promises in return. Saecsen promises!' I blurted, and fell silent.

'You think me a fool.' Arthur's voice was quiet.

'God love you, Arthur, I know you are no fool. That is why this troubles me so. You are not yourself since you returned from Ynys Avallach.'

Arthur did not reply directly, but turned away to study the far horizon, his face as hard as the rock cliffs in the distance.

'What happened to you at Ynys Avallach?' I asked. I did not know if he would tell me, and at first I thought he would not.

But at last he spread his hands towards the distant shore and said, 'I saw a vision, Bedwyr. I saw a land alive with light. I saw a land blessed of the Living God, where all men lived as kinsmen and brothers. I saw a land — *this* land, this Britain — at peace under the rule of Justice and Right.

'I saw this, and much else besides. And I vowed to make it true. I have pledged my life to it, Bedwyr. My life is a sacrifice to the Summer Realm, for I am the Lord of Summer.'

What could I say to this? If he saw a vision, he saw a vision. But was this the right way to go about it?

Arthur laughed suddenly. 'So maybe I am a fool after all, eh?'

'God's truth, Bear, I do not know what to think.'

'I will tell you something else, shall I?' he raised his eyebrows and jerked his head back towards the sea cliffs. 'The north is very far away from the south, you know.'

'Well I know it. We would not be on this leaky tub if it were otherwise.'

He nodded, his mirth turning waggish. 'No one has yet discovered a way to fight the Picts and Angles in the north while the Saecsens raid in the south. Jesu knows that I cannot be in two places at once.'

'Meaning?'

'The war will be fought and won in the north. Our freedom will be won in the north, or lost there.'

He saw by the expression on my face that I thought this unlikely. 'You doubt me?' he asked. 'Consider this, then: every invasion has always come from the north. It is the swiftest way into the heart of Britain. The Romans understood this — just as they discovered that it is impossible to defend.' He flung a hand to the wavering coast. 'There are ten thousand bays and coves on this sea — and each one a hiding-place for Sea Wolves. They have only to make landfall and the Picti, or their own kind, will welcome them.'

'Aelle and Colgrim attacked the south,' I pointed out.

'Did they?'

'You know that they did.'

'Are you like the others? Think, Bedwyr! How were they able to strike so quickly? How were they able to order their attack so?'

I stared blankly back at him, for I did not know.

'It is too far to come from Saecsland. The sea journey is too difficult — and then to fight at the end of it? It cannot be done. So what did they do? Think, Bedwyr!'

'I am thinking, Artos! What did they do?'

'It is so simple! They made landfall in the north and wintered there. This they were able to do because they had friends waiting for them. They gathered their forces from those who had come before; they amassed ships and weapons and men through the summer. Then, when they were ready, they swept down from the north to attack the brittle defences of the south.' Arthur smiled grimly. 'As I said, the swiftest, surest way to the south is through the north.'

Yes, it was true what he said. I had not thought of it that way before, but I recognized the truth now that he explained it to me. What is more, this was the Arthur I knew and remembered. I told him so.

'You think because I want peace I have lost the craft of war?' He shook his head slowly. 'I have not changed, my friend — not enough anyway.'

'So what are we doing now? What can we accomplish in the north, just the three of us?'

'We are going to hold council with King Lot of Orcady.

He is a strong lord, with many ships and a good warband. I would see whether he will support me.'

'Ships? You have horses, now you want ships?'

'I want as many ships as I can get — as many as Lot will give me. Then I mean to build the rest. I want a fleet such as the great Caesar had when he came to the Island of the Mighty.'

'But we cannot fight on ships.'

'Oh yes, we can. And, what we do not know of it, we shall learn. Even if we do not fight with our ships, we must have some way to move horses and men more swiftly than over land. That is too slow, and — '

'I know: the north is very far from the south, and you cannot be in two places at once.'

Arthur grinned and slapped me on the back. 'Well done! I was beginning to think you slow witted.' He rose from the railing and stretched. 'But all this talk has made me thirsty. Let us have some beer.'

I watched him move off along the deck, thinking, *Do I know this man, after all?* He turned and called, 'Not thirsty?' And, never one to turn away a cup, I hurried after him.

The Orcades are a huddle of bare rocks that poke from the northern sea like the heads and shoulders of drowned giants. They are covered with a green crust of earth, so that the scrawny sheep have something to eat. It is an unlikely place to find a lord of Lot's repute. More a hoarding of small settlements than a realm. Yet the lords of Ynysoedd Erch have ever held their own with a fierce and justifiable pride.

I wondered what our reception would be. Certainly, Lot would welcome an alliance with the south. His position could hardly be comfortable in the best of times — with Picti and Angli between him and the southern lords. But he existed, some said, by trade and friendship with the Angli and Saecsen. Mind, I have never known anyone to make that accusation to Lot's face.

As our ship neared Llyscait, where Lot's stronghold overlooked the deep stone-lined bay, the sun dimmed as it passed behind the clouds. The quick chill off the water made me shiver. But it was not only the cold, I think.

We were met by a small boat which came out to us from the rock-strewn shingle. The boatmen hailed us and called for news. Some of our ship's hands obliged them, and then Myrddin bade them take us to Lord Lot.

This they were happy to do, although it meant that we were made to slither over the side of the ship, to drop ingloriously into their boat, whereupon they rowed us to shore. As we bumped to a halt on the shingle, there appeared a welcoming party.

'Greetings, and God's blessings be on you, my lords, if you come in peace,' said the foremost among them. His words were gracious, but I saw that those with him wore swords and had long knives tucked into their belts.

'God be good to you,' replied Myrddin, 'peace is our sole ambition.'

'Then may it go well with you while you shelter here among us. Will you greet our king?'

'We would like nothing better. And you can tell Lord Lot that the Duke of Britain has come to hold council with him.'

Lot's adviser cocked his head to one side. 'Are you the Arthur we hear of?'

Myrddin shook his head slowly and put out a hand to the young man beside him. 'This is Arthur.'

The man's expression changed from wary acceptance to astonished disbelief. 'You? You are Arthur?'

'I am,' the Duke answered.

'We have come a long way, and we are tired,' said Myrddin.

The adviser turned at once to Myrddin. 'I am sorry, Emrys. Forgive me, I — ' he began, for he realized at once who Myrddin must be.

'It is of no importance. Please, take us to Lot.'

'At once, Emrys.' The man turned on his heel and we were escorted from the beach and up a long, snaking passageway cut in the rock to a caer walled in stone and surrounded by gorse. The gate stood open and we passed through into a small, well-ordered yard.

Lot stood in the centre of the yard, arms crossed on his chest, scowling at three horses standing at halter before him. He turned his head towards us as we entered, and,

182

like his man on the beach, his aspect altered at once — but not entirely for the better.

Although he threw open his arms and embraced Myrddin, I could not help thinking that his greeting was forced. 'Myrddin, you look well. It has been long and long since we last met. You are welcome here.' Lot smiled, but his smile did not touch his coldly distant eyes.

'Thank you, lord,' replied Myrddin. 'Time has been a boon to you. I see you have prospered.'

Lot nodded, but did not reply. Instead, he turned abruptly to Arthur. 'This can only be Duke Arthur, of whom so much is told.' He extended the same chilly greeting to Arthur, then looked to me.

'I am Bedwyr,' I told him. 'God be good to you, lord.'

'Ah, Bedwyr ap Bleddyn of Rheged. We have heard of you, too,' Lot said, and barked an awkward laugh. 'Do not look surprised. We are not so solitary as it seems. The commerce of these little islands rivals that of Londinium itself, I believe. We hear much, and see more that passes unnoticed elsewhere.'

'Much indeed,' I said, 'if you have heard of me.'

These formalities observed, Lot turned his attention once more to the horses, explaining, 'These animals have been sent me from a trader in Monoth. I can find no fault with them. Still, I am not liking what I see.' The king appealed to Arthur, saying, 'Perhaps you can show me what I am missing.'

'I will help if I can,' replied Arthur. He approached the horses and walked around them for a moment, pausing to stroke each one and feel its flesh. I studied them, too, for I knew horses well.

'The two on either side are well enough, if a little light in the hindquarters. They would be swift, but I think they would tire quickly over rough ground. The one in the centre, however, is the one you should choose.'

'Oh? That, to my thinking, is the one least suitable of all.'

'He is young still,' replied Arthur, 'but he will flesh out, given time.'

'See how he stands — as if his legs hurt him,' protested Lot mildly, showing, I thought, a good deal more discernment than he admitted to.

'It is his shoes,' explained Arthur. 'I suspect he was shod just before bringing him here, but the work was hurried, and carelessly done.'

Lot approached the horse, stooped, and lifted a foreleg to examine the hoof. 'It is true,' he said, letting the hoof drop. 'The shoe is too big and the nails are poorly placed. It is a marvel he can stand at all.'

'Have him re-shod properly and you will see a different animal.'

'I commend you, Duke Arthur; you know horses,' said Lot, regarding Arthur carefully. 'Do you know ships as well?'

'I know that ships are faster than horses in reaching the far places where the enemy hides. I know that the Angli and Irish must come here in ships, and can be stopped with ships. I know that the shipwrights of Orcady build the finest ships in the Island of the Mighty.' Arthur paused, and then added with a shrug. 'Beyond this, I confess that I am ignorant of ships. That is why I have come.'

Lot appraised Arthur through narrowed eyes, as if to take his measure against the words he had uttered. Satisfied at last, the king held out a hand towards the hall. 'Come, Duke Arthur, I think that we must talk.'

FOUR

'Not since the Romans have ships been built in Muir Guidan,' said Arthur. 'But the shipyards are still there — I have seen them on the Fiorth near Caer Edyn. The fishermen use them for harbourage in the winter, and occasionally someone will build a boat there.'

Lot nodded, deep in thought. 'If it is as you say, it could be done.' He was silent a goodly while. 'There is good timber nearby?'

'More than we could ever use were we to build ten thousand ships.'

'My shipwrights would have to return here in winter to repair my own ships.'

'I will see to it, and gladly. What do you say?'

'I say you had better begin finding men to pilot your ships, for Britain will soon have a fleet once more.'

Beaming, Arthur loosed a wild whoop of pleasure, and Lot's normally icy demeanour melted under the sun of Arthur's joy. The king opened his hand towards Myrddin, as if begging the Emrys' blessing on the pact he and Arthur had just made. Myrddin gave his encouragement by way of clapping Lot on the back and saying, 'From the union of two strong lords the defeat of the enemy is enjoined. The Gifting God be praised!'

Lot then called his stewards to bring us drink and serve the meal, even though the sky was still light outside. For indeed, daylight lingers long in the northern isles — sometimes through the night. At midsummer the sun never truly sets at all!

We drank and began talking of where and how the ships could be used most effectively. I noticed Myrddin lay aside his cup, rise, and withdraw from the company. I waited until Myrddin had left the hall and then went out to him.

I found him standing in the centre of the yard, gazing at the vast northern sky. 'What is wrong, Myrddin?' I asked, as I came to stand beside him.

He answered, but did not take his eyes from the cloudless, amber sky. 'Arthur has his ships — or soon will have, and Lot has been won as an ally. What could be wrong?'

'You distrust Lot. Why?' It was merely a guess, notched and let fly. But it struck nearer the mark than I knew.

Myrddin turned his eyes away from searching the heavens and applied the same sharp scrutiny to me. 'I do not know Lot. It is hard for me wholly to trust someone I do not know.'

This I thought a reasonable answer, and true — as far as it went. But I knew Myrddin. There was more to it than that. 'He has troubled you in the past,' I said. Another guess.

'Troubled me?' Myrddin began to walk towards the fortress gate, which still stood open. I fell into step beside him. 'No, not that. But he has often confused me. You will have heard it told, I suppose, that few kings supported me for the High Kingship. It is true; only a very few. But Lot was one of them. And him with less reason than any of the others. . . That perplexed me — as it does to this day.'

'You suspect treachery?'

'I suspect. . . ' He stopped as we walked past the gates and down the track towards the sea. Upon reaching the rock shingle he stood gazing out at the dusky sea. The waves lapped at the rocks and the air smelled of salt and rotting seaweed. We stood together for a long while, and then Myrddin swung his golden gaze to me. 'You have a brain in your head,' he told me. 'What do you make of Lot? Do *you* trust him?'

Now it was my turn to be silent for a spell. Did I trust Lot? What did I make of him? I weighed the scant evidence for and against him in my mind. I tried to be fair.

'Well?'

'It seems to me,' I began slowly, 'that Lord Lot is unused to having people enjoy his company. He is tolerated, perhaps, and obeyed, certainly — he is king, after all. But he is not loved. Likely, he has no friends at all.'

Myrddin nodded. 'Why is this, do you think?'

Living in Orcady was part of it. Remote, isolated from the rest of the world, cut off by the sea and the barren northern wastes, it was difficult to maintain friendships and alliances with the noble houses of the south. For this reason, and others, the southern lords remained suspicious. Northerners were held in little regard in the south; they were thought to be backward, coarse and low. Little better than Picts, if no worse.

From what I had seen of Lot and his men, they were none of these things; they were simply different. Yet, despite their differences, just as civil and refined as any southern lord and his tribe. But living on their barren, sea-surrounded rocks made them severe, in the same way their limited contact with the south made them wary and brusque — always expecting the veiled insult, and finding it, whether intended or not.

These things I thought, and told to Myrddin. 'King Lot has no friends,' I concluded, 'because he suspects everyone of trying to do him harm. No, it is not guile at work in him — it is suspicion.'

'Suspicion, yes. And there is something else: pride.'

'Suspicion and pride,' I said, 'two dogs that lie uneasily together.'

'Indeed,' said Myrddin, 'and neither one to be crossed.'

At last I thought I had discovered what Myrddin was worrying about. 'But that is not why I am uneasy,' he said.

'No?' Myrddin always does this. Just when you think you have cracked one hard nut, he pulls another from his pocket, tougher than the last. 'What else, then?'

'In truth, Bedwyr, it has little to do with Lot, and yet everything to do with him.'

That is something else he does: mutters in obscure riddles. Myrddin dearly loves enigma and paradox.

'Nothing and everything,' I observed sourly. 'We will be here all night.'

'It is Lot's father — rather, it is his father's wife.'

'Lot's mother, you mean?'

'Did I say that? No. I said Lot's father's wife. King Loth had two wives. The first was Lot's mother and she died. Loth's second wife was a woman named Morgian.'

'Speak plainly, Myrddin. Who or what is this Morgian to us?' Indeed, in all the time I had known him, I had never heard the name pass his lips. But then, there was much about Myrddin that no one knew.

Myrddin did not answer. Instead, he asked, 'Do you know why men call these islands Ynysoedd Erch — the Islands of Fear?'

I looked around at the forbidding rocks and the shadowy fortress rising above the sea. The Orcades were a forlorn and lonely place. Certainly, that was reason enough for such a name, and I told him so.

'No. It is because of her, Morgian, Queen of Air and Darkness.'

Now, I am a man who does not shrink from much. But I have always found it disturbing to invoke evil, even in jest. So, when Myrddin spoke that name, I felt a chill quaver in the air as if rising suddenly from the sea. But it was not sea air that sent the flesh creeping upon my scalp.

'You know her?'

'I do — and wish to Heaven that I did not!' The vehemence with which he spoke took me aback. I also heard something in his voice I had never heard before: fear. The Great Emrys was afraid of Morgian — whoever she might be.

'Myrddin,' I said gently, 'what is she to you?'

His head whipped round and he glared at me. His mouth was a grimace of revulsion, and his eyes were hard, bright points of pain. 'She is my death!'

The next days were given to planning how best to commence shipbuilding on the Fiorth. Arthur and Lot were to be seen head to head in Lot's chambers, or strolling the grounds of the stronghold, lost to the world in their ardent schemes and strategies. While it was clear that Lot and Arthur were becoming fast friends, it was also evident that Myrddin was less and less happy about our stay.

He made me uneasy. I would see him walking out on the wind-blown hills of the island, or sitting brooding on the rocks overlooking the sea. He rarely spoke in our company; and when he did it was only to utter a curt reply.

Arthur appeared not to notice. But I noticed.

Days passed with little to do. Time weighed heavily on me, and I began to grow impatient to return to Caer Melyn. There, I knew, work aplenty waited for me: there were men to train, horses to break, supplies and provisions to sort and, not forgetting — irate kings to pacify. No doubt Cai and Pelleas had their hands full while I sat idle.

More and more, I found myself wishing for something to do. And in the end I got my wish. Immediately, I regretted it.

We were given no warning. A ship just appeared at dawn one morning and made for the harbour. This caused a mild stir in Lot's court and some men went down to meet it on the shingle below the caer. The ship was scarcely anchored when word came back: Irish had landed and were pushing inland to join the Picti.

Hearing this, I dashed to Lot's hall, where I knew he and Arthur were concluding their business. I entered just behind Lot's principal adviser, who called out, 'Lord Lot, Gwalcmai has returned with dire news: Sea Wolves have put ashore in numbers and are raiding inland. The Picti have welcomed them.'

'Where is this?' asked Arthur.

'In Yrewyn Bay.'

This answer took me aback, for this bay is but a short distance from my home in Rheged. 'Have they attacked Caer Tryfan?' I asked, but my question went unheeded.

'What of Gwalchavad?' asked Lot.

Just then the door to the hall burst open and a young man hurried in, his bright blue-and-green cloak flying. One glance at his black hair and fierce aspect and I knew him to be Lot's kinsman. The silver torc at his throat gave me to know that he was nobly born.

'Gwalcmai!' called Lot. 'Where is Gwalchavad?'

'He has taken the warriors we had with us to follow the Sea Wolves — to keep watch on them. Have no fear, he promised to stay out of sight until we come.'

The relief in Lot's face could only be that of a father for a beloved son. This guess was proven true a moment later, when Lot turned and said, 'Duke Arthur, I present to you my son, Gwalcmai, who has just returned from Manau, where we trade.'

The young man — no more in years than Arthur or myself — inclined his head in greeting. 'Duke of Britain,' he said. 'Long have I desired to meet you — though I never expected to see you here.'

'I give you good greeting, Prince Gwalcmai. What else can you tell us of this invasion?'

'The Irish entered Yrewyn Bay and came inland up the river — thirty ships we counted. They seem to be gathering their forces. I think they are waiting for something.'

'The *cran tara* has gone out,' said Myrddin, stepping from the shadows of the hearth. 'They wait for the other tribes to join them.'

'Then they will not strike before midsummer. We have time yet,' replied Arthur.

'Little enough,' I observed. It was less than a month away.

Arthur turned to the king. 'Lord Lot, I will need your ships sooner than expected.'

'They are yours,' Lot replied. 'And my warband with them.'

'I am yours to command, Duke Arthur,' said Gwalcmai, placing himself under Arthur's authority. 'My ship is ready and waiting in the harbour.'

'Then we leave at dawn.'

We had hoped to engage the enemy before they could achieve full strength of numbers. This was not to be. Upon reaching Caer Melyn, Arthur sent messengers to the British kings, summoning their warbands. His own Cymbrogi were ready at once, of course, and Arthur sent them on ahead with Cai, Pelleas and Meurig, riding overland and taking most of the horses with them. The warbands of the other kings were slow in coming.

God save them, they were angry with Arthur for making peace with Aelle, Octa and Colgrim, and thought to punish the Duke by withholding aid. Also, they were reluctant to commit warriors to the defence of the north. After all, it is just foul moors and heather bogs — let the Irish and Picti have it. This is what they thought.

In the end, however, they were forced to uphold their pledge to Arthur as War Leader. So, four days before midsummer, we gathered at dawn on the strand at Abertaff near Caer Dydd, men and horses, weapons and supplies. Three kings came with us: Idris, Bedegran, and Maglos.

Old Bishop Gwythelyn, and his renowned pupil Teilo, led us in a special warriors' mass. From his nearby abbey the revered Illtyd came also to give his blessing. The holy men emboldened us with heartening words from the sacred texts, and commended us to the Lord Jesu. Then we all knelt there among the windswept dunes, the sound of the surf and gulls in our ears. We knelt, each and every one of us, and prayed to the Almighty God for swift sailing and swifter victory.

When the prayers were finished, we all rose up and sang a song of praise to the Saviour God. Ah, there is nothing finer than the voices of the Cymry lifted in song, I can tell you. We were three thousand strong. And that is a mighty voice before the Throne of Light.

Then, as the sun crested the far hills across Mor Hafren and the first red-beamed rays stretched across the water, we boarded the ships and set sail for the north. Forty-five ships in all — most of them Lot's, but Arthur had found a good few others. Not since the days of the Romans had such a fleet been seen in the Island of the Mighty. This, and the first of Arthur's ships had yet to be built!

Forty-five ships! Blessed Jesu, it was a sight to behold.

FIVE

We entered Yrewyn Bay at dusk and came ashore to make camp. The fires were kept low and we posted watchmen in the hills above the bay, lest a rearguard of Irish had been left behind. But the night passed quietly.

At dawn the next day we began the march inland to meet Cai and the Cymbrogi. We had arranged to come together at a place I knew: a ford where the River Glein joins the Yrewyn as it flows down from the mountains into the vale of Yrewyn.

There are no settlements in that region — the people were driven off long ago by the relentless raiding. We formed up in two long columns, after the Roman fashion. Arthur's *ala* — the mounted warriors — leading, foot soldiers coming after, and the supply wagons following. Since we had come by ship, we had only four wagons with us, and only a hundred horses — fewer than we would have liked, to be sure. But, as we intended joining Cai in a day or so, we thought we could sustain ourselves at least that long.

It was not until we reached the Glein that we realized our mistake.

'There must be ten thousand down there,' I whispered. Arthur and I sat our horses on the ridge, gazing down into dusk thickening in the Yrewyn vale. We had ridden into the foothills to spy out the land below — and a good thing, too! The numbers of the enemy ranged around the ford appeared as a dark smear spreading along either side of the river. The smoke from their innumerable fires blackened the air. 'I have never seen so many Irish in one place. I did not think there *were* so many.' The *cran tara* had indeed gone out, and it had been answered in force.

'They are not all Irish,' said Arthur, his eyes narrowed to

the distance. 'Look — see how they form two camps, there and there?' He indicated the dark mass on the left. 'The fires are larger and ranged in a great circle. And there — ' he pointed to the other smudge, 'the fires are smaller and scattered; those are the Irish.'

'So who are the others? Saecsen?' Saecsens often built circular camps around a central fire.

'Angli,' answered Arthur.

'Angli — Saecsen? What is the difference? They are barbarians, are they not?'

'Oh yes,' agreed Arthur with a grim laugh, 'they are barbarians. But if they were Saecsen I would know that Aelle and Colgrim had broken the peace.'

'Cold comfort,' I remarked. 'What are we to do now, Bear? They are camped where we are to meet Cai in a day's time.'

'We will ride south a little way to meet him.'

'What are they doing down there?'

'Waiting.'

'I can see that. Why, Exalted Duke, are they waiting, do you suppose?'

Arthur gave his head a slight shake. 'I do not know, and that worries me.'

'Will you offer them peace?'

'Yes. Why fight for peace if it can be achieved without bloodshed?'

'That may be, Artos,' I agreed, 'and I truly pray that it is. But I do not think they are going to down weapons and sail away peacefully. They have come to fight, and I think they mean to have their way.'

'I fear you are right.' Arthur lifted his reins and turned his mount. 'Come, we will go tell Myrddin what we have seen.'

Our own camp was but two valleys to the east of the enemy encampment. Twilight had fallen and the valley was darkening, although the sky still held light in the west. Arthur rode in, calling for the kings to meet him in his tent, and for the cooking fires to be put out at once.

Myrddin met us outside Arthur's tent, and held our horses as we dismounted. 'Well, was it to your liking?'

'You did not tell us there would be so many,' said Arthur

lightly. He might have been describing a herd of sheep he had happened to meet.

'How many?' asked Myrddin, cocking his head to one side.

'Ten thousand,' Arthur replied.

'So?' wondered the Emrys.

'I counted them myself,' I assured him. 'Every one.'

Myrddin shook his head slowly. 'It was not to begin this way. This is not how I saw it.'

'It does not matter,' said Arthur. 'This will be to our benefit.' Just then Idris ambled up, and Maglos behind him. 'We will hold council in my tent,' Arthur told them, 'when Bedegran has joined us.'

The two entered the tent and Arthur turned to Rhys, his harper and steward. 'Have food brought to us, and something to drink.'

Inside the tent, the lamps were already lit, casting their thin reddish glow over the rough board that had been set up to serve for his council table. Our cups were there, but empty yet. Idris and Maglos sat across from one another, leaning on their elbows.

'You have seen something, yes?' Idris asked, as I settled on the bench next to him.

'I have seen the vale of Yrewyn,' I told him. 'It is a sight worth seeing.'

He regarded me sceptically for a moment and then shrugged. 'Sooner ask a stone.' He turned away and began talking to Maglos.

I had come to like Idris — at least, I no longer disliked him as much as I once had. He had a good way with his men, whom he treated with all respect. It was unfortunate he had sided with Morcant and Cerdic in the beginning. But I sensed he was deeply sorry for this — which was why he had chosen to ride with us. He was trying to make amends for his lapse by fighting for Arthur every bit as hard as he had fought against him.

He was a strong man, though slender, and wore his hair and moustache long, like the Celts of old. And, although he had never set foot inside a church in his life, he had learned reading and writing from the brothers at the monastery at Eboracum.

Maglos, on the other hand, was nearly as broad as Cai, though not nearly as tall. He sat his horse like a stump. But, like a stump, his roots went deep. Maglos ap Morganwg of the ancient Dumnonii possessed his people's easy confidence — brought by long association with wealth and power — but surprisingly little of their stiff-necked pride. Also, he was seldom to be found in an ill humour.

We had not fought alongside these men before, and I wondered if they would be able to place themselves under Arthur's authority as easily as they had placed their warbands under his command. That we would see.

The tent flap opened and Arthur entered with Gwalcmai, Bedegran and Myrddin. The Duke carried a jar of beer in his hand and began pouring the cups with his own hand, then sat down and began passing the cups to the others. Myrddin did not join us at the council table, but remained standing behind Arthur. Gwalcmai sat down at Arthur's left hand, across from me on his right. Bedegran sat next to me.

Arthur lifted his cup and drank deep. He refilled it and let it stand before him. 'We cannot meet Cai and Meurig at the Glein ford,' he said. 'Yrewyn vale is full of Irish and Angli.'

'Angli?' Gwalcmai lowered his cup in surprise.

'They are there,' I told him. 'In numbers.'

'How many?' asked Idris.

'Ten thousand.'

The words hung in the air as those gathered round the board struggled to envisage this number. Arthur let them work on it for a while before he said, 'I will send to them with an offer of peace. We will pray that they accept it.'

'And if they do not?' asked Idris.

'If words of peace do not speak to them, perhaps they will heed British steel.'

The table fell silent, calculating our chances of surviving against such numbers.

'Of course,' continued Arthur, 'Cai would be unhappy to miss such a glorious battle.'

Maglos laughed. 'I can think of a few others who should be sorry to miss such.'

'Therefore, tomorrow you will ride south to wait for Cai

and the Cymbrogi. Bedwyr and I will take the willow branch to the Irish and Angli camp.'

I breathed a silent thanks to him for this singular honour.

'What if the enemy moves from the vale?' asked Bedegran.

'We will stop them.'

'We cannot engage them,' insisted Bedegran. 'We are too few.'

'Yet I tell you they will be stopped,' replied Arthur, evenly.

Bedegran opened his mouth to speak again, but thought better of it and took a drink from his cup instead.

Arthur glanced at each of the others, to see if anyone else would challenge him. When no one did, he continued. 'Cai is expected in the next few days. He is following the Roman road up through Caer Lial on the Wall. We will ride south and east to meet him where the road ends.'

'All respect, Duke Arthur,' said Idris, clearing his throat. 'Should we not wait for others to join us? At ten thousand they are more than three to one against us. I know I would fight easier with a few more warriors beside me.'

'My father and brother will soon arrive with the warband of Orcady,' offered Gwalcmai.

'How many? Three hundred?' asked Idris hopefully.

'Fifty — '

'Fifty! Is that all?' sputtered Idris. He turned in appeal to Arthur. 'Fifty — '

'Peace, Idris,' said Maglos. 'You above all men should deem yourself fortunate. With fewer kings to divide the plunder, we all get more.'

Idris glared at him. 'Tell me if it is fortunate you feel with ten foemen hanging on your sword arm at every stroke. They will cut us to strop leather.'

'Where is your courage, man?' said Maglos. He lifted his cup and said, 'The battle is before us, there is glory to be won. Bring it on! Hie!' With that, he tossed down his beer, and wiped his sopping moustache on his sleeve.

'Pray to God that this battle may be avoided,' said Arthur, rising in dismissal. 'Pray all of you that peace triumph.'

The next day, while the others broke camp, Arthur and I mounted our horses and rode to the enemy encampment.

We paused at the riverside to gather willow branches. I cut the biggest ones I could find, lest there be any mistaking our intentions. Still, I had no great hope that the barbarians would honour them.

Then, crossing over the river, we rode on to meet the enemy. They saw us coming, of course, and we were met by a company of Irish and Angli chieftains. They scowled at us, and jeered, but did not kill us outright, and for that I was grateful.

'I am Arthur, Battlechief of Britain,' Arthur told them. 'I want to talk to your *Bretwalda*.'

At his use of the barbarian word for war leader, the Angli glanced at one another. Then up spoke one of the barbarians. 'I am Baldulf,' he said, and his speech was not good. 'What do you seek?'

'I seek peace,' replied Arthur, 'which I gladly grant to you.'

Baldulf muttered something to one of his advisers, who muttered back. The Irish, of the tribe called Scoti, frowned mightily but said nothing.

'What are your terms?' asked Baldulf.

'You must leave this land. As you have done no harm here, I will suffer no harm to come to you. But you must go from here at once.'

Again Baldulf conferred with his chieftains. Then, turning with a haughty sneer, he said, 'If we do not go?'

'Then you will all be killed. For I have given my promise to God that there will be peace in this land.'

'Kill us then, if you can,' replied Baldulf bravely. 'Maybe it is you and your god who will die.'

'I have given my pledge to you. Peace will abide in Britain, whether won by word or deed. Today, I give you your lives, tomorrow I will take them. The choice is yours.' So saying, Arthur and I turned our horses and rode back to camp.

Everything was ready to move; they were only awaiting our return. Arthur chose sentries to watch the enemy camp, and we left the valley and started east to meet Cai.

The sun had risen fair in the sky, but clouds came in from the sea laden with rain, and by midday the ground beneath

197

our feet was soft mud. The wagons became enmired and time and again had to be dragged free. The going was miserable and slow.

This should have been a warning to us.

But the first hint of trouble came when one of the sentries returned on the gallop, his mount lashed to a lather. He flew directly to where Arthur and I rode at the head of the columns. 'They are moving,' he gasped, out of breath from his wild ride.

Arthur halted. 'Which way?'

'Moving up the valley — to the east. . . '

For the space of a heartbeat Arthur froze, bringing the image of the valley before his mind. The next instant he was all action.

'Bedwyr!' he called, wheeling his horse. 'Follow me!'

'Arthur! Where are you going?'

'If they leave the valley, we are lost!'

I called after him but he did not hear. A moment later I was flying down the ranks halting the columns and turning them onto our new course. I rode to the end of the columns and shouted at the men tending the wagons. 'Leave the wagons here! Fetch your weapons!'

Bedegran and Idris appeared. 'What is happening?' demanded one. 'Why are we turning?' asked the other.

'The barbarians are moving. Arm your men.'

'We are not going to attack them!' Bedegran gaped at me, as if I had lost my wits.

'I do not see why — ' began Idris.

'Arm your men, and follow!' I shouted, and rode to tell Maglos and Gwalcmai, before racing after Arthur, who was quickly disappearing over the broad hump of the hill. Myrddin was with him.

I caught up with them as they sat looking over the vale of Yrewyn — a good deal east of where we had been the day before. There were no Irish or Angli to be seen.

'It is as I hoped,' Arthur was saying. 'They are slower afoot than we are. We have come in time.'

The vale had narrowed to little more than a glen, and I saw Arthur's plan immediately. If the enemy were moving east along the river, they would come through this pinched-up place where we would be waiting for them. Then their superior numbers would not avail them, for we could not easily be surrounded.

'Do we establish ourselves down there along the river — or wait in the hills?'

'Both,' Arthur said. 'Let the footmen be ready down there. We will hold what horse we have here and here — ' he pointed to the steep slopes on either side of the river, 'and then sweep down upon them when they try to come around us.'

The Duke turned to Myrddin. 'Will you uphold us?'

Myrddin nodded, his golden eyes dark. 'You have no need to ask. I will uphold you by the power of the Three.' He sat looking at the sky to the east, and across the hills to the south. 'We will be aided by the weather,' he observed. 'With the ending of the rain the mist will rise. If they be long in coming, we will be well hidden near the river.'

It was true. The rain from the west was ending but, behind us to the east, a thick damp fog was already winding along the river; low dark clouds were scudding in from the south and the wind was turning cold.

The first of the horsemen began arriving and I set Idris and Maglos across the valley. Gwalcmai and I held to the near side — fifty horse on either hand. Arthur and Bedegran led the footmen down into the glen and set about hiding them.

Mist or no, in a few moments, when I looked, I could scarcely make them out. Nine hundred men vanished in the glen in the blink of an eye. And with their going an unnatural calm fell upon the narrow valley as the mist rolled in.

Well down behind the crest of the hill, I closed my eyes and prayed to the Saviour God — as I do before a battle. It helps to settle the mind and put courage in the heart.

In a little while, I felt a touch on my arm, and heard Gwalcmai's whisper in my ear. 'They are coming.'

Flat on my belly, my face so close to the ground I could smell the sedge, I crept forward to peer over the crest of the hill. The first of the enemy was entering the narrow valley from the west. They came on unheeding, a straggling mass, moving in thickened clusters which defined their battlelords. The Irish came first, the Angli after, and slowly. The Picti I did not see, and this caused me to wonder.

'They are so careless,' remarked Gwalcmai, his voice filled with contempt at their stupidity.

'But they are so many,' I reminded him.

He smiled, his teeth showing white in the gloom. 'The more glory for us, friend Bedwyr.'

'Listen!'

The blast of a horn echoed in the glen. It was Rhys, with Arthur's hunting horn — the signal to attack. And suddenly there he was, springing up out of the river mist and hurtling into the startled barbarians. All along the river men rose as one. Their shout carried to the hilltops and echoed along the glen.

The barbarian host was thrown into confusion at once. Those leading were forced back into the mass behind. The Britons thrust ahead, following Arthur at a run. He had taken a white horse, so that he could be more easily seen in the murk, and he flew at the enemy like a harrying hawk.

The sight of him driving fearlessly into the churning wall of foemen made Gwalcmai gasp. 'Is he always so daring?' he asked in astonishment.

'It is his way.'

'I have never seen the like of it. Who can match him?'

I laughed. 'No one. He is a bear in battle — a great mad bear. No one matches him for strength or valour.'

Gwalcmai shook his head. 'We heard he was a stout battlechief, but this. . . ' he fell silent for want of words.

'Beware,' I warned, 'he expects no less of the men who follow him.'

'*I* will follow him if he will have me,' Gwalcmai vowed solemnly.

I clapped the prince on his shoulder with a gloved hand. 'Well, you are indeed a fortunate man, Gwalcmai ap Lot. For today you have the happy chance to prove yourself worthy.'

So saying, I rose and drew on my war helm. I walked back to the picket, mounted my horse and took up my long spear, then gave the signal to the others who were already mounted and waiting. We advanced to the crest of the hill and poised there, ready to sweep down into the fray.

We did not wait long, for the first ranks of Angli had already seen what Arthur was about and were running up the side of the hill to evade the chaos choking the centre of the glen, hoping to surround the Cymry. As yet, no one had crossed the river to come at him from the other side.

I raised my spear to heaven. 'For God and Britain!' I cried, and my cry was answered in kind. And then I was racing down the hillside, my cloak rippling out behind me, the wind singing from my dark-glinting spearhead.

So heedless were the Angli that they did not see us until we were right on top of them. The first ranks of warriors went down before us like wheat ripe to the scythe. The speed and force of our charge carried us well into their quickly scattering swarm.

We reformed the line and galloped up the hillside, turned, and came sweeping down upon them again. The Angli saw what we intended and fled before us, running, stumbling, rolling, picking themselves up and running again. We drove them before us like so many sheep for the slaughter.

They did not even try to fight.

I reined up and gathered the horsemen to me. 'Let them go! Let them go! We ride now to support Arthur!' I pointed with my spear down the hillside where the main force laboured. The Irish, by dint of numbers alone, had succeeded in halting Arthur's advance. By cutting in from the side, we could divide the Irish force and keep the Angli penned behind, where they could do nothing.

Oh, Arthur had chosen the battle place well. The land worked for us and against the enemy; their greater numbers were no use to them now.

Setting my spear, I wheeled my horse and charged. I heard a wild war whoop beside me and Gwalcmai galloped past, his face alight with the battle glow. I lashed my horse to match his pace and the ground trembled beneath us. The beat of our steeds' pounding hooves sounded like a throbbing drum.

Down and down we came, plummeting like eagles, swifter than the wind. The terrified Irish heard the terrible din of our coming and threw their round shields before them — as if this could stop the thunder breaking over their heads.

The clash of our meeting sounded like a thousand anvils being struck at once. Steel flashed. Men screamed. The air shuddered with the shock. I thrust with my spear again and again, opening a wide path before me.

Gwalcmai rode at my right hand, matching me thrust for thrust. Together we drove straight into the heart of the battle, where Arthur's white horse reared and plunged. Any who came before us fell — either to our spears or to the swift and deadly hooves of our battle-trained horses.

I will tell you how it is to fight on horseback, shall I?

You feel the enormous surge of power beneath you and the rhythmic roll of the beast's flanks as its legs stretch and gather. The strength of the great creature becomes your strength, rising through you and through the shaft of the spear in your hand. With the enormous weight of the animal behind it, that hardened length of ashwood becomes indestructible; the flared iron leaf of the spear head penetrates anything: wood, leather, bone.

As you begin the charge, the enemy appears as massive and faceless as a wall. As you close, the wall begins to splinter and fall inward upon itself. Then you see individual timbers — men — as they collapse before you. There is a terrible instant when you see their eyes bulge and mouths gape as they go down. And then they are gone and you are free.

The shock of the clash washes over you like a sea wave, swelling, cresting, rolling, and moving on. The sound of the battle is a roar in your ears and a blur before your eyes. You see the glint of metal. You see the point of your spear like a point of light, like a Beltane firebrand, as it thrusts and thrusts.

You smell the thick, salty sweetness of blood.

You are at once greater and more powerful than you can imagine. You expand to fill the whole of this worlds-realm. You are formidable. You are invincible. You are God's own idea of a warrior and his hand is beneath you, upholding you. His peace flows from your heart as from a wellspring.

All these things and more I knew as I hurtled like a flaming star to Arthur's side. The Irish fell before me and many did not rise again.

'Arthur!' I cried, scattering the last of the foe before me as I fought to his side.

'Good work!' he shouted. The press of battle was thicker

here and the spear was no help. Arthur's sword was in his hand and I saw his arm rising and falling in deadly rhythm. I shoved my spear into its holder beneath my leg and drew my sword, unslinging my shield at the same time. Then I settled into the grim business at hand.

All around us the Cymry hacked at the foe, who fell back and back before us. They were giving ground and that was good. Oh, but it was slow going. We pushed on, and it was like wading to shore against an outrushing tide.

And then, all at once, the tide changed and we found ourselves being pulled along with it. I looked out across the glen to see what the cause might be and I saw Idris and Maglos sweeping down the hillside to meet an Angli counter-attack from the other side of the river. The attack was crushed before it could begin.

Seeing their hope extinguished so quickly and efficiently, the Irish abandoned the fight.

'They are retreating!' shouted Arthur. 'Follow me!' He raised his sword and his war cry was lost in the shouts of retreating Irish. I saw his white horse leap ahead and we gave chase.

We pursued them all the way back to the ford at the Glein. Here the valley widened and flattened, and here the Angli chose to halt their retreat and give battle once more.

We halted a little distance away to view the battle array, and to catch our breath before attacking. The kings gathered round us to hold council. 'They think to take us here,' observed Arthur.

'And they may just do it,' remarked Idris. 'Look at the length of that line. We cannot equal it — we will be stretched too thin. They can easily surround us.'

I, for one, had had enough of his crabbed lack of faith. 'If this be courage, Idris,' I told him, 'you show it in a most peculiar way.'

Gwalcmai laughed, and Idris subsided, his mouth pressed into a bloodless line.

'We will strike them in the centre, there,' said Arthur, who had been studying the enemy; he pointed to the thickened mass before us. 'The Angli fight like Saecsens, but they are even more afraid of the horses. Therefore, the *ala* will force them back across the ford and cut the line in two.

When this happens the two ends will be drawn in together to fill the void.'

'They will circle and surround us, Duke Arthur.' It was Maglos this time.

'Yes,' replied Arthur coolly, 'and when that happens our footmen will come at them from behind.'

'But we will be trapped,' Bedegran insisted.

'There must be some bait in a trap,' Gwalcmai told him, thus saving me the trouble, 'or the rat will not put his nose in.'

'I do not like it,' sniffed Idris. 'It is needlessly risky.'

I turned on him. 'They fear the horses! Have you not seen how they flee the sight of them? By the time they close on us, our own warriors will be at their backs and they will be the ones surrounded!'

I turned to find Arthur staring at me. 'What? You think yourself the only one who knows the head of a spear from its butt?' I demanded.

Arthur turned to the others. 'Well? You have heard Bedwyr. He will lead the charge to the centre. Bedegran and I will lead the footmen as before. May God go with us.' And he rode off to join the foot soldiers waiting beside the river.

Idris was right: Arthur's plan was risky. But it made the best possible use of our few horses. By using them to keep the enemy off balance, so to speak, our fewer numbers were not such a disadvantage.

The Angli thought to attack while we were still undecided. And with a tremendous roar they came at us on the run. 'Spears ready!' I called, sheathing the sword and retrieving my spear. I threw the reins forward and my horse lumbered into a trot. The *ala* formed up in wings on either side of me.

Gathering pace, the trot became a run and the run a gallop. Gwalcmai's voice rose above the thunder of the hooves, and an instant later we were all wailing in that high, eerie war chant of his. I felt the hot blood rising in my veins and the icy calm of the battle frenzy descend over me.

And it was no longer Bedwyr riding headlong towards the onrushing enemy. I was a flame, a burning brand flung into the wind. My heart soared within me with the song of battle.

My movements were immaculate, my thoughts bright and sharp as crystal.

The eyes in my head looked out and noted the battle array before me. We were closing. . . nearer. . . nearer. . .

CRACK!!

I was through the line and pulling up hard. A dozen Angli sprawled on the ground around me: some of them dead where they had dropped, others struggling to rise.

I saw one foeman staring stupidly at his shield which seemed to have become stuck to his chest. He pulled at it and the shield fell away, revealing a slender length of a broken spear, jutting out from between his ribs. My own spear had mysteriously lost half its length. I threw it down.

Drawing my sword, I wheeled my horse to survey the carnage. The force of our charge had indeed collapsed the centre of the line: the damage fifty horse can do is considerable. What is more, we had not lost a single rider.

But our assault had carried us further into the centre than I could have believed possible; we were at the ford, almost in the water. The Angli were not slow to react. Instantly, they closed on us and we were surrounded. Yet, even as they filled the rents we had made in their battle line, I heard Arthur's hunting horn sounding high and clear.

I gathered the *ala* to me and we formed up to fight towards Arthur. The battle had become close. We were pressed on all sides, but the Cymry kept their heads and we moved forward, slowly, and with difficulty, for the Angli, in their desperation, gave ground grudgingly.

Then, when all was committed to Arthur's plan, the worst thing possible happened: the Picti, so far absent from the fight, suddenly appeared, streaming down from the hillside, coming in behind Arthur. As soon as they were within striking distance they loosed their hateful little arrows.

So there we were, outnumbered and twice surrounded. Of all possible positions for an army, there are not many worse.

Arthur did what he could, sending Idris' troop to deal with the Picti. Naturally, this weakened his own force. Seeing Idris break away, the Angli and Irish responded with almost hysterical fury.

Giving forth a tremendous howl, the barbarian rose up

like a great sea wave and Arthur was inundated. I saw him at the head of his troops on his white horse rising above them, and then he was gone.

'Arthur!' I cried, but my voice was lost in the battle roar. The seething waters of the enemy host closed over the place where he had been.

SIX

The *ala* drove into the thick of it. On the strength of steel alone we pushed a way clear — over the thrashing bodies of the foeman. May God forgive me, my mount's hooves scarce touched the ground!

We reached the ford. The water ran red; the river foam blushed crimson. Corpses floated, their limbs drifting. Caught on the rocks, the dead gazed with profound blindness into the darkening sky.

Once in the water, the going was easier — but only just. The Angli flung themselves at us with the ferocity of wild beasts. Swinging their axes, stabbing with their long knives, bawling, lunging, grappling.

We hewed at them like standing trees and they fell. But always there were more and more.

I strained into the welter, searching for Arthur. All was a chaos of flailing limbs and flashing weapons. I did not see him.

Now we were within range of the Picti arrows — though Idris had succeeded in moving them back somewhat, the wicked missiles still struck with deadly accuracy. The warrior to my left was struck in the shoulder, and one arrow glanced off my shield boss.

Grimly, we laboured on. The leaden sky deepened to the colour of fire-blackened iron. The wind gusted, driving the mist along the river. Rain began pelting down. The ground beneath our feet grew slippery. Blood and water mingled, flowed away. The battle proceeded.

Ever and again I cried out, 'Arthur! Arthur!'

In response I heard only the thunder of the fight, loud and sharp, pierced by hot oaths and agonized cries. And under it, the dull, droning rumble of running feet and horses' hooves. . .

Horses' hooves. That could not be what I heard, and yet I know the sound as well as my own heartbeat.

I raised my eyes. Out of the mist I saw a herd of horses racing into the valley, their shapes made ghostly by the rain. Swift as diving eagles, they thundered headlong into the midst of the fight.

Could it be? I looked again and saw the reason for this marvel. At the head of the stampede I saw two figures — one obscured by the mist and rain, but the other I knew: no one sits a saddle like Cai.

The enemy saw the horses at the same instant I did. A heartbeat later they were fleeing across the river. By the hundreds and thousands they fled, trampling over one another as they struggled across the ford.

We hacked at them as they fled, but they were no longer resisting. Stupid with fear, they abandoned themselves to our swords without thought.

The horses were careening closer. I saw Gwalcmai leading a phalanx of warriors to turn the stampede. And above the tumult I heard voices strong and brave, lifted in a Cymry battle song. It was the Cymbrogi, driving the horses before them and singing as they came.

The battle was broken. I halted to catch my breath and watched the immense tide of barbarians flowing away across the Glein and into the hills. Some of the Cymbrogi continued the rout, riding them down as they fled, but the enemy escaped by the score. This I regretted, but I did not have it in me to give chase. I was exhausted.

As they did not require my help, I turned again to the task of finding Arthur. The rain stopped as suddenly as it had begun. The mist cleared, and there he was before me.

He was on foot. His horse had been cut from under him, and he had been forced to lead his men on foot. The Bear of Britain saluted me when he saw me, raising his red-streaked sword.

'Hail, Bedwyr!' he called, and promptly sat down on a rock.

I tried to salute him back, but with the weight of the sword in my hand, my arm would no longer move. I slid from the saddle and leaned against my horse. 'God love you, Arthur,'

I said, wiping the sweat from my brow with the back of my glove, 'I thought you were dead. If Cai had not arrived we all would be meat for crows.'

Arthur leaned on his sword, gulping air. 'Yes, and now we shall have to share the plunder with him, I suppose.'

'Share it! He can have it all. It is as much as my life is worth to see him driving those horses.'

Just then Myrddin appeared. 'Here you are.' He examined us closely, and, satisfied that we were alive and well, dismounted and slipped to the ground. 'What did you think of the mist?'

'A most excellent mist,' declared Arthur. 'Forgive me if I do not make more of it.' He made to rise, but could not manage the effort, so settled back on the rock with his elbows on his knees.

I shook my head in disbelief at Myrddin's indifference. 'Do you know we were almost massacred here? Those cursed Picti and their arrows very nearly slaughtered the war host of Britain.'

'That is why I thought of the horses,' explained Myrddin placidly. 'The Picti believe horses contain the spirits of the dead and are reluctant to kill them lest they become haunted.'

'Listen to you, our sword brothers lie dead and you wag on about mist and horses!'

Myrddin turned to me. 'Look around you, Bedwyr the Bold. We have not lost a single man.'

Quick anger flashed up in me. I stared at him. 'What! Are you mad?'

'You have but to look,' Myrddin said, throwing wide a hand in invitation.

I turned my eyes to the fallen around us, and. . . it was true. Lord and Saviour, Blessed Jesu be praised! It was true!

Wherever I looked — the river, the glen, the hillsides, the rocks in the water — the dead were Irish and Angli. Not a single Briton could be found among them.

It was a miracle.

Dark came upon us. By torchlight we worked among the dead, retrieving gold and silver and the special treasure which we h d quickly learned to value: the Angli war shirt.

The Angli had learned to make a singular kind of battle-dress. Forged of thousa ds of tiny steel rings, the shirts protected the wearer yet allowed free movement. Mostly, only Angli kings and nobles wore them, for they were highly prized.

I walked over the battleground, rolling corpses to inspect their limbs and clothing. Sometimes the barbarian carry gold coins or gemstones in their mouths and the jaw must be broken to get them; or they hide them in little leather pouches which have to be pried away. The dead do not mind, I kept telling myself as I cut rings from swollen fingers and stripped battleshirts from stiffening backs.

Searching corpses is a grisly business, but necessary. We sorely needed the plunder and the war shirts. The one to pay for the support of the warband, and to keep men like Idris and Maglos happy. The other for defence against sword cuts and arrows.

The Cymbrogi returned from harrying the enemy. Pelleas and Meurig greeted us with the report that the barbarians appeared to be regrouping and moving north.

'What are we to do about the dead?' asked Maglos. 'We would wear ourselves out digging graves for all of them.'

In the fluttering torchlight Arthur cast an eye to the sky. The clouds were breaking up and in the east the moon was rising fair. 'We will have light soon,' he said. 'Shallow graves would not tire us overmuch.'

Bedegran grumbled; mild Maglos sighed, and Idris snorted. For once I agreed with them. 'You may be able to toil both day and night like Weland's Smithy. But we have fought most of the day, and tomorrow we must pursue the enemy. We are fainting with hunger. We need food and rest.'

It went against him to leave the dead unburied, even enemy dead. But there was nothing for it. 'Let it go, Bear,' I told him. 'There is no dishonour in it.'

Still, he hesitated. Myrddin came forward and put his hand on the Duke's shoulder. 'They are right,' Myrddin said. 'Come, let us leave this place to God and his servants. Let the Cymbrogi go ahead of us and make camp, so that it is ready when we come.'

Arthur consented. 'I yield to your counsel,' he said. 'Give the order, Meurig.' Then he turned and moved off in the darkness.

It was late when we arrived at the camp, a short distance to the east along the river. But there was hot food for us and a dry place to lay our heads. We slept the sleep of Bran the Blessed that night. The next morning we moved north in pursuit of the enemy.

This region is well known to me, for it borders on Rheged, the realm of my fathers. Now that Cai and the Cymbrogi were with us we had horses for four hundred, and we moved much more swiftly, marching back along the Yrewyn the way we had come. At Yrewyn Bay we met King Lot and Gwalchavad, who had come in time to see the Angli passing north in retreat, and had stayed to guard the ships lest they be tempted to steal or destroy them in their flight.

'They took no notice of the ships,' Lot told us upon joining us on the strand, 'but hastened themselves north.'

'It is as we thought,' remarked Cai. 'But in the dark we could not be sure.'

'They are following the glen of Garnoch,' said Gwalchavad. 'We may yet catch them if we hurry.'

I had to look at him twice to be certain it was not Gwalcmai dressed in different clothing. Lot's sons were twins, each no more different from the other than a man and his reflection. Gwalchavad — his name means Hawk of Summer — seemed to me more cautious, or more deliberate than his brother. But that is the only difference I ever noticed between them.

'I would have you stay with the ships,' Arthur told Lot. 'They will try to reach the shore.'

'Let us move the ships, then,' advised Gwalchavad.

'Can you move so many?' wondered Arthur. For there were more than fifty ships in all now, not counting the Irish ships we had taken.

Lot laughed. 'You have much to learn of ships, Duke Arthur. Yes, we can move them with no more than the men I have with me.'

'Then take them to the shipyards at Caer Edyn,' Arthur ordered. 'We will come to you there when this is finished.'

With no more parley than that, we turned at once to the

north-branching Garnoch, and followed Garnoch Glen in the direction the barbarians had fled. The trail was easy — a blind man could have followed it. All the way I kept pondering why they had turned north. Why not take the ships and flee?

The only reason I could think of was that they did not consider themselves conquered, merely discouraged. In this, I was not far wrong. We had surprised them the first time. They had been waiting — I remembered talking to Arthur about this, and he said it had worried him. Now it worried me. What had they been waiting for?

Two days later, when we came to the great River Clyd, I looked out across the plain towards Caer Alclyd and I knew the answer.

The Clyd valley forms a passage which cuts the northern wilderness east to west from Caer Alclyd at the Clyd estuary all the way to Caer Edyn. This vale also separates the hills of the south from the mountains of the north at the island's narrowest place. Anyone wishing to pass from one side of Britain to the other quickly must travel the Clyd valley.

Or, put another way: control the Clyd valley, and the whole of the north is yours. It is that simple. The barbarians knew this and they had been waiting for the spring flood at the Aberclydd to ebb so that they could lay siege to Caer Alclyd, the ancient fortress that guards the entrance to the passage to the east — as Caer Edyn guards it to the west.

We had forced them to act sooner than they might have done, that is all. They had not given up, and had no intention of leaving. Our appearance had not caused them to abandon their plan. What is more, gazing upon them as they were ranged about the caer, it became apparent that they had been joined by other hosts. Perhaps Angli had been hiding in glens and valleys all through the region, waiting to come together at this time and place.

Well, our numbers had increased, too. With Lot and his fifty, the Cymbrogi, and. . . I was struck by a sudden thought. 'Arthur — ' I said, turning suddenly to Arthur on my left, 'who is that in Caer Alclyd?'

'Do you not recognize the banner above the rampart?'

I squinted to gaze at the distant rock with its fortress on top. There was indeed a long banner hanging from a

212

spearshaft fixed to the wall. It swung and fluttered in the wind, and I caught a glimpse of gold and blue. 'Bors?'

'None other.'

'Bors! What is he doing here?'

Arthur only shrugged. 'That we will have to ask him when we see him face to face. But it appears we must first clear these barbarians away from his gate so that we can talk.'

He made it sound as if it were but a moment's chore. God's truth, it was but the beginning of a work that would last the rest of the summer.

We met the enemy three times and three times defeated them. But they were determined, for they knew the importance of the fortress: whoever held it commanded the western half of the valley.

The first battle liberated Bors at Caer Alclyd. He had arrived from Benowyc only a day or two after Arthur had sailed north from Caer Melyn. So he had followed with his ships, thinking to meet us at the Clyd estuary. Upon coming into the river, however, he encountered the Angli host and had quickly sought refuge in the old fortress. The enemy then laid siege to it, and there the matter stayed.

This is how we found them: arrayed on the plain of the river, their camps ringing the great stronghold, or dun, as it is called in that region. Arthur gave orders for the glen to be blocked, and sent swift messengers south to Custennin in Celyddon, and to the lords of Rheged, bidding all to attend him. We settled down to wait until the British lords should arrive.

The lords of Rheged, my father included, joined us as soon as word came to them that Arthur was fighting in the region. Lord Ectorius, Cai's father, joined us from Caer Edyn. Custennin of Celyddon came with a warband of two hundred.

As soon as these last arrived, Arthur gathered the Cymbrogi together and led us in a prayer of victory. Myrddin held his hands above us in blessing, whereupon we pulled on our battle dress and mounted our horses. Then, taking our places at the head of the massed warbands, we left the glen and rode out onto the plain.

The charge was masterfully made. Long had Arthur observed the enemy encampment from our vantage of the glen. He knew how the battle lines would form, he knew — even before the barbarians knew it themselves — how they would respond to the charge. He knew it in his blood and in his bones.

Thus was that first battle short and sharp. Baldulf was beaten before he could mount a defence. Our *ala* simply ran through them, and not once only: time and time again, charge upon charge. Great was the carnage, great the slaughter.

The flat plain was death to them. They could not stand against us. The siege broken, Bors swooped down from the rock fortress with his warband, sweeping all before him into the Clyd where many were drowned.

Seeing that his warriors could not fight us, Baldulf ordered the retreat, thinking to flee south to his ships. But Arthur had foreseen this, and our own footmen sealed the glen. In desperation the Angli and their minions fled to the north.

The barbarians were retreating to the forests of the lake region above the River Clyd, there to lose themselves in the dense and hidden pathways of those dark hills. Arthur called us to him while still on the battlefield.

'Cai, Bedwyr, Pelleas, Bors — assemble warbands and divide them among you. We will give chase.'

Idris and the other kings joined us, and up they spoke. 'Those forests are dangerous. The enemy can ambush us in there; they will lie in wait,' Idris complained.

Bedegran echoed his concern. 'Horses cannot manoeuvre in such thick woods. We would only do ourselves harm.'

Arthur could not quite hide his contempt. 'Since you fear, you will not be asked to undertake such dangerous duty. I have something else in mind for you.'

They did not like the way he scorned them, but it was their own fault. 'What is it that you require of us?' asked Maglos.

'You are to accompany Lord Ectorius and Myrddin back to Caer Edyn. I would have the shipyards protected and restored.'

'We are to become seamen?' sneered Idris. He thought it beneath him.

'Before this land is free, all my chieftains will be sailors. We will all fight as readily on the deck of a ship as from the back of a horse.' So saying, Arthur dismissed them to return with Myrddin and Ector, and we began the long and difficult task of running the barbarians to ground.

Idris and Bedegran had not overstated the danger, but had belittled the need. It had to be done: every barbarian who succeeded in eluding us would return to slay and burn again. They spurned Arthur's offer of peace, and had chosen the blade instead. Therefore we harried them mercilessly, allowing them neither rest nor respite. We pushed deeper and deeper into the wild hills driving the barbarians before us.

The hills north of the vale of Clyd are steep-sided and close set. The lakes are narrow, long, deep and cold: black-water realms ruled by keening eagles. Into these desolate hills we followed the enemy, pushing them further and further each day. And many days passed.

After many more days, we came to a place where a vast hump of land rises between two long lakes. The one is open to the sea and has no name; the other is called Lomond. A river called Dubglas joins them, running through a deep defile. And it was on this river that the barbarians chose to rally.

In this Baldulf showed wisdom. The cleft of the river was narrow, preventing a charge by the horses. And it sloped sharply up, giving the enemy the high ground they covet — if they cannot find a ford, a hill is best. And here they stood.

We attacked from below and the barbarians rushed down upon us. We fell back — as if overcome by their strength. Baldulf, eager to avenge himself for his defeats, pursued us. I still remember the gleam of their weapons in the hard sunlight as they plunged headlong down the scree-filled defile, screaming in triumphant rage. Those inhuman cries woke the stillness of the forest and made it quake. Down they rushed, with but one thought: to crush us utterly.

That was their mistake.

Arthur had held the second division in abeyance until Baldulf should commit himself. As the barbarians fell upon us, the hunting horn sounded and Pelleas, Cai, and Bors appeared up in the pass behind Baldulf. They had come round the hill and worked up the river pass from the opposite side.

Now Baldulf was trapped between two forces, and the larger of them held the high ground. Oh, the speed with which those cries turned to wails of anguish as the barbarians realized what had happened!

If at first they fought for revenge, now they fought for their lives. The battle was fierce, the fighting bitter and hot. With my spear I drove into the clash. My shield rattled with the blows rained upon it. My arm ached. But I struck and struck again, deadly, each stroke a killing stroke. The enemy fell before me.

The glens round about echoed with the clash of steel on steel, and the cries of the wounded and dying. With the larger force bearing down upon the barbarians from above, we gave ground below, coming at last to stand on the grassy banks of the lake.

This opened a way for Baldulf, but there was no place to run. Behind and on either hand stood Arthur's war host, and before him the deep waters of Lake Lomond, shining like polished silver. I do not know what I would have done in his place, but Baldulf fled into the lake. The lake!

It is not as foolish as it sounds. For there are a score or more islands in the Lomond waters. Some of these are mere rocks, fit only for gulls; others support huge stands of trees, and men might hide there. And by running from island to island they might cross the deep water and escape to the far side, which in some places is no great distance at all.

Cai came red-faced at a run. 'They are getting away. Do you want us to go after them?'

We stood on the shore and watched the enemy floundering across the water. Arthur did not reply.

'Please, Artos, let us finish it here, or we will be fighting all summer.'

Cai was right, of course. But in his excitement he had not thought it out.

'What would you do?' I asked him. 'Swim after them?'

'They are escaping!' he complained, thrusting his sword at the lake.

Arthur turned to Cai. 'Take the Cymbrogi and ride the

south track round the lake to the other side. Kill any who will not surrender.'

Cai saluted and hurried off to do as he was bid. Turning to me, the Duke said, 'Mount the rest of the warband and follow me.'

'Arthur, no!' I called after him. For I had guessed what he had in mind. 'It cannot be done.'

He stopped and turned round. 'Has anyone ever tried?'

'Well, no — I do not think so. But — '

'Then how do you know? An angel told you, perhaps?'

'Do not talk to me of angels, Arthur. God love you, I am in earnest!'

'I am in earnest, too, Bedwyr. I mean to end this battle without further loss of life. I can do that and no one even need get wet. I call that a victory.' He turned away again and called for Rhys to signal the formation. We mounted up at once and rode south, following Cai.

At intervals of a hundred paces Arthur placed one horse-man, and one footman every fifty paces between them. In this way he surrounded the whole southern half of Lake Lomond. Upon reaching the eastern shore we met Cai riding back along the lakeside.

'Did anyone come across?' asked Arthur.

'Only a few. Most drowned. They would not surrender, so they were put to the sword. The rest have taken refuge on the islands. I will continue south, lest they slip away from us.'

'There is no need,' Arthur replied.

'But they can swim across while we sit here talking. Once in the forest we will never find them again.'

'There is no need,' I explained, 'because Artos here has surrounded the lake.'

'Surrounded the lake!' exclaimed the red-haired firebrand. 'Am I hearing you aright?'

'You are,' I assured him sourly. I did not much esteem the idea of surrounding large bodies of water.

Cai sputtered for a moment, but could think of no suitable reply. In the end he sighed — a noise like a hornful of beer poured onto a bed of hot embers. 'Well, what are we to do now?'

'Wait,' said Arthur. 'Only wait.'

'We could wait here all summer!' Cai complained. His temper, bless him, was never far from the surface. 'Those islands have game and birds on them. There is water to drink. They could feed themselves for months!'

'Then we will wait months,' Arthur said firmly. 'We will wait until snow rises to our chins before I let another of my men be killed rooting out Baldulf.'

There could be no moving him when he got like that. So I let be. On the eastern bank of Lake Lomond we made camp and pitched our tents in among the tall pines and burly oaks.

Waiting for someone to starve to death is a tedious business. I do not advise it.

The expense in patience alone is staggering, and it is a cost that must be weighed carefully. I have never liked sieges for the same reason. Better a battle sharp and quick — a spear thrust to the ribs, the swift chop of a sword — than a lingering death and slow.

Twice a day riders took food to the groups of watchers ranged about the lake; this task alone proved most formidable — the food must be prepared, loaded onto a wagon, and delivered to the sentries. Every other day the sentries were relieved and other warriors took their places, for it was an onerous duty.

For the rest, we occupied ourselves as best we could. We hunted in the forests and fished the lake. The warriors wrestled and disported with one another in various games of skill and chance. And, above all, we watched.

Now and then we would catch a glimpse of the enemy on one of the islands. Usually this was at dusk or early in the morning. Mostly they stayed out of our sight — though once at the end of a long, rainy day there arose a cry from the islands and the barbarians came down to the water's edge to jeer at us and rouse us to come and fight them.

Cai was all for it, but Arthur would not. We watched them, and as night came on the calls died away. All through the night there were renewed cries, and we saw torches and fires burning on the islands. But these too died away in time, and night closed around all.

One morning I saw Pelleas sitting on a rock at the water's edge, gazing at the largest island before us. 'It is a poor way to die,' he said, as I sat down beside him.

'They do not have to die at all,' I pointed out. 'They can surrender. All they have to do is swear peace and Arthur will let them go free.'

'It is hard for men who hold no truth among themselves to believe anyone else will hold to it,' Pelleas said.

'Is it harder than death?'

'That we will see, Bedwyr ap Bleddyn,' he said thoughtfully.

Many more days passed. I knew we were coming to the end of it, however, one night when, a little after midnight, we heard splashes in the water and the next morning found bodies floating near the shore. Whether they had been killed by their own hand, died at the hands of their own people, or had drowned trying to escape, we could not tell. But it served to warn us that the end was nigh.

Arthur gave orders for the bodies to be fished from the lake and buried in the forest. Then he got into a boat and paddled out into the lake a short way. He stood in the boat and called to Baldulf.

'*Bretwalda*! Listen to me! I know you are starving. I know that you have no more food. Listen! You do not have to die. Swear peace to me and you will go free from this place. Peace, *Bretwalda*!'

Baldulf emerged from the foremost island. He waded out into the water to stare balefully at Arthur, and others crept out behind him. 'You mean to kill us! We defy you to the death!' His words spoke boldly, but his shoulders sloped and he stood as one who dares not hold his head erect. He was a beaten man.

'Why speak of death, *Bretwalda*, when you can live? Swear peace to me and go free.'

Baldulf was still standing in the water, trying to decide what to do when some of the men behind him threw themselves into the lake and began swimming to Arthur's boat. Others came towards where we stood on the shore. None of them had weapons.

When they reached the shore they lay on the rocks, gasping, exhausted, unable to rise even to drag themselves from the water, let alone raise blade against us. Their strength was gone.

Those standing behind Baldulf saw Arthur pulling their sword-brothers from the water and giving them places in his boat. They saw us hauling their companions from the lake rather than dashing out their brains with the butts of our spears. They saw that we did not kill them, and when they saw this all hesitation ceased; they flung themselves into the lake and swam to join their kinsmen on the shore. Thus, whether Baldulf would or no, the siege of Lake Lomond was finished.

We were most of the day gathering them up. Once the trickle started, the flood came from all directions. Of those who had followed Baldulf, only three thousand were left, mostly Angli. There were few Irish, and no Picti. The Picti, I believe, had succeeded in escaping into the forests and had not stayed to fight as the Angli did.

Baldulf was the last to come ashore, but he came in Arthur's boat. And he came with his proud head held high — as if *he* were the conqueror. Arthur helped him from the boat with his own hand.

Oh, but it is a strange sight, I tell you. To see blood-sworn enemies standing together as if never a harsh utterance had passed between them, as if the grim battles were but a grievance, as if good men and brave did not sleep in turf houses in ground hallowed by their own blood. . . as if war were only a word.

But Baldulf stood beside Arthur as if he had done nothing wrong. And it is the measure of Arthur's mercy that he offered his enemy the life his enemy would have denied him. Baldulf would not have hesitated a heartbeat in plunging the sword through Arthur's throat, and everyone knew it.

Arthur showed true nobility of spirit as he faced Baldulf and made peace between them. His terms were simple: leave Britain and never again come here to raid. When this was agreed to, Arthur ordered the barbarians to be fed and allowed to rest.

We stayed by Lomond lake two more days and then began the long march back south to the Clyd, and from there to Caer Edyn and the shipyards on the Fiorth where the Angli ships had been gathered.

In all it was a long, slow march, but we came to Caer Edyn in due time and put the Angli into the ships, charging them once again never to return to the Island of the Mighty on pain of death. We stood on the strand, watching the sails until they disappeared beyond the swells.

'It is over,' I told Arthur. Great was my relief to see the barbarian ships vanish from my sight.

'Pray God the peace holds,' Arthur replied, then turned to the warriors gathered there with us. He made to speak a word to them, but the Cymbrogi began cheering him and the cries of acclaim drowned out his voice. The cheering turned quickly to singing and Arthur was lifted up on the shoulders of his men.

In this way we entered Ector's fortress: our voices ringing in bold song, Arthur lifted high above us at our head, his fair hair shining in the sun, the gold of his torc ablaze at his throat and his sword, Caledvwlch, thrust towards heaven.

SEVEN

Myrddin was not at Caer Edyn when we arrived. 'He left seven days ago,' Ectorius reported. 'I think he was going back to Caer Melyn, but I am not certain. He did not tell anyone where he was going. I offered to send an escort with him, but he would not.'

Arthur wondered at this, but Myrddin is his own man and no one can ever tell what he is thinking, let alone what he will do next. Whatever it is, this much is certain: it will be the thing least expected.

'That is unfortunate,' replied Arthur, somewhat disappointed. 'I would have him share in the victory feast.'

The Duke was inclined to let the matter rest there, but Pelleas would not. 'Lord Arthur, I must go to him.'

'Why, Pelleas?'

'He may need my help.' Beyond that, Pelleas could make no answer. But I remembered Myrddin's strange behaviour at Lot's court and I, too, sensed something of the apprehension he felt.

'Of course,' replied Arthur slowly, gazing at Pelleas intently, 'if you think there is cause.'

Pelleas was not often insistent. He became so now. 'I do think so, lord.'

'Then go, and God go with you.' Arthur said. 'Choose six to accompany you, however. These hills are hostile yet. Better still, take one of the ships; it will be faster.'

The seven left as soon as fresh horses could be found and provisions gathered and stowed aboard the ship. I watched them go, feeling sorry for the warriors who would not now share in the feast they so richly deserved. But Arthur saw to it that the six who accompanied Pelleas received gold

222

armbands and knives for their portion, and they all departed happily.

The feast lasted three days and the battle was recounted in tales of valour and in song by Rhys, Arthur's harper. Though I still thought the hunting horn — which he so nobly sounded on the battlefield — more appropriate to his skill, I had to admit that he had improved his art by a fair measure. Indeed, to my surprise I found it no longer annoyed me to listen to the lad. At least, I could listen to him longer without becoming annoyed.

Ah, but he was no Myrddin Emrys.

The other kings had their harpers with them, too, so we suffered no lack of vaunting praise in our ears. Good Ectorius' brown beer and rich golden mead flowed freely. We drank up his entire winter's supply, I suspect. But it was to good cause.

I like a feast as well as the next man, but after three days I began to weary of celebration. This is rare, I know, but once and again I found myself wandering down among the ships — all of them tethered at the tideline in rows. Some rode at anchor further out in the Fiorth. Others had been beached, so that they could be put to better repair.

At dusk the fourth day, I was again drawn to the shipyard. The clean, sunwashed sky shone a burnished bronze, and the fresh sea wind blew away the smoke of Ector's hall that lingered in my hair and clothing. The solace of the shore was broken by the sharp cries of the wading birds that worked the mudflats for their suppers.

Arthur found me on the deserted deck of one ship whose keel was sunk in the slime of the tidewash. 'Hail, Bedwyr!' he called, slogging through the muck towards me. 'What do you here, brother?'

'I am thinking what it will be like to swing sword and heft spear on the rolling deck of a ship,' I replied, offering my hand as he pulled himself up over the side. 'And I am thinking it will take some getting used to.'

'No worse than a horse,' he observed, and laughed suddenly. 'Do you remember the shameful thing we did to Cunomor?'

I did remember. No more than twigs, we were just beginning weapons training with some older boys — one of them an insufferable braggart of thirteen summers named Cunomor ap Cynyr, the son of a small king in Rheged. After enduring this pompous ass and his bloated arrogance for a month or more, Arthur and I tampered with his tack and weapons, so that the heads fell off all his spears, and his saddle slipped sideways on his horse as he cantered round the practice field. He was made to appear so ridiculous that he could not hold his head erect all the rest of the summer.

'Poor old Cunomor,' I remarked, as Arthur's words brought the image of that red-faced youth to mind. 'I wonder if we will look as foolish trying to fight in these ships as he looked trying to maintain his toplofty dignity on that sliding saddle?'

'Worse!' laughed Arthur. It was good to see him happy. Arthur seemed to have come once more to himself — as Myrddin had said he would. Although the uncommon gravity of character persisted, it had sunk beneath the surface somewhat. He was building himself anew, I suppose, and the holy vision of the Kingdom of Summer was his solid foundation.

As if to confirm my observation he said, 'But we will prevail, Bedwyr. We must. Or Britain is lost — and much else besides.'

'I do not doubt it, Bear.' I turned my eyes away from his to view the wide, shimmering sweep of Muir Guidan. It was peaceful and good, with the soft light slowly fading in the deepening sky.

'We will leave soon,' Arthur said, scanning the horizon with me. 'After Lugnasadh.'

That was not many days hence. 'So? But, I thought you wanted to see the shipyards restored.'

'Ector has everything well in hand. Lot has agreed to stay on and oversee the building of the first ships. I am needed elsewhere. We have tribute to collect and horses to break before winter.'

'The tribute!' I had forgotten all about that. 'I would rather fight Picti than collect tribute!'

'We cannot do the one without the other,' Arthur said.

'Then you do not believe the peace we have made with Baldulf will hold?'

The Duke shook his head slightly. 'No, we have not seen

the last of Baldulf. And as for the Scoti and Picti — when did they ever heed a treaty?'

'We should have killed them and been done with it.'

'They would return in any case. This way they may learn something. Anyway, if we have to fight again I would prefer an enemy I know. But take heart, Bedwyr, the fighting is over for this year.'

'You are certain of that?'

'Yes.' He grinned and slapped me on the back. 'And we have won glory and honour — not to mention very much gold. We have done well.'

A few days after the autumn festival of Lugnasadh, we sailed for Caer Melyn with the morning tide. Arthur bade each battlechief take three or four ships under our command so that we could begin learning that subtle craft. Saints and angels, but they were more unwieldy than whales! It was like leading a warband mounted on pigs.

Arthur thought to serve warning that Britain's coasts were guarded once more, so we took our time, calling in at various ports along the way and taking every opportunity to allow our presence to be felt. We did learn something of the command of ships and collected tribute from the coastal realms as well, so it was time well spent.

Nevertheless, upon reaching Abertaff, I was glad to be quit of the pitching beast and set foot on solid ground again. We unloaded the horses and rode to the caer, tired, full of the pleasure of homecoming, eager to settle before the hearth with a jar and a fresh warm loaf.

As we entered the yard — oh, the greeting we received from those who had stayed behind! — Arthur became uneasy. 'What is wrong, Artos?' I asked. The loud halloos still filled our ears as the warriors greeted kith and kin.

He glanced quickly around as one expecting to see his hall in ruins, or a roof aflame. 'Myrddin is not here.'

'No doubt he is inside, pouring out the beer,' I ventured.

'He would be at the gates if he were here.' Arthur threw himself from the saddle and rushed into the hall. 'Where is Myrddin?' he demanded of the steward, a gaunt stick of a man, named Ulfin.

'The Emrys is gone, Duke Arthur,' Ulfin replied.

'Where?'

'He did not consult me, my lord.'

'Did he say when he will return?'

'He did not,' replied Ulfin stiffly. 'You know how he is sometimes.'

'Then where is Pelleas?' Arthur's voice rose.

'Lord Pelleas came here but left at once. He went in search of the Emrys, I believe.'

Alarm tingled along my spine. 'When did he leave?' I asked, thinking that wherever they had gone, one or the other should have returned by now.

Ulfin cocked his head in calculation. 'Just after Lugnasadh, my lord. A few days after. And he went alone.'

Arthur dismissed the steward and turned to me. 'I am not liking this, Bedwyr. Something is wrong. I am going to find them.'

'I will go, Artos,' I said. 'You are needed here. The kings will want an accounting of the northern battles.'

The Duke hesitated, fighting the logic. 'Where will you begin?'

'At Ynys Avallach,' I replied. 'Fret not, Bear, I will fetch them back before you know I am gone.'

'Take Gwalcmai with you,' Arthur replied, acquiescing at last. 'Or Bors — both, if you prefer.'

'Gwalcmai will serve.'

One night's sleep with a proper roof over my head, and I found myself in the saddle and on the trail once more. We departed in the grey dawn with the sun a vague rumour in the east, striking off for Ynys Avallach away to the south. To hasten our journey, I piloted one of our ships across Mor Hafren. Though another sea voyage was the last thing I would have chosen, it saved a good many days in the saddle. And I proved myself no mean pilot.

On making landfall, we rode with all haste, stopping only for water and food, and then moving on again without rest. In this way, we arrived at the Tor at dusk the second day from starting out. Evening mist rose from the lake and marshland round about, encircling the high-peaked Tor which poked through the vaporous white fog like an airy island rising above a flat sea of cloud. The steep green hill topped by its graceful palace seemed an enchanted realm — one of those Otherworldly mounds that appear and vanish as they will in the sight of bewildered men.

Now, as I have said, I had never been to the Glass Isle — though from both Myrddin and Pelleas I had heard about it since I was old enough to hear about anything. I felt I knew the place. And I experienced the uncanny sensation of returning after long absence to a home I had never seen before. The druids have a word for this, I think. I do not know what it is.

But, as we climbed the twisting path to the Fisher King's palace in the crimson and purple sunset, I found myself remembering small particulars as if I had grown up there — even to the lark song falling from the fiery sky high above the Tor. Gwalcmai was agog, with eyes the size of shield bosses as he gawked up at the soaring walls and towers. The polished gates — good old familiar gates I had entered a thousand times, and never once before — stood open, and we rode in to be met by the servants of King Avallach.

'They all look like Pelleas!' observed Gwalcmai, in hushed exclamation. 'Are all the Faery so made?'

'Why do you think they are called Fair Folk?' I asked him. Still, it was no less a marvel to me. While we had grown used to Pelleas and knew the truth, seeing others of that race made me want to believe all the idle and ignorant tales told about them.

'Look at that one!' Gwalcmai all but shrieked, as we entered the hall. He was beside himself with excitement. But then, he was from the Orcades.

'Stop pointing! That is the Fisher King,' I hissed. 'Is it the stables you are wanting for your bed?'

King Avallach advanced, dressed all in scarlet satin with a wide belt of silver plates like fish scales, the dark curls of his hair and beard oiled and glistening. His handsome face wore a smile of welcome and his arms opened wide to receive us. Though he could not have known who we were, I felt the quick warmth of his joy.

'God be good to you,' said Avallach, in a voice that came from somewhere deep in his broad chest as from inside a hollow hill. 'Rest and be welcome, friends.'

'Hail, King Avallach, I give you good greeting!' I said, touching the back of my hand to my head in salute.

'Do you know me?' the Fisher King asked.

'We have never met, Lord Avallach. I know you in name and appearance only. Myrddin Emrys has told me of you.' At my mention of Myrddin, the king nodded. 'I come to you in the name of Arthur, Duke of Britain.'

'Yes, yes,' replied Avallach. 'You are friends of Arthur's?'

'I am Bedwyr ap Bleddyn of Rheged, and — '

'So at last I meet the renowned Bedwyr!' roared the great king in his delight. 'God's blessing on you, Bedwyr ap Bleddyn. Arthur has told me much about his sword-brother.'

'This is Gwalcmai ap Lot of Orcady,' I said, indicating the dumbstruck northerner beside me.

At this the Fisher King stiffened and his gaze narrowed; he regarded Gwalcmai as if he were a new kind of serpent, whose fangs had yet to be tried for poison. I wondered at this and then remembered what Myrddin had told me: Morgian, Queen of Air and Darkness, was Gwalcmai's grandmother. His kin!

Stupid! I groaned inwardly and kicked myself for the fool I was. Why, oh why, had I not realized this before now? I could not have chosen a worse companion for this journey!

'Welcome, Gwalcmai ap Lot,' intoned Avallach tersely.

I do not think Gwalcmai noticed his cool reception. I do not think he noticed anything at all — except the entrancing beauty of the woman approaching from across the hall. She had entered from behind Avallach and walked towards us purposefully.

I know that I have never seen a woman more fair in face and form. I know that I never shall see another the equal of the Lady of the Lake — for it was she. I knew her, as I had known Avallach, from Myrddin's descriptions. Oh, but his words did not tell the tenth part of her elegance and grace.

Her hair was long and golden, like sunlight falling on a spring-flowered lea. Her skin was white as the snowcrest on a bending bough, or rarest alabaster; and her lips were red as the petals of winter roses against the milky whiteness of her skin. She looked upon us with eyes the colour of forest pools, and just as calm. The delicate arch of her brows spoke of nobility and pride.

She wore a long tunic of sea-green silk, worked in the most wonderfully ornate filigree of red-gold, and over this a sleeveless mantle of russet, embroidered in gleaming silver. At her throat she wore a slender torc of braided gold, such as a Cymry queen would wear. But she *was* a queen, of course, or once had been.

'Truly, she is a goddess!' Gwalcmai croaked in a stricken whisper.

'She is Myrddin's mother, mind,' I told him, finding it difficult to credit the truth of it myself.

Charis came to me and kissed me on the cheek in greeting. 'May the peace of Christ be yours, Bedwyr,' she said, in a voice soft and low.

'You know me, lady?' I gasped, astonished that she should utter my name.

My features must have trumpeted my amazement, for the lady laughed nicely and said, 'How should I not?'

'But I have never been here before this moment,' I stammered.

'Not in the flesh, no,' Charis agreed. 'But you were the unseen spirit at Arthur's shoulder when he sojourned here last winter.'

'He spoke of me?'

'Oh, he spoke of you to be sure,' replied Avallach. 'If he spoke about nothing else, he waxed vocal of his brother Bedwyr.'

'That is how I knew you,' Charis said. 'And it is the same way you knew me — from my son, no doubt.' She turned her eyes to Gwalcmai, who stood entranced beside me.

'I present to you Gwalcmai ap Lot, of Orcady,' I said, nudging him in the ribs with my elbow. But it was no use, he gawked at her as if he were dull-witted and mute.

At the mention of his name, a change came over Charis — although I noticed no outward alteration of expression or demeanour. Yet I felt something flow out from her as a sudden rush of warmth directed at Gwalcmai. Looking him steadily in the eye, she placed a fair hand on either of his shoulders, put her face close to his and kissed him on both cheeks.

'May the peace of Christ be yours, Gwalcmai,' she said.

'And with you also, my lady,' he whispered, his cheeks blushing red as foxglove.

'You are welcome here,' she told him solemnly; then brightened at once and declared, 'Come, this is a pleasant end to a good day. We will sup together and you will tell me how my son has fared in the wider world since last I saw him.'

By this I knew that neither Myrddin nor Pelleas had stopped at the Glass Isle, and that our search must quickly continue.

We were conducted to a smaller chamber off the hall, where a long board had been set up with chairs around it. There was red wine in a crystal jar and cups of silver beside it. The wine was poured and we drank, and began to describe all that had happened since Myrddin and Arthur had visited Ynys Avallach last winter. And there was much to tell.

Gwalcmai picked at his food with his knife. Had he been a bird I know he would have eaten more heartily. But he sat limply in his chair and gazed at the Lady of the Lake, with such a rapt and insipid expression I wonder that she neither flew from his sight, nor shamed him with scornful laughter.

I was mightily grateful that I was not a maid that must endure his bland and sickly glances. But then, the lady Charis was twice the lady I would have been!

Despite Gwalcmai's bad manners, the evening passed agreeably — indeed, it seemed as if it fled like the too-brief melody of a nightingale. We slept that night on beds of finest linen over fresh-cut rushes, and I awoke the next morning thinking that no man ever slept better or more comfortably.

But awake I did, and when we had broken fast I uttered my regrets that we must continue our journey that very day. As I did not wish to alarm Charis — how could I live with myself if I caused that fairest lady pain! — I told her nothing of our search for Myrddin, but merely affirmed that we were about the Duke's business and must press on with all haste.

We made awkward farewells and soon were winding our

230

way down the side of the Tor and across the causeway as the new day's light pearled the eastern horizon. 'Myrddin has not been here,' I told my companion. 'I feared as much.'

Gwalcmai started, as one awakening from a dream. He peered back over his shoulder at the looming Tor. 'Have you any idea where he would go?'

'To Llyonesse,' I answered, for the dread in my heart was growing and I remembered where and when I first had felt it: that day on the shore when Myrddin told me about Morgian.

I began to sense that where Morgian was to be found, that is where I would find Myrddin. Pelleas had guessed it too, and that is why he had been so anxious about Myrddin, and so eager to go after him.

'Where is this place Myrddin has gone — this Llyonesse?' wondered Gwalcmai.

His question swung me round to face him. 'You have never heard of it?' I asked.

'If I knew, I should not ask where it is,' he replied lightly, with innocence I judged genuine. 'Do *you* not know where it is?'

I stared at him hard and decided he was telling the truth, then turned back to the track before us. 'It is in the south; that is all I know.'

Llyonesse. This was the source of my fear, the touchstone of my deepest dread. I knew it now: Myrddin had gone to confront Morgian. Well, my path was clear before me. I must go to Llyonesse to find him.

We stopped at a small settlement not far from the Tor to ask the way, and were curtly told by the chief — while the people made the sign against evil behind their backs — to keep on south and west and I would find it. . . if that is what I desired.

I remember little of the journey. The days and nights were all one to me. It seemed as if we rode through a world gradually dying. Barren moorland stretched before us and the lonely wind moaned; at night it cried softly as it passed. With every laboured step the sense of futility and oppression increased. The weight! The weight on my heart dragged at my spirit.

We came at last to a Fair Folk stronghold and my heart

231

rose for a moment with the hope that we might find Myrddin, or at least hear word of his passing. To my dismay, the palace and fortress were deserted. I did not bother searching. There was nothing to be found — even the gorse had shrivelled and died.

In any event, Myrddin was not there. So we pressed on, following the coastline further south. Gwalcmai attempted to lift our spirits, but his songs died on the wind. No fair word could be uttered in that place.

For we passed through a wasted land: stunted, twisted trees; barren, rock-crusted hills and vacant hollows; stinking fens, vile bogs oozing like pus-filled wounds. In many places gaping rents had opened in the earth and these steamed with a noxious yellow mist that seeped along the trailways, obscuring the way so that we feared plunging headlong into one of the hell holes.

Nothing green showed. No bird called. No creature large or small made its home here any more. All was death and desolation — a ruined realm made hideous by the evil practised within its boundaries. It was beyond my imagining even to consider what might have caused such devastation. Whoever or whatever Morgian was, she apparently possessed a maleficent power above anything I might conceive.

Fear quickened like a viper in my breast, but I rode on, not caring any more what might happen to me. I prayed. I called upon the Great Good God to defend me. In silence I chanted the mighty psalms of strength and praise. I called down Jesu's grace upon that evil-blighted place.

Gwalcmai rode close beside me and we upheld one another. In whispered confidences I told him of Jesu, the Saviour God. And that son of Orcady believed. Whatever might happen to our bodies, our souls were safe in the Sure Strong Hand. There was some small comfort in that, at least.

Despite all, our steps grew slower, the way less clear. And then, when I thought we must abandon the track altogether, I saw a sea crag rising up just ahead, sharpsided, restless water surging around its jagged roots. Sea birds soared high above it and, strangely, many crows among them.

Carrion birds! By this I knew where Myrddin would be

found. Alive or dead, I knew not, but our search had ended.

'Stay with the horses,' I told Gwalcmai. He made no reply, but dismounted and tethered the horses to a blasted stump. I left him sitting on the stump, with his drawn sword resting across his knees.

A prayer on my lips, I began the long climb up the rough headland, stopping to call out from time to time as I climbed. I expected no answer and heard none. . .

I found Myrddin perched on the topmost cliff, hunched upon a rock, his ragged cloak wrapped tightly round him though the day was stifling. Shattered scrags of heat-scarred stone lay heaped and toppled like ruins round about. He was alive, God be praised! And he turned his face towards me as I scrambled to him.

I beheld his face and nearly fell into the sea. His eyes — sweet Jesu! The eyes in his head were dead embers, cold, extinguished, the once-bright lustre of those matchless golden eyes leached white as ash!

His brows were singed, his lips blistered and cracked, the skin over his cheeks burnt and peeling. His hair was ragged and matted with blackened blood.

'Myrddin!' I ran to him, sobbing, half with relief to find him alive at all, and half for pity at what had been done to him. 'What has happened to you? What has she done to you?' I gathered him in my arms, like a mother cradling a dying child.

When he spoke, his voice was a harsh, brittle whisper forced out with great effort. 'Bedwyr, you have come at last. I knew someone would come. I knew. . . I thought it would be Pelleas. . . '

Pelleas! What had happened to Pelleas? I scanned the cliffside, but saw no sign of anyone anywhere.

'I have been waiting. . . waiting. . . I knew Arthur would. . . send someone. . . to me. . . Where is Pelleas?'

The pitiful sound of that fine voice, now broken, brought tears to my eyes. 'Do not speak, Emrys. Please, rest you now. I will care for you.'

'It is well. . . she is gone. . . '

'Morgian?'

He nodded and licked his bruised lips. This started the

blood seeping down his chin. He struggled to form the words.

'Please, Emrys,' I pleaded, weeping freely. 'Do not speak. Let us go from here.'

Myrddin clutched at my sleeve, and his dead white eyes wandered unseeing in his head. 'No. . .' he rasped. 'All is well. . . she has fled. . .'

I did not at first credit what he was telling me. 'Gwalcmai is with me; we have horses. Let us bear you away from this hateful place. She may return.'

'She is gone. . . her power is broken. I have faced her. . . Morgian is beaten. . . gone. . . she is gone. . .' He shivered and closed his eyes, leaning heavily against me. 'I am tired. . . so tired. . .'

Swoon or sleep, it was blessed relief to him. With difficulty I carried him on my shoulders over the rocks and down to where Gwalcmai waited with the horses.

Gwalcmai shuddered upon seeing Myrddin. 'What happened to him?' he asked in a horrified whisper.

'I do not know,' I answered, bending the truth as far as it would go. How could I tell him Morgian, his blood kin, had done this? 'When he wakes he may tell us.'

'Where is Pelleas, then?' he asked, lifting his head to regard the sea crag once more.

'Perhaps Pelleas was delayed elsewhere. We will pray that this is so.'

Night came too quickly to that blighted spit of land thrust out into the sea. We made a camp in one of the pocked hollows and Gwalcmai dragged in enough dead wood to keep the fire through to morning. I found water and made a broth with some of the herbs we had among our provisions. This I heated in my clay bowl and roused Myrddin, so that he could drink it.

He seemed the better for his sleep, and drank down all the broth and asked for some of the hard bread we had. He ate it in silence, then lay back and slept once more.

I watched him through the night, but he slept soundly. Towards sunrise I slept while Gwalcmai watched, awakening a little while later. Myrddin stirred as we were making ready to leave.

'You must help me, Bedwyr,' he rasped, and I noticed his voice was somewhat stronger.

'I will do whatever you ask, lord.'

'Make some mud and bind my eyes.' I hesitated and he flung out a hand to me. 'Do as I say!'

With the water and clay I made some mud and daubed it over his eyes as Myrddin directed me. Then, tearing a length from my tunic, I bound his eyes, mud and all. Myrddin felt his bandages with his fingers and pronounced my work well done.

In this way we began the journey back — blind Myrddin sitting the saddle, erect, silent — Gwalcmai and I taking it in turn leading his horse, making our long slow return to the land of the living.

EIGHT

Three days later, at the end of our scant provisions, we passed out of Llyonesse. I did not look back. That melancholy land had left its dark stain on my soul.

Myrddin held his own counsel all the while. He sat upright in the saddle, straight and silent, eyes wrapped in the mud-stained cloth, his mouth twisting now and then in a grimace of pain — or loathing.

We journeyed through the day, and the night. When we finally stopped for rest, we had put a fair distance between us and the borders of that dismal, desolate land. I made camp near a stream and Gwalcmai killed two plump hares for our meal. These we roasted and ate in silence, too tired to speak. There was grass for the horses, and good water for us all.

Though the night was mild, I made a small fire — more for the light than the warmth. We sat together as the stars kindled in the deep autumn sky. Slowly night drew its dark wing over us, and Myrddin began to speak. In a voice as dry as winter husks, he began to declaim:

'Myrddin I was; Myrddin I remain. Henceforth all men will call me Taliesin.

'Earthborn am I, but my true habitation is the Region of the Summer Stars.

'I was revealed in the land of the Trinity; and with my Father I was moved through the entire Universe. I shall remain until Doomsday upon the face of the Earth, until Jesu returns in triumph.

'Who is there to say whether my flesh is meat or fish? For I was created from nine forms of elements: from the Fruit of Fruits, from the first fruit of the Lord God at the world's beginning.

'The Magician of magicians created me.

'From the essence of all soils was I made, renowned blood flowing in me. Peoples are made, re-made, and will be made again. Fairest Bard, I can put into song what the tongue can utter.

'Hear my bold telling:

'At my calling the small-souled scattered like sparks from a firebrand flung from high Eryri.

'I was a dragon enchanted in a hill; I was a viper in a lake; I was a star with a silver shaft; I was a red-scaled spear in the grasp of a Champion.

'Four fifties of smoke will follow me; five fifties of bond-maids will serve me.

'My pale yellow horse is swifter than any sea-gull; swifter than the hunting merlin.

'I was a tongue of flame in fire; I was wood in a Beltane blaze that burned and was not consumed.

'I was a candle; a lantern in the hand of a priest; a gentle light that glows in the night.

'I was a sword and a shield to Mighty Kings; a blade of excellent craft in the hand of the Pendragon of Britain.

'Like my father, I have sung since I was small. The harp is my true voice.

'I wandered; I encircled. I called upon the Swift Sure Hand to deliver me. I attacked.

'Righteousness was my only weapon; the courage of the Saviour burned in me. The battle frenzy of Lleu was not more glorious than my golden rage.

'I wounded an enchanted beast: a hundred heads on it, and a fierce host at the root of its tongue — a black, forked tongue; nine hundred claws it raised against me. I slew a crested serpent in whose skin six fifties of souls are tortured.

'I shall yet cause a field of blood, and on it seven hundreds of warriors; scaly and red my shield and blade, but bright gold my shield ring.

'A warrior I have been; a warrior I will be.

'I have slept in a hundred realms and dwelt in a hundred hill forts; a hundred hundred kings will yet salute me.

'Wise Druid, prophesy to Arthur!

'Tell the Days of the Bright Champion: what has been, what is to come; was, and will be.

'The Brilliant Shining One will make his people; they will be called by his name: the Sure Hand. Like lightning he will quicken the Host of Forever!'

I stared at him in wonder. Myrddin, a man I knew well and seemed now not to know at all. The bard's *awen* was on him and his face glowed — whether with the light of the fire, or with its own mysterious light, I could not tell. He sat, nodding his bandaged head to the cadence, hearing the echo of his words in the empty reaches of the night.

'Why do you wonder at what I tell you?' he asked abruptly. 'You must know that I speak the truth. Nevertheless, guard yourself against the wiles of the Enemy, my friends. Oh, but never fear. Never fear! Hear me, Bedwyr! Hear me Gwalcmai! Hear the Soul of Wisdom and know the power of the High King we serve.'

So saying, he began to tell what had happened in Llyonesse. Blind, his eyes bound, he lifted his raw voice to the glittering sky, and he began to speak it out, slowly, haltingly at first, but more quickly as the words formed in a strong and steady stream. This is what he said:

'I observed evensong in the Shrine of the Saviour God, something I have long wanted to do. I regretted passing so close to Ynys Avallach and not stopping to see Charis and Avallach, but I could not let them know what I intended.

'Upon entering Llyonesse, I rode to Belyn's palace and found it — like the Fair Folk settlement in Broceliande — deserted. But why? That is what I could not understand.

'What had happened to the Fair Folk? What disaster had overtaken them? How could it have been accomplished? What purpose was served in their murder? Oh, yes, that is how I came to see it: wilful and wanton murder. And so it was. But why? Great Light, why?

'I could not rest. The more I thought about it, the more

troubled I became. That some dread design of Morgian's lay behind it, I did not doubt — '

'Morgian!' Gwalcmai gasped.

'I am sorry, Gwalcmai,' said Myrddin softly. 'It is true. But you need feel no shame — the fault is hers alone.'

Gwalcmai's contrition was pure. He knelt down before Myrddin, bowed his head and stretched forth his hands in supplication. 'Forgive me, Emrys. If I had known. . . '

'But you are guiltless, lad. I blame you not, neither should you hold yourself to blame. You did not know.'

'What of Morgian's design?' I asked, itching with curiosity to hear the rest.

Myrddin shook his bandaged head. 'I could in no wise determine what that design might be. Waking or sleeping, the questions assailed me like hornets disturbed in their nest. Why? Why? Why?

'I prayed to the Illuminating Spirit to teach me this purpose. I fasted and prayed to learn it. I fasted and prayed like a very bishop, all the time riding deeper into Llyonesse.

'Then, upon waking one morning, it came into my mind that Morgian, Queen of Air and Darkness, was fear driven. It is so simple! Why did she act now after all these years? Because something drove her to act — and that something was fear. Morgian was *afraid*.

'Now what could cause such fear? Think! What does darkness fear but the light that reveals its secret empty heart? What does evil fear but goodness?

'I ask you, Bedwyr: who then stands between Morgian and her dread desires? Who is the Summer Lord? Whose reign signals the beginning of the Kingdom of Summer?'

'Arthur's,' I answered; I had heard him say as much.

'Yes. . . oh, yes. It is Arthur she fears. His power waxes greater in this worlds-realm and she cannot abide that. For Arthur's power to grow greater, hers must decrease. And that is the thing most hateful to her.

'She fears Arthur, yes. But more she fears *me*. For I am the one who upholds Arthur in his power. This is the way of it: such power as Arthur has is my own. Without me he would fail, for he is not strong enough yet to stand alone. So, if she would conquer Arthur, she must first destroy me. And she is ravenous with hatred and fear.

'By reason of this driving fear, I determined, she had destroyed the Fair Folk settlement. Why? Because out of the remnant of Atlantis' lost children will come her doom. It is true. This much I have seen — though in essence only; I know not its form.

'Therefore she must destroy all the Fair Folk if she is to save herself. In the same way, I weened, she must soon move against Avallach and Charis at the Tor — as she had moved against the Fair Folk in Broceliande, and against Belyn in Llyonesse. She must destroy them all if she is to earn a measure of rest from her unrelenting fear. And again, she must also destroy me.

'A poisoned draught and a knife — but Pelleas prevented it. That was a clumsy, childish attempt. No credit to me, it nearly succeeded — for the obvious fact that I expected more from the Supreme Bitch Goddess than infantile trickery.

'That in itself is a riddle. But the answer is perfectly simple. Pelleas and I once stood within the very circle of her power, yet we had not been destroyed. Why? I will tell you: she had not the strength to do it. It was a lie! Everything about her is a lie! She could enchant, she could charm and beguile; but she could not destroy outright. I tell you she could not, or surely she would have done so.'

Myrddin seemed to forget who was there with him and imagined instead that it was Pelleas. It did not matter. I was fascinated by all he said. For I heard in his words the veiled brightness of truth too dazzling for utterance.

'How stupid I have been! Like so much else about Morgian, the depth of her vaunted power was a lie! Yet, in all events, it was sufficient to the task. And it had grown more potent of late. Broceliande was the first warning of what was to come.

'Oh, Morgian had not been idle. Gathering the scattered threads of her force, concentrating the far-flung strands of her energies, marshalling the vast, twisted array of her weaponry — this had been all her work since her failed attack on me. And she had grown mighty through it.

'Make no mistake, she meant to finish what she had begun. And that soon — before Arthur grew too powerful in the Light, before the flowering of the Summer Realm rendered her weak and harmless.

'So she must seek me out and destroy me. Once that was accomplished, there would be nothing to restrain her any more. She would grow from strength to strength as her seeds bore fruit. And her evil would be beyond imagining.

'I despaired. I tell you the truth, I did. I knew all this; I saw it all clearly, but I was powerless to prevent it. Probably I was already too late. My spirit cried within me. I wept for my weakness.

'Yet, by the courage of the Living Light, I gazed into the very shadow of despair, into the black ugly heart of the thing I have hated and feared all my life. And I saw. . . this I saw: glory to the Saving God, I saw that my solitary hope lay in taking the fight to her. I must be the one to confront her.

'A scant hope, you may think. But it was, I considered, the only weapon I had, and all that would be given me if I did not take it. Well, I took it. I embraced it. I tell you, I gloried in it. I prayed to the All-Wise God for the wisdom to use it well.

'Then I waited. I fasted and prayed, and when I felt the quickening of my soul I came here to this place.' By this, I think he meant the sea crag where I had found him. 'Taking no thought for myself — whether I might live or die, I tell you it did not matter any more! I would gladly give my life to banish the Darkness once for all.

'Curiously, once my feet were on the path, comfort was granted me in the form of understanding. For at last I understood that Morgian was trapped by her fear — her fear of Arthur and of me, and of the Kingdom of Summer — and she was far more desperate than she could allow anyone to know.

'Lord and Saviour, it is true! Do you see? It is the fear — the insatiable fear that is companion to great evil. She that must ever appear Sovereign of Fear, is herself its servant.

'And this is her failing. Great Light! This is her weakness! The Queen of Air and Darkness can never admit her fear, her unbearable weakness, even to herself. She must appear to hold the very power she lacks. She must seem always to possess the very thing which remains for ever beyond her grasp.

'Oh, but I have feared. Great Light, you know *I* have felt the terror of death and the despair of weakness. I have known failure and grief. I have borne the pitiable short-fall of frailty, yes, and the loathsome impotence of the flesh.

'I have known and endured these things. I have drained the cup that was poured out for me, and I did not thrust it aside. I understood that this was my strength. By this I would conquer.

'Do you see it now? It is beautiful, is it not? The designs of God are ever subtle, but beautiful in their subtlety. . . ever glorious. So be it!

'I tell you I rejoiced in this knowledge. I made it my battle song; I forged sword and shield from it. I wore it like a helm and battleshirt. And I rode to meet the trial I had avoided for so long.'

Here Myrddin paused, reached out a hand for his cup. I gave it to him and he drank. It was full dark now. The night air had turned cool. The dew would form heavy tonight, but the fire would keep us dry.

I tugged Myrddin's cloak closer about him, took the cup from his hand when he had finished, and poured more water into it. Then I settled back, pulling my own cloak round my shoulders, and I waited for Myrddin to speak again. From the branches of a nearby tree, a nightingale began its lilting song. The voice of melancholy; sweet sorrow in melody.

As if this were the signal he had been waiting for, Myrddin began to speak again. But his voice had changed. There was sadness in his tone, and pain. A pain deep and wide as grief.

'I did not know where or how I should meet her. Nevertheless, I considered that she would know of my coming and likely would meet me before I wandered very far, for she could not abide the light that was in me. In this I was not mistaken.

'I thought it would be at night, in darkness. I trusted her to choose her element, and she did.

'In the time between times, when the veil between this worlds-realm and the next grows thin, she came to me. I had camped for the night in the ruin of an oak grove. I had slept a little, but grew restless and awoke. The moon had slipped low in the sky, but it shone enough to see by.

'She rode a black horse, and was dressed much as when we had met that day in Belyn's court: black cloak and mantle, tall black boots, long gloves, her face hidden beneath a hood. She had come alone, and this surprised me. For she certainly knew why I had come.

'She knew, but her self-deception argued for boldness, and her debauched pride exulted in her superior strength. She came alone because her vanity demanded it.

'Yet, if she was wary, she was also calm. The swarming force of her hate did not gather at once. Curiosity, I think, held it back for the moment. She could neither understand nor credit my intention. Such is her intelligence, however, that she would not attack a foe until she knew the weapons he would use.

'Of course, my weapons were unknown to her: courage, hope, faith. I displayed them fully and without guile, but she could not discern them.

'I spoke first. "So, Morgian," I said, rising as she approached. "I knew you would find me; I prayed it would be soon."

'She answered me. "You are far from home, Myrddin Wylt," she said, as she swung herself down from the saddle. I could read nothing from her tone.

'"Perhaps," I allowed. "We are both strangers here, I think."

'She rankled at my suggestion. "You flatter yourself too highly if you think we meet as equals. I am as far above your small powers as the sun above the barren earth you toil over, as high as the hawk above the flea that troubles your wretched flesh. We are *not* met as equals."

'"Once you offered me friendship," I replied. A strange thing to say; I do not know why I said it. Could it be that God's mercy is such that it could embrace even Morgian? On Jesu's behalf then, I made the offer. "It is not too late, Morgian. Turn back, I will meet you. You can be redeemed."

'She scorned it, as I knew she would. "Do you think to bind me with that, dear Myrddin? Do you think your contemptible god interests me at all?"

"'The offer of peace has been made, Morgian. I do not withdraw it."

'She let fall the reins from her hand and approached me slowly. "Is that why you have come?" I could feel the icy heat of her hatred begin to burn.

"'Why do you hate me so?"

'She made a motion with her hand and my camp fire leapt higher. Whereupon she lifted the veil from her face so that I should admire her dire beauty. Such wasted splendour, such tainted elegance. Oh, her allure is astonishing, dazzling; and as potent as her spite — and that is well nigh boundless. Yet, to see her is to know the mocking futility of the gilded tomb.

She pouted, and even her frown was beguiling. "But I do not hate you, Myrddin. I feel nothing for you at all. You are nothing to me — less than nothing."

'It was a lie, of course. Mistress of Lies, she owned no other language. "Then why waste the breath to tell me?" I asked. "Why bother to confront me now?"

'Morgian's eyes flashed. "What I do, I do to please myself. If it amuses me to speak to you, that is reason enough." She sidled round me, her palms pressed together, gloved finger-tips touching her lips. "Besides, we are kin, you and I. What would people say of me if I refused hospitality to a kinsman?" She was still uncertain. She suspected treachery who could no longer apprehend the truth.

"'You elude my question, but I will answer for you, shall I? You hate me because you fear me, Morgian. In this you are one with the rest of unenlightened humanity: fools hate what they fear."

"'You are the fool, cousin!" she hissed. The words were knife pricks. "I do *not* fear you! I fear no man!" The flames jumped still higher. Then, as if the fit had never occurred, she smiled and lightly stepped closer. "I told you, I feel nothing for you."

"'No? Then why have you come to kill me?"

"'Kill you?" She affected a laugh. The sound was wretched and pathetic. "Dear Myrddin, do you imagine your life means anything to me? Your existence is beneath my regard."

"'You tried to destroy me once and failed," I reminded

her. "It was a child's trick, and still you could not succeed in it. You need not bother to deny it, Nimue."

'She laughed again; the flames crackled ominously. I sensed that she was very close to striking, but I did not know how the blow would come. "Oh, well done, Myrddin! I compliment you on your great sagacity. You guessed that it was me at last, did you? Well, Wise Myrddin, this time you will not fare so well. This time your precious Pelleas will not interfere."

'I was expecting her to strike, and still she caught me off my guard. The force of her hatred hit me like a physical blow. My lungs were squeezed by a tremendous pressure, and I felt as if I were falling beneath the weight of the world — as if Yr Widdfa itself had been dropped upon my chest. I staggered backwards, fighting to stand upright, struggling to breathe. My vision dimmed. The crushing weight forced me to my knees.

'Morgian was delighted with her handiwork. "You see? I could crush you without a word. . . But I will not."

'Instantly, the weight left me. I pitched forward on knees and elbows, lungs aching, my breath coming in raking gasps.

'Morgian stood over me. "Death is but the beginning, my love," she whispered. "I have often contemplated your destruction, and I mean to savour it to the full. I have waited so long."

'She began circling round me slowly, drawing off her gloves. Then, holding her hands shoulder high, palms outward, she began to chant in the Dark Tongue. I saw eyes — scars burned into her flesh and painted in black and silver on her palms in the form of eyes. As she spoke, these seemed to glimmer and gleam as if alive.

'And swelling up behind her I saw the form of darkness — a spreading darkness surrounding her — everywhere she moved it moved with her; it was alive, I tell you! This thing, this living shadow began to seethe and writhe. Like a mass of snakes it drew together and separated.

'I looked, and there now stood around her six huge forms — demons they were, called from some nameless hell to witness her great victory. They stood with her, watching,

245

the frigid vapours of their awful malevolence seeping into the air.

'Dread they were, but beautiful to behold. Achingly beautiful. Like Morgian, they were exquisite in their perfection. But it was the perfection of empty precision; soulless and insensate, lethal, immaculate in its vanity.

'To see them — oh, just to see them stopped the warm heart beating in my breast. I grew cold; my flesh tingled with the terrible malice of their presence. The stench of rotting corpses filled the air. Tears streamed down my cheeks.

'Morgian stepped nearer. She was in the full flowering of her fell glory. Gloating, her eyes dancing with malice, she exuded venom. The eyes excised on her palms radiated the force of her wickedness like waves rippling out from a stone plunged into deep water. This was calculated to unnerve me.

'But I was not unnerved, neither did I fear. In truth, once I had weathered the first storm of her hatred, I knew that she could not touch my soul. She might kill me — Ha! Any brute barbarian can do that with a sharpened stick! — but Morgian could not destroy me. She could not make me renounce the Light, or die cursing my Lord.

'I found my voice. "Do your worst, Morgian. I will not be moved. In the name of Jesu, Son of the Living God, I possess the strength to defy you."

'These words had scarcely left my mouth when I became aware of wings around me. Strange, I know — but there is no other explanation. Wings! Enfolding me, sheltering me, protecting me. Whether the wings of angels, or of the blessed Christ himself, I cannot say. But I was surrounded. Peace flowed out to me. Peace in that place of horror. Think of it! I knew beyond all doubt my Lord and King stood over me. His Swift Sure Hand upheld me.

'Morgian sensed the shift in the battle. It made her angry, though she could not see the source of my courage. "Words! Words! Fool of a Prophet! Your insipid god cannot save you. No power on earth can save you now!" She raised her hands and crossed them above her head, and began calling down the powers of the Air and Darkness.

'She chanted her ghastly incantations, and I heard the frozen scream of the howling void.

'So strange, but even then — at the very moment her power had reached its full height, she had lost. I had not given in to her. In the face of her hate, I did not hate. Neither did I cower or flee.

'Great Light, the Enemy's power is so fragile! The devils can use only what we ourselves will give them. Do you see? Give them nothing, and their power fails; it falls like a spent arrow, like a blade broken and blunted.

'Morgian railed at me, she cursed. She summoned the demons of hell to her bidding. Oh, you should have seen her. It was terrible to behold. But the wings enfolded me, I did not fear.

'She summoned a gale of fire. The rage! The rage and hate surged out of her in a vile and poisonous stream. Dark lightning flashed and the blighted grove began to burn. Branches flamed and fell around me; trees became torches and toppled one over another. But I felt no heat; no flame touched me!

'Emboldened, I called to her. "You see the truth at last, Morgian: by the power of the Holy One, the True God, I am saved. You cannot harm me. Greater is He that is in me, than he that is in you. All honour and glory and power belong to Him. So be it!"

'This she could not abide. Neither could she stand against it. For so quickly had she consumed her strength that she now had nothing left; she was exhausted. She could not even hold up her hands any longer.

'I taunted her. "Come, Morgian!" I cried. "Your lords are watching. Show them how their creature wields the weapons she has been given."

'Her eyes were wild with madness and fury. The fire mounted still higher. Trees burst with the savage heat. But the grass beneath my feet did not so much as wither. Cool, sweet air bathed me.

'Exultation swept through me; I opened my mouth and sang. I sang hymns of praise to my Lord. I sang a song of victory to my King. And I danced before him. The demons crowding behind Morgian shimmered in the lashing heat, then faded and vanished.

'Morgian's face went black as the evil swelled within her; murderous rage held her in its jaws and shook her. She screamed and her scream could have felled an army!

'She leapt at me, her fingers like claws, raking. I threw my arms up to protect my face, but attack did not come.

'I heard a voice call her name. "Morgian!" The sudden shout stopped her. I lowered my hands and looked; a man appeared on a horse, galloping towards her through the flames. . . '

Myrddin paused; at the mention of the man his voice had become heavy with grief. 'You recognized the man,' I said.

'I knew him,' Myrddin replied. 'May God save him, it was Lot.'

'Lot!' Gwalcmai and I shouted together.

Myrddin bent his head slowly. 'It was. Even through the smoke and flames, I knew him.

'He called to her. Morgian stood frozen in her malice. But Lot raced to her, leaned low and gathered her up; he hauled her up before him in the saddle. The horse reared, hooves flashing at me, and they fled.

'I called to her: "Come back, Morgian! Let us finish what you have begun." But they did not turn back. Anger surged up within me. And, God help me, I went after her. I did not want her to escape.

'At the edge of the grove they stopped and half-turned towards me. I thought that Morgian would face me. But she had one charm left. She threw her hands over her head and screamed the spell. Hideous, it was a last cry of defiance and despair.

'I halted. Lot wheeled the horse away. In the same instant lightning fell from the sky and gouged a crevice in the earth between us. They fled together. And I lay on the ground for a long time, dazed, shaken, my skull ringing like a sounding bell. I opened my eyes and I could not see. The lightning burned and blinded me.'

He raised his finger-tips to his eyes. 'My sight is gone — my foresight also. I can no longer see the scattered pathways before me; my feet will no more tread those Otherworld places. All is dim, the future is featureless and void. I am twice blind.' He paused and shook his head sadly. 'Well, I am to blame. I abandoned the protection of my Lord to seek her death. And now I bear the scar of my folly. Oh, but I was loath to let her go.'

Gwalcmai, his face ashen — even in the firelight — turned stricken, tear-filled eyes to me. 'I will avenge this wrong,' he vowed softly, little knowing what he said.

'How can you accuse yourself?' I asked Myrddin. 'Surely, Morgian is responsible; *she* did this to you. She is to blame.'

A mocking smile touched Myrddin's lips. 'Do you not see it yet? This was never my battle! It was between the Prince of Darkness and the Lord of Light, between the Enemy and Jesu. I had no part in it.'

'No part in it? If not for you she would have triumphed long ago!'

'No,' Myrddin shook his head slowly. 'That is what I believed, too. For a long time I have carried that burden in my heart and soul, but it was a lie! Yes, that too was a lie.'

'I do not understand,' I said firmly.

'It was never my battle,' the Emrys explained gently. 'My own pride, my vanity, my puffed-up importance kept me from seeing that.' Myrddin gave a bitter laugh and raised a hand to his eyes. 'I was blind before, but now I see quite clearly: my Lord is All-Sufficient to his own defence. He did not need my help. It is he who saves and protects, not me, never Myrddin.'

He paused, as if reflecting, then added, 'I tell you, it is the Enemy's delight to make us think otherwise. But it was only when I knew my own weakness, when I came alone and unprotected to this place, with no other plan or purpose but to stand against Morgian — only then was my Lord free to act.'

'But you did it. You faced her.'

'I did *nothing*!'

Silence. The crackling of the fire and the quiet rippling of the nearby stream grew to fill the night.

'I did nothing, Pelleas,' he said again softly.

'Lord,' I said, putting my hand on his arm, 'Pelleas is not here. It is me, Bedwyr — and Gwalcmai.'

Myrddin Emrys reached a hand to his head. 'Oh,' he said, 'of course. But where is Pelleas?'

'I do not know, Emrys. He set out to find you — before Lugnasadh it was.'

Myrddin rose and stumbled a few paces forward. 'Pelleas!' he cried, lifting his face to the night. With a mighty groan he crashed to his knees. 'Oh, Pelleas, fair friend, what has she done!'

I rushed to his side. 'Myrddin?'

The pain in his voice was a knife to carve the heart from the breast. 'Pelleas is dead. . . '

My spirit shrank within me, and I heard the sinister echo of Morgian's words to Myrddin: *This time your precious Pelleas will not interfere.*

Blessed Jesu, I prayed, let that be a lie, too.

NINE

Charis was thankful to have her son returned to her alive. She mourned his blindness, but set to work at once to heal him. The normal serenity of life at the Tor yielded somewhat to the urgency of Myrddin's injury as the Lady of the Lake searched her wide knowledge of medicine and consulted with the good brothers of the Shrine.

Yet, in the end, they were forced to the conclusion that if Myrddin's sight were to be returned, it would be at the pleasure of the Gifting God. The efforts of men would avail little, so he must wait and let God work his will. Until then, Myrddin would wear a blind man's bandage.

Morgian was not destroyed, but her power was broken. She had fled and would trouble us no more. Myrddin did not think she could ever recover her powers. Once exhausted, he explained, they rarely return. In this, he may have been optimistic. But he knows these things better than anyone.

And then there was the problem of Lot. It was possible that Lot could have come to Llyonesse: he might have sailed the moment we left Caer Edyn. Considering the time we took on the way, it would not have been difficult for him to go ahead of us.

Still, I thought it unlikely. Gwalcmai was too deeply ashamed to say one way or another what he thought. He felt that his noble name had been dishonoured and his clan disgraced. Wretched and humiliated, it was all he could do to hold his head up. He dragged himself around the Tor — fairest of abodes in this worlds-realm! — the very image of despair. I tried my best to cheer him, but my words were little comfort. The wound to his northern pride cut deep.

I talked with Myrddin about this. 'Of course it is not Gwalcmai's fault. I do not condemn him. But I saw what I saw, Bedwyr. I cannot change that,' he insisted.

'But might you have been mistaken? Might it have been someone else?'

'Of course, it is possible,' he admitted. 'But this someone else wore Lot's face and spoke with Lot's voice — someone else so very like Lot that he must be Lot's twin.'

While Myrddin conceded that he might be mistaken, it did not get us very far. For Lot, as far as I knew, did not have a brother.

Nor was Gwalcmai any help. 'My father has no brother,' he confirmed sadly, 'Loth had but one son, and I have never heard of another.'

This was a problem without an immediate solution. So, I left it to God's care, and went about my own affairs. Myrddin would be well enough to travel in a few days' time, and I was anxious to return to Caer Melyn as swiftly as possible. The weather had turned windy and wet. The days were growing colder. As pleasant as it is, I did not wish to winter on the Glass Isle. We must leave soon if we were to leave at all before spring.

Charis, fearing for her son, was reluctant to let us go. Yet she understood our need and showed me how to change the cloth over Myrddin's eyes, and how to prepare the mud mixture that would soothe her son's burned flesh. From the thick-wooded west side of Shrine Hill, I cut a long staff of rowan for him, so that he would not stumble; it gave him the look of a druid of old, and many who saw him took him as such.

Avallach gave us the pick of his stables; and we took a horse for Myrddin and left the first clear day. The ship waited where we had left it. I paid the fisherman who kept it for us; and we settled the horses on board and then pushed off.

The day was bright and the wind fresh. Yet, when I saw the land receding behind us, a pang of grief pierced me like an arrow. For we were leaving Pelleas behind, and I knew in my bones that we would never see him again.

If my grief throbbed like a wound in my flesh, how much greater was Myrddin's?

'He is gone,' he lamented in a voice so soft it broke my heart to hear it. 'A bright star has fallen from heaven and we will see it no more.'

'How can you be certain?'

'Peace, Bedwyr,' he soothed. 'If he were still alive do you think I would spare myself, even a moment? When in my madness I cowered in the forest, it was Pelleas who found me. He searched for years and never gave up. How could I do less?'

Gwalcmai heard all this and, upon disembarking at Abertaff, he mounted his horse with us, but soon turned onto a southern track. I called after him, 'Caer Melyn is this way! Where do you think you're going?'

He paused and looked back. 'To find Pelleas!' he answered. 'I will not sit at meat with Arthur until I have found him.'

'Gwalcmai!'

The headstrong young warrior set his face to the south and raised his spear in farewell. 'Greet my brother for me, and tell him what has happened.'

'Tell him yourself! Gwalcmai, come back!'

'Let him go,' said Myrddin. 'Let him do what he must.'

'But you said Pelleas was dead.'

'He is.'

'Then his search is senseless.'

'No,' Myrddin said. 'His search is redemption itself. He may not find Pelleas, but perhaps he will find and reclaim his honour. I tell you the truth, if he stays he will sicken with remorse. Let him go, and he will come back to us a champion.'

Few there are who can stand against the Emrys' inscrutable wisdom. I am not one of them. I did as I was told and granted Gwalcmai leave to go where he would.

Arthur accepted this decision. In view of all that had happened he could do no less, though it chafed him to lose so fine a warrior as Gwalcmai had shown himself to be. He lamented Myrddin's blindness, but was glad to have him returned alive. And Caer Melyn was so busy with preparations for winter that we could not dwell over-long on the mystery of Lot's treachery. We had neglected the stronghold for the whole of the summer, and there was much to do before the icy winds howled down from the north.

We were kept busy during the long winter, too: mending weapons and making new ones, and repairing tack, equipment and wagons. What with all the hammering, sharpening, burnishing and polishing, we might have been such a city of smiths as Bran the Blessed encountered in one of his fabled journeys.

But Arthur knew the coming campaign would be hard fought. He wanted everything to be ready. When Bors returned from Benowyc in Armorica, the Duke aimed to sail to Caer Edyn. For the next attack, he reasoned, would come at Britain's new shipyards.

In this he was not wrong.

Snow still clung to the sides of the mountains when we set out. The wind that filled our sails also cut through our cloaks and set our teeth chattering in our heads. The coastal waters were not as rough as we expected and, after only a few mishaps wherein one or another of our inexperienced seamen floundered or lost the wind, the fleet made good time.

Ectorius had not been idle through the winter, either. He rode down to the new docks to welcome us with the report that five new ships awaited our inspection in the Fiorth.

'Come and see these sleek-hulled beauties,' crowed Ector. 'Lot's wrights are a marvel. As long as we kept them supplied with timber, they worked. Why, we cut the trees and they worked right through the winter and never a grumble about the cold.'

'But I gave them leave to return to Lot in the winter,' said Arthur.

'Is that not what I am saying myself?' replied Ector. 'Lot deemed it best to keep them here. You driving off the barbarian horde saved his ships, so he had no need of them in Orcady.'

'When did Lot leave Caer Edyn?' I asked, hoping to resolve the mystery of his appearance in Llyonesse.

'Well. . . ' Ector pulled on his red beard. 'It was late.'

'How late?' Arthur asked. He understood what I was after.

'Well, now I think of it, not all that late. Before the Christ Mass, it was.'

'How long before the Christ Mass?'

'Not long — only a few days.'

'And the rest of the time he was here?'

'Where else would he be?' Ectorius was becoming suspicious.

'Are you sure?' I demanded. 'Lot did not leave and come back perhaps?'

'He was here, Lord Bedwyr. You yourself saw him. He was here, and here he stayed until the Christ Mass — or a little before, as I say.'

'You are certain?' said Arthur.

'It is God's truth I am telling,' swore Ector. 'Now then, what is this about?'

Arthur was reluctant to say, so I answered for him. 'Lot was seen in the south — after Lugnasadh, but well before the Christ Mass.'

'No,' Ector shook his head adamantly, 'it is not possible. I know who it is that sits at my board. Lot was with me here.'

So, instead of helping solve the mystery, I had only deepened it. Naturally, we did not speak a word of this to Gwalchavad, who had wintered with Ector and was there to greet us on our return from the south. We told him that his brother had gone in quest of Pelleas, but no more than that. Still, we wondered: who was this second Lot who had rescued Morgian?

The old Roman shipyards lay a short ride east along the coast. We heard the clangour of hammers and the shouts of the labourers before ever we saw the docks. But, coming upon them suddenly around a bend in the shoreline, I would have vowed the Romans had returned.

A whole forest of trees had been felled and stripped, and the logs stacked along the shore, where scores of men shaved, split and trimmed them. Fifty huts and lodges had been built — some to house the workers, some to house ships so that work could continue in bad weather. New wooden docks had been erected on the old stone pilings, and the channels dredged of silt so that the ships could be brought up for repair, or launched without waiting on the tide.

Everywhere I looked I saw men with tools of one sort or another. And the noise! The sawing, the chopping, the shouting — men bawling orders and answering with bellows, yells and roars. The gulls shrieked and chattered overhead, and windblown waves slapped the pilings smartly. The air smelled of fresh-cut wood and sweat, of sea-salt and sawdust. It was as if the world had suddenly woken from its long winter sleep and begun to work at shipbuilding.

Ectorius was proud of his accomplishment. And Arthur was at pains to praise him highly enough. 'You have worked a marvel here, Ector,' Arthur said. 'I will send you a fourth part of the tribute.'

Ector held up his hands in mild protest. 'Please, Duke Arthur, save what you have for your men. You will need it.'

'No.' The Duke was adamant. 'You cannot support this work alone. It is not right. From now on you will receive a portion of the year's tribute, and even then I will not think to repay the service you have done me.'

'What I have done,' said Ector, 'I have done for you, it is true. And for the saving of Britain. You are the only hope we have, Arthur.'

The Bear of Britain put his arm on Ector's shoulder, and the lord of Caer Edyn embraced his one-time fosterling. 'Give me but twelve men of your like,' said Arthur, 'and I will restore the empire.'

'I care not for empires,' replied Ector, solemn and low. 'But I will live to see the High Kingship in your hand. That is my pledge and bond.'

'Then let us see these ships you are so proud of,' said Arthur lightly. 'Perhaps they will speed the day.'

The ships rode low in the water. Five tight new vessels: clean-lined and ready rigged to sail. They were of Saecsen design for the most part, but their masts were sturdier and their prows sharper. Saints and angels, but Ector had braced those sharp prows with iron! I could see each one slicing the waves like the blade of a sword.

'They are made for fighting,' explained Ector. 'They will carry neither cargo nor horses, but try to outrace them and you will sooner catch the wind.'

Arthur scrambled down onto the dock and aboard the nearest ship. He stood on the planking, feet apart, fists on hips. 'I like it!' he called. 'You have done well, Ector, Ship Builder. I cannot wait to swing sword and heft spear from this sturdy sea fort!'

The Duke's words must have been carried across the sea on a swift wind, for they were heard as a challenge in the land of the barbarians, who rose up to answer in force.

Not five days later our feet were pounding onto the planking, and our hands slipping the mooring ropes, loosing those swift ships like hounds eager to meet the charging boar.

We had never fought aboard ship. And the sight of those blue-tinted sails and dark hulls slicing towards us did little to embolden us. But Arthur had taken the lead ship, and he ranged the other ships — commanded by Bors, Cai, Gwalchavad and myself — around him like the divisions of his Cymbrogi. We were a seaborne *ala*!

The five new ships formed the sharp spearhead in the centre, moving out like gulls skimming the wavetops. The other ships — thirty in all, with thirty men each — followed in a solid wall behind us.

The Angli had fifty ships. At our sudden appearance, they turned to the south and made for the nearest shore — a wooded headland at the entrance to the Fiorth called Basas for the shallows surrounding it. Basas, an interesting name. . . it also means death.

The five foremost British ships drove straightway into the exposed flank of the enemy. If the Angli had known how fast were Arthur's ships, I think they would have retreated instead. But they had no way of knowing.

Each of Arthur's five struck an enemy vessel amidships. Bone-shattering, teeth-rattling collision! Screams of men! Deadly lurching and shuddering shock! Our iron-prowed warsteeds splintered the thin hulls of the Angli, crushing them like eggshells. The first five we engaged sank like stones.

We pushed away from the wreckage with our spears while fending off barbarians struggling in the water. The closer

257

ships turned on us and we ducked behind our shields as the cruel axes of the Angli clattered against the hulls. Grappling-hooks of iron snaked through the air, caught, tightened, and drew those same ships to their ruin. With staves and swords and spears, we battled the Angli. Their narrow timbers were soon sluiced with blood.

Hefting spear and swinging sword on the heaving deck of a ship is, as Arthur suggested, not so very different from the back of a plunging horse. The Angli, as abashed at our sudden appearance as by our forceful challenge — the sea was *theirs*, they were used to running free rein along the coasts — shrank from the attack.

Enemy ships further off made for the shelter of a great rock standing by the towering headland, or *law*. Din-y-bas, it is called: Fortress of Death. And we immediately saw why it deserved its name.

For the Angli ships, heedless of the danger, drove into the shallows. The rocks waiting just below the surface of the water did their remorseless work. Pierced hulls cracked and men pitched into the water. Great the turmoil, loud the tumult!

Oaths to the hideous, one-eyed devourer, Woden, mingled with screams of anguish. The Angli abandoned their crippled ships and began swimming to shore. Several British ships broke formation and swept towards the pebbled shingle, intent on pursuing the landed invaders. The rest drove steadily on, surrounding the wallowing enemy fleet.

The rearmost Angli — caught between the rocks of Din-y-bas and the seaborne fury of Arthur — dropped sail and, with oars churning, began moving off the rocks. They swung and met Arthur head on. Alas, there were only five British vessels, or we might have made an end of it.

But it was twenty against five. And while we engaged the first five to reach us — sinking two of these outright — the others escaped. They did not even try to help their own, but made for the open sea. Perhaps the closing net of British ships behind Arthur discouraged them, or perhaps the disaster of their ruined attack had unnerved them. Whatever it was, the barbarians fled.

In all, twelve enemy vessels were sunk and eleven more foundered on the rocks. We counted it a victory, although twenty-eight ships escaped. Arthur did not give chase, because the only British vessels with a hope of catching them were the new ones and out in the open sea those five would easily be outmanned. Prudently, the Duke settled for a defensive victory and let the barbarians limp home to lick their wounds.

Ector and Myrddin had watched the battle from the ramparts of Caer Edyn. I say watched, for although Myrddin did not actually see it, Ectorius described what was happening in such detail that Myrddin well knew everything that had taken place.

The two of them were waiting on the new dock when we returned to the shipyard. 'Well done!' shouted Myrddin, thumping his rowan staff on the oak planking of the dock. 'Well done, Pride of Prydein! Long has it been since the warriors of Britain ruled the water marge, but that is changed from this day. Henceforth and to the Day of Doom will Britain reign over Manawyddan's bright realm. Welcome, glorious heroes! Praise and welcome!'

Myrddin's salute was heartening, but his praise was over-eager. For, though we had dealt the foe a staggering blow, they did not return to their home-shore. We learned later that, once out of sight, they simply turned south and sailed down the eastern coast where they were accustomed to finding unprotected bays and estuaries. And where also small barbarian settlements waited to welcome and aid them.

This they did, coming into the mouth of the Twide and running to ground in the dense forests that cover the Celyddon Hills. They hid there and waited while their messengers called forth weapons and warriors from their heathen homeland across the sea.

They waited, nursed their wounds, and grew strong with the passing months. By midsummer we began receiving reports from Custennin, Lord of Celyddon, of their presence and activity. Arthur listened to the reports and concluded that they had were moving slowly inland up the Dale of Twide to circle in behind us at Caer Edyn.

Arthur increased our forces through the summer. Custennin of Goddeu, my kinsman Ennion of Rheged, Owain of Powys, and Ectorius. Out of kinship and unity of purpose, these had begun calling themselves the Men of the

North. There were also several kings from the south: Cador ap Owen Vinddu of Cerniw, Ogryvan of Dolgellau, and Ceredig of Gwynedd with his son Maelgwn, as well as Maglos, Meurig, and Idris. Other nobles and chieftains joined us, too, so our ranks grew as the grain in the fields.

When the last of all these had assembled with us in Caer Edyn, we strapped sharp iron to our hips and helmed ourselves for battle. Cai, Ector, Bors, Gwalchavad and Cador boarded the ships, and we needed every one. As the sails dwindled on Muir Guidan, we mounted our horses and turned our faces towards the Eildon Hills and the dark forests of Celyddon beyond. Then did we ride out, fifteen thousand Britons, to face an enemy sixty thousand strong.

The way the bards have it, the glory was ours for the taking. Well I, Bedwyr, fought in every bloody battle and it is a far different song that I will sing.

TEN

Deep in the twisted pathways of black Celyddon the barbarians waited. They had not been idle. Merciful Jesu, they were more than ready for us! Baldulf had once again taken command of the combined foe, and had forced his horde to labour long in preparation for the battle.

They thought to have the dark treacheries of the forest on their side. And they did. But we had Myrddin Emrys on ours.

Myrddin had lived in Celyddon for many and many years, before ever Arthur came. And he knew the hidden trails and byways of that dark wood. Every mound and stream, every valley and overgrown glen, every rock and tree and weed-grown pool was known to him. And, even in his blindness, he could describe those familiar features as closely as the lines of his own face.

Nor was Arthur ignorant of the great forest. He had hunted there often. The hills of Eildon he knew as well as the hills of Dyfed in the south. The ruins of old Trimontium, the Roman fortress on the Twide, and the nearby monastery at Mailros were as much a home to him as Caer Edyn and Caer Melyn.

So, as we advanced along the Megget, Arthur and the Emrys riding at the head of our great army, we sang the songs of the Cymry — the ancient songs of battle and victory; the songs of honour and valour and courage. And our hearts soared within us, as the eagles riding the high winds above the steep-sided green glens around us.

Three days we marched, giving time for the ships to come round and for Cai's contingent to secure the eastern coast before striking inland to join us. On the fourth, the day before the battle would commence, we camped on the banks of a silvered lake.

We ate well and slept in the afternoon. Many bathed and sported in the cold, clear water of the lake. Some fished, and others looked to their weapons and armour.

From the hillside above, I gazed down upon our thousands ringing the long crescent lake and pride rose within me. Myrddin and Arthur were nearby, playing a game of gwyddbwyll on the grass. 'Has ever such an army of Britons been raised in the Island of the Mighty?' I asked aloud. 'Look at them! Southerners and Men of the North fighting together, side by side, under the command of one war leader. Angels and archangels, it is a stirring sight!'

'There was a time, once,' answered Myrddin presently, guiding sightless eyes to the sound of my voice. 'Aurelius united the kings to fight the Saecsen Hengist and his brood.'

'Were there as many?'

'No,' admitted the Emrys, 'but then, there were fewer Saecsen, too.'

Arthur raised his head from the board and scanned the hillside. Everywhere were tents scattered on the slopes, and behind them long pickets of horses. Supply wagons formed a wall along the water's edge, where the cooking fires were lit and whole oxen roasted day and night to keep the bellies of our warriors filled. Oh, it was indeed a marvellous sight.

'What do you feel, Artos, to look upon such a thing?' I asked, sitting down beside him on the grass.

'I feel — ' he paused, his blue eyes drinking in the vista before him, 'I feel humble and afraid.'

'Afraid!' I hooted. 'Why afraid? There are ten thousand down there and not a man among them who would not gladly give his life to protect yours. You are the safest man in all Britain.'

'I do not fear death,' Arthur said. 'I fear displeasing God. I fear losing his favour.'

'How so, Bear?'

'When much is given a man, much is required in return. I fear giving less than I have been given,' he explained, and I began to see it. He raised his hand and spread his fingers out across the lake. 'And look you, Bedwyr, my brother, I have been given more than any man in Britain. What will be required of me, do you think?'

'Any man as desperate to please God as you are, Bear, cannot fail.'

The Emrys sang that night beside the lake, his voice echoing in the empty hills, the moon high and fair to look upon, the wavelets shining silver at his feet. The harp nestled against his shoulder poured forth its matchless gift of song, and our hearts soared high in the star-flecked sky. Myrddin sang of battles fierce and hot, of courage, valour, and honour. He sang us the victory and the glory. He sang the old songs, and some I have never heard.

He sang of the Kingdom of Summer and its excellent king. His clear, strong voice conjured images in our minds and the images lived. His song took life and grew until it became more real to us than the dull earth beneath our feet. To hear the Emrys was to see, and to see was to believe.

The Summer Realm lived in our midst; the yearning of our hearts gave it shape and substance. We tasted the sweetness of its fragrance on our lips, and heard the gentle music of its fair winds rising within us. The gleam of its unfailing light filled our eyes.

We were made for this, I thought. We were made for the Kingdom of Summer, and it was made for us. Sweet Jesu, let it be.

We awakened to a blood-red dawn and a white mist upon the lake. We ate the food that had been prepared for us through the night: fresh barley bread and brose, and good roast meat. Fare to fill a warrior's stomach with warmth, and his spirit with courage.

Arthur walked among the men, talking to them, laughing with them, stirring their mettle with bold words, praising their valour, encouraging them, exhorting them.

The other kings saw how he was with his men — and how the Cymbrogi repaid his respect — and they began to follow the Duke's example. When the time came to don battle dress and mount horse, the battle flame had already begun to burn in our hearts.

I do not think a more gallant army will ever be seen in

the Island of the Mighty than the one that rode along the lake that brilliant, sunlit morning. We moved like a great silence through the empty hills. The forest lay directly ahead of us to the east. We marched swiftly along the Yarow river towards where the Yarow water met the Etric and the forest together — a good flat place of wide shallow water surrounded by thick-wooded hills behind, and Celyddon before.

Upon leaving the glen we came upon something very strange and little seen any more: a band of Hill Folk. We saw them on the ridgeway above us and, as we passed by, three of their number rode down to meet us on their shaggy, thick-legged little ponies. Arthur, Myrddin and I turned aside to receive them while the army continued on.

Although I was there and heard every word, I will not pretend to know what they said. I heard only the words *kentigern* and *tyrfa drwg gelyn ffyrnig*. I would not have understood those but for the fact that they were repeated several times with great emphasis. Still, the airy ripple that passes for speech among those quaint folk was meaningless to me.

'What do they want?' I asked Arthur. 'And who are they?'

Arthur turned to Myrddin at his right hand, who did not answer but held conversation for some moments with the Hill Folk leader. This gave me the opportunity to observe them carefully, which I did with great fascination. They were small men, yet fair of form; straight of limb, fine featured, and fully grown — yet none of them above the height of a boy of twelve summers. They were dressed in scraped skins and wore gold liberally about them: gold ear-rings and neck rings, armbands and bracelets. Each had a small blue mark on his right cheek: four tiny slashes.

When they finished speaking, Myrddin turned to Arthur. 'They are of the Wolf Clan,' he explained, 'and have come looking for the leader of Bear *fhain*. That is you, Arthur. They want to fight the beast-men who have been destroying their *crannogs* and killing their children.'

'But how do they know me?'

'They heard that the Ken-ti-gern, the Wise One of the Tallfolk — that is me — had raised a mighty son who is to drive the beast-men into the sea. They have come to see this miracle, and to lend their aid.'

'Their aid?' I wondered in amusement, regarding the slender bows and short, fragile-looking reed arrows the Hill Folk carried. 'What can they do?'

'Do not dismiss them lightly,' Myrddin warned. 'The flint arrowheads carry a poison that kills with the slightest scratch. And their accuracy with the bow is astonishing.'

'But can they fight?' asked Arthur.

'Oh, yes. In their own fashion. Their ways are different, but most effective. They mean to join the battle whether you will or no, so you need not question their courage.'

Arthur laughed. 'If that is the way of it, then I give them full freedom to join us.'

Myrddin inclined his head, as if in deference to Arthur's judgement, and loosed a long string of wispy sounds. Whereupon the Hill Folk turned their ponies and galloped off without a blink. They disappeared over the ridge with their tiny warband and we did not see them again.

When we regained the head of the army, the dark, bristled mass of Celyddon lay directly ahead. And across a flat meadow and the dull-glinting Etric water, stood the barbarian host in the accustomed wedge-shape. Baldulf, with his kinsmen Ebbisa, Boerl and Oesc, and the Irish king Fergus, had drawn up before the forest at a wide ford on the river.

Arthur gazed on this sight for a long moment, and then turned to the waiting troops behind us. 'The enemy is before us, brothers!' he cried. 'There is glory to be won! For Holy Jesu and Britain!'

Lofting his spear in the air, Arthur signalled Rhys, who raised the hunting horn to his lips and gave forth a rousing blast. Arthur turned his horse and began trotting towards the ford. He had no need of ordering the warbands. We all knew what to do. The armies of Britain arrayed themselves even as we flew to join the enemy — the *ala* in a strong double line going before; the foot soldiers, seven thousand in all, advancing behind.

The earth trembled with the pounding of hooves and the drumming of feet. The sun blazed high overhead in a blue-white haze of sky. The ford spread before us the colour of hard iron, and beyond it the innumerable ranks of the foe-men. Before that day, I had never seen so many barbarians in once place.

The thunder of our charge was nothing to the world-splitting lightning of our clash. Saints and angels bear witness! The foe scattered before us like sheep — retreating from the first charge!

We pursued them as they fled into the forest, and learned too late the reason for their seeming cowardice.

Row upon row of sharpened stakes had been planted on the forest fringe. The cruel shafts tore at the legs and ripped the bellies of the horses. We lost scores before we could halt the charge. Down they went, the ranks riven by the brisk brutality of the trap. All around me were men and horses impaled upon those hateful pikes.

Fortunate were those who died outright. The screams of agony were terrible to hear. More terrible still was the sight of those brave horses and riders thrashing, struggling to free themselves from the death trap, their flanks and chests pierced by the wicked stakes; the blood and entrails of the brave spilling freely upon the earth.

I was saved only by the narrowest chance. To think of it chills the marrow in my bones even now. I saw the brutal stakes before me and jerked back the reins with all my strength, lifting my mount's head and forelegs in an insane leap. The nearest stake raked the hide from the animal's belly, but we landed untouched in the only clear place that I could see for dozens of paces in any direction.

The cold cunning of the barbarians took us by surprise. They feared our horses, and that fear inspired them to new depths of savagery. At the sight of our *ala* faltering in bewilderment, our precise formation collapsing in chaos, the enemy roared in delight and leapt upon our helpless warriors. They hacked the defenceless with their sharp war axes, and flung the severed heads at us.

Carefully, carefully, we fought through the trap, picking our way among the stakes, advancing slowly over the bodies of our own. The enemy gave ground, but stubbornly. Each small advance was made at heavy cost.

And then we were through the trap and into the forest. And here the barbarians triggered the second of their deadly stratagems. For, the moment we cleared the forest's edge, the foe turned and ran, vanishing into the wood.

We had no choice but to follow if we were to maintain our advantage. So we plunged blindly after them. This was our second mistake.

As I have said, the barbarians had laboured through the early summer, and as we drove deeper into the forest the fruit of those labours became apparent. All summer they had hewed trees and delved soil to build a perfect mazework of earth and timber. They had opened ditches and constructed elaborate walls and barriers against us.

We careened into the forest, storming headlong into the ditches and walls. The barbarians stood on top of the timbers and hurled stones and tree trunks down upon us. Suddenly we discovered our attack halted and overwhelmed. In a single swift moment our horses were made useless and we were impossibly outnumbered.

Yet we fought doggedly on. We charged the barriers and threw ourselves against them as if to break them down by force of will alone. We slew and were slain, but could gain no advantage. The cunning barbarian mazework kept us separated and confused. We tried to circle round the earthworks, to breach the furthest edge, but the forest prevented us. It was too thick and the way too easily lost. So we charged the barriers. Again and again and again. . . we were thwarted. Each time we came away leaving more dead in the ditches than the time before. Our efforts grew erratic, frantic, reckless.

Arthur had no choice but to order the retreat. Rhys blew the long quavering note and riders began streaming past me out of the wood. Arthur was last among them.

'We can do nothing against this,' he said, his voice husky with fatigue. 'We must find another way.'

Out of the forest, I saw our troops streaming across the ford. It was a dismal sight. Battered bloody, and limping with exhaustion, they dragged themselves to the far bank and collapsed. Food and drink had been prepared by the camp cooks and these were hastily brought and given the warriors where they dropped.

Rhys sounded assembly, and the battlechiefs sought us

where Arthur had planted his spear on the riverbank. Grim-faced, they slid from their saddles, wiping sweat and blood from their eyes. The lords came to stand in a ring, with Arthur at the centre.

The curses with which they greeted the Duke spoke their despair. They blamed Arthur for the retreat, or rather its necessity, and wasted little time telling him how they felt about it. Arthur took their abuse, but the Emrys frowned and raised his staff.

'Did you think yourselves invincible?' inquired Myrddin sourly. 'No? Then why condemn Arthur for your own weakness?'

'Weakness!' Idris cried. 'You blind bastard! I own no fault in this. Half my warband was cut down by those cursed stakes.'

Ceredig grumbled agreement, and Owain tactfully suggested, 'Our War Leader should have known better.'

'Did *you* know better?' I demanded hotly. 'Or you, Ceredig? Ogryvan? I did not hear your protests when Arthur laid the battle plan.'

'It is our fault, is it?' wailed Maglos, his voice thin and pathetic. They were hurting and did not know what they were saying, it is true, but it rankled me to have them blame Arthur.

'I cannot see it serves any purpose to accuse each other — ' began Custennin, his voice quickly drowned in the railings of the others.

Myrddin made to speak again, but Arthur laid his hand on the Emrys' arm. 'I am with you, my lords,' he declared loudly, so as to be heard above them. 'I should have seen the traps sooner. I should have guessed. I own the fault. But we are in it now and must decide what is best to do. We are beaten where we stand if we fall to fighting among ourselves.'

'Hear him!' said Custennin and several others. Meurig added, 'Let us save our fury for the foeman.'

Tempers were brought to heel, and a sullen silence settled over the lords. The stewards came with cups and we were given cold water to drink. 'Now then,' began Arthur, draining his cup in a gulp, 'what did you want to say to us, Wise Emrys?'

'The pit that snares the wolf, may also capture the hunter. And there are many, many traps in Celyddon,' Myrddin said.

'Spare us your riddles, Bard,' growled Idris.

'What the Emrys means,' explained Arthur, 'is that perhaps we can turn the traps to our advantage.'

'How?' demanded the surly kings. 'Our horses are no use to us in the wood. You can scarce swing a sword without tangling blade and arm in the branches.'

'You are right,' soothed Arthur. I looked and saw the light come up bright and fierce in his eyes. 'Listen, Baldulf thinks to use the forest against us; very well, we will take up the weapons of the forest: darkness and disguise, secrecy and stealth.'

I do not know how Arthur did this. Was it in his mind, waiting to be called forth at need? Did it come to him fresh from the Otherworld — like the *awen* of a bard? Or did he simply invent it as he spoke it out? As many times as I saw him do it, I cannot say. But when at need a plan of genius was required, genius we received.

As Arthur began to elaborate on his plan, all grumbling and vexation ceased. The kings crowded in closer to hear the scheme and their disappointment soon turned to delight.

Although our shadows stretched long on the meadow, we reformed the battlelines according to Arthur's orders and advanced once more into Celyddon — all except the troops under my command. For as soon as the first ranks reached the forest and the fighting began again, those with me broke to horses, mounted, crossed the ford, and began galloping west and south along the Etric glen.

There were a thousand with me under the younger battlechiefs: Idris, Maelgwn, Maglos. We followed the river a goodly way before finding the place Myrddin had described to us — a small dingle where the Etric met a smaller stream, one of countless thousands of burns that flowed out from the forest. This was our entrance.

Abandoning our horses, we took our spears and headed into Celyddon along the burn. We ran reckless through the undergrowth, now in and now out of the water. Our only thought was to reach the battle as quickly as possible. But the burn wandered in the wrong direction! We were moving away from the fray.

'Damn his eyes!' shouted Idris, 'That meddling bard has sent us the wrong way!'

I halted and whirled on him. 'Shut up, Idris! We see it through.'

The others caught us. 'I say we go back,' insisted the stubborn Idris.

Maglos stood undecided, though inclining more towards Idris than Myrddin. But Maelgwn spoke up, 'A blind bard is to be trusted above all else. Who else sees the world so clearly?' He planted the ash haft of his spear between his feet and would not be moved.

I glared at Idris, furious with him for halting our march and provoking the warriors to doubt. I could have run the spear through his arrogant heart. 'I said we will see it through, Idris. Follow me.'

I turned and continued on. Maelgwn followed without hesitation. Maglos and Idris remained stubbornly behind, but when the warriors began passing them, they came along.

The burn continued bending away from the battle site. I trusted the Emrys with my life, but as the sound of the clash diminished, doubt began to creep in. Perhaps Idris is right and Myrddin has misremembered, I thought. Celyddon is so vast; there are so many brooks and burns perhaps this is not the one he thought it was. Or perhaps we have come to another. . .

No, we must go on. There was no other way. The lives of our kinsmen depended on it. The battle depended on it. If we failed the battle was lost. I clenched my teeth and kept running.

And then, the sound of the battle faded away altogether. I strained after it, and heard only the drum of blood in my ears, and my own rasping breath. Please, God, I prayed, do not let us fail. I kept my eyes on the track ahead and ran, my feet pounding the soft earth even as my heart pounded in my chest. My mouth went dry and my lungs burned, but I swallowed the pain, lowered my head and ran on.

Then all at once we were running uphill and the burn

became a straight and open pathway. The trees arched overhead and the water ran swift. Above the sound of rushing water came the faint din of the fight.

The sound grew to a mighty roar. By this I knew we were coming to the battle-place — but now we were behind it. Heaven bless your Most Excellent Bard, he has remembered aright!

There was a pool ahead which the barbarians had used for water, now dark in the failing light. Beyond the pool rose the central bulwark of the earth and timber mazework Baldulf had constructed to thwart us. I could see it through the trees, and I could see the swarming host upon it.

Around the mounded structure, like vast contorted limbs, lay the immense timbered walls of the mazework. It was as Arthur had suggested — the maze had a centre which, because it served to protect the other sections, would not be protected itself. The enemy had trusted the forest to prevent an assault from the unprotected side.

Before me the chaos of battle raged unrestrained. The British warriors struggled against the barriers, gained them, and were time and again turned back. Our Cymbrogi fought bravely. The battle din was a ground-trembling roar, the clash of shield on shield and sword on axe a steadily pounding drum. Fierce was the fight, dread the slaughter.

It was all I could do to keep from dashing in at once and attacking the unsuspecting enemy. But that was not the plan.

Instead, we knelt at the edge of the pool and kindled the brands we had brought with us. This stole precious moments from the fight. Father of Light, kindle your wrath against our enemies and let it burn as brightly as the torches in our hands.

At last, when every man held a flaming brand, up I stood and cried the charge. My shout was answered by a thousand throats and a thousand pairs of feet sprang forward as one.

The startled barbarians turned to see a blazing wall of fire rushing towards them. We fired their camp as we passed through. The flames leapt high and the smoke curled black and thick.

The barbarians quailed to see it. Our sudden appearance

inspired alarm, and the blaze of our torches greatly magnified our numbers in their eyes. For in the fading light of the forest they thought themselves surrounded by a numberless fiery foe.

But they quickly gathered courage. Some abandoned their earthwork defence and raced to join battle with us. The charge was ill-timed and inept. It did nothing to halt us, or even divert our path. We drove straight to the timbered mound whereon Baldulf stood to direct the battle.

Upon reaching the foremost earthwork we seized the clay jars at our belts and smashed them against the timbers, spilling oil everywhere. We thrust the torches forth and held them. The oil sizzled and burst into flame. Greasy smoke billowed into the air. Curtains of shimmering flame leapt high. The smoke rolled to heaven. Everywhere along the timbered mazework the assault was repeated and the timbers began to burn.

Now were the barbarian hosts entrapped in a maze of their own making. Battle taunts became shrieks of terror. Men plunged through the flames to the ground and we ran among them with sword and spear, cutting them down.

We had prayed for confusion, and were granted chaos.

Angels and archangels bear witness, we gave the barbarians a taste of the burning hell that awaited them! Oh, it was terrible to see!

The disordered ranks of Angli and Irish collapsed. The Irish screamed and flew to the refuge of the forest. The Angli raged and began slashing at one another in utter hopelessness and frustration. In all, the enemy hordes behaved foolishly, for if they had simply held firm for a moment they would have seen how few we truly were, and how scant the fire.

But it has been said, and indeed proved true, that for all their ferocity and cunning, the barbarians are easily discouraged. They lack the spirit to stay the course. Let their scheme be thwarted and they surrender wildly to despair. They fall away; they die. Myrddin says it is because they do not know how to hope, and I believe him.

We had only to run shouting at them, throwing our torches into their midst, and they faltered. Our simple surprise unnerved them. They yielded not to our swords, but to fear. And it was their doom.

They might have rallied given time, but Arthur snatched that chance clean away. For the instant the barbarians turned to glance behind them at our onslaught, the dauntless Cymbrogi swarmed up and over the embankments. Fire on one side, Arthur on the other — little wonder that so many chose the flames.

With deft, sure strokes we hewed them down. Though they had been a forest, we could not have felled them so swiftly. All around us the enemy wailed. Where one or two brave battlelords stood to fight like men, a dozen others deserted king and kin. Thousands bolted into the dark refuge of the forest.

'*Bretwalda*!'

I heard the familiar voice and searched the melée for it. Not a hundred paces before me stood Arthur at the foot of the central mound, Caledvwlch streaming red in his hand. I ran to his side.

'*Bretwalda*, I challenge you!' the Duke called boldly.

From the earth mound above us came a great cry of rage. We looked up through the shining veil of smoke and flame and saw a knot of foemen clustered about the skull-and-bones standard of the *Bretwalda*. Out from the midst of his house carles roared Baldulf like a bull, his helm gleaming in the firelight, his axe shining dull red; blood drenched his sinewy arm to the elbow. Trampling without heed over the corpses of his kin, the battlechief plunged down the hillside straightway, so that the force of his assault might be the greater.

Arthur faced him unafraid. And when the *Bretwalda* leapt through the flame-curtain, his loathsome axe high in the air, the wily Arthur dodged aside, leaving only the sharp edge of his sword behind.

Baldulf's steel shirt saved him from the fatal thrust, but the frenzy of his attack carried him beyond Arthur. In trying to stop, his feet slid in the blood-soaked earth and he fell onto his back. Arthur was there and ready.

Caledvwlch sang in the air. The thirsty blade bit deep, and Baldulf's head rolled cleanly from his shoulders.

Seeing their mighty *Bretwalda* slain, the barbarians fled, howling in despair and anguish. Their flight to the forest became a migration. The hundreds, thousands — abandoning the field like dogs running from a scalding.

Arthur strode to the severed head of his enemy and lifted the helm from its face. The bulging eyes that stared at him were not those of Baldulf. The face belonged to another man: Boerl, the *Bretwalda*'s kinsman.

'They must have taken one another's helms and weapons,' I observed.

Arthur nodded. 'It matters not. Baldulf has doomed himself.'

The Duke signalled Rhys, who raised the hunting horn to his lips and sounded the rout. The Britons pursued the fleeing foemen into the darksome tracks and game runs of Celyddon. The wood echoed with the screams of the unfortunate. It was the sound of miserable defeat. I do not know any warrior who likes hearing it.

But twilight comes early to the forest and we could not run the enemy to ground. Many escaped in the dark.

ELEVEN

'We will camp in the meadow and continue the pursuit at dawn,' declared Arthur. 'I will have Baldulf in chains, or see his body in the earth before I put up this sword.'

He then ordered the care of the wounded and the plunder of the dead, and we worked steadily into the night, stripping the corpses by torchlight. The enemy dead were thrown into the earthwork ditches. The British fallen were wrapped in their cloaks, carried to the mound, and honourably put to the flame by the priests of Mailros. As the pyre lit the darkling sky the good priests prayed the souls of our sword brothers on their way. Thus the bodies of our kinsmen and Cymbrogi did not suffer the gross humiliation of birds and beasts.

When at last we staggered back across the river to the meadow, a pale moon shone through wisps of cloud. The camp fires had been banked high; hot food and cold drink awaited. The war host of the Island of the Mighty sank gratefully down upon the cool grass, too tired to stir. The Duke made certain his men were well supplied with all they needed before turning to his own refreshment.

The other lords did likewise, and I saw the clustered masses of our troops spread out along the river and across the meadow. Fewer, Dear God, than had marched out this morning — an age ago that was. I felt old and weak.

Arthur and I dragged ourselves to the place where Arthur's tent had been set up. Myrddin waited there before the fire, and rose when we came near. 'Sit you down,' he commanded. 'I will bring food.'

Without a word, Arthur collapsed into Uther's camp chair. He sat there too exhausted to move. We had washed in the river, but the blood stains on our clothing shone black in the firelight and we were speckled with dark, crusted blotches.

'It is a filthy business,' Arthur murmured, staring at his hands.

I nodded. 'That it is, Bear, that it is.'

Myrddin returned with two stewards carrying meat and bread on a wooden tray, and beer in a huge jar. He quickly dismissed the stewards to other duties and began serving us with his own hand. Blind though he was, the Emrys moved quickly and without hesitation. When I asked him how he knew where to find us, he laughed and answered, 'By the smell of you, Most Fragrant Bedwyr! How else?'

It was meant to cheer us, and did not fall far short of the mark. But I was too tired to laugh, and could not even manage a suitable smile. I drank my beer in silence, and ate some bread, forcing my jaws to chew. I think I have never eaten bread so tough; although it came apart in my hands easily enough, it was all I could do to choke it down. The venison was no better.

While we ate, some of the other lords, having settled their men, joined us. Maelgwn and Maglos were first, and they were followed by Owain, Ogryvan, Idris and Ceredig. These were eager for the division of the spoils, which they thought should take place at once as they saw no reason to delay.

Arthur was not inclined to disappoint them, although I could see that his heart was not in it. 'Bring the plunder here before me, and I will divide it out.'

That is what they wanted to hear. Indeed, they were only waiting on Arthur's word, for all at once men bearing armloads of treasure appeared. They came before the Duke and placed their burdens before his feet. Others came with mealbags full of objects collected from the barbarian camp and corpses — gold and silver, brass, bronze and pewter, bright coloured, with gems and with clever inlay: cups, bowls, trays, torcs, arm rings, bracelets, brooches, mead jars, pins, knives, swords, belts, finger rings and rings for the ear, necklaces, cauldrons, pots, fine furs, combs, hair ornaments, collars for dogs and for valued slaves, coins, mirrors, statues and idols of Woden, Thor and Freya, razors, discs and plaques, spoons, circlet crowns, ingots large and small in the shape of axe-heads. . . and on and on.

At first the gathered throng cheered to see the rich hoarding. Bag after bag and load upon load was brought forward and the pile rose higher and still higher — the heap was fully as tall as Arthur himself! But as the trove swelled the laughter and the cheering became less. The last trinket was placed upon the stack in total silence.

Awed and abashed, we gazed upon the wealth we had won. Then the shame of it stole over us and the sweet taste of victory turned bitter in our mouths.

The treasure was ours by right, but it was covered in blood — much of it British blood, since the barbarians had stolen it from those they had marauded all summer. We took back only our own, and there was little cheer in the taking.

It was slow going through the forest. And though we left at first light — as soon as we could read the trails through the tangled wood — our pursuit did not raise any of the escaping enemy, who by now must have reformed into warbands. But we kept at it, and by midday began making eerie and unusual discoveries: barbarian corpses drained white and hanging from the branches of trees.

At first only a few, and then more. . . by the scores. . .

I called off the pursuit and ordered the Cymbrogi to return to the Twide valley. 'Leave be,' I told the men, 'we will find none left alive. We ride for Mailros.'

It was early in the afternoon when we rejoined the main force. Arthur was surprised to see us return so soon. 'What is it, Bedwyr? Poor hunting?'

'Oh, aye,' I told him, swinging down from my horse. 'Spoiled, more like. Someone has poached the game from your hunting runs, Lord of the Hunt.'

The Duke regarded me with a quizzical look. 'What happened?'

'The Hill Folk have collected the blood debt that was owed them, I expect. We came upon the bodies along the pathways — each one pierced by a Hill Folk arrow and hung up to bleed like carcasses of beef. The *bhean sidhe* slew hundreds, Bear, but we neither saw nor heard anything of them.'

'You were right to come back,' agreed Arthur. 'Leave the Hill Folk to fight their battle in their own way.'

Of Baldulf we had no sign. For, despite the ghastly grove of corpses I had seen, I did not for a moment consider that he might be dead. Too many had escaped into Celyddon — thousands in all. At least half the barbarian host was still alive to fight again.

A short while later the scouts which the Duke had sent out before dawn returned with the report that Baldulf had fled east to his ships waiting on the coast. As confirmation of this fact they brought with them the Irish king, Fergus, and the tattered remains of his warband. Fergus and his men had been captured making for Abertwide.

British lords and warriors hastened to Arthur's tent to see what the Duke would do. They pressed close about in a tight ring around Arthur. Some shouted and jeered at the Irish, but most remained quiet.

Fergus, his hands bound with leather straps, was hauled forward and made to kneel before Arthur. But the Duke took one look at the pathetic sight and raised the king to his feet. He took the knife from his belt and cut the thongs that bound him. Then, staring him full in the eye, Arthur said, 'If I were in your place I know you would kill me. Do you deny it?'

Fergus knew the northern tongue and answered, 'I do not deny it, lord. I would kill you.'

'Then why have you allowed yourself to be brought here like this?'

The Irish king raised his head and with eyes full of defeat and humiliation replied, 'Because I heard that you were a just and merciful man, Duke Arthur.'

'You call me just and merciful, O King. And yet you made war against me. How can this be?'

'I am not lying when I tell you that I am far from wealthy. Once the name Fergus mac Guillomar meant something in the world. But the tribute we must pay to the *Bretwalda* has bled us dry. Now my lands are poor; my crops fail and my cattle die, and the crops and herds of my people do no better.

'This, and the tribute is never decreased by so much as a kernel of wheat. We starve, lord, for want of grain and meat. Baldulf said he would waive the tribute if I joined him in raiding. He promised much plunder.' Fergus lowered his

278

head in misery. 'Please, lord, if you will not grant mercy to me, grant mercy at least to my warriors, who have done nothing but follow their king.'

Arthur pulled on his chin for a moment and then motioned for me to come near. 'What do you think, Bedwyr?'

'An unlikely tale, it seems to me.'

'But might there be some truth in it?'

I thought for a moment. 'Well,' I said slowly, 'the Irish need little enough encouragement to raid. Even in the best of times they seldom prosper.'

'That is so. What else?'

'The part about paying tribute to Baldulf rings true. It would explain much.'

'I agree. So what do we do with *him*?' the Duke jerked his head towards where Fergus waited.

'Ask Myrddin. He is your Wise Counsellor.'

'I am asking you. What would *you* do, Bedwyr?'

'I do not know, Artos. Kill him, I suppose. These greedy heathen must know that they cannot make war on Britain and hope to escape without swift and severe punishment. Strength is the only thing they respect.'

Arthur put his hand on my shoulder. 'Your answer is the Soul of Wisdom, brother. A man would be a fool to go against it. And yet that is what I shall do.'

'You mean to let him go?'

'Yes.'

'Then why ask what I think? What difference does it make what I say?'

'I needed to hear it, Bedwyr. That is all. You speak the hard law of war. But there is a higher law we may invoke.'

'Which is?'

'When a man asks for his life, you must give it — even if it were better in your eyes for that man to die.'

He turned away quickly and bade Fergus kneel down before him. The Cymry gathered close around murmured to themselves, speculating on Arthur's decision.

'Do you swear, O King, on pain of death, never to practise war upon Britain again? And will you with whatever oaths you deem binding swear fealty to me, and promise to uphold me and pay me tribute as long as your life endures?'

Fergus glanced up into Arthur's face, and I saw a rare

sight — one that is not often seen in this world. I saw hope kindled in a man who knew himself doomed, who had no right to hope at all. This hope was born of mercy. And I could see by looking at the Irish king that Arthur had won a loyal friend for life. Fergus swore his oaths, bound his life to Arthur's, and rose a happy man.

Against all reason, Arthur fed the captives and sent them home — without an escort. There was nothing to prevent them from breaking faith and turning back to raiding the moment they moved from our sight. This caused many in our camp to grumble against Arthur, but when did the complaints of others ever sway the Bear of Britain?

We rested on the wide, grassy lee of the sparkling Twide, taking time to refresh ourselves and heal our wounds. It remained sunny and warm, and the long northern day stretched soft and golden before us. Arthur spent it with the Cymbrogi, eating and drinking and singing with them. He gifted them with gold rings and armbands, and silver cups for their valour. He gave liberally of his share of the plunder, keeping nothing for himself.

So, after a supper of stewed leeks, roast venison, the coarse camp bread, and cheese, Myrddin Emrys took up his harp. The entire camp gathered on the riverbank, crowding one against another to the edge of the water so that no one could move. None seemed to mind the cramp, so intent were they on the Emrys' song.

Myrddin stood before them on a flat-topped rock, the waters of the Twide swirling below him. Straight and tall he stood before the battle host of Britain, idly strumming the harp, dead eyes downcast, searching among the tales in his vast store for the one he would share tonight. It was ever the same with him; Myrddin would try to fit the song to his listeners, so that it would speak to them a word they could treasure in their souls.

His long fingers played over the harp strings, drawing a melody from the singing heart of the harp as lightly as a maid coaxing a smile from her lover. Then, raising his head, he began the tale. And this is what he sang. . .

In the First Days of Men, when the dew of creation was still fresh on the earth, Bran the Blessed, son of Llyr, was king of Gwynedd and Lloegres and all Ynys Prydein besides. He was as just and fair as the sunlight that falls from heaven, and a better king was not known since kingship began in the Island of the Mighty, and this is the way of it. . .

One day, as Bran sat on the rock of Harddlech overlooking the sea, accompanied by his kinsmen and such men of rank as ought to surround a very great king, he spied thirteen Irish ships coming to him from over the sea and making for the coast, running before the wind with all the grace and ease of gulls.

Seeing this, Bran bestirred himself and said, 'Friends and kinsmen, I see ships out there boldly approaching our lands. Go you down to meet them and discover what these visitors intend by coming here like this.'

The men of Bran's company equipped themselves and went down to await the Irish ships. 'Lleu smite me,' exclaimed one of the men as the ships came closer, 'if I have ever seen ships as fine as these.' And all agreed that they were handsome ships indeed.

The foremost ship drew ahead of the others and they saw a shield raised on the deck as a sign of peace. The ships then stood off from shore and put out boats filled with strangers who proceeded to land.

'Lleu be good to you,' called Bran in greeting from his rock as the foremost stranger strode up out of the water, 'if you seek peace, you are welcome. Whose ships are these, and who is your leader?'

'Lord Sechlainn, King of the Ierne,' came the reply. 'It is he who owns these ships — and many more like them, since you ask.'

'What does he seek by coming here?' demanded Bran. He had learned through bitter experience not to trust strangers from across the sea. 'Will he come ashore?'

'No, lord,' the emissary answered. 'My king has a request of you and will not set foot upon these lands unless you grant it.'

'Well, am I to know this request?'

'Great lord,' the emissary said courteously, 'King Sechlainn seeks to make an alliance with you. As proof of your friendship, he has come to ask for Bronwen, daughter of

Llyr, to be his wife, that your houses be for ever bound by ties of blood and honour. In this way will Ierne and the Island of the Mighty be made stronger.'

'Tell your lord that he had better come to my dun where we can discuss the matter properly.'

King Sechlainn heard this and came ashore at once, his counsellors and men of rank with him. And great was the host in Bran's hall that night.

First light next day, the men of the Island of the Mighty met in council. They decided that the incessant warring with the Irish must cease, and the sooner the better for all. If the alliance with Sechlainn could accomplish this, it should be sought. Still, they were greatly sorrowed to let Bronwen go from them, for she was one of the Three Great Queens of the island, and widely known as the most beautiful woman then alive.

Nevertheless, it was decided that she should become Sechlainn's queen for the good of all. And so a feast was declared to celebrate the joining of the two most powerful houses in all this worlds-realm.

For his part, King Sechlainn brought seven of his ships near to land and began unloading them. 'What is swimming to shore?' wondered the British men. 'Please tell us, for we have never seen creatures of their like before.'

'These noble animals are called horses,' replied the Irish men. 'Well you might wonder to look upon them, for they are a gift to us from Lugh of the Sure Hand himself; they come to you straightway from the Otherworld.'

The British men were amazed to see such beautiful creatures climbing out of the waves and foam, glistening in the sunlight as if gilt with the gold of heaven. The horses and their grooms were received with all honour and respect and put at once in the finest fields and glens that Bran possessed.

And Bronwen, his sister, was married to Sechlainn the Irish king that very day. As proof of their marriage, the couple slept together that same night and thus joined the noble kingdoms of Ierne and Ynys Prydein.

During the wedding celebration — which lasted so many days that men lost count — Lord Evnissyen, Bran's quarrelsome cousin, arrived from his travels and saw some of the horses. 'What are these ugly beasts?' he demanded. 'And who has brought them here to waste our land with their upkeep?'

'They are the bride price paid for Bronwen, who is now become the wife of King Sechlainn of Ireland,' answered one of the grooms.

Evnissyen, the Bent One, frowned, which he was ever known to do, and growled at the groom. 'What! Have they given away that excellent woman without my consent? Indeed, my cousin could not have hit upon a greater insult to me if that had been his sole ambition. Very likely it was.'

So saying, the ill-tempered Evnissyen began smiting the horses with his fists, striking first their jaws and heads, then their flanks and backs, and finally their hocks and tails. This he did with such vengeance and malice that the once-proud creatures were disfigured beyond all value.

News of this outrage took wings to King Sechlainn, who wondered at the atrocity of it. 'This insult to my gift is no less insult to me. More, if this is how they respect my highest treasure, I fear I will fare no better,' he said, shaking his head. 'My path is clear: there is nothing to do but make for the ships.'

King Sechlainn took his wife and men and hastened to his realm across the sea. The ships became specks on the sea and disappeared altogether before Bran learned of his leaving. But he did learn, and he said, 'It is not fitting that he should leave in such unseemly haste. Therefore, we will not let him go.'

Bran sent messengers out in his fastest ships to plead with Sechlainn to return and favour Bran's court with his presence.

'That I will not do,' replied King Sechlainn from the deck of his handsome ship, 'until I know who has cast this slander on my name by destroying my good gift.' And he told them about the injury done to the horses.

When Bran heard the messengers' report, he was heard to remark, 'I smell the evil of Evnissyen at work here. Lleu knows he was ever a trouble maker.' So once again he sent out the messengers — Manawyddan ap Llyr, Heveydd the Tall, and Unig Strong Shoulder — to offer his apology for his kinsman's bad manners, saying, 'Tell the king of Ierne that if he will overlook Evnissyen's insult I will give him a staff of silver as tall as he is, and a platter of gold as broad as his own face. Or, if he will not accept that, let Sechlainn come to me and name what he will accept and we shall make peace on whatever terms he deems best.'

These swift messengers sailed with all speed to Sechlainn and offered Bran's words in a friendly way. The king listened and his fair wife pleaded with him, 'My brother is an honourable man, my husband. Allow him to prove himself in this matter and you will not be disappointed.'

The Irish king pulled on his chin, puffed out his cheeks, and cast an eye upon his beautiful wife. In her he found favour and so replied, 'As this is a strange thing from the beginning, it pleases me to have an end to it. Very well, I will return to Bran and hear him out.'

The Irish flew once more to the Island of the Mighty, but they were cautious and anxious lest any further insult befall them. Bran saw that they were listless at their food and conversation. 'My friend, you are not so light-hearted as you were before. Is it because you consider your compensation too small? If so, I will add as much as you like to make you happy.'

'Lugh reward you, lord, I believe you mean what you say.'

'I do. And as pledge of my word, I will give you my chief treasure, a great cauldron of gold wherein resides this peculiar property: if a slain warrior is put into the pot today, he will fight as well as ever on the morrow. Only, he will not be able to speak a word.'

King Sechlainn thanked Bran graciously and was so well pleased with his new treasure that he forgot the insult done him. The feast continued as many days as before, and an enjoyable feast it was. But the time came to take his leave, and the Irish king embraced the British king like a brother and said, 'Come you to my court when you will, lord, and I will return the favours you have accorded me tenfold. You may prove me in this, and I hope you do.'

Then, after many heartfelt farewells, King Sechlainn and Bronwen set out. Thirteen graceful Irish ships sailed from Aber Menei and flew away over the sea to Ierne where they were greeted joyously by one and all.

Soon it became voiced about all the kingdom that Sechlainn had taken a wife of rare and surpassing beauty. And everyone who came into his court from the first day received from Bronwen's hand a ring of gold, or a polished jewel, or a fine enamelled brooch, or some such treasured gift as would please them. Oh, and it was a marvellous sight to see these precious gifts being carried off!

Bronwen's renown as a kind and generous queen grew in the land, and small wonder. King Sechlainn's realm flourished as never before with goodness and peace. Great the honour thereof! And this king liked and loved his lady well.

In due time Bronwen's belly swelled with child which she bore most regally, and at the end gave birth to a son named Gwern. After the custom of those days, the boy was sent to the best house in all the realm to be reared as a nobleman ought.

Bronwen's cousin, Evnissyen, wicked as the night is long, bethought himself how things had turned out, and how Bran had healed the split he had made. And he became jealous of Sechlainn's happiness and good fortune. 'Govannon smite me with his hammer if I do not settle this matter between us for once and all.' And taking a small coracle, he set out at once for Ierne.

There are trouble makers in Ierne, just as everywhere else. And Evnissyen had no great difficulty finding them and stirring them up with hateful words and false promises.

This was only too easily done, for because of Queen Bronwen's kindness and honour, and the heir she had given their king, these small-souled creatures were already halfway down the trail to jealousy by reason of Sechlainn's happiness. In less time than it takes to tell it, the grumblers, led on by smooth Evnissyen, fastened on the insult done their king while in Bran's court. The more they thought about it — and they thought about little else — the angrier they became.

Did they keep their anger to themselves? No, they did not.

Very soon they were flapping their tongues here and there all over the realm, and causing others to do the same. This poison spread as it will do, and in time reached Sechlainn's ears. He grew sad to hear it, and at first refused to take offence at this insult that had been so handsomely redressed by the gift of the enchanted cauldron.

But the evil words did not cease. And as the waves pounding on the rock wear it down bit by bit to pebble size, so too after a time Sechlainn could no longer look at his beautiful queen without thinking of the wrong done him.

But the makers of trouble did not let it rest there. They continually hounded the poor king to his misery by demanding that the disgrace to his kingdom be avenged so that his honour, and theirs, might be restored.

In short, they raised such an uproar and ferment throughout Ierne that in the end unhappy Sechlainn yielded to them — more to earn a space of silence than anything else. And this is the revenge he took: Bronwen was struck once on the cheek and driven from his chamber. A queen no longer, she was given a place in the kitchen and made to cook for the court.

For this reason, the blow Bronwen suffered was ever after known as one of the Three Unjust Slaps of Britain.

But, as everyone knows, it could not stop there. 'Now lord,' said the malcontents, 'word of this must not reach Bran or he will surely come and make war on us to avenge his sister.'

'What do you propose?' asked Sechlainn sadly. He no longer cared what happened to him or his kingdom. The light had been snuffed from his life.

'You must forbid all ships from going to Ynys Prydein, and all ships coming from there must be seized, so that no one can take word to Bran. Do this and we will be happy at last.'

'You may be happy, but I will not. While you are at it you might as well call me Mallolwch, Most Wretched, from now on, for I can no longer be Sechlainn and feel the way I do.'

'That is your decision,' replied the evildoers. 'We certainly never wanted it this way.' But of course they did.

Evnissyen, having sown his evil far and wide, departed at once and no one knew where he had gone. Poor Bronwen, bereft of friendship and forsaken in her own house, grew weary and sick at heart. 'Lleu knows I have done nothing to deserve this. My kindness has been repaid with loneliness, and my generosity with endless work. This will not do at all.'

As it happened, Lleu, flying overhead in his accustomed form — that of a huge, black raven — heard Bronwen's lament. Well he remembered her former glory, and so swooped down to see if the affair might benefit from his intervention.

Alighting on Bronwen's kneading-trough as she toiled at the bread, he watched her with a bright black gem of an eye. She saw the raven and offered it a scrap of meat, which it gulped down at once and croaked its gratitude. She poured out some milk and gave it to the raven to drink, which it did with all speed. 'At least, my labours are appreciated by someone,' sighed Bronwen mournfully. 'I give you good day, friend raven.'

Up spoke the raven. 'Daughter, who are you to toil without ceasing? Surely, you were born for better than this?'

'I am Bronwen, daughter of Llyr, and Bran the Blessed is my brother. You have spoken the truth, though you may not know it. For I was once a queen in my own land, and a queen here as well — and highly respected, though I say it myself.'

'What happened to bring you to this low estate?'

'You are wrong if you think that I caused my own undoing. I tell you truly, I am not loved in this place. Once, but no longer — owing to the wicked men who slandered me most cruelly.' She looked at the raven suspiciously. 'Not that it is anything to you.'

'Indeed, Sister, it is everything to me.'

'Who are you, bird, to take an interest in my sad plight?'

'Never mind about me. What are we to do about you?'

'A most vexing question. In vain have I sought for an answer through many long days of contemplation. For not only am I a slave here, no one may pass across the sea. My kinsmen might as well live in the Otherworld for all I can reach them.'

'Say no more,' croaked the raven. 'Ships may be prevented from sailing, but no one yet has discovered a way to hinder a bird from flying where it will.'

'Will you take a message to my brother, then?'

'Is that not what I am saying?'

'Well, I hope you speak more plainly to him than you do to me,' she snapped.

'Give me the message,' said Lleu in his raven's guise. 'Then stand you back and watch what will happen.'

So Bronwen told the raven all about her plight, then described Bran and what kind of man he was and where to find him. Away winged the big black bird to that fairest land across the sea.

The canny raven found Bran in his stronghold and spoke to him in private. Bran listened, becoming most distressed and outraged at his sister's disgrace. He thanked the raven and in the selfsame breath called for his advisers and counsellors and druids and any within the sound of his voice to assemble, whereupon he told them what had befallen Bronwen at Sechlainn's hands.

'How this could have happened, I cannot understand. I had the highest respect for that Irish king, and now this. Well, there is no trusting those quarrelsome dogs. Speak, Wise Sages! What say you, Counsellors? Advise me, Advisers! What am I to do about this?'

They all gazed in dismay at one another, then answered with a single voice. 'Your way is clear, lord and king. You must take your warband across the sea to save your sister and bring her back if you are to end this disgrace.'

Bran agreed. He raised his warband — and a better warband has not been seen on the Island of the Mighty from that time to this — and they steered their ships from Aber Menei to Ierne; each man among them armed and helmed, and each a better warrior than the last.

Now, Mallolwch's swineherds were down by the sea tending the pigs and they saw Bran's fleet coming. They threw down their staves and let the pigs scatter where they would, and ran to their lord who was holding court with his advisers.

'Lugh be good to you,' the Irish king said in greeting. 'What news do you bring me?'

'We have seen a wondrous sight, lord. And a more wondrous sight would be difficult to imagine,' the swineherds said.

'Tell me then, for I would hear of it.'

They answered straightway, saying, 'Do not think us

drunk, lord, but we have seen a forest arising on the sea where never was seen so much as a single tree. What is more, the forest is hastening this way. Think of that!'

'A strange sight, indeed,' replied Mallolwch. 'Did you see anything else?'

'In the centre of this forest, surrounded by it, we saw a mountain. Lightning broke from its brow and its crags were filled with roaring thunder.'

'A storming mountain surrounded by a forest,' mused Mallolwch. 'Coming this way, you say?'

'We do say it. What do you think it means?'

'On my life, I cannot think what it means. But the woman who was my wife is an intelligent being. Let us ask her.'

So the king and his advisers besought her, saying, 'Lady, tell us the meaning of this wonder we have seen.'

'Though I am no longer a lady,' she replied, 'I know well enough what it is. Lleu knows it is a sight that has not been known in this worlds-realm for all these many years.'

'Will you tell us yet?'

'I will. It is nothing more nor less than the gathered warband of the Island of the Mighty, sailing to battle. I believe my brother Bran the Blessed has heard of my sore plight and is coming for me.'

'What is this forest we have seen?'

'That is the masts and oars and spears of the ships and the warriors on them.'

'What is this mountain?'

'That is none other than Bran himself in his towering rage.'

The Irish men heard this and were afraid. 'Lord, you cannot allow them to make war on us. They will slaughter us most frightfully.'

Mallolwch answered them bitterly. 'Lugh knows it is no more than you deserve for the trouble you have caused.'

'Fret us not with that,' the evildoers answered. 'Rather do your duty and protect us.'

'Because of you, that will not be easy to do. By Toutatis, you are a vile lot! I wish I had never known you. Nevertheless, I will do what seems best to me, and it is this: I will offer my kingship to my son, Gwern, Bran's own kin. He will not make war on his sister's son.' With this Mallolwch charged his messengers to bear these words to Bran when he came ashore.

The messengers obeyed and greeted Bran kindly as he waded ashore, his sword naked in his hand. 'What answer shall we take to our lord?' they asked when they had delivered their message.

'Tell your lord he shall have no answer from me until he brings me a better offer than I have heard just now.'

Back went the Irish men to their lord with the sound of ringing steel in their ears. 'Lord and protector,' they said, 'Bran says he will not give you an answer until he hears a better offer than the one you gave just now. Our advice is for you to prepare a better proposal, for we are not lying when we say that he will have none of the one you sent.'

Mallolwch nodded sadly. 'Then tell my brother Bran that I will build him the greatest stronghold this world has ever seen — with a hall big enough to hold all his people in one half, and all of mine in the other. Thus, he shall rule over Ierne and the Island of the Mighty, with me as his steward.'

The advisers came before Bran with this proposal, which pleased him when he heard it. The result was that he accepted it at once. In this way, peace was made and work begun on the stronghold and its enormous hall.

The men of Ierne toiled away to raise the timber, and they fell to discussing things, as workmen will do. Evnissyen, disguised as a workman, began complaining of the unfairness of Bran, and the harshness of his rule. Inspired by Evnissyen, they were soon saying things like: 'It is not fitting that our lord and king be made a steward in his own realm. This is a great dishonour for him, and for us as well, come to that.'

So the workmen set a trap. On every peg of every timber of the hall they fixed a large leather bag; inside every bag they put one of their most ferocious warriors.

When the hall was finished, Mallolwch sent word to Bran to come and take up residence. Evnissyen heard the summons and made certain to enter the hall before all the others. He scowled at the magnificent hall as if it were the most contemptible shepherd's bothy. And turning his cunning eyes on the leather bag nearest him, he said, 'What is that?'

'Barley,' replied one of the workmen.

On the pretence of examining the grain, Evnissyen reached into the bag, found the warrior's head and squeezed hard until he perceived his fingers crushing bone and sinking into brain.

As he did to that first bag, he did also to each bag in turn, until every one of two hundred warriors were killed and none were left in the land of the living. 'Now,' he smirked to himself, 'let the Irish men find this and they will howl with rage to think what Bran has done to their kinsmen.'

By this time the host had arrived. The men of the Island of the Mighty sat on one side of the great hearth, and the men of Ierne sat on the other. Peace was made and the Irish King removed his torc and held it out to Bran.

When Bran saw this he relented and said, 'I have a torc, lord, and lands and people enough. Only let my sister be reinstated in her proper place and I will be content.'

Mallolwch heard this and wept for joy. 'Truly, you are a blessed man,' he cried. 'You treat me better than I deserve.'

'How should I treat my own kin badly?' answered Bran.

'In token of your honour to me,' said the Irish king, 'let my son, your nephew, be brought forth. He will be crowned in my place, and I will serve him as I would serve you.'

Little Gwern was brought forward, and Mallolwch placed the torc upon his son's neck instead. Everyone who saw the boy loved him, for a more fair and honest boy there never was.

Up spoke Evnissyen, whose spirit writhed within him to behold the amity between the two peoples. 'Why does not my young kinsman come to me for a blessing?' he called, and the boy, fearing no harm, went to him gladly.

Ha! said the evil trickster to himself — be assured there was not the smallest grain of goodness in him — not even Lleu himself could foresee the outrage I will perform next. So saying, he seized the boy and threw him head first into the enormous fire, before anyone could lay a hand on him to stop him.

Bronwen saw the flames close about her dear little son and she cried out in horror and leapt towards him, as if to throw herself into the fire to save him. But there was nothing to be done. The flames were kindled hot and swiftly reduced the child to ashes.

Up jumped the men of Ynys Prydein with a shout. And this shout was echoed by the Irish men who, with Evnissyen's help, had discovered their murdered sword brothers. And never was there a greater commotion in all this worlds-realm than the one that followed, as each man reached for his weapons.

The fight, the battle, the slaughter that was made that night was worse — oh, far, far worse than any since the world began. The din sounded like thunder, the clash like a tempest. Blood rose to the thighs of the warriors and still they slew one another cruelly.

Meanwhile, Evnissyen was not idle. For when the battle raged white-hot, he crept into the shadows, striking here and there, stealing a life with every blow of his poisoned dagger. He saw Bran protecting his sister Bronwen between his shoulder and his shield, and he struck them both from behind, laughing as they fell from his blade.

More good men went to their deaths, and more good women were made widows than heaven has stars. When the men fell, their women took up arms, so that man, woman, and child fought to their deaths.

Bitter was the battle, and bitter the tears that followed. And long, long the mourning.

The sun shone raw and red and the sunrise like a wound in the east when the last foe laid down his arms for ever. Seven men only remained, staring at one another with blood in their eyes and on their hands.

Then the Bent One saw the survivors place the Cauldron of Rebirth upon the hearth, and they began putting the dead into it. Fearing that all his toil would be for nothing, Evnissyen crept in among the bare-bottomed corpses, lay down, and was tumbled into the cauldron with the rest.

Once inside, Evnissyen stretched out full length, pressing hands and feet against the sides of the cauldron. He pushed with all his might until the marvellous cauldron burst into four pieces and was ruined. As it happened, the wicked man's heart burst also and he died ignobly.

The survivors, all British men, came upon Bran who lay dying beside fair Bronwen. They fell on their knees and wept over him. 'Lord and king,' they wailed, 'the cauldron has burst and now we cannot save you.'

'Listen to me, my brothers,' Bran said, 'and do what I tell you. When I am dead, cut off my head and take it back with you to Ynys Prydein. There let you bury it on the White Hill overlooking Mor Hafren, where it will guard that sea gate from any intruder.

'I tell you the truth, for so long as you do not dig up the head no enemy will ever harm you. You will feast in the land of your fathers, Rhiannon's birds will sing to you, and eighty years will be as a single day. In this way, the head will be as good a companion to you as ever it was, for your joy and prosperity will be assured.

'But let anyone uncover the head and plague and war will come once more to the Island of the Mighty. And, once uncovered, you must hasten to bury it again where no one will ever think to find it, lest worse befall you.

'Now then, it is time for me to die. Do at once what I have commanded you.'

Sorrowfully, the British men did what their lord commanded. They sailed back over the sea to their homeland and buried the head where Bran had told them. And they buried Bronwen a little apart, but near the place where her brother's head rested, so that they could be together.

And, all at once, up sprang a great palace with walls and floors of polished stone that shone like gemstones in the sun. Inside they found an enormous hall and food of all kinds laid upon the groaning board. There was wine and mead and beer to drink. And whether food or drink it was the finest they had ever tasted. As they began to feast, three birds appeared on golden perches and all the most wonderful singing they had ever heard was like empty silence compared to the singing of these marvellous birds.

And the men forgot the sorrow of their lost kinsmen and companions, and remembered nothing of the grief they had seen and suffered, nor any other hardship in the world.

For eighty years they lived like this, their wealth and kin increasing, their joy abounding. The eighty years was called the Assembly of the Wondrous Head. By reason of this, the burial of Bran's head was called one of the Three Happy Concealments. For as long as the head remained undisturbed neither plague nor enemy came to the shores of Britain.

So ends this branch of the Mabinogi.

The song finished, Myrddin lowered his harp in utter silence. The assembled kings and warriors deemed themselves in the presence of a True Bard and were mute as deer, eyes glowing as if enchanted, and perhaps they were. For certainly they had been held by this tale, and it had worked its subtle spell inside them.

And inside me as well. I, too, felt the tale as a living creation; I knew it to be alive in the way of all true tales. More the dread because of it! For I understood the deeper significance of the song, and I knew what it was the Emrys had sung:

Arthur's troubled reign, and the Enemy's hand in it.

TWELVE

With Cai and Bors before and Arthur behind him, Baldulf's choices were few. Cut off from reaching their ships on the eastern shore, the escaping barbarians turned northward. They hoped to pass unnoticed through one of the many hidden dales and glens that seamed the lowland hills.

They did this and reckoned themselves more than fortunate, for they happened upon a ruined Roman fortress. There are no less than half a dozen of the old marching-camps in the hills, camps that served Trimontium, the largest stronghold in the region. Nothing remains of Trimontium save a hump in the grass near the Twide, but the smaller forts were made of stone and withstood the wind and weather. It was one of these that Baldulf found — Caer Gwynnion, the White Fort. Though the wooden gates were long gone, those solid stone walls still commanded the dale below.

The second day after the battle, Cai's forces joined us. We broke camp the next morning and marched north up the dale of the Aloent towards Caer Gwynnion. In all we were lighthearted: our forces were replenished, the foe was in retreat, and our prospects for a decisive victory and an early return to the south good. So we passed along the green-sided hills and the rushing water, and sparkling lark song filled our ears. What could be better?

We had never attacked a Roman fort before. And although we knew well how to defend one, assault is a different matter. Small wonder the Celts of old never won a war. Even in ruins, those strongholds are devilishly difficult to defeat.

Indeed, the barbarians learned a new tactic. Nevermore did we face them in the field — they knew they could not win there! After Celyddon the fighting would be from behind the sheltering walls of a fortress.

The Angli had been deserted by their allies. The Picti had long since fled the battle and had vanished into their high moorland wilderness. The Irish, all that remained, had gone home. Only Baldulf and his kinsmen, Ebissa and Oesc, were left with their host — now pared to fewer than thirty thousand.

The British host had diminished, too. We numbered little more than ten thousand: two thousand horse, and the rest on foot. But a good few of those were fresh troops, who had been with Cai and Bors. These had seen no fighting yet, and were eager to win their mead portion and a share of the plunder.

The siege of Caer Gwynnion commenced on a cold, wind-swept day of the kind that come so frequently and suddenly in the north. Light rain whipped at our faces. The trails became slippery with mud. The horses and wagons were left behind in the valley below, where Arthur directed the camp to be established. An *ala* in full flying gallop is not much use against the stone walls of a fortress.

We were not foolish enough to storm the walls unaided. That is madness and defeat, as anyone knows. So Arthur turned his memory back to the same Romans who had built the fortress, adopting a tactic the legionaries used with unrivalled success against the timber hill forts of the Celts. We laid siege to the stronghold, and then set about constructing battle machines.

Myrddin's knowledge served us here, for he knew how such machines should be made, and he directed their construction. We made a wheeled tower with a doorway slightly higher than the walls of the fortress. We also built an *onager* with which to hurl stones into the walls and yard.

The machines were made of timber that had to be dragged up from the dale below by horse. It was slow and tedious work, but in five days they were finished and the battle could begin in earnest.

When the barbarians saw the tower erected they set up a hideous howl. But when the first stones began streaking from the sky like comets, they screamed in rage and frustration. They stripped naked and ran along the tops of the walls, presenting themselves openly, hoping to draw us into range of their axes and hammers and stones.

But Arthur remained unmoved. He commanded that no man should approach the walls and we all stayed well back and let the war machines do their work. We kept the stones flying day and night, moving the *onager* continually, so that the enemy could find no safe refuge within the walls.

Within three days they were well battered and hungry. When the seventh day had passed, they were weak and stupid with hunger. Then did Arthur order the tower to be wheeled to the wall. The best warriors were inside the tower, led by Cai, who demanded the privilege of directing the battle.

God love him, he argued so ardently and so well that Arthur gave him Caledvwlch to wear, to show that Cai had the Duke's full authority in command.

The warriors formed the *tortoise* — a simple manoeuvre by which a barrier of interlocked shields is raised over the heads of those who must approach the wall — and advanced slowly, pushing the great tower before them. Arthur and I watched the battle from the fair vantage of a rock outcrop nearby.

Brave I am, foremost in battle, yet I cannot say I would gladly have been the first to leap through the tower door onto the wall. Cai did that, showing magnificent courage, battling with a dozen or more alone until one by one his men joined him. I do not know how he was not killed the moment his foot touched the wall.

Gwalchavad, Cador and Owain led their warbands into the tower next, followed by Maelgwn, Bors and Ceredig. Once these first gained the fortress wall, we could not keep the rest away. The other kings crowded one another for places beneath the tower, so that a long line of warriors stretched back from the fortress wall.

The first fighting took place on the wall itself, as I have said. But the battle quickly carried to the yard below, and that was dreadful. There was no room to swing a sword without hitting foe or friend alike, so the Cymbrogi worked with their spears. Had they been threshers they could not have taken a greater harvest! The barbarians thought to crush the attack by sheer weight of numbers and so threw their naked bodies against the British spears. The bodies fell one upon the other — a wall of twitching limbs — before Cai and the Cymbrogi, and the enemy were forced to crawl over the corpses of their kin to fight.

The British were swarming over the wall now, hurling spears down into the churning chaos. There were so many Angli pent up within the caer that our warriors killed with every throw.

'There is no honour in this,' I observed. 'It is a slaughter of unknowing beasts.'

'Baldulf is as stubborn as he is proud,' Arthur said. 'But it will be ended soon.'

As if to make a prophet of Arthur, the gate — which had been stopped up with rocks and rubble, suddenly collapsed outward in a white cloud of dust and the enemy stormed out. The British kings were ready. Custennin, Ennion, Ogryvan and Ceredig ran forth to engage the foe. The sound of the clash reached the rock where we sat.

'Are we going down there?' I indicated the battle spreading before us.

Arthur gave his head a sharp shake. 'There is no need. We will let Cai and the kings have this victory.' He turned his horse away. 'Come, we will await them in the valley.'

Baldulf's stubbornness cost him the battle. His pride cost him his life.

The barbarian would not surrender and, even when the battle was well lost, he refused quarter. Cador killed him and set the *Bretwalda*'s head on the end of his own skull-and-bone battle standard. He then set the standard over the corpses heaped before Caer Gwynnion.

Arthur received the victorious host in the dale. Cai, Cador, Bors and Gwalchavad led the long march down to the camp. Arthur set up his camp chair before the ford and, when the warriors crossed, he welcomed them as heroes and champions and gave them all gifts.

Cai and the others were well pleased, for the pickings were meagre on the hill. Not so much as a gold ear-ring or even a brass pin did they get there. Arthur made up the lack from the share of plunder he had saved for them. He then proposed a victory feast.

Ah, but our hearts were not in it. Weary of battle, our

thoughts were on the homeward road. Harvest time was drawing near; the kings were anxious to return to their realms. They had been gone from their affairs long enough. The war, for this year at least, was won. It was time to go home.

So we formed ranks and traversed the long, wide dale of Twide eastward to where the ships lay at anchor on the coast. Then we set sail for the south.

Highest Heavenlies, be praised! Our return to Caer Melyn was all golden gladness and sweet joy. The people gathered at Arthur's hill fort and thronged the track from the ford to the very gates of the stronghold. They cheered and sang as we passed among them. Most of them were Meurig's folk, with a good few from surrounding cantrefs as well. But their welcome was every whit as genuine and heartfelt.

Arthur, first in generosity, feasted them and stood the celebration of our summer's victories out of his own treasury. The other kings enjoyed his largesse, but none offered to help provide so much as a pig or a goat for the feast.

If that is all their renown is worth, so be it. For myself, I would not care to risk a bard's mocking tongue for the price of a few pigs or bullocks.

After the feast the kings departed to their own realms, and we set about ordering the stores — for the tribute had already begun to flow into Caer Melyn from all who had pledged to uphold the War Leader. The news of Arthur's victories had stirred the lords of Britain to something resembling extravagance.

Though the winter proved dark and cold, and the snow deep — as deep as ever I have seen it, I think: clothing the hilltops and mountains in cloaks of purest white, and enfolding the valleys in mantles of thick fleece — we did not mind. The fire burned bright in Arthur's hall, and Myrddin sang the songs of valour and great deeds. Our hearts soared.

At mid-winter we observed a fine and holy Christ Mass. The new-made Bishop Teilo performed the mass, joined by Illtyd and other churchmen of renown in the region. Indeed, the church seemed especially eager to lavish its blessing on Arthur's golden head, for they saw in him the preservation of their sacred work from the ravages of the barbarians and their loathly idols. Indeed, the good brothers were the first to suffer the slaughter and torture of the heathen; always it was a priest's blood spilled on the ruined altar, the monk's body put to the flame.

So, the churchmen were right to bless Arthur, and eager to offer up every prayer for his continued good health and long life. In all, the Christ Mass at Caer Melyn that year gave us all a foretaste of Arthur's reign. And a more blessed and joyous realm I could not imagine, nor hope to find anywhere.

The winter proved far too short for my pleasure. Warmth crept back into the land; the sun lingered longer in the lifting sky. Rivers swelled with rain, the wind gentled, and the green land blossomed.

As soon as the trackways cleared, I rode to the hill-hidden breeding runs to oversee the year's colting. The breeders and trainers had done their work well: two hundred horses stood ready to join the *ala*. Arthur's warband would not have to walk to battle this year — nor, from the look of it, for many years to come.

I did not deceive myself that the war was over. Even with their *Bretwalda* dead, the Angli would not give up. They would simply choose a new leader and the war would begin again.

Had I possessed Myrddin's exalted Sight, I could not have foreseen who that leader would be, nor how powerful.

The ships began guarding the coastline as soon as the winter gales ceased for good. From Muir Guidan to the Wash, all along the Bernich coast the ships kept a restless watch. Alas, that was not how the enemy would strike this time. There would be no more sea raids, no more massed attacks on the open field, no more pitched battles at fords. The barbarians respected Arthur's genius that much at least. From now on we would fight a different war.

One morning just after Beltane a small retinue arrived at Caer Melyn. Dressed in their best finery, I did not at first know them: a dozen men in red-and-black checked cloaks, and bright tunics and trousers of blue and orange. Their hair was greased and braided, and their beards trimmed short. Gold and silver glinted from their arms, necks and ears. They held themselves erect, proud and haughty, men and women both astride stocky, winter-shagged ponies — a company of thirty in all, including a grey-mantled druid going before to lead them.

'They are a colourful brood,' I remarked, observing the strangers from my place beside Arthur. 'Who are they?'

Arthur's blue eyes narrowed as he scanned the group gathered in the yard. All at once, recognition broke like sunrise across his face. 'Fergus!'

The Duke strode forth to receive his visitor, while I stood gaping in disbelief. Fergus? Here? I thought that we had seen the last of him.

'Hail, Duke of Britain! I give you good greeting,' called Fergus mac Guillomar in his thickly accented tongue. He spoke with due formality, but then swung down from his horse and embraced Arthur like a kinsman.

'What do you here, Irishman?' asked Arthur mildly. Yet the question was direct.

'I have come with my retinue to pay the tribute of gold and hostages that I owe.'

Arthur grinned, obviously pleased. 'I own the right of tribute, it is true. But I have made no demands on you.'

'Am I a barbarian that I repay honour with dishonour?' Fergus demanded. He turned quickly to his retinue, now dismounting, and called one of them forth.

A dark lanky youth with a long, serious face and deep-set black eyes under brooding brows stepped forward. He carried a long spear with a gleaming silver head. Across his shoulders he wore a cloak made from wildcat skins. The torc of braided silver at his throat spoke of nobility.

'This is Llwch Llenlleawg,' said Fergus proudly. 'He is the champion of our people. He is also my sister's son, my fosterling and kinsman. I deliver him as hostage to you. May his service bring you great reward.'

Arthur appraised the young man thoughtfully — not wishing to offend Fergus by rejecting his offer outright. But, before he could speak, the Irish king beckoned another to him: a slender young woman.

I have known and admired many young women, but this one was like no other I had ever seen. Her hair, so black it shimmered with a blue sheen in the sun, was pulled back to fall around her graceful neck and shoulders in a mass of braids: deepest jet against the pure alabaster of her flawless skin. She wore a disdainful expression, her lips pressed firmly together and her chin outthrust, as she regarded Arthur with keen grey eyes the colour of a dove's wing, or the mist that comes down from the mountain in the morning. The high, noble sweep of her brows and straight nose gave her the aspect of a queen.

Her long slender fingers held tightly to the haft of a spear. She carried a golden dagger on one smooth hip, a short sword on the other, and a small bronze-bossed shield on a braided cord over one slim shoulder. Her cloak was soft wool, dyed deepest red, gathered in an enormous golden brooch upon her breast. Most surprising of all, she wore a shirt of Angli mail, but the ringlets were small and exquisite, made of silver. It gleamed as she moved, like shining water rippling over her fair form.

She was dazzling, and despite her battle dress, easily the most beautiful woman I have ever seen. She advanced slowly and came to stand beside Fergus, though her gaze never left Arthur. The look she gave him could have cut steel, I think, but the Duke seemed not to notice.

'This is Gwenhwyvar,' Fergus said, 'my daughter.'

He signalled the druid who came forth with a bundle of cloth in his outstretched hands. The druid gave the bundle to Arthur, and then unwrapped the cloth to reveal four golden torcs of the most remarkable quality and design — each more beautiful than the last.

It was clear that Fergus was giving Arthur his most highly prized possessions: his champion, his daughter, the ancient treasures of his people.

Arthur was rightly speechless. He stared at the gold, and then at the girl and the warrior, and back to Fergus. 'I am honoured,' he said at length. 'Your tribute shames my small kindness.'

'I have pledged my life, Duke Arthur, and I know well what my life is worth,' replied Fergus proudly.

'I accept your tribute and your fealty, O King.'

What have you done, Arthur? I wondered. We will never see the end of this now!

Arthur gripped Fergus' arms like a kinsman. 'Come, my

friend,' he announced boldly, 'we will share the guest cup.'

Fergus beamed his pleasure, gratified to be treated this way by Arthur. I stood in the yard, gazing after them as they all moved into the hall. I was not the only one disturbed by this development. For, as I turned to follow the others, I saw Myrddin standing a little away.

'Did you hear?' I asked.

'I heard.'

'Well?'

'There is much in this that I do not like.'

'Oh, it is trouble,' I agreed. 'All saints bear witness, nothing good comes of accepting gifts from the Irish.'

Myrddin frowned, dismissing my observation with a distracted wave of his hand. 'It is more than that, Jealous One.'

He turned away, and I charged after him. 'Jealous! Me? Why do you call me jealous?'

But Myrddin would not answer. He made his way into the hall and to his place beside Arthur at the hearth table. The cups had been filled and were passing from hand to hand. I reluctantly joined the odd celebration and drank when the cup came to me. I noticed that Myrddin did not drink, however, but hovered at Arthur's shoulder like a guarding angel.

It was not until late afternoon that Myrddin gained opportunity of speaking to Arthur in private. 'A word, Arthur,' he said, and moved off towards the Duke's chamber at the end of the hall. Arthur rose, and since he did not bid me stay, I went with him.

'It is a mistake,' the Emrys said at once, his tone low and serious. 'You cannot accept the tribute.'

Arthur spread his hands helplessly. 'But I have already done so.'

'Undo it.'

'I cannot, even if I wanted to — which I do not.'

'You can and must.'

'What is it, Myrddin? What is troubling you?'

Myrddin was silent for a long moment. 'It is the woman,' he said at last.

'What about her?' asked Arthur innocently. 'I saw nothing in her to cause such dread.'

'She is a queen. . . '

'She is Fergus' daughter — '

'It is the same thing with them. Do you not know this? By accepting her, you are agreeing to marry her. Fergus would not have given her to you otherwise.'

Arthur gaped stupidly at his Wise Counsellor.

'Well? Nothing to say, Mighty Duke? Did such a thing never occur to you?'

'On my life, I confess that it did not,' replied Arthur indignantly.

'It is true. This champion, Llenlleawg — he is Fergus' champion, yes; but he is the queen's protector first. And the gift of gold — her people's wealth,' said Myrddin in a softer tone. 'Arthur, it is her bride gift, and a greater gift could not be made. Fergus honours you highly — perhaps too highly.'

'What do you mean?' asked Arthur suspiciously.

'Among the Irish the kingship is passed through the woman to her husband.'

'Ha!' I crowed. 'You would be king of Ierne, Bear! Think of that!'

'It is no small thing!' snapped Myrddin. To Arthur he said, 'Think! The High King of Britain must have a British wife.'

Arthur glared at me and stiffened. 'That is my decision, surely. No man will tell me who I shall take to wife.'

'Your arrogance will cost you the High Kingship. The lords of Britain will never own you king with an Irish queen for your wife. By accepting Fergus' daughter, you are declaring her above all the noble women of Britain, and so exalting Fergus above all the kings of Britain.'

The Duke folded his arms across his chest. 'Then so be it! What British king has ever treated me with half as much respect as this enemy has done?'

'Think what you are doing, Arthur. Give her back to Fergus,' Myrddin urged.

'My honour will not allow it!'

'It is pride you are talking about, not honour,' Myrddin Emrys told him flatly. 'If you take this woman, your precious honour will be ruined beyond all hope of repair. It will mean your kingdom and much else besides.'

The Duke glared at us, but said nothing.

'Please, do as your Wise Counsellor suggests and think about it, at least,' I told him, 'before you do something we will all regret.'

Myrddin and I left him there alone. 'Will he heed us, do you think?' I asked.

'The truth? No, I do not expect that he will,' the Emrys said. Something in his voice made me wonder: sadness? despair? What did he foresee from this? Why would he not speak it out?

Well, he is like that. I do not presume to reckon his ways.

Arthur did not back down, and he did not decline Fergus mac Guillomar's tribute, though it would have saved him much pain, and not a little peace of mind to do so. But then, in so doing he would not be Arthur.

Fergus also brought another gift — no less valuable in its own way: news, which he shared with us over meat that night.

The Picti, he said, were massing in the northern wastes and appeared likely to strike southward before the summer was out. Ships had been seen slinking along the western coast and darting among the western islands. 'They seek blood vengeance for the defeat you gave them in Celyddon,' Fergus suggested. 'I would not be surprised if the Angli joined them in this. They will have nursed their defeat into hatred through the winter.'

'Have you word that the Angli will attack?' asked Arthur.

Fergus wagged his head from side to side. 'I do not. Neither do I have word that day will dawn in the east, yet I think it unwise to assume differently.'

Arthur thanked Fergus for these tidings, and nothing more was said at the time. But three days later, as the Irish made ready to leave, Arthur called Gwalchavad to him. 'Ready the remaining ships, we are sailing north with the tide.'

This he did as Cai and Bors assembled the warband. Myrddin and I held council with the Duke in his chambers. 'Wait at least until the kings can attend you,' I said. 'We should not be seen rushing into an ambush.'

'You doubt Fergus?'

'I do not doubt Fergus, but neither do I trust the Picti. We must strike quickly, I agree — but we must strike with force.'

'Every day we delay the enemy grows more daring. We will guard the coasts and harry them until the other kings join us.'

Myrddin leaned forward on his staff. 'It is not too late, Arthur. Send the woman and her protector back with Fergus. I will do it, if you like. Fergus will have no cause for offence.'

The Duke replied softly. 'I have given my word. I will not take it back.' That was the end of it certainly. But Myrddin was not finished.

'If you are determined, Arthur, let the lady and her treasure be escorted to Ynys Avallach. She will be safe there, and out of the way. My mother will welcome the company — perhaps she may even educate this fiery maid to some British manners.'

Arthur happily accepted this suggestion. 'So be it, Myrddin. I bow to your counsel.'

I was less than pleased, for in the same breath Arthur turned to me and said, 'You will take Gwenhwyvar to the Glass Isle, Bedwyr.'

'Me? Arthur, be reasonable! It is no fit task for a battlechief. You will need me with you. Let someone else go. Send Cai or, better yet, send Bors — he deems himself a hero with women. Any of your warriors will serve as well.'

Arthur clapped a big paw onto my shoulder. 'It must be you, my brother. I will not insult Fergus or his daughter by sending less of a man than my own champion.'

'It seems to me you put too much faith in that Irish rogue,' I grumbled. 'You worry more about imagined offence to your enemies than genuine insults to your friends.'

Sooner pour out your heart to a stone; I grumbled to no avail. Arthur's mind was made up and he would not be moved. I had no choice but to strike off at once for Ynys Avallach.

If I was unhappy with the arrangement, Gwenhwyvar was furious. She saw the preparations for battle and fully expected to fight. To be indifferently hauled away like a sack of grain kindled her wrath full well. I have never seen a woman so angry.

Her eyes blazed and her cheeks and throat blushed crimson. One look at the horse standing saddled before her and she dug in her heels. Her fingers became claws and her tongue a sharp and skilful lash with which she flayed the ears of those around her — Arthur especially, I think, as his name bubbled to the surface regularly. Unfortunately, much of her complaint was in the Irish tongue so I did not understand the finer shadings, but the general flow was manifestly clear.

I lightly touched her arm to move her towards the horse, and almost lost my hand. Her knife was out and in her hand quicker than a flick. She turned on me, livid and spitting. The dagger would have found its home in my heart if Llenlleawg had not put himself between Gwenhwyvar and me at that moment.

He spoke a sharp word or two and she subsided. The dagger slipped back to its sheath. Without another glance the queen swung herself into the saddle and jerked the reins smartly.

The Irishman turned to me. 'It was not seemly. . . I am sorry.'

His apology took me aback. 'It does not matter. But I want no further trouble.'

'I am your servant, Lord Bedwyr.'

'You know me?'

'Who has not heard of Bedwyr, Bright Avenger, Swift Sword of Arthur?' Llenlleawg moved away at once and mounted his horse. I stood looking after the tall young Irishman and wondering how far I could trust him. They are known to be a deceitful and wicked race, and the truth is not in them. Still, I wondered.

We left Caer Melyn at once. I wanted to deliver the hostages to Ynys Avallach and return as quickly as possible, so that I could join Arthur in the north. Therefore I took only three others with me and we hurried down to the shipyard at Abertaff, where we boarded one of the smaller ships to cross Mor Hafren.

Once aboard ship, Gwenhwyvar went to the prow and stood there, rigid, arms folded across her breast, face set, eyes staring straight ahead. If she had been carved of solid stone she could not have been more adamant and unyielding.

I took Barinthus, Arthur's foremost pilot, because after leaving Ynys Avallach I wanted a swift journey north. Barinthus steered a close course and landed us well up the Briw river, not far from the Glass Isle. We camped on the riverbank that night, and rode on to the Tor the next day. Gwenhwyvar maintained an active and hostile silence all the while.

'You are welcome here,' said Charis graciously. 'May the peace of Christ be with you.' Swathed in deepest green, with a flowing mantle of shimmering gold, she seemed a queen of the Otherworld to my eyes. She greeted each one of us with a kiss, drawing us into the glimmering hall. At once I felt the gentling spirit of the place grace my soul.

Gwenhwyvar, too, was cowed by Charis' kindness and elegance. I prayed the Irish maid would remain so, and trusted that she would, for the Tor had already begun to work its mysterious enchantment upon us all.

Much as I would have enjoyed sojourning in Avallach's palace, Barinthus was waiting with the ship to take me back. So I left the hostages in the care of King Avallach and the Lady of the Lake and returned with the escort to the ship at dawn the next morning.

Upon reaching the ship, I hailed the pilot, and the men settled the horses aboard. But, as Barinthus made to cast off, he stood suddenly and pointed at the track behind me. I swung round and saw Llenlleawg riding to join us.

'You are to remain at Ynys Avallach!' I shouted as he came near, running forward as if to bar his way further.

He gazed placidly down at me from the saddle. 'I am the queen's champion. She has commanded me to attend the Duke.'

'And I have commanded you to stay!'

He shrugged and climbed down from his horse. 'It is my life to obey the queen,' he replied easily and, stepping round me, proceeded to take his horse onto the ship.

I should have sent him back, but I was anxious to be away and in no humour to argue with him in front of the men.

'Arthur will deal with you,' I told him darkly, and let the matter rest there for the moment.

I gave Barinthus the order, and we pushed off from the bank. We hastened away, reaching Mor Hafren with the tideflow. Whereupon we turned west into the setting sun, hoisted sail, and made for the open sea.

THIRTEEN

The Picti had swarmed Caer Alclyd and seized the old fortress, intending to establish a stronghold against us. Like the Angli, they had abandoned open-field battle. They thought to secure themselves in the rock dun and make us root them out from behind stout walls.

By the time I reached the plain below the rock, the battle lines were drawn and Arthur had laid siege to the fortress. He had not attacked the caer, but was inclined to let the siege run its course. This plan enjoyed a double benefit — the Duke would not risk warriors unnecessarily, and he could wait until the British kings joined him and his forces reached full strength.

Ships rode in the Clyd and warbands ringed the great grey rock as we sailed into the estuary. Arthur had camped to the north of the dun, where he could oversee both the water and the rock, and I sought him out the moment my feet touched dry land. It was nearing dusk and the clear northern light shone all honeyed and golden as I rode up the rise to his tent.

He sat in his camp chair outside his tent talking to Cador, who had arrived earlier in the day with a warband of five hundred. Arthur rose as I slipped from the saddle. 'Hail, Bedwyr, my brother! I give you good greeting!'

'Hail, Bear of Britain! What do you here, my Duke? You take your ease while the vile Picti thumb the nose at you?'

'Better their noses than their arrows.' He wrapped me in a rough embrace and clapped me on the back. He broke off abruptly and said, 'I thought to commend you, Bedwyr, but it appears praise might prove overhasty.'

I glanced back over my shoulder and followed Arthur's gaze, to see lanky Llenlleawg trotting up the hill. He had followed me from the ship. 'Oh, him,' I said. 'I can explain.'

'There is no need,' Arthur said. 'I can see what has happened.' He stepped away from me and squared off to meet the headstrong Irishman, his face and manner becoming stern.

But, upon reaching the Duke, Llenlleawg threw himself from his horse and quickly drew his short sword, which he placed at Arthur's feet, then stretched himself face down upon the ground. Arthur turned to me, a curious smile on his lips. I spread my hands helplessly.

Arthur observed the prostrate form before him. 'Get you up, Irishman,' he said. 'I will not demand your head — this time, at least.'

Llenlleawg rose slowly, retrieved his sword and replaced it beneath his cloak, keeping his dark eyes downcast all the while.

'What have you to say?' demanded Arthur, not altogether severely.

'On pain of death I am commanded to serve you, Lord Duke.'

'Who has so commanded you?'

Llenlleawg cocked his long head to one side, as if this should have been self-evident. 'Queen Gwenhwyvar has commanded me.'

'You are *my* hostage,' Arthur reminded him.

'The Duke holds my freedom, but the queen holds my life,' the Irishman replied. 'I am here to serve you, lord.'

'What good is a servant that I cannot command?'

'If I have displeased you, Lord Duke, I offer my life.' Llenlleawg made to withdraw his sword again.

Arthur stopped him. 'Put up your sword, Irish Fool. You dull the edge dragging it out like that all the time.'

Llenlleawg removed his hand and knelt on both knees before the Duke. 'I am your man, Duke Arthur. I will swear fealty to you by whatever oaths your people hold most honourable. I will serve you faithfully in all things save one only: I will not harm nor see harm done to the queen.'

'Then arise and serve me with a whole heart, Irishman. For no harm will come to your queen through me as long as she remains in my care.'

311

Cador stared at Arthur as if he had lost his sense. 'You cannot think to take him at his word!' I charged. 'They could be plotting against you, for all you know.'

'So could you, Bedwyr,' Arthur replied. 'So could Cador. Idris and Maglos and others already have!' He stretched forth a hand to Llenlleawg. 'If you would pledge to me, swear by this: your faith on the life of your queen.'

Still kneeling, the Irishman said, 'I, Llenlleawg mac Dermaidh, pledge fealty to you on my life and the life of my queen, Gwenhwyvar ui Fergus. May both be forfeit if I prove false.'

'There,' said Arthur. 'Are you satisfied?' To Llenlleawg, he said, 'Take the horses to the picket, and then find yourself something to eat. You may return to me here when you have finished.'

Arthur and Cador returned to discussing the siege, and I dragged up a camp stool and listened. Cador had come by nearly the identical route that I had travelled, and gave the same report. 'We saw no ships at all, Duke Arthur,' Cador said. 'Though the enemy can ply between the western islands with impunity and we would never see them.'

'What word from the ships on the east coast?'

'No word yet. But I have sent messengers to Ectorius at Caer Edyn, informing him of my plans. They will return in a day or so with any news from that quarter.' Arthur paused, watching the stewards who had set about kindling his fire for the night. 'But one thing troubles me in this. . . '

'Which is?' I asked. The Duke gazed long at the dusky sky. Lark song spilled down from the blue heights. But for the smoke rising ominously from the great rock, I would have thought the world composed and perfectly at peace.

'What do the Picti want with this fortress?' Arthur said at last. 'It is nothing to them.'

'Control Caer Alclyd,' Cador suggested, 'and they can control the whole valley to the Fiorthe.'

'Not without Caer Edyn,' Arthur pointed out.

'Perhaps they hope to win here and go on to take Caer Edyn as well.'

'That is very ambitious of the Picti, is it not?'

It was true. Though fierce, the Painted People were not known for cunning. A savage growl and a club to the skull — that was their way. Overpowering the guard and seizing a fortress was not like the Picti; they preferred slicing throats and slinking away into the forests and heathered moors.

'What does it mean, Bear?' I asked.

'It means, I think, that someone is directing them.'

'Who?'

Arthur lifted his shoulders. 'That we shall have to discover.'

Over the next few days the British battlelords began assembling on the Clyd: Owain, Idris, Ceredig, Ennion, Maelgwn and Maglos. British ships filled the estuary and British warbands encircled Dun Rock on every side. The Picti did not seem discouraged or upset by this show of force. They kept themselves well hidden behind the walls and waited. When the first of Arthur's messengers returned, we began to understand their unusual behaviour.

'Caer Edyn is besieged, Duke Arthur,' the messenger reported. The British chieftains gathered in council in Arthur's tent fell silent. 'I could not reach Lord Ectorius.'

Cai, sitting next to me, leapt to his feet. 'Ector besieged! Damn the heathen! Who has done this?'

The messenger's eyes shifted to Cai's. 'They were Angli, for all I could see. And some Picti.'

'How did things appear at the caer?' asked Arthur. 'Was there fighting?'

'No fighting that I could see, lord. The stronghold appeared secure. I turned and rode straight back, but was twice delayed by warbands coming up from the south. I followed to see where they would go.'

'What did you see?'

'They were making for the old fortress at Trath Gwryd.'

'Indeed!' exclaimed Arthur. 'Then they have learned real warfare at last. Who has taught them this, I wonder?'

'This is not the calculation of a barbarian mind,' remarked Myrddin. 'Someone who has fought with British kings is leading this war.'

Who could that be? Most of the nobility of Britain was either fighting alongside Arthur or supporting him. Only one was conspicuous by his absence: Lot. Could it be Lot? That made no sense: Lot had given us ships, and shipwrights. His own sons had taken service in the Duke's army. I glanced at Gwalchavad, who appeared just as concerned and angry as the rest of us. There was no guile in him, nor treachery that I could see. Blessed Jesu, I would stake my life on it!

So the mystery remained: who could it be?

'They will have taken Trath Gwryd,' said Arthur, upon dismissing the messenger to food and rest, 'and have laid siege to Caer Alclyd and to Caer Edyn. This they have done with stealth and silence. They have chosen their positions well: fortresses instead of fords — our mounted warriors are all but useless. And, except for Caer Edyn, they have the advantage.' Arthur paused, his blue eyes sweeping the assembly before him. 'If they succeed,' he continued, his voice low, 'all we have done till now is less than nothing. Britain will fail.'

He had spoken the cold heart of fear. Now he spoke the bright fire of hope. 'Yet they have not won. The battle remains to be fought. We are not beaten because they have outwitted us this once. He of the Strong Sure Hand will uphold us, brothers, for we fight for peace and freedom, which is ever his good pleasure.'

Arthur raised his hands like a priest giving benediction, and said, 'Go now to your tents, and to your prayers, for tomorrow we begin. And once we have begun we will not cease until the Day of Peace has dawned in all Britain.'

The others left, but Cai, Gwalchavad, Bors, Myrddin and I stayed, for the Duke wished to speak to us privately. 'Will you drink with me, friends?' Arthur asked.

'Sooner ask if a pig would grunt,' said Bors, 'than ask if Cai would drink!'

'Sooner ask that pig to fly,' replied Cai, 'than ask Bors to pass the cup!'

We all laughed, and drew our chairs round Arthur's board. The steward brought in jars and cups and placed them at the Duke's right hand.

As soon as we had drunk a cup together, we fell to discussing what was foremost on our minds: tomorrow's battle.

'A few of those machines Myrddin made for us last year would aid us now,' said Bors. 'We could make some.'

314

'No time,' said Cai. He was thinking of Caer Edyn, and his father besieged there. 'We must assault the walls.'

'You would brave those Picti arrows?'

'I am not afraid of their arrows.'

'You are welcome to them, then,' said Gwalchavad. 'In Orcady it is said: the Picti have only to see a bird to shoot it out of the sky.'

'Even the Picti cannot shoot what they cannot see,' put in Arthur.

'Then perhaps we should fight at night!' I said. Arthur smiled and slapped his knee.

All eyes turned to Myrddin, as a single thought gripped our minds. 'The moon will rise tonight,' he told us, 'but not until after the third watch.'

'We attack *tonight*!'

Never have I seen a sky so ablaze with stars, never so alive with light. Although the moon had not risen, the cloudless night seemed like bright midday to me. We all wore dark cloaks, and our faces were blackened with mud. We crawled over the cold rock on our stomachs, our swords hidden, our spearheads and shield bosses muddied. We hugged the ragged stone to our chests and climbed on elbows and knees towards the looming walls above.

Jesu preserve us, the Picti sentries regularly looked down over us! But their attention was occupied with the show of fire Arthur had contrived to conceal us: down in the camps men danced with torches and sang raucous songs. Their voices carried to the dun and urged us on.

Arthur, despite the objections of his chieftains, led the assault himself — up the cragged east side, well away from the narrow gate track. Once we reached the walls, one of us would go up and over to open the gate.

The one chosen for this was Llenlleawg. He volunteered almost before the words were out of Arthur's mouth, and the Duke was bound to let him do it or defame the Irishman by refusing. Since we had no reason to deny him — other than the fact we did not completely trust him — Arthur agreed. So Llenlleawg carried the braided rope and iron hook beneath his cloak.

After what seemed an age, we reached the perimeter of the wall. Huddled under cover of its shadowed roots, we waited.

I do not know how it happened: one moment I was looking down onto the firelit plain, and the next Picti arrows were whispering around me, striking the rocks and shattering their flint tips. I pressed myself flat against the wall, and others took what cover they could.

All at once I heard a shout. Out of the corner of my eye I saw someone stand. A rope snaked out and was pulled taut. The lone figure began to climb. . .

Llenlleawg! The mad Irishman was proceeding with the attack. Arrows flying, he had secured the hook and was climbing the wall. . . Jesu save him, he would be killed the instant he reached the top!

I expected next to see his pierced body plummet from the walltop to be dashed upon the rocks and, with him, our hopes of taking the fortress quickly.

But Llenlleawg somehow skittered up the sheer rock face and gained the top. A body fell — but it was not Llenlleawg's. I could tell it was a Pict, even in the darkness.

Somehow all this took place in silence — yet a more noise-battered silence I never want to hear! An entire age passed in the space of a few terror-fraught heartbeats.

Llenlleawg disappeared over the rim of the wall. And then. . .

Nothing.

A figure rose from the gloom beside me. Arthur's voice whispered urgently, 'Make for the gate! Go!'

I edged my way along the rough wall face, moving as quickly and quietly as possible. From the walltop above I heard not a sound — only the echoed shrieks rising from the camps. The dun was entered from the north by a single narrow door. I peered cautiously round the eastern corner and saw no sign of a guard above. I ran to the gate, reached it, and pressed my ear to the thick wood. I heard nothing from within.

I hunched down before the door and waited, signalling the others behind me to stay well back. An age passed, and another. . . I was about to go back to Arthur, when

I heard a slight scratching noise on the other side of the door.

I pressed myself against the coarse wood. The scratching sound became a sharp rap, followed by another, and the muffled sound of someone cursing under his breath. It was Llenlleawg — the gate was stuck!

Seeking to help him, I pushed with all my might, and one of the warriors behind joined me and together we heaved our weight at the gate. But it would not budge.

'Get back!' came a hushed cry from the other side.

There came a whir in the air and the dull chunk of an arrow striking into the wooden planking of the door. Then another.

The Picti had found the Irishman! Our attack was discovered.

'Get back!' Llenlleawg called loudly — silence was no use to us now. 'You are pushing the wrong way!'

I stumbled back, and at once the door swung wide. The gate opened outward! How was I to know that?

I dived through the narrow opening, rolled on the stone flagging and came up with my sword in my hand. Warriors followed on my heels. Arrows whirred around our heads like bees, chunking into the wood or shattering against the stone and bursting into stinging fragments.

We swarmed into the yard and onto the walls. The Picti, newly roused and wakened, raised the alarm with their piercing battle wail as we hewed into them.

Suddenly, there was torchlight all around. More and more Picti were pouring into the yard. Their blue-stained bodies writhed in the dancing light, garish as nightmares. They rushed upon us with their long knives and double-headed axes. They howled in rage at our invasion.

Before I knew it we were being forced back out of the door by the press of enemy. 'Hold ground!' I cried. 'Hold, Cymbrogi!' But there were too many of us jammed in the gateway and those behind could not get in. We were trapped between the enemy and our own warriors. And there we would die.

A torch sailed high through the air towards us. I ducked aside as it struck the ground at my feet, and made to reach for it. But the brand was snatched from me and carried off. I looked and saw the torch become a shining trail of flame, whirling and spinning into the barbarian host.

Sparks of fire showered all around, and wherever the torch struck, a body fell. The fire gambolled as if alive. Driving, smashing, reeling, twisting, and twirling away before the enemy could react. The barbarians screamed and fell back before this dreadful killing apparition.

In the fireshot mist of shattered shadow-light I saw the face of our deliverer: Llenlleawg, the Irishman. It was a visage I shall never forget — stark and terrible in its rage, burning like the torch in his hand, eyes bulging with madness, mouth contorted and teeth bared like the fangs of a wildcat! It was Llenlleawg, and the battle frenzy was on him.

'Cymbrogi!' I screamed, and dashed forward into the surging turmoil of the Irishman's bloody wake.

I slashed and thrust with my sword, striking out in the confused darkness at any bit of exposed flesh. I knew my strokes succeeded from the weight that first hindered, then fell from my blade. The ground beneath my feet became slick with blood. The smell of blood and bile hung thick in the air.

I could not see Arthur.

I fought forward, little heeding if any came behind me. My only thought was to overtake the battle-mad Irishman. I hewed mightily but, each time I looked, I found him further ahead — the whirling torch dancing lightly as windtossed thistledown. I heard his voice rising above the battle blare, quavering, calling, swooping like a hunting bird: he was singing.

'Cymbrogi! Fight!' Over and over I shouted, and my cry was answered by the high clear note of Rhys' horn. The forces waiting below the dun had seen the fight commence and had stormed the rock. Now they were shoving in through the gate, and swarming over the walls on ropes and the laddered poles we had prepared. The Picti were thrown into panic, rushing here and there, striking wildly and foolishly.

I lost all sight of anything but the tangled limbs of the enemy before me. I chopped with my sword as if hacking through the dense and knotted snarls of a bramble thicket.

I laboured long, ignoring the ache spreading from shoulder to wrist.

Smashing with my shield, stabbing with my sword, lunging, plunging headlong into the howling enemy. . .

And then it was finished.

We stood in the fire-reddened yard, Picti corpses piled around us. The stink of blood and entrails in the air and on our hands. Black blood, shimmering in the light of a rising moon. The enemy dead. . . all dead. The caer quiet.

I raised my head and saw three men struggling with a fourth, and went to lend my aid, thinking it must be the captured Picti chieftain. But it was Llenlleawg. He was still deep in his battle frenzy and, though the fight was over, he could not stop. Cai and Cador had found him lopping the heads from the corpses and heaving them over the wall.

'Irishman!' I shouted into his face. 'Peace! It is over! Stop!'

He could not hear me. I think he could no longer hear anything. There was no sense in him any more. I ran to the nearby trough and lifted a leather bucket, returned and dashed the water into Llenlleawg's face. He sputtered, stared, gave a sharp cry and fell back limply.

'He must be wounded,' said Cai, pushing his helmet back. 'A blow on the head.'

'I do not see any blood,' replied Cador, holding close the torch he had wrested from the Irishman's hand.

'No blood? He is verily drenched in it!'

'Stay with him,' I told Cador, 'until he wakes up, then have him taken back to camp.' To Cai I said, 'Get some more torches and begin searching for wounded. I am going to find Arthur.'

I could have saved my breath, for already scores of warriors were beginning to carry out the wounded. Due to the closeness of the stronghold not all of our attack force could crowd into the yard. Most, it appeared, had remained outside and only now were able to move in. These carried torches and hastened to the task of caring for their fallen sword brothers. Arthur stood on the wall above the gate directing them.

I climbed the steep-stepped rampart and joined him. 'We have taken the fortress, War Leader.'

'Well done, Bedwyr.' He made it sound as if *I* had done it single-handed. He surveyed the torchlit yard beneath him. The flickering shadows made it seem as if the fight still raged silently all around us. The growing heap of enemy corpses told a different tale.

'Is Llenlleawg still alive?' the Duke asked presently.

'Yes,' I answered, weariness beginning to seep into my arms and legs. 'He lives, and not a scrape on him that I could see. How? I do not know. Did you see?'

'I saw.'

'He is mad,' I said. 'I can well see why he was Fergus' champion. Who can fight a whirlwind?'

Later, when all the British dead and wounded had been removed, and the Picti wounded killed — it is a hard fact of war, but we put the enemy wounded to the sword, for we were leaving the next day and they would have received no care; better the quick thrust that sends them across the Western Sea to the Fortunate Isles, or wherever they go, than the lingering torture of a slow death. We burned the bodies of our countrymen in the fortress where they fell, and threw the enemy over the southern wall to the tide flats below. Govannon would take them to feed his fishes.

We stood aloft on the walls of Caer Alclyd and watched the flames reach towards heaven. Blind Myrddin stood with his arms extended over the pyre the whole time, chanting a psalm of victory in death. The Cymry lifted their voices in the song of mourning, which begins as a sigh, grows to a wail, and ends as a triumphant shout. In this way, we sang the souls of our fallen into Blessed Jesu's welcoming arms.

Then we went down to our camps to sleep. The sun was rising, pearling the night vault in the east to glowing alabaster. The dawn was fair, and the grass inviting; I stretched out on the ground outside Arthur's tent. Exhausted as I was, I could not sleep, so lay gazing up into the sky at the slowly fading stars. In a little while the Irishman, Llenlleawg, crept silently to Arthur's tent. He did not know that I was awake, so I watched him to see what he would do. He drew his sword. Was it treachery?

My hand went to my knife. But no, I need not have feared. Llenlleawg placed the sword at his head and lay down across the entrance, as if to protect the Duke while he slept.

At midday, after we had eaten, we broke camp and moved off along the overgrown track of Little Wall — called Guaul in that region — the northernmost wall built by the Romans and then abandoned. It is a ruin mostly, a grass-covered hump; and the old road is not good. But to the east lies a good road running north and south. Reaching this, we turned north to the old fortress of Trath Gwryd.

And I turned my thoughts once more to the mystery at hand: who was directing the war against us?

FOURTEEN

There has been a fortress at Trath Gwryd from ancient times. Like Caer Alclyd on the west coast and Caer Edyn on the east, it is built atop an enormous rock above a river, and stands between them in the centre of the invasion route. And like Caer Alclyd the Picti had seized the old rock-top fortress, intending to defend it against us.

Upon reaching the sands of Gwryd, below the rock, we camped and laid siege to the rock. Almost at once Arthur's scouts began returning with further reports about the enemy siege at Caer Edyn: Ectorius still held the fortress, and seemed in no immediate danger; the stronghold remained solid and secure.

King Custennin of Celyddon arrived with more disturbing news: others were coming into the war. Along with the Angli there were Jutes, Mercians and Frisians from across the northern sea; Scoti and Attacoti from Ierne; and Cruithne joining with the blue-painted Picti. In short, all the old enemies of Roman Britain. The new *Bretwalda*, whoever he was, had stirred the pot well.

God's mercy, there were no Saecsens. Somehow the peace in the south held true, or the fight would have been finished before it began.

Anxious to move on to the defence of Ector at Caer Edyn as soon as possible, Arthur dealt with the rock fort quickly, using the same night raid tactic with which we had reconquered Caer Alclyd. The battle was short and sharp, and we prevailed. The fortress duly secured, we turned east to the rescue of Ectorius.

We passed through several small holdings and settlements along the way. The barbarians had been there before us and had left behind the black mark of their passing — a smouldering scar of destruction, bleak and terrible, a bleeding wound upon the land. Crops burned, cattle driven, goods plundered and carried off, and all else ruined.

Bitter smoke and ashes filled our mouths; tears filled our eyes. For in each of the holdings the bodies of men, women and infants lay strewn among the debris. Not content to fire the buildings and slaughter the people, at each place the barbarians left a grisly reminder of their cruelty and hate: a disembowelled corpse lying in the centre of the road, stomach carved open and lungs spread out upon the chest, liver pulled out and placed between the lungs, the heart severed and laid on top, the genitals cut off and stuffed in the mouth.

It was a sight to sicken, to dishearten, to taunt. Not a man among us who saw it failed to imagine himself or his sword brother or kinsman lying dead there — dismembered and dishonoured. Fear and humiliation were kindled by the ghastly spectacle and spread like a noxious stench through our ranks.

But, in each place where this atrocity was practised, Arthur acted forthrightly. He ordered the body to be wrapped in a clean cloak and decently buried, with prayers spoken over the body.

This helped ease our dismay, but did not banish it. Daunted and sick with dread we drew near Caer Edyn. Custennin had warned us, and we were ready. Yet the first sight of the besieging host encamped upon low hills below the caer stole the light from our eyes and the warmth from our hearts.

'They were not lying when they told you the whole barbarian realm had come to Caer Edyn,' Cai said. 'How did so many escape our ships?'

Arthur's face hardened like flint. His eyes turned the colour of Yr Widdfa in storm. 'Breathe the air, my friends,' he said. We drew a deep breath of the fresh, salt-tinged breeze. 'It tastes of triumph, does it not?'

Seeing the black smoke curling into the blue-white sky and the loathsome masses swarming about the roots of Ector's strong fortress brought the sour gall to my lips. 'It tastes of death, Artos,' I replied.

'Death or triumph, I will embrace one or the other before this day is done.'

At this moment the barbarian host sent up a deafening screech. 'This sound, so hateful to our ears, will no more be heard in Britain,' observed Myrddin, sitting his horse, hands folded calmly before him. His golden eyes, as ever, were bound in a length of white linen. 'I have seen the face of the *Bretwalda*: it is a Briton's face and its features are well known to us all.'

This the Emrys spoke as if dropping a remark about barley bannocks. 'Is that all? A name! Tell us who it is, Wise One,' I said.

'The name you know already. I will not defile my tongue to utter it.'

'Wise Emrys,' pleaded Cai, 'I would hear spoken the name of the dog who has raised this outrage against my kinsmen.'

It was no use asking, Myrddin would say no more.

Arthur began at once to order the attack. Down on the narrow plain the enemy was already forming the battle line. I could see that they had chosen the field well. Even if they did not possess the fortress, the rock wall at their backs gave them good protection, and the deep-riven dells would make it difficult for our horses.

Nevertheless, the *ala* moved into position, forming three divisions of four ranks each. I led one division, Cai another, and Bors the third — each of us with two kings under our command. Arthur, with Llenlleawg beside him, would lead the warriors on foot — we all knew that once the horses had served their purpose the battle would be waged on foot.

At Rhys' signal we galloped forth, spears levelled, shields dressed. The thunder of hooves drummed in our brains and blood. I settled into the saddle, gliding with the rhythmic rock and sway of the fearless animal beneath me. My hand, my arm, my eye — all of my being became the sharp spear-head glinting at the end of the ashwood haft, slicing air before me.

Closing with merciless speed, the first rank went down before me, mouths agape, eyes wide in wonder and terror. As in all the other battles, I fought through the knotted confusion of bodies, the clash keen and loud in my ears, the blood mist in my eyes. I slew the enemy before me, taking them on the point of my spear. And when that broke, I used my sword.

I hewed mightily. I laboured like the farmer when the thunder and lightning threatens his ripe field. But no planter ever reaped such grim harvest, or gathered a loathlier crop.

We were lions! We were charging boars in battle! Our first attack, fierce and furious, broke the barbarian line in four places. It sagged inward as if to draw us in and crush us against Edyn's Rock — and well they might have, for there were more than enough of them! — but Arthur, swift and sure, drove into them from behind.

The barbarian resistance collapsed in chaos and they began to scatter. I steered my division back towards Arthur's position, carrying all before me. And then I saw it, springing up directly in my path — the *Bretwalda*'s skull-and-bones standard. And beneath it, surrounded by his house carles, the *Bretwalda* himself. And, God help him, I recognized the face beneath the iron helm: Cerdic ap Morcant.

It was Cerdic!

Bile surged up into my gullet and into my mouth. Rage, hot and black, dimmed my sight. I lashed my mount forward, hoping to attack him before he saw me. But the craven's carles closed around him and bore him away before ever I could reach him. Indeed, the barbarians were scattering, fleeing south and west. Confusion must have gripped them, for they were running away from the coast where lay their ships!

I made directly for Arthur. 'I have seen him, Bear,' I shouted. 'I have seen the *Bretwalda*.'

His head whipped towards me. 'Who is it?'

'Cerdic ap Morcant,' I told him. 'I saw him with the Angli.'

Arthur bristled. 'That coward will curse the day of his birth,' he muttered. Then said, 'It is well. If he will not hold with me in life, let him keep faith with me in death. Either way, I will own his fealty!'

'Sound the pursuit! We can catch him,' I cried, preparing for the chase.

To my surprise, Arthur merely shook his head. 'No,' he said. 'I will not ride into ambush. Reform the *ala* and care for the wounded, then gather the chieftains and come to me at the caer. I will hold council in Ector's hall.' He rode off, leaving me to sputter after him.

A moment later, Rhys raised the signal to reform, and the pursuit broke off; riders began returning to the field. Once the wounded were under care — mercifully, there were few of them; the battle had been brief — I assembled the lords and we rode up to the caer. The gates were open and Ector was standing in the yard, talking to Arthur.

At our approach they finished and Ector hurried into the hall. The Duke turned suddenly and spoke a word to Llenlleawg, who ran to his horse, leapt into the saddle and raced away.

I dismounted and threw my reins to one of Ector's men. 'What is it?' I asked, hurrying to Arthur's side.

'There are Saecsens here.'

'Saecsens!'

'So Ector believes. He will tell us more.' He glanced towards the gate where the first of the lords was arriving. 'Bring them in. We will hold council in the hall.'

Once settled inside, we clutched our cups and listened to Ector speak the words most dreadful to our ears. 'Before the siege, word came to me that Saecsen warships had been seen on the water below Traprain Law. I took ten ships and we made for the coast there, but we found no sign of them.'

'Your report was accurate?' asked Owain.

'There was no doubt.'

'Yet we saw no Saecsens in battle today. They must have turned back. Your ships scared them away,' suggested Ceredig.

'We saw no Saecsens, because we were not *meant* to see them,' declared Myrddin Emrys. 'There was no battle today.'

'No battle?' demanded Maelgwn. 'It seemed a battle to me!' Everyone laughed. 'What did we fight against then?'

'You fought against a shadow,' replied Myrddin.

The Emrys' strange words worked in me and in that instant I saw the subtle shape of the trap that had been set for us. Oh, Cerdic had bethought himself well. Long had he nourished himself with cunning, and groomed himself with treachery. I saw it in an instant: the siege of Caer Edyn, like Trath Gwryd and Caer Alclyd, was meant only to distract us and wear us down while he moved us into position. The real battle he had saved to the last.

Shrewd Cerdic, deft in deceit. He who would not rule under Arthur, turned traitor against him and against his own people. Devil take him, he was always a bad seed.

'A shadow?' The lords of Britain stared in disbelief, then laughed scornfully.

'Listen to the Soul of Wisdom,' commanded Arthur. 'Has it not occurred to you that we have succeeded too easily? These first fights were but annoyances — vexations to divert us from the true battle. Had we given chase today, we would now be food for ravens and wolves.'

The lords muttered loudly at this: accusations of weakness and indecision. Some complained aloud that Arthur imagined too much. If there were Saecsens, they said, why did they not show themselves? Why did we turn aside when we had the battle won?

Let them mutter and accuse as they might, the Bear of Britain would not be moved. He crossed his arms over his chest and faced them down, each and every one. When order was restored, he turned to me. 'Bedwyr, tell them who is *Bretwalda* to the barbarians. Tell them who you saw beneath the skull-and-bones today.'

'I saw Cerdic ap Morcant,' I said loudly.

Some, like Idris and Maglos who had been friend to Cerdic and had ridden with him before joining Arthur, refused to believe. 'Impossible! You are surely mistaken.'

'I know who I saw. It is a face I have seen more than once across the field of battle.'

'He would not slaughter his own people,' maintained Idris, albeit weakly.

'He fought against *us* in the beginning! Or have you forgotten,' I spat. Anger splashed up hot within me. 'Since he could not prevail that way, he has joined the enemy. I do not find that so difficult to believe.'

That gave them something to chew on. Mighty God, they can be a thick-headed lot! But they cavilled to nothing but their own dishonour, for it showed how little they esteemed Arthur. Still! Even after all he had done.

Bors, Gwalchavad and Cador, who had been tending to the Cymbrogi, joined us now. Custennin took advantage of the momentary interruption to move the council along. 'Whether it is Cerdic,' he proclaimed, 'or whether it is someone else, does not matter for the moment. If there are Saecsens waiting in ambush, then we must decide quickly what to do. Arthur is our War Leader, we must listen to him.' Turning to Arthur, he said, 'Tell us, Duke Arthur, what would you have us do?'

Arthur rose to stand over us. 'We will send scouts to discover where the enemy have gone. Once we know th — '

'We *know* where they have gone!' said Owain. 'Every moment we delay strengthens them.'

Arthur struck the board with the flat of his hand. The slap rattled the cups the length of the board. 'Silence!'

The lords fell silent at last. Arthur glared at each one and continued, 'I will *not* ride into battle until I know the field, how it lies, and who is arrayed against us. With your own ears you have heard that there is some deception at work here. Since we know not what it is, I mean to be wary.' He straightened and folded his arms across his chest. 'I thank you for your trust, my lords, and I will summon you when I am ready.'

This is no way to enter a battle. Bitterness and strife in command can leech the strength of an army more quickly than fear. There was little we could do about that now. It was already too late.

The scouts were sent out and returned just before nightfall with word of the enemy's position. And that word was not good to hear. Arthur assembled the lords and the scouts told what they had seen: the barbarian host had passed west along the Fiorthe to the place where Guaul met the river mouth, then they had turned away from the coast into the wooded hills to the south.

'This does not appear to be a heedless retreat,' observed Arthur, when the scouts had spoken. The lords were forced to agree that the enemy had behaved with unusual fore-thought. 'Did you see where they stopped?'

'They stopped,' reported the foremost scout, 'in a region of lakes. I saw two hills with ancient forts on them. It appeared that they were met by some already waiting there.'

'Did you see who was waiting?'

'They seemed to be Saecsens, Duke Arthur.'

The trap! Yes! Arthur's cool instinct had saved us from a fatal mistake. I would have ridden into it.

'How many?' asked Arthur.

The scout hesitated. 'I cannot say, lord.'

'More than ten thousand?'

'Yes, lord, more than ten thousand.'

'More than twenty?'

Again the scout paused. I could well understand his reluctance. 'Yes, Lord Arthur, more than twenty thousand. I think it was Octa and Colgrim.'

Arthur dismissed the scout, and turned to the lords. 'They were met by Saecsens, twenty thousand strong, at least. Probably more.'

'I know the place,' said Ector. 'There are two hills — rather one hill with two peaks, and the ruins of an old fortress. The hill is called Baedun.'

'Twenty thousand!' scoffed Maelgwn. 'We would have heard long before now if that many barbarians were loose in the land.'

'Not if our eyes and ears were distracted elsewhere,' I reminded the council. At last, the peril became apparent to them as they grasped the gravity of our position.

'What are we to do?' asked Maglos.

'We must assemble more men,' said Owain, and several others agreed. 'Send to the south for more men.' Others had other ideas and spoke them out.

Arthur let them have their say, and then told them how it would be. 'We cannot wait for more men. The enemy must not think they have frightened us. We strike quickly, and we strike boldly. Order your men, tomorrow we carry the battle to Cerdic and his barbarians.'

Baedun Hill rises above the woodlands, a big, rough, rock-strewn, double-humped tor. It is steep and flat-crested. Its chief advantage to the foemen lay in its size and the strong walls of its two old fortresses: they were enormous, large enough to hold the thirty thousand assembled there. And the walls, though they were not high, were double banked and made of stone.

I saw at once why they had chosen the place. The deep ditches ringing the mound made the uphill grade perilous, and the stone-scattered slopes made them treacherous for our horses. From the heights the enemy could rush swiftly down upon us as we struggled upward.

Yes, the battle site was wisely chosen. Cerdic had bethought himself well. To know that this treachery was practised upon us by one of our own made the fire leap in my belly. That he had caused the Saecsen to break faith with Arthur was the worse.

'A double fortress,' I said. Arthur and I had ridden ahead to view the enemy encampment. 'There is not another like it in all Britain. If we attack one side, they will come at us from the other. We are forced to divide our forces before the battle begins. What will you do?'

'I will make them yearn for peace. Long will they regret raising war against me.' The hollow cast of his voice sent the chill along my spine; it did not sound like Arthur. But his countenance remained unchanged, his brow lowered, his jaw firm. He jerked the reins back, wheeling his horse. He had made up his mind. 'Come, Bedwyr, we will return to the men.'

'What will you do?'

'You will see!' Arthur called back.

I hastened after him and we returned to the place where the combined warbands of Britain waited in the shelter of the wood below the lake, a short distance north of Baedun Hill.

The lords had gathered to await Arthur's return. The waiting had made them anxious and uneasy. They rushed to us as Arthur dismounted and demanded to know how he would order the battle. 'What do you intend?' they asked. 'Will you attack at once? What did you see? What are we to do?'

But Arthur would make no answer. 'Exalted lords,' he said, 'let tomorrow care for itself. Tonight we sup and sing, and embolden our hearts with high words.'

They did not like this answer, but it was the only one they received. Arthur did not heed their mutterings, but retired to his tent to rest. A little while later, Llenlleawg returned, his horse lathered and exhausted. He went directly to Arthur, and Myrddin joined them. The three remained together for a long time, talking.

Towards dusk, Arthur emerged from his rest. He had bathed, and bound his hair. And he had put on new clothing: red trousers and a mantle of white. Around his waist he wore a wide belt of gilded leather, and a cloak of deepest red across his shoulders. He carried his sword, Caledvwlch, at his side.

The cooking fires burned brightly, near the wagons where the stewards were busily preparing the meal of venison and onions. The air hung heavy and blue with smoke, spreading over the camp like a softly undulating roof. Gone was the usual noise and bustle of camp. Everywhere, men drew together; some talked, others looked to their weapons, still others sang softly — not battle songs, but the gentle home-hallowing melodies of fireside and family. Their thoughts carried back to those whom they might never see again. Every warrior's mortality weighs on him before a battle. It is natural, and necessary in a way.

Arthur walked among the men, speaking to them, encouraging them with good words, calming them, sharing out his spirit as if it were a treasure he might divide among them. To see him was to behold true nobility, and everyone who saw him took courage and their hearts were lifted up.

We ate our simple meal on the shore. The lake stretched out smooth as a mirror, and deep-hued black like iron. The dark wood crowded close, but at the lakeside the light lingered, reflected in the water. When we had eaten, Myrddin came with his harp and we sang with him beneath the stars, and the singing was sweet to hear.

Then arose Arthur and gathered the Cymbrogi before him at the lakeside. 'My countrymen!' he called. 'My kinsmen, listen to me. Tomorrow we will meet the enemy — those who call themselves Woden's Children — and we will fight.

'A thousand years from now the bards will sing of this battle. Our names will echo in the halls of mighty kings, and our deeds will live in the hearts of men yet to be born. So I ask you, my brothers, how will you be remembered?'

Men turned puzzled faces to one another.

Arthur began striding along the shore. The wavelets, all silver-flecked in the starlight, lapped quietly at his feet. 'As much as any warrior among you, I thirst for glory. But what glory? I ask you to consider now.'

A hushed murmur worked through the gathered ranks. We have never heard Duke Arthur speak like this to us, they said. What is the Bear of Britain saying?

'Yet a thousand years is a long time,' Arthur continued. 'A long time and much may be forgotten: who won the battle or how it was lost, the field where we fought and those who fought against us. All that will remain — if anything at all remains — is what manner of men we were.'

At this some of the men smacked their thighs with their open hands in approval. Here surely would come the word of courage and valour, of honour and bravery. But Arthur had something else in mind.

'I ask you to consider now, my brothers, what manner of men are we?' Arthur paused long, letting them work out an answer. Then he stopped pacing and held his arms out wide. 'My kinsmen, my brothers, what manner of men are we?'

'We are Britons!' someone shouted. 'Cymry!' cried another.

'Cymbrogi!' others called. 'Companions of the Heart!'

'Hie! Hie!' came the resounding agreement. 'We are Cymbrogi!'

Arthur held up his hands for silence and, when it was regained, he said, 'Oh, we are Fellow Countrymen, aye. But this is not our country of origin. Our true home is the heavenly realm wherein the Saviour God waits to greet all who own him Lord.

'Listen to me! Tomorrow we join battle with the barbarians. They will call upon their repulsive idol, Woden. But I ask you now, my brothers, who will you call upon?' He lowered his hands to shoulder level and indicated the gathered throng with a wide sweep of his arm. 'Who will hear *your* cries in the day of strife?

'Consider wisely now. For I tell you truly, whatever glory we achieve will die with us unless Jesu the Christ goes before us. But if we are called by his holy name, his glory will cover us like a mantle of gold — and though we die our deeds will be remembered for a thousand years, and a thousand thousand after that.'

Llenlleawg stepped close, bearing the Duke's shield. Arthur took it, turned it towards us and held it up above his head. Upon the new white washed surface had been painted a great red cross, the symbol of the Christ. 'From this day, I wear the cross of Jesu. By this, he goes before me into battle. If the High King of Heaven fights for us, who can prevail against us?'

The Cymbrogi were silent. Behind them stood throngs of others who had heard Arthur's voice and, drawn to it as to a beacon fire, had pressed closer to hear what he said.

Arthur planted the shield before him on the shore. He lifted a hand heavenward, pointing over their heads into the twilit sky where new-kindled stars burned. 'Look! The feet of the Holy One are already on the path. He will lead us if we follow him. I ask you, my brothers, who will follow?'

Up they rose, as one man. The Cymbrogi surged forward and by press of numbers forced Arthur into the lake. He stood in water up to his knees, but heeded it not. 'Kneel Cymbrogi, and swear everlasting allegiance to the High King of Heaven, who has promised to save all who own him lord! He will be your strong arm and your wise counsellor; he will be a shield to cover you, and a sword to defend you!'

They knelt by the hundreds, there in the shallow water. Some of the priests from Mailros who were with us — they had taken refuge with Ector when the barbarians arrived — began moving among them, cupping water in their hands and baptizing the new believers into the Fellowship of Faith. I looked on in awe, my heart beating in my throat, for Arthur's words had wakened in me the thirst for the divine glory he described.

I was of the Christianogi already, so had no need of another baptism, but I went down to the water, too, to ask forgiveness for my sins so that I might enter battle with a spotless soul. Many another Christian among us did the same, while others began singing a hymn of praise to the Gifting God, and the dusky hills echoed with the holiest of sounds.

FIFTEEN

We rose before dawn and broke fast. We donned leather and mail; we helmed ourselves with iron and strapped steel to our hips. We slung our heavy wooden shields over our shoulders and bound our arms and legs with hard leather. We saddled our horses, formed the ranks, then moved silently through the wood to Baedun Hill.

Before daylight we assembled below the hulking flanks of Baedun and looked long upon the two dark fortresses rising above us. The enemy sentries saw us gathering below the hill on the eastern side and sounded the alarm. In moments the screams assaulted our ears as the massed barbarian hosts — Picti, Angli, Irish, Saecsen and others — raised their hideous battle cry.

Rhys on his left hand, Llenlleawg on his right, Arthur advanced slowly up the slope. The grade rises sharply half-way up, and here Arthur halted the army, dismounted, and walked forward alone. He walked boldly to the bank of the first ditch and stopped. 'Cerdic!' he called. 'Come down! I would speak to you.'

'Speak, Bastard of Britain!' came the sharp reply. 'I can hear you.'

'I stretch out my hand to you in peace, Cerdic,' said the Duke. 'I stand ready to forgive you and all those with you if you will swear fealty to me.'

'Whorespawn!' screamed Cerdic. 'I have no need of your forgiveness or pardon. I will swear only to your death. Come up here, if you are not afraid, and we will see who bends the knee.'

'I have offered peace, and I am reviled,' said Arthur. 'Yet I will have peace in the end.' With that he turned and walked back to his horse.

Once remounted, he signalled Rhys, who raised the horn to his lips, giving forth the long, ringing call to battle. Arthur drew Caledvwlch and lofted it high. The sun's first rays struck the well-honed blade and set it aflame. 'For God and Britain!' he cried, and his cry echoed along the line on either hand and down from the stone wall above.

The battle call sounded again, and his horse trotted forward. The *ala* surged forth behind him, the doubled ranks of footmen behind them. The trot became a canter and then a gallop.

The combined warbands of Britain stormed up the rock-strewn slope and reached the first ditch. Down we plummeted, and up we rose, scrambling for a foothold on the opposite side. Then we were up and over, and climbing steeply. The mighty battle horns of the Saecsen — great bullroarers to shake the dead in their graves! — trembled the cool dawn air. I felt the pounding thump of the war drums in my stomach and the cool rush of air on my face.

But my hands were steady on my spear; my shield was solid beside me. I gave my mount his head and let him choose the ascent. The terrain was so rocky that I could not guide him and fight at the same time. Ahead I saw the leading bank of the second ditch. I stole a glance to either side to see that my men were with me, and then we plunged into the ditch together.

As in previous battles the *ala* was formed into divisions, each led by one of Arthur's battlechiefs: Cai, Bors, Gwalchavad and myself, two kings each below us. Arthur and Cador, and the remaining lords, led the footmen, coming on behind us as swiftly as they could. Even above the thunder of the horses' hooves, I could hear the dull pounding of their feet on the earth.

The second ditch was deeper than the first, its sides steeper. Several horses stumbled, throwing their riders; a few more balked at the climb and fell back. But all the rest cleared the ditch and charged ahead.

Seeing that our approach was not greatly hindered by the ditch, the barbarians leapt over the wall and flew down the hill to meet us. The steep downward slope lent force to their blows and let them inflict wounds more easily. This they did.

Many fell in the first assault. Difficult terrain and the ferocity of the foe conspired to bring good men down to their deaths. Thus was our first foray turned back.

At the rim of the upper ditch I reformed my division. Quickly scanning the higher slopes, I saw that the other divisions had fared no better. All along the hillside we were being forced back.

Upon my cry, the *ala* charged once more.

This time we let the foemen hurl themselves at us. We held back at the last and they plunged headlong onto our spears. It was a simple trick, but it worked laudably well. The barbarians learned quickly enough and reeled back — leaving hundreds dead and wounded upon the ground.

Still, though we pushed after them, our horses foundered on the higher slope. We fell back once again and the enemy pursued us, striking wildly at our backs. Upon reaching the bank of the upper ditch, we were met by the footmen charging up from below.

I gave command of the division to Owain, and rode quickly to Arthur. 'It is no good,' I told him. 'We cannot carry an attack up here — it is too steep and there are too many of them.'

Arthur saw that I spoke the plain truth. 'It is as I feared. Very well, save the horses. We may need them later. We will carry the attack on foot.' His blue eyes searched the wall line looming above us, and his finger pointed. 'That place there — do you see it?'

'That low place? I see it.'

'We will centre the attack there. Follow me!'

I hurried back to my division and passed on Arthur's order. Rhys signalled the dismount and a moment later we were racing back up the hillside, scrambling over the rocks, falling, picking ourselves up, running on.

The enemy saw that we had abandoned our horses and took this as a good omen for them. They raised their evil screams with renewed vigour, and danced their frenzied war dances along the top of the wall. They were frothing mad with blood lust.

As soon as we came within range the enemy loosed their throwing axes at us. We threw our shields before us and stumbled on. Some among us picked up the hateful axes and hurled them back. More than one barbarian was killed with his own weapon.

The sun had risen higher and I could feel its warmth on my back. My blood pounded hot in my veins, and I drew the cool morning air deep into my lungs. It was a good day for a battle, I thought, and then remembered that in numbers and position Cerdic boasted the advantage.

The place Arthur had found proved the only weak place that side of the wall. He had chosen the eastern side for assault because the incline was easiest, but the enemy realized this, too, and had built up the wall on the eastern side. The low place Arthur saw was a section that had been hastily repaired and some of the stone had fallen in when the first foemen swarmed over.

We drove towards this place, all of us, our force becoming a spearhead to thrust up under the enemy's defences and into his heart.

It nearly worked.

But there were simply too many barbarians, and the incline too steep. Though we stood to our work like woodmen felling trees, we could make no headway. Picti, Cruithne, Angli and Scoti, Saecsen and Frisian and Jutes. . . there were too, too many. We could not come near the wall.

For every pace we advanced, the enemy pushed us back two. For every foeman we killed, three more sprang up before us. Our warriors were being dragged down by the enormous crush of the enemy host. They rushed down upon us, hacking with their cruel axes: eyes wild, mouths twisted, arms swinging like flails.

But our warriors had fought barbarians before and were not unnerved. We lowered our heads and stood to our grim toil. And the battle settled into its awkward, lurching rhythm.

The day passed in a haze of blood and havoc. As the sun descended westward, I heard Rhys raise the retreat and knew that we were beaten. I gathered my division and we withdrew with our wounded; everywhere warriors were streaming down the hillside to the refuge of the wood.

The enemy seemed eager to give chase at first — would that they had done so! We would have cut them down with the *ala*. But Cerdic knew enough to halt the pursuit at the lower ditch, and the barbarians returned to the hill fort.

While the warriors lay under the trees recovering strength and having their wounds bound, the cooks and stewards brought us meat and bread and watered ale, and we ate. My limbs ached and my head throbbed. My clothing was sodden with sweat and blood. I stank.

A still and sinister dusk settled over the land. The trees around us filled with crows from the battlefield, croaking grotesquely over their ghastly feast. But that was as nothing to the wild cries of victory from the hill fort above us. Fires leapt high into the darkening sky as the victory celebration commenced.

We slept fitfully that night, the sound of savage revelry loud in our ears. At dawn we awoke, broke fast, took up our weapons and climbed the hill once more. The barbarians allowed us to crawl so far and then fell upon us, hurtling down from the heights, axes whirling.

We took them on the points of our spears and swords, and struck them with our shields. But many a warrior fell, his helm or shield or mail shirt riven asunder. The carnage was appalling, the tumult deafening.

Once again the flanks of Baedun Hill blushed crimson with the blood of the brave.

And once again, as the sun passed midday Rhys signalled the retreat and we withdrew to the wood to lick our wounds. The warriors sank to the grass and slept. The stewards crept among them with water jars and woke the sleeping soldiers to drink. The wood grew still, given only to the hum of flies and the flutter of birds' wings in the branches above. On Baedun, the enemy was silent.

When they had refreshed themselves and put off their weapons the lords of Britain held council with Arthur.

'I say we must lay siege to the hill and send south for more men.' This was Maglos' suggestion, and after the heavy going of the morning, several agreed with him.

'If we could only take the fortress,' began Ceredig, but he was cut off by the scorn of the others.

'Take the fortress!' Idris shouted. 'What else were we doing up there? It is impossible — there are too many! I agree with Maglos: we should lay siege and wait for more men.'

'No,' said Arthur. 'That we cannot do.'

'Why not?' demanded Idris. 'It worked at Caer Alclyd; it worked at Trath Gwryd. . . '

'It will not work here,' Arthur told him flatly.

But Idris gave no heed to the iron in Arthur's voice. He persisted, saying, 'Why? Because you want to exalt yourself over Cerdic?'

'If that is what you think — ' I snapped, jerking my head toward the hill, 'join him!'

Myrddin, leaning on his rowan staff nearby, stirred and came near. 'This hill is cursed,' he intoned softly. We all quieted to hear him better. 'There is distress and calamity here. The slopes are treacherous with torment, and disaster reigns over all.'

We all glanced over our shoulders at the looming hill. The clouds playing across its surface gave it a brooding, dangerous aspect. Certainly, the corpses scattered on its rock-crusted slopes argued eloquently for disaster. Myrddin did not need sight to know our torment — but what else did he see?

'In older times armies have fought upon this troubled mound. A great victory was won here through betrayal, and the wicked defeat of good men clings to the earth and rocks. The mountain is unquiet with the evil practised upon it. Cerdic's treachery has awakened the vile spirit of this place to work again.'

'Tell us, Emrys,' said Custennin. 'Give us benefit of your wise counsel. What are we to do?'

It was the formal request of a king to his bard. Myrddin did not fail to oblige. 'This battle will not be won by stealth or might. It will not be won by bloodshed alone. The spirit abiding here will not be overthrown except by the power of God.'

The lords peered helplessly at one another. 'What are we to do about that?' they demanded.

'We must pray, lords of Britain. We must erect a fortress of our own whose walls cannot be battered down or broken. A caer that cannot be conquered. A stronghold of prayer.'

Some of the lords scowled at this, embarrassed at their

lack of faith and understanding. But Arthur rose and said, 'It will be done as you say, Wise Counsellor.'

Myrddin placed his hands on Arthur's shoulders. 'I will do all to uphold you — as I have ever done to this day.'

Though men may scoff, it is no small thing to be upheld by the Chief Bard and Emrys of Britain.

The next morning, as we arrayed ourselves for battle, I saw the solitary figure of Myrddin toiling up the hillside, picking his slow, blind way with his staff, his cloak wrapped tightly around him. For the day broke grey and misty, and a chill wind blew at us out of the north.

'Do you want me to go after him?' I asked, fearful for Myrddin's safety.

'Wait here. I will go to him,' replied Arthur, starting after the stumbling Emrys.

I watched Arthur stride out upon the hillside. Cai and Bors saw him and came running to where I stood at the edge of the wood. 'What is he doing?' asked Bors. 'Does he think himself invisible?'

'I do not know,' I answered.

'I am going to bring him back,' said Cai.

'He said to wait here. But signal Rhys to be ready to sound the attack. If the barbarians come over the wall, I want the Cymbrogi to move at once.'

Llenlleawg, who had been lurking nearby, came to stand beside me. He spoke not a word and his eyes never left the hill, but he gave me to know that our hearts beat as one for Arthur.

'Now what are they doing?' wondered Bors aloud. 'It looks as if they are gathering stones.'

God's truth, that is what they were doing. Arthur, after a brief word with Myrddin, stooped and began piling rocks upon the ground. Myrddin laid aside his staff and, kneeling down, began to heft rocks onto the pile.

'They are building a cairn,' observed Cai, eyes wide with disbelief.

'Not a cairn,' I said. 'A wall.'

'Bah!' huffed Bors, who was having none of it. 'They will get themselves killed out there as soon as the enemy stirs.'

The leaden sky had lightened somewhat with the rising

sun. Arthur and Myrddin toiled openly on the slope. The enemy must have observed their presence by now. Our own army had gathered at the edge of the wood to view the strange proceedings.

'We cannot let this continue,' blustered Bors. 'It is not meet for the Duke of Britain to heap rocks on the ground.'

'What do you propose?' I asked.

'You must stop him!'

'*You* stop him.'

Bors drew himself up. 'Very well, I will.' So saying, he stalked from the wood.

Gwalchavad came running to us. 'What is happening? What are they doing out there?'

'Building a wall,' Cai replied.

Gwalchavad opened his mouth to laugh, and then stared in amazement. 'They are!' he declared. 'They will be killed!'

'Possibly,' I allowed.

'Is no one going to stop them?'

'Bors is going to do that,' said Cai.

Gwalchavad gaped at us as if we had lost our reason. Out on the hill Bors picked his way among the tumbled stones. 'Well, he will need help,' Gwalchavad said, and hastened after Bors, who had reached the place where Arthur and Myrddin toiled.

The lord of Benowyc waved towards the hilltop stronghold and then in the direction of the wood. Arthur raised his head, spoke a word, and Bors stopped gesturing. The Duke returned to his labour and Bors stood looking on.

'Look at that,' scoffed Cai. 'Bors has certainly stopped them.'

Gwalchavad reached the three on the hill and fell to work beside them at once.

At the appearance of Gwalchavad running out upon the hillside, the floodgates opened and others began moving from the cover of the wood. By twos and threes they went, then by dozens and scores to see what was happening.

'Well, Gwalchavad has persuaded them beyond all doubt,' Cai observed. 'What are we to do now? Our army is advancing without us.'

Llenlleawg turned to me. 'It is the supreme dishonour for a battlechief to fall behind his warriors.'

'Cai, are we to be taught our duty by an Irishman?'

'Never!' Cai cried. 'Flay me for a Pict! I will not have it flaunted about that we neglected our duty.'

'Brave Cai,' I said, 'foremost in war and wall building!'

Together we marched from the wood. Llenlleawg fell into step beside us. I confess, I had begun to warm to that man. He was Irish, there is no denying it, but a deal less vile than others of his race. The soul within him was noble, and his heart was true. More the shame for men like Cerdic: when the barbarian reveals higher nobility than right-born Britons!

We advanced to where Arthur and the others laboured at the rocks. 'What do you here, Bear?' I asked.

Arthur straightened. 'I am building a wall.'

'This we have observed,' said Cai. 'Are we to know the reason for this unseemly toil?'

The Duke hefted a stone and lifted it above his head. He stepped onto the pile of rocks he had raised. 'Men of Britain!' he called. 'Listen to me!'

Warriors pressed close to hear him. The cold wind fluttered the red cloak about Arthur's shoulders; mist pearled in his hair. 'Look in my hand and tell me what you see.'

'A stone!' they cried. 'We see a stone!'

Arthur lofted the stone before them. 'No, I tell you it is not a stone. It is something stronger than stone, and more enduring: it is a prayer!

'I tell you,' Arthur continued, 'it is a prayer for the deliverance of Britain. Look around you, my brothers; this hillside is covered with them!'

We scanned the rough and rocky steeps of Baedun as Arthur directed. Baedun was, as he said, covered with stones — as if we had not known this already!

'You ask what I am doing. I will tell you: I am gathering up the prayers and making a wall with them. I am raising a stronghold to surround the enemy.

'Our Wise Emrys has decreed that we must erect a fortress whose walls cannot be battered down or broken — a caer that cannot be conquered. My countrymen, that is what I am doing. When I have finished, not a single barbarian will escape.'

With that Arthur stepped down and placed his stone upon

the pile he had made. Men regarded him as if he had become mad. The wind whipped through the crowd and uttered sinister whispers against the Duke. The silence grew dense with accusation: he is mad!

Then, throwing his cloak over his shoulder, Cai stooped and, every sinew straining, lifted an enormous rock and, grinning with the exertion, heaved his rock on top of Arthur's. It fell with a solid and convincing crack. 'There!' Cai declared loudly. 'If stones be prayers, I have sung a psalm!'

Everyone laughed and suddenly other stones began toppling onto the pile as one by one we all stooped to the stones at our feet and lifted them to top the foundation Arthur had made. In this way, the wall was begun.

The lords of Britain held themselves aloof from this toil, but when they saw the fervour of their men, and the zeal of the Cymbrogi, they put off their cloaks and directed the work. It was a triumph to see them — Ennion and Custennin, Maelgwn and Maglos and Owain, Ceredig and Idris, all of them barking orders and urging on the men.

We are a song-loving people and labour is long without a melody to lighten it. Once the work began in earnest, the singing began. Holy songs at first, but when these gave out we turned to the simple, well-known songs of hearth and clan — and these I believe are holy too. The wall rose stone by stone, each stone a heartfelt prayer.

High up in the hilltop stronghold, the barbarians looked down upon our strange labour. At first they did not know what to make of it, and then as the line of the wall appeared and stretched along the hillside, they began to shout and jeer. When the wall began to rise, their jeers became angry taunts. They threw stones and shot arrows at us, but we were beyond hurtful range and the stones and arrows fell spent long before reaching us. They raged, but they did not leave the protection of their fortress.

Now, two men working diligently can raise a twenty-pace section chest high in a day. How much more, then, can three thousand times that many accomplish? Saints and angels, I tell you that wall raised itself, so quickly did it appear!

See it now: hands, thousands of hands reaching, grasping, lifting, placing, working the rough stone into a form.

Backs bending, muscles straining, lungs drawing, cheeks puffing with the effort, sweat running. Palms and knuckles roughened, fingers bleeding. The wind billowing cloaks, rippling grass, curling mist and rain.

Dusk fell full and fast. And though dark clouds swirled about the hilltop, light, clear and golden, shone in the west. In that light's last gleam we placed the final stone on the wall and stood back to see what we had done. It was marvellous to behold: a long, sinuous barrier rising to shoulder height and surrounding the entire hill.

The enemy wailed to see it. The barbarians howled in frustration. They cursed. They screamed. They saw themselves surrounded by stone and called upon one-eyed Woden to save them. But their cries were seized by the wind and flung back in their faces. The wall, Arthur's Wall, stood defiantly before them, encircling Baedun with its stern message: you will not leave this battle ground. Here you will die, and here your bones will lie unmourned for ever.

My arms ached, and my legs and feet and back. My hands were scraped raw; my arms were cut. But I looked upon that wonderful wall and my small agonies were less than nothing. It was more than a wall — it was faith made manifest. I looked upon the work of our hands and I felt invincible.

The barbarians looked upon the wall and despaired. For they saw that Arthur had cut off his own retreat — no one does that who doubts the victory. Thus was Arthur telling them: your doom is sealed; you are lost. They keened their death songs into the gathering gloom. And then, though the day was far spent, they attacked.

Why they waited so long I will never know. Perhaps God's hand prevented them. Perhaps Arthur's Wall of Prayer daunted them. But all at once they swarmed out from their stronghold and flew down the hill towards us. Rhys signalled the alarm and we snatched up our weapons, turned and formed the line, then raced to meet them. The shock of the clash shuddered the mountain to its roots.

Fighting at night is difficult and strange. The enemy has a shape, but no face; a body of limbs, but no features and no definite form. It is like fighting shadows. It is like one of those Otherworldly battles the bards sing about, where invisible armies meet in endless combat on a darkling plain. It is strange and unnatural.

We fought, though exhaustion hung like a sodden cloak upon us. We fought, knowing that all our work would be for nothing if we could not now shake off our fatigue and keep the enemy from reaching the wall. Indeed, the barbarians seemed more intent on gaining the wall than in fighting us. Perhaps they thought to escape. Or perhaps they saw in Arthur's Wall something which they could not abide — something they feared worse than defeat or death.

Gloom enwrapped the hill. The wind shrieked in our ears and rain drove down. The barbarian host pressed us back and back. Heedless of danger, heedless of death, they swarmed before us, driving at us out of the storm-tossed darkness. On and on and on they came, torches flaming, forcing our backs to the wall our hands had raised.

Clear and high, Arthur's hunting horn sounded; short blasts cutting through the tumult: the rallying call. I looked to the sound and saw Arthur — his white shield a gleaming moon in the darkness; Caledvwlch flashing as his arm rose and fell in graceful, deadly arcs; crimson cloak streaming in the wind, muscled shoulders heaving as he leaned into the maelstrom. . . Arthur.

I could not see his face, but there could be no doubt. He fought like no other warrior I had ever known. Such controlled ferocity, such deadly grace; the dread purity of his movements, spare and neat, each flowing into and out from the other, became a dazzling litany of praise to the fearful hand that had framed him.

It came into my mind that it was for this Arthur was born; *this* was why his spirit was given. To be here, now, to lead the battle in just this way. Arthur had been created for, and summoned to, this moment. He had heard his call and he had obeyed. Now all was delivered into his grasp.

I wanted to be near him, to pledge faith to him with my blade and with my life. But when I fought to his side, he was gone.

I also saw Llenlleawg. He had taken up a Saecsen torch and now became once more a whirling firebrand of a warrior: torch in one hand, short sword in the other, he danced in his mad battle ecstasy. The enemy fell before him and on every side, scattering like the sparks that flew from the flame in his hand.

Garish faces came at me out of the darkness — tattooed Picti and blue-painted Cruithne, fair-haired Saecsen and dark Angli, all of them writhing and grimacing with hatred, livid with blood-lust, inflamed with death.

The blood ran hot in my veins, drumming in my ears, pounding in my temples. My sides ached and my lungs burned. But I struck and struck again and again and again, sword rising and falling in deadly rhythm: falling like judgement from the night-dark sky, falling like doom upon the heads of the unheeding.

With each stroke I grew stronger — like the ancient hero Gwyn, who increased in strength as the day wore on. I felt the ache leave my muscles, melting away in the rain that drenched me. My hands were no longer stiff on the grip of my sword and shield. My head cleared. My vision grew keen. I felt the heat of life rising in me, the battle glow which drives out all else.

My men pressed close beside me; shoulder to shoulder we hewed at the enemy. To be surrounded by brave men faithful through all things is deeply to be wished, and my heart swelled within me. We laboured in combat as we had laboured on the wall, matching thrust for thrust, and stroke for stroke. I felt their spirits lift with mine. No longer were we being driven back. We had somehow halted the advance of the enemy and now stood against it.

Though the darkness round about was filled with the howls of barbarians and the shrieks of berserkers and the dire blast of Saecsen battle horns, we did not give ground. The enemy became the sea surging angrily against us as against the Giant's Steps. Like the sea they battered the rock, washed over it and whelmed it over, but when the waves broke the rock remained unmoved.

Wild the night, wild the fight! Buffeted by wind and battle roar, we stood to the barbarian host and our swords ran red. I killed with every thrust, every blow stole life. My arm rose and fell with swift precision, and at each deadly stroke a soul went down into death's dark realm.

The foemen fell around me and I saw all with undimmed clarity. I was fierce. I was cold as the length of steel in my hand. Jesu save me! I slaughtered the enemy like cattle!

I killed, but I did not hate. I killed, but even as they fell before me I did not hate them. There was no hate left in me.

Dawn drew aside the veil of night and we saw what we had done. I will never forget that sight: white corpses in the grey morning light. . . thousands, tens of thousands. . . strewn upon the ground like the rubble of a ruin. . . limbs lifeless, bodies twisted and still, dead eyes staring up at the white sun rising in a white sky and the black blurs of circling, circling crows. . .

Above, the keen of hawks. Below, the deep-stained earth. All around, the stink of death.

We had won. We had gained the victory, but there was scarcely a hair's breadth of difference between the victors and the vanquished on that grim morning. We leaned upon our spears and slumped over our shields. Wide-eyed and staring, too tired to move. Numb.

Anyone coming upon us would have thought that we were one with the dead. Though we lived, it was all we could do to draw breath and blink our swollen red eyes.

I sat with my back to a rock, my sword stuck in my unbending fingers. My shield lay beside me on the ground, battered and rent in a hundred places. 'Bedwyr!' A familiar voice called out my name and I looked and saw Arthur striding towards me. I drew up my knees and struggled to rise.

Grey-faced with fatigue, his arms criss-crossed with sword cuts, his proud red cloak rent to rags and foul with blood, the Duke of Britain hauled me to my feet and crushed me to him in his bear hug. 'I have been searching for you,' he whispered. 'I feared you must be dead.'

'I feel as if I am.'

'If all the barbarians in the world could not kill you, nothing will,' Arthur replied.

'What of Cai? Bors? Cador?'

'Alive.'

I shook my head, and my gaze returned once more to the corpse-choked field and the glutted crows swaggering upon the pale bodies. My stomach turned and heaved; I vomited bile over my feet. Arthur stood patiently beside me, his hand upon my back. When I finished, he raised me up and led me aside with him.

'How many are left?' I asked, dreading the answer. But I had to know.

'More than you think.'

'How many?'

'Two divisions — almost.'

'The kings?'

'Maglos and Ceredig are dead. Ennion is sorely wounded; he will not live. Custennin is dead.'

'Myrddin?'

'He is well. Do you know — when the battle began he climbed up on the wall and stood there the whole night with his staff raised over us. He upheld us through the battle, and prayed the victory for us.'

'What of Gwalchavad? He was near me when the battle began, but I lost him. . . So much confusion.'

'Gwalchavad is unharmed. He and Llenlleawg are searching the bodies.'

'Oh,' I said, though his meaning at the moment escaped me.

We walked a little down the hill and I saw others moving about, slowly, carefully, picking their way sombrely among the silent dead. As we approached the wall there came a shout from behind us up the hill. Gwalchavad and Llenlleawg had found what they were looking for.

We turned and made our way to where they stood. I saw the skull-and-bones standard lying beneath the body and knew what they had found.

Arthur rolled the body with the toe of his boot. Cerdic gazed up into the empty sky with empty eyes. His throat was a blackened gash and his right arm was nearly severed above the elbow. His features had hardened into a familiar expression: the insolent sneer I had so often seen on him — as if death were an insult to his dignity, a humiliation far beneath him.

He was surrounded by his Saecsen guard. All had died within moments of each other — whether in the first or last assault no one could tell; no one had seen him die. But Cerdic was dead, and his treachery with him.

'What are we to do with him?' asked Gwalchavad.

'Leave him,' said Arthur.

'He is a Briton,' Gwalchavad insisted.

'And he chose this place for his tomb when he made war against me. No one forced him to it — it was his own choice. Let him lie here with his barbarian kin.'

Already men were removing the bodies of our comrades for burning. As a witness and warning to all future enemies, the corpses of the barbarians would be left where they had fallen. They would not be buried. So Arthur decreed; so was it done.

The westering sun stretched our shadows long on Baedun's hillside as the funeral flames licked the wooden pyre on which was placed the bodies of our countrymen. Priests of Mailros Abbey prayed and sang psalms, walking slowly around the burning pyre with willow branches in their hands.

Myrddin walked with them, holding a thorned length of rose cane before him. The rose, called Enchanter of the Wood, signified honour in druid lore, the Emrys explained; and to the Christians it symbolized peace. Peace and honour. These brave dead had earned both.

The ashes were glowing embers and twilight softly tinted the sky when we finally left Baedun Hill. We did not go far for we were tired and sore, and the wagons bearing the wounded could not travel any great distance before dark. But Arthur would not stay another night beside that hill, so we went back through the wood to the lake where we had baptized our sword brothers and consecrated ourselves for battle.

There beside its placid waters we made our camp and slept under a peaceful sky in the Region of the Summer Stars.

BOOK
THREE
ANEIRIN

ONE

In the day of strife, the heathen swarms gazed across the wave-worried sea to this green and pleasant land and coveted the wealth of Britain. Their oar-blades churned the bright water in their haste to forsake their wretched shores and despoil ours. Of bloodshed and battle, plunder and pillage, rape and ravage, death and destruction, flames and fear and failure, there was no end.

Great the disgrace, the lords of Britain were no better. Full many a petty king ruled in this worlds-realm, and ever waging war each upon the other wasted all the land — till Arthur came.

Scoff if you will! Mock me, viper's brood! But the Kingdom of Summer was founded on the rock of Jesu's holy name.

Do I not know the truth? Does a bard forget his tales? Well, I was a bard. I was a warrior, too. I am a learned man. Aneirin ap Caw is my name — though now I am known by a name of my own choosing.

I was born in the year of Baedun. Therefore I am a man of fortunate birth, for I began life in that happy time when all wars ceased and peace greatly abounded in this worlds-realm.

Baedun. . . a word for triumph in any tongue.

At Baedun's summit, the Duke of Britain halted the slaughter in what the bards now deem foremost of the Three Great Battles of Ynys Prydein. I tell you the victory was not yet one day old when Arthur retired to the ruined chapel at Mailros to pray thanks for the Almighty Father's deliverance.

Arthur, High King of All Britain; Pendragon of Rheged, Celyddon, Gwynedd, Dyfed and the Seven Favoured Isles;

353

Emperor of Alba and Lloegres, Bear of Britain; Arthur of the Double Crown, of whom perpetual choirs sing.

Not many alive today realize the significance of this: Arthur was crowned twice. The first time on a hill above his northern capital at Caer Edyn; the second time in the south at Londinium. Both crown-takings were conducted before God in a rightwise manner and in all holiness. But each was different from the other as gold from grain.

The reason for two king-makings? Simple necessity. 'I am king of all, or king of none,' Arthur declared. 'North and south have been separated too long. In me, they are united.' To prove his word he had himself crowned conspicuously in both regions so that neither could claim superiority over the other as had been done in elder times.

His king-making in Caer Edyn was all a prince could hope for. But his crown-taking in Londinium nearly incited a riot in that arrogant city. Alas, it was but the first of the troubles to come! Arthur, King of Summer, who bought peace for Britain with his own toil and sweat and blood, was not to know a moment's peace himself.

Listen well, you dull of hearing. Heed the truth, you slow of understanding. Here is a tale worth the telling, a true tale, The Song of the Summer Lord. Hear and remember! This is the way of it. . .

Coming up from the Vale of Twide and Baedun, Arthur and the remnant of the Cymbrogi rode to Caer Edyn. High summer it was; full-leafed, green and golden, blue and clear the sky, calm the sea. The dark smoke-clouds of war had dissolved and now only God's pure light shone upon Britain.

Of course, it would be some time before they realized this. All these battle-weary warriors knew was that the fighting had ended for the year. They did not know that Arthur had led them to their greatest victory; they did not ween it a victory for the entire world. They only knew there would be no more battles that summer.

Lord Ectorius feasted the victors at his table. Three days and three nights they tasted the firstfruits of peace. But even then Arthur's spirit was being revealed. In the presence of his trusted Cymbrogi, Our Lord the Christ showered his favour upon Arthur, and those around him marvelled greatly to see it.

On the shoulders of his warriors Arthur was borne out from Ector's fortress and carried up to the top of the rock that now bears his name. There he was given to sit on a throne of living stone and the remnant of his warband passed before him one by one and pledged their lives to him. The kings of Britain who had endured with him drew their swords and laid them at his feet; they stretched themselves upon the ground before him and Arthur placed his foot upon their necks and became king over them.

The Cymbrogi, also, brought their spears and laid them down before Arthur. They knelt and stretched forth their hands to touch his feet and swore fealty to him upon their lives. He took them to be his subjects and they took him for lord.

Myrddin the Emrys raised the rowan rod over him, and decreed Arthur High King. Then he spoke out the holy words of kingship, saying, 'All praise and worship to the High King of Heaven, who has raised up a king to be Pendragon over us! All saints and angels bear witness: this day is Arthur ap Aurelius made king of all Britons.

'Kneel before him, fellow countrymen! Stretch forth your hands and swear binding oaths of fealty to your lord and king on earth — even as you swear life and honour to the Father God of All Creation.'

When this was done, Myrddin bade Dyfrig, Bishop of Mailros, come forth. He approached Arthur with a torc of gold between his hands, and called out in a loud voice. 'Declare this day before your people the god you will serve.'

'I will serve the Christ, who is called Jesu. I will serve God, who is called the Father. I will serve the Nameless One, who is called the Holy Spirit. I will serve the Holy Trinity.'

'Will you observe justice, perform righteousness and love mercy?'

'With Blessed Jesu as my witness, I will observe justice; I will perform righteousness; I will love mercy.'

'Will you lead this realm in the true faith of Christ, so long as you shall live?'

'To the end of my strength and the last breath of my

mouth, I will lead this worlds-realm in the true faith of Christ.'

'Then, by the power of the Three in One, I raise you, Arthur ap Aurelius. Hail, Arthur, Protector of Britain!'

And all those gathered on Mons Agned shouted, 'Hail Arthur! Protector and Pendragon of Britain!'

Myrddin placed the torc of kingship around Arthur's throat to the loud acclaim of all. Then Arthur passed among them, giving gifts to his Cymbrogi, and to the kings and warriors who served him in battle. He gave them gold and silver brooches, and knives, and rings with precious stones. These things other princes do upon their crown-taking; Arthur did more.

He decreed that the chapel burned by the Picti at Abercurnig should be rebuilt, and the abbey at Mailros. From the spoil of war he paid for this, and established a chapel near Mailros, in full sight of Baedun, to sing psalms and sacred songs and pray good prayers for Britain perpetually, by day and night, until our Lord Jesu shall return to lead his flock to paradise.

Arthur took himself to the small holdings round about, where women lived whose men had been killed by barbarians. To these he gave such gifts as were welcome: gold and silver to some, cattle and sheep to others; in all he provided for the widows through his lords that they should be cared for and their children raised without hardship.

Returning to Caer Edyn, Arthur and his lords sat together at meat and drink. It was here, when the company waxed joyful in celebration, that Myrddin Emrys stood up before all and called out, 'Pendragon of Britain, may your glory outlast your name which will last for ever! It is right to enjoy the fruit of your labour, God knows. But you would find me a lax and stupid counsellor if I did not warn you that away in the south men have not yet heard of Baedun and know nothing of your king-making.'

'Peace! I have only this day received my torc,' Arthur laughed. 'Word will reach them soon enough.'

'But I am persuaded that men believe their eyes more easily than their ears,' Myrddin replied, and the lords slapped the board with their hands and voiced their approval.

'So it is said,' agreed Arthur. 'What is your meaning?'

'Fortunate are the men of the north, for they have ridden beside you in battle and they know your glory. The men of the south will not be won with such news as comes to them in time.'

'There is little I can do about that, I think. A man may be made king but once.'

'That is where you are wrong, O King. You are Pendragon of Britain now — you can so order what is to be.'

'But I have already taken the crown here,' complained Arthur good-naturedly. 'What need have I of another king-making?'

'What need have you of two eyes if one sees clearly enough? What need have you of two hands if one grips sword tightly enough? What need have you of two legs if one runs swiftly enough? What need have you of two ears if — '

'Enough! I understand.'

'But it is not enough,' replied the Exalted Emrys. 'That is what I am saying.'

'Then tell me what I must do to quiet you, and you may be certain that I will do it at once.'

At this the lords laughed aloud and clamoured their acclaim of Arthur and his Wise Counsellor. When they had quieted, Myrddin announced his plan. 'Summon the lords of the south to attend you in Londinium and witness your crown-taking there. Then they will believe and follow you gladly.'

This is exactly what they did. They enjoyed their feast that night and at dawn the next morning up they rose, saddled their horses, and rode to the shipyards of Muir Guidan. They sailed that very day. Messenger ships raced ahead, stopping at settlements along the coast to announce the king's summons.

In due time, Arthur arrived in the vicinity of Londinium, now called Caer Lundein, and ordered his fleet to be anchored on the Thamesis. Upon making landfall, he assembled his Cymbrogi, made his way towards the city and came boldly to the gates.

As the Wise Emrys had foretold, the men of Caer Lundein and the south did not esteem Arthur greatly. They knew nothing of the great battle at Mount Baedun. Neither did they have a care for any northern trouble, holding the fortunes of life between the walls but a thing of small consequence. This is blindness and folly, it is true, but they were men of little intelligence and less understanding.

But Aelle and the lords of the Saecsen Shore, who had not rebelled at Baedun, knew full well that Arthur was their rightful king. At Arthur's summons, they assembled their house carles and their wives and children, and marched at once to Arthur's summons — much to the shame of the Britons.

Still, the crowds of Caer Lundein, like crowds everywhere, loved a spectacle. At Arthur's approach they thronged the narrow streets and gathered on the rooftops of the ancient city, straining for a glimpse of the tall young man who paraded his subject lords before him.

'Who is he?' they asked one another.

'A Pict from the northland,' some answered. 'Look at his clothes!'

'No, he is a Saecsen,' said others. 'Look at his braid and his fair hair.'

'He rides a horse!' they said. 'He is certainly this Arthur we have been hearing about.'

To which others replied, 'But he is young yet. This must be that famous warrior's son or nephew.'

On and on it went. No one could decide who it was riding into their city with his warbands and retainers. All they knew for certain was that they were seeing someone the like of whom they had never seen before, and never would again.

But not all who looked upon the fair stranger that day were pleased to see him. Far from it! Long had they forgotten the slim young man who had drawn the sword from the stone seven years before. They had forgotten the Council of Kings, and the strife which gripped the kingdoms of Britain and held them powerless.

They had forgotten and so they reviled what they saw with their eyes. Does he think himself a Macsen Wledig riding into Rome? they demanded. Does he think himself emperor?

Who is he? Arthur? What kind of name is that? They

say he has defeated the barbarians. Who has he defeated? There are Saecsens walking around Caer Lundein bold as day! Look at him! He is too proud, too arrogant! He is a pretentious oaf and we will not be deceived by any northern conspiracy.

These things and more were muttered against Arthur, and some far worse. Arthur heard their mumblings and, though they stung him like the hairs of the nettle, he was not deflected from his purpose.

'I see they have learned no love for me,' he said to Bedwyr, riding beside him.

'Truth to tell, Bear, I have learned no love for them. Take the crown and let us be gone from this miserable place.'

Cai grew indignant. 'How long do they think their precious walls would stand if not for you, Artos? Let the Picti have it and be done.'

'I have come here to receive my kingship in the place where my father took the crown. When I have done what is required, we will leave this place.'

Arthur was received by the governor of Caer Lundein, a fatty haunch of pork named Paulus, who viewed all the world beyond the portico of his palace as unbearably backward. But Paulus had not scaled the height of his ambition without learning the uses of deceit. So he welcomed Arthur, his round face wreathed in jowly grins, right hand raised in friendship, left hand grasping the dagger behind his back.

Governor Paulus only waited to see which way the wind blew to know how to deal with Arthur. A battlechief from the north country was an unusual sight in Caer Lundein. *Dux Britanniarum* someone said — very impressive, very Roman. High King? Well, there were kings, yes; some were officially recognized. Pendragon? How charming, how quaint. Very rustic, in all; very refreshing.

Bedwyr was not misled by the fulsome governor's effusive welcome. 'He is a lizard, Artos. Do not believe a word he says. I would not drink a drop of his wine either, if I were you.'

'We satisfy the law in coming here,' Arthur told his retinue. 'Nothing more.'

'What law?' wondered Cai.

'The law established when the great Caesar first set foot on this island.'

'Which is?' asked Bedwyr.

'Every ruler must conquer Londinium if he is to hold Britain.'

'I have never heard any such law,' scoffed Cador. 'What is so exalted about this crumbling heap?'

'It stinks of urine and slops,' sneered Gwalchavad. 'From what I can see, the citizens of Caer Lundein are kin to barbarians.'

Arthur heard their complaints and explained patiently yet again. 'We are not staying here a moment longer than necessary. Once I have done what I came to do, we are away for Caer Melyn.'

When they had supped with the governor, Arthur and his retinue left the palace precinct and rode to the church — the same in which Arthur had stood and divers times pulled the sword from the stone. That keystone was now firmly in place in the central arch. Hundreds of people passed beneath that stone every day without realizing it. To them it was just an ordinary block of stone in an ordinary arch.

This is how many men perceived the Kingdom of Summer. Since it did not wear its great goodness emblazoned in shining gold, they did not esteem it. They simply passed by without a thought or glance at the very thing which kept the roof from crashing down upon their stupid heads. They passed by and knew it not.

Upon reaching the church, which had been besieged by the Cymbrogi, Arthur was met by the Bishop Uflwys and gaunt Archbishop Urbanus. Both men were genuinely happy to see Arthur. They had heard from the monks who served with the Cymbrogi how Arthur had conducted himself honourably in war, and how he had given gold for the rebuilding of the ruined churches. They were pleased to welcome him and bless him as was right.

Like Aurelius before him, Arthur shunned the governor's palace and embraced the church. He lodged there until his crown-taking could be completed.

The great Emrys was already at work making the necessary arrangements. He had sent to Dyfed for good bishop Teilo, the saintly Dubricius, and his young helper Illtyd.

This was not done to slight Urbanus. The plain fact was that the ever-ambitious archbishop had compromised himself by grasping after earthly power and could no longer serve God with a whole heart.

Myrddin Emrys wisely set Urbanus aside, saying, 'As Arthur is a man of the west and north, and will return there to rule, it is only fitting that those who must serve with him also commission him to his service.'

Urbanus may have felt affronted by these words, but he could not argue with them. Also, he was somewhat relieved not to be seen commending Arthur. Who knew what might befall? If Arthur proved unworthy it would be better not to have had anything to do with him. Relief battled with wounded pride — relief won. 'Yes, I do agree with you, Myrddin Emrys,' the archbishop said politely. 'I will leave it in your hands, and in God's.'

I am not lying when I tell you this was the best thing Urbanus could have done.

While these matters progressed, kings, lords, nobles and chieftains began descending upon the city. Some had ridden with Arthur in battle and already owned him king, others had supported him through tribute and were ready to acknowledge him, still others knew nothing of him and the summons caught them unawares. Nevertheless, they all came. For a new High King was to be crowned; and, whatever they thought of Arthur, this was not to be missed.

From Lloegres, Berneich, Rheged, Gwynedd, Dyfed, Mon, Derei, Dal Riata they came. They all came, yes, and from the Saecsen Shore came Aelle, now *Bretwalda* of the Saecsen kind, with his carles and kinsmen: Cynric and Cissa and Cymen.

Others came too: Ban and Bors of Benowyc across the sea; Cador of Cerniw; Samson, Bishop of Eboracum, and his abbot, Caradoc of Carfan, together with a fair company of monks and priests; Meurig of Dyfed and Silures; Ulfias of the Dobuni; Brastias of the Belgae; Idris of the Brigantes; Cunomor of Celyddon; Fergus, King of Ierne; and many more — each with a goodly retinue.

Of gifts there was no end. Each lord strove to embarrass the other with feats of generosity. Gold and silver glittered in the form of armbands, torcs, brooches, bowls, and ornaments of innumerable kinds. There were colourful gemstones and pearls of great value, enamelled pins of cunning filigree, and boxes of scented wood carved with the interwoven figures of fantastic animals; new-made spears by the score, horn bows and flights of arrows, trained hounds for hunting, shields embossed with gleaming brass and painted cowhide; casks of golden mead, and vats of ale; gifts of grain and leather, butter, salt, honey; and also beef, pork, lamb and fowl. More, in short, than can be told and believed.

Arthur's second king-making was as near to his father Aurelius' as the Wise Emrys could make it. He even schooled the churchmen in the words they should pronounce. The ceremony was performed in the church and witnessed by the assembled lords, the Cymbrogi, and as many of the self-appointed dignitaries of Caer Lundein as could squeeze themselves through the doors.

What they saw is well known. It has been reported from one end of this worlds-realm to the other — and even in Rome and Jerusalem!

At dawn, on a spotless morning in the height of summer, Arthur entered the church, accompanied by Bedwyr and Cai on his left and right, and Myrddin walking slowly before him. Though the Exalted Emrys was blind, he had learned such craft with his rowan staff that it served him better than sight. Behind Arthur came Illtyd, bearing a circlet of gold.

The four walked the length of the church, passing among a congregation struck dumb by the singular sight of Arthur: tall, erect, regal in every stitch and sinew, arrayed in a tunic of pearl white over trousers of leaf green, a belt of red-gold disks at his waist and a golden torc at his throat; his cloak of deepest red. His fair hair was trimmed and brushed back from his temples. His placid blue eyes were fixed on the altar ahead and filled with reverent joy.

At Arthur's entrance, the holy brothers of Urbanus' order began chanting the *gloria*. 'Gloria! Gloria! Gloria in excelsis Deo! Gloria in excelsis Deo!'

Glory! Glory! Glory to God in the high realms!

Before the altar Dubricius and Teilo waited, lit candles

in their hands. The entire church shimmered and danced with candlelight like tongues of apostolic flame kindling the spirits of all who gathered there with holy fire.

The throng bowed down as Arthur passed, falling to their knees upon the tessellated stone flags in homage. Upon gaining the altar, Arthur knelt and the priests placed their right hands upon his shoulders and prayed silently for him.

Then, Myrddin raised his hands in invocation, his voice — a true bard's voice — swelling to fill the church with its rich, resonant sound.

'Great of Might, High King of Heaven, Lord of the High Realms, Maker, Redeemer, Friend of Man, we worship and honour you!'

Then, turning to the four quarters of the church, he began the prayer that was first prayed by the Blessed Dafyd for Aurelius, High King of Britain and Arthur's father. Calling out aloud, he cried:

> 'Light of sun,
> Radiance of moon,
> Splendour of fire,
> Speed of lightning,
> Swiftness of wind,
> Depth of sea,
> Stability of earth,
> Firmness of Rock,
> Bear witness:

> We pray this day for Arthur, our king;
> For God's strength to steady him,
> God's might to uphold him,
> God's eye to look before him,
> God's ear to hear him,
> God's word to speak for him,
> God's hand to guard him,
> God's shield to protect him,
> God's host to save him
> From the snares of devils,
> From temptation of vices,
> From everyone who shall wish him ill.

We do summon all these powers between him and
    these evils:
Against every cruel power that may oppose him,
Against incantations of false druids,
Against black arts of barbarians,
Against wiles of idol-keepers,
Against enchantments great and small,
Against every foul thing that corrupts body and soul.

Jesu with him, before him, behind him;
Jesu in him, beneath him, above him;
Jesu on his right, Jesu on his left;
Jesu when he sleeps, Jesu when he wakes;
Jesu in the heart of everyone who thinks of him;
Jesu in the mouth of everyone who speaks of him;
Jesu in the eye of everyone who sees him.

We uphold him today, through a mighty strength,
the invocation of the Three in One,
Through belief in God,
Through confession of the Holy Spirit,
Through trust in the Christ,
Creator of all creation.

So be it.'

Then, coming once more before Arthur, he said, 'Bow
before the Lord of All, and swear your fealty to the High
King you will serve.'

Arthur prostrated himself face down before the altar,
stretching out his hands to either side in the manner of
a vanquished battlechief before his conqueror. Teilo and
Dubricius came to stand at either hand, and Illtyd stood
over Arthur at his head.

Dubricius, at Arthur's right hand said, 'With this hand
you will wield the Sword of Britain. What is your vow?'

Without lifting his face, Arthur answered, 'With this hand
I will wield the Sword of Britain in righteousness and fair
judgement. By the power of God's might and through his

will, I will use it to conquer injustice and punish those who practise harm. I will hold this hand obedient to my Lord God, used of him to do his work in this worlds-realm.'

Teilo, at Arthur's left hand said, 'With this hand you will hold the Shield of Britain. What is your vow?'

'With this hand I will hold tight to the Shield of Britain in hope and compassion. By the power of God's might and through his will, I will protect the people who keep faith with me and hold Jesu for their lord. I will hold this hand obedient to my Lord God, used of him to do his work in this worlds-realm.'

Illtyd, standing at Arthur's head said, 'Upon your brow you will wear the Crown of Britain. What is your vow?'

'Upon my brow I will wear the Crown of Britain in all honour and meekness. By the power of God's might and through his will, I will lead the kingdom through all things whatever shall befall me, with courage, with dignity, and with faith in the Christ who shall guide me.'

Whereupon the three priests replied, 'Rise in faith, Arthur ap Aurelius, taking the Christ to be your Lord and Saviour, honouring him above all earthly lords.'

Arthur rose, and Illtyd placed the slender golden circlet upon his head. Dubricius turned to the altar and took up Caliburnus — that is Caledvwlch, or Cut Steel, Arthur's great battle sword — and placed it in the king's right hand. Teilo took up Prydwen, Arthur's great round battle shield, which had been white washed anew and painted with the cross of Jesu.

Myrddin held before Arthur a wooden cross. 'Arthur ap Aurelius ap Constantine, who would be High King over us, do you acknowledge the Lord Jesu as your High King and swear him fealty?'

'I do,' replied Arthur. 'I pledge fealty with no other lord.'

'And do you vow to serve him through all things, as you would be served, even to the last of your strength?'

'I vow to serve him through all things, as I am served, even to the last of my strength.'

Myrddin nodded solemnly and continued. 'And will you worship the Christ freely, honour him gladly, revere him nobly, hold with him in truest faith and greatest love all the days that you shall live in this worlds-realm?'

'I will worship my lord the Christ freely, honour him gladly, revere him nobly, and hold with him in truest faith and greatest love all the days that I shall live in this worlds-realm,' declared Arthur.

'And do you pledge to uphold justice, grant mercy, and seek truth through all things, dealing with your people in compassion and love?'

'I do pledge to uphold justice, grant mercy, and seek truth through all things, dealing with my people in compassion and love, even as I am dealt with by God.'

Upon receiving Arthur's vows, Myrddin stepped close and unfastened the cloak from Arthur's shoulders. Teilo and Dubricius brought forth a fine new cloak of imperial purple with gold edging. This they fastened at Arthur's shoulder with a great silver stag-head brooch. Myrddin raised his hands and said, 'Go forth, Arthur, to all righteousness and good works, rule justly and live honourably, be to your people a ready light and sure guide through all things whatever may befall this worlds-realm.'

Arthur turned, holding the sword and shield, the new purple cloak falling from his shoulders to brush the floor stones.

'People of Britain, here is your High King! I charge you to love him, honour him, serve him, follow him, and pledge your lives to him, even has he has pledged his life to the High King of Heaven.'

The people stood and opened their mouths to acclaim him. But before anyone could raise voice the heavy doors of the church burst open with a loud commotion and in swept twelve fierce warriors with spears. Cai and Bedwyr rushed forth with swords drawn, and would have fallen upon the strangers. But Dubricius put out a hand to stay them, saying, 'Hold, men! There will be no bloodshed on this holy day. Put up your weapons and we will see what they desire in coming here like this.'

The strange warriors advanced fearlessly to the very altar of the church where Arthur stood. Without a word they ranged themselves around the altar and stood with their spears raised high. Then appeared a most unusual sight: sixteen beautiful dark-haired maidens, arrayed all in white, each holding a white dove in her hands and walking barefoot towards the altar.

Upon reaching the place where Arthur stood, the maidens halted and turned to face one another. No sooner had they done this than approached three tall battlechiefs dressed all in green and black. Each held a naked sword upright at arm's length, and each walked backwards.

Turning neither right nor left, these men took their places beside the dove maidens. Thereupon the twelve warriors brought their spears down upon the stones with a sharp, resounding crack. At once appeared another maid, this one more beautiful and more graceful than all the others, carrying a new-burnished spear in one hand and a dove in the other.

This singular maid wore a cloak the colour of fine emeralds, edged in purple, and a long mantle of yellow bright as sunlight. Her raven hair was loose and long, and plaited with summer wild flowers of white and gold; her fair cheeks blushed the colour of foxglove on the moor; her noble brow was high and smooth and white, lifting with noble pride, and her eyes held a playful gleam. She wore no shoes but nevertheless walked purposefully, yet with great elegance and dignity, to the altar.

Everyone in the church strained eyes to see this strange maid; they murmured aloud to one another, 'Who is she? Who can she be? Why does she carry that spear? What does she want?'

'But Arthur knew who she was, and though her appearance surprised and amazed him, he knew also why she had come.

'What is it?' demanded Myrddin of Bedwyr in a harsh whisper. 'What is happening? Tell me, man!'

'It is Gwenhwyvar,' Bedwyr replied uncertainly. 'She has come to honour Arthur, I think.'

'Honour him!' sneered Myrddin. 'She has come to claim him!'

Gwenhwyvar halted before Arthur and bent low, laying the spear cross-wise at his feet. She straightened and placed the white dove in Arthur's hands. Then she reached out a bold hand and took from the High King the Sword of Britain, which she grasped by the blade, wrapping her long fingers around the bright steel. And, raising Caliburnus to

367

her lips, she kissed the crosspiece of the hilt and then cradled the naked blade to her breast.

It was so swiftly done. No one suspected what had taken place — except Myrddin, who knew well what the swords and doves signified; and Arthur, who knew in his heart that he had found the one woman in all the world his full equal in courage, and above all others worthy of his love.

In this way was Arthur made High King of all Britain. And in this way was Arthur also wed.

TWO

Gwenhwyvar brought with her a wedding gift: a tabled rotunda — a structure of cunning craft and of a design unknown in Britain. That is, she brought the builder's drawings for this edifice: five vellum scrolls of ancient age wrapped tightly in fine linen. These drawings had been treasured by the kings of Ierne through many generations. As far as is known, there is only one other rotunda like it in all the world, and that is in the City of Constantine in the east.

A strange gift, certainly, for a wedding. But appropriate for a Warrior Queen like Gwenhwyvar. She had conceived the idea while sojourning with the Fair Folk at Ynys Avallach where she came to know Charis, Myrddin's mother and daughter of Avallach the Fisher King.

Myrddin was given the task of overseeing the construction of the tabled rotunda; the Great Emrys was the only man in this worlds-realm with knowledge and subtlety enough to raise the building. This work became the cornerstone of Arthur's reign, and it was meet so to do.

Building also began at Caer Melyn, Arthur's southern capital, and at Caer Lial which he had taken for his northern seat. The High King decided that he would maintain two principal courts, so that Britain should remain united. Caer Lial, old Caer Ligualid, City of the Legions in the north, was a wise choice. It was on the Wall, yet also near a sheltered bay which could serve the fleet. Seven roads met there, allowing rapid travel to all parts of the Island of the Mighty.

Caer Lial, long abandoned, lay in grey ruins: streets silent, tumbled houses roofless, garrison yards weed-grown, doorways deserted, forum vast and empty. The people of the area had from time to time pulled down parts of its walls for building-stone, but mostly the once-proud city was left to its own slow decay.

It was to Caer Lial that I came with my father, Caw, lord of Trath Gwryd, who had his realm from the High King. He had brought me to serve with the Cymbrogi as he was beholden to do.

Trained as a bard since I could speak — though also learned in Latin — I felt my heart beat high with the thought that I might sit at the feet of the Exalted Emrys, Chief Bard of Britain. The day I arrived in the Pendragon's city is one I shall never forget.

My father and I rode down from Trath Gwryd with two of my older brothers who were also to join the Cymbrogi. Caw had nine sons and all but one served the Pendragon faithfully; at thirteen, I was youngest of all.

Caer Melyn was a stronghold of timber, but Caer Lial was a city of stone. A marvel of the stone-mason's craft, jewel of the north. Everywhere I looked, the brightness of Arthur shone in his fair city. Even the streets gleamed!

Once past the gates, we dismounted out of respect and led our horses through the city to the High King's palace — the former regional residence of an Imperial Legate, now restored. We were received by Cai, King Arthur's seneschal, who informed us that the Pendragon was away but expected to return at any time.

'I welcome you in the name of the Pendragon,' he said, 'and I accept the tribute of your sons, Lord Caw.' He gripped the arms of my older brothers, but ignored me altogether. 'We are ever grateful for good fighting men among the Cymbrogi.'

Caius ap Ectorius of mighty Caer Edyn was a champion many times over. Hair red as flame, and quick green eyes, he was a huge man, with a generous, open countenance which spoke of a guileless heart and an easy mind. Still, I reckoned, he would be a formidable foe in battle. A man to make his enemies curse the day of their birth. I felt weak and unworthy, just standing next to him. And this though I had been raised in a lord's house with warriors for brothers!

Cai summoned one of his stewards and, after my father's

farewells, my brothers were led away to the warriors' precinct, opposite the enormous training field behind the
palace. My father and Cai talked for a time, and eventually
their talk turned to me.

'What of the Great Emrys?' my father asked. 'Aneirin here
is also pledged to Arthur's service, but as he is a mabinog
and will soon become a bard we thought the Chief Bard
might sooner find a place for him.'

Cai clapped a hand to my shoulder, rattling my frame, and
grinned. 'A *filidh* for Myrddin, eh? Splendid! I have been
telling him he needs assistance. There is simply too much
to do and Rhys unfortunately has not mastered the art of
being in three places at once. It will be good to have you
with us.'

I thanked him and plucked up what courage I possessed
at the age of thirteen. 'If you tell me where he is, I will go
to him and recommend myself with your blessing.'

Cai laughed at my presumption. 'Oh, you will do, boy.
But the Emrys is not here. He is at work on the rotunda.
He resumed work this spring as soon as the snow cleared
the valleys, and vows that he will nowise return until it is
finished.'

'If you will tell me where he is to be found, I will go to him
and give myself to his service.'

Cai's grin became secretive. 'Oh aye, that is the problem,
is it not — where is the Table Round?'

The whereabouts of Arthur's shrine was being kept secret.
A holy place, it was to remain hidden from the world of
men. Since part of its function was as burial vault for great
warriors, the High King did not want its hallowed ground
desecrated by curious wayfarers, or jealous pagans. He did
not wish it to become a place of pilgrimage, for although a
sacred site, it was to be first and foremost a sanctuary for the
gallant who had given their lives for Britain, and so earned
their blessed rest. Inasmuch as he also planned to be buried
there at the appointed time, the Pendragon did not want its
peace disturbed.

'It would not do to have just anyone about the place,' Cai
continued, regarding me suspiciously. 'But if you are to be
a help to Myrddin — '

'Lord Cai,' I interrupted, 'would it not be better to

address the Exalted Emrys by his rightful title?' My impertinence was boundless!

'You think *me* insolent?' Cai folded his arms across his vast chest. 'Well, I tell you this, boy. If I make bold to speak his name it is because I have earned the right. Let us pray that when you reach my height and years you can do the same with me!'

My ears burned, as well they should. My father gave me a look of strong reproof. 'Forgive me, Lord Seneschal,' I replied meekly, my cheeks crimson with embarrassment.

Cai softened immediately. 'Still, if you are to be a help to Myrddin it is no doubt best for you to be where he is. Since he is not here, you must go there. It will be arranged.'

My father and I thanked him heartily, whereupon Cai said, 'In Arthur's name I extend to you the hospitality of the High King's hall. You will sup with us tonight. Tomorrow is soon enough to begin your journey.'

I remember almost nothing about that first night in Arthur's hall — except drinking too much wine before meat and falling asleep face down in my bowl. I awoke next morning in a strange part of the palace, near the kitchens, and found my way once more to the hall. The hall was empty, but I heard voices echoing from the doorway beyond and went out onto a portico to find my father and Cai saying farewell to one another.

With throbbing head I, too, bade my father farewell, and apologized to Cai for my embarrassing behaviour of the night before — whatever it had been. 'You will think me low and untutored,' I said, 'and I would not blame you. But I assure you I mean to be worthy of the honour of my service, Lord Seneschal.'

The big battlechief placed his hands on my shoulders and held my gaze with his eyes. 'Then *be* worthy, boy. No one stands between you and honour. Take it, seize it! It is yours if you want it.' And so it was.

I broke fast on bread and water — I could stomach nothing else — and I was given to the care of one of the Seneschal's stewards. My horse stood saddled and ready in the yard, so we left the city and rode north on the old Roman road into the Rheged wilderness. As we rode along, I learned that my companion's name was Tegyr. He had been a warrior once, but had lost his right hand in the Battle of Baedun Hill. Now he was Cai's chief steward and proud of it, for, as he said, 'I would have given my right hand anyway to serve the Pendragon. It is but small loss to bear.'

I liked him at once, and asked him about Caer Lial and the Pendragon. He answered me forthrightly and began to tell me about the ordering of the Pendragon's house and all I should know to be part of it.

He also told me about the Great Emrys, although I had been hearing stories of him since I was old enough to hear anything. The more he talked, the faster beat my heart to think that soon I would be meeting this exalted person in the flesh. I was nearly overwhelmed by the thought. Me, Aneirin, serving the Chief Bard of the Island of the Mighty!

At midday we left the old track and turned due west into the hills. But a while later we dropped down into the vale of Nith and followed the river a little south, to a sand-bounded peninsula. Here, on the foundation of an ancient hill fort was Arthur's rotunda erected. As we approached I could see the shapely form rising sharp against the sky. The hill on which it sat overlooked the sea, and at first I wondered at the wisdom of placing this secret edifice on a promontory where any passing ship could see it. But upon reaching the place I learned that although the expanse of sea was in full view of the hill, the rotunda itself remained below the crest of the mound, well out of sight of the casual observer.

We dismounted at the foot of the hill near some tents which had been set up for the labourers who worked on the shrine. These were empty now; there was no one else around. So, as Tegyr set about tethering the horses, I walked up to the shrine for a closer look.

The rotunda itself appeared strange to my eyes. Certainly, I had never seen a building like it: fully round, constructed on a series of circular stone foundations or tables of diminishing size, narrower at the entrance and then swelling gracefully out before curving inward as it rose to meet the sky. At first sight the thing appeared nothing more than an immense beehive of the kind often made of braided rope — but far more graceful and imposing. Indeed, the size and beauty of the rotunda and its situation on the sea inspired peace. The eye savoured the rising curve of the dome, the sea played upon the ear, and the soul drank in the tranquillity of the holy place.

I gazed upon the sacred edifice and felt my spirit yearn to be part of all that this holy shrine symbolized: peace, beauty, honour, valour, courage. . . It was the Kingdom of Summer distilled into stone.

And such stone! The subtle blues and grays and whites were so worked to give light and colour and shape to the whole, in such a clever way that I did not wonder men passing by would not see it. The hues of sky and sea and cloud were its colours, and in certain lights and at certain times of day it would all but vanish.

If my first glimpse of the shrine awoke in me the desire to draw near and pray, my first glance at the Wise Emrys provoked the opposite effect. He came charging out from the interior of the rotunda, a mason's hammer in his upraised hand. 'Halt!' he called, in a voice that would have cowed a charging bull. I stopped and he flew towards me.

He was tall, much taller than I expected, and much younger. He was reputed to be of the Fair Folk, yet I had imagined him a very old man. He had known Vortigern; he had known Saint Dafyd; he had met Macsen Wledig! He was ancient!

Yet the man bearing down upon me was no older in appearance than my own father. His hair was dark and full, with only a fleck of silver here and there. Though his brow was lined, his countenance was still unwrinkled, and there were no creases about his eyes. His eyes! They were clear and deep and the colour of bright gold. I thought immediately of the soaring hawk and hunting wolf.

'I thought you were blind!' I blurted out the first thing that came into my head.

'I was, but no longer,' he replied. 'Who are you and what do you want here?'

Tegyr, who had been tending the horses, came running to my aid. The Emrys turned on him. 'Tegyr, it is you. Why do you come here like this?'

'Forgive me, Emrys. I should have signalled our arrival.' He glanced at the shrine soaring above us. 'The work is going well, Emrys. It is beautiful.'

The Emrys turned and glanced over his shoulder. 'It is nearly finished — at last,' he said. 'Only a few small matters remain.' Then he turned back to me. 'But you, boy — you have not answered me,' he said abruptly.

'My lord?'

'Your name — if you have one. What are you called?' He gazed so fiercely into my eyes that I felt his touch upon my soul and quite forgot who or what I was.

'An- Aneirin,' I stammered uncertainly. My own name sounded strange and unnatural in my ears. 'I am Aneirin ap Caw, Emrys.'

The Great Emrys tossed his head. 'You are well named, boy. Aptly named.' To Tegyr he said, 'Why is he here?'

'Cai has sent him, Emrys. He is to help you. If you do not wish him to stay, I will take him away.'

The Emrys regarded me narrowly. I could already feel myself in the saddle and heading back to Caer Lial. My heart sank to my feet. Most wretched of men, I felt myself rejected.

But the Emrys needed the help of two willing hands. I do not flatter myself that it was anything more than that. Yet it was enough for me. 'Since he is here, let him stay,' the Emrys said, and I was saved.

'Emrys,' said Tegyr, 'I must return to Caer Lial at once. Is there anything you require? I will have it brought.'

'Only this: bring word when Gwenhwyvar has returned. I will have a message for her then.'

'It will be done, Lord Emrys.' Tegyr turned and hurried away. I saw that he took my horse with him.

I turned to find the Emrys already striding up the hill. I ran after him. 'What would you have me do, lord?'

Without stopping or turning round, he called back, 'Do you know how to make a broom?'

I had never made one, but I had seen it done often enough by the women at Trath Gwryd. 'I think so,' I answered.

'Then make one!' the Emrys said, and continued on. I spent the rest of the day gathering the various twigs and sticks I would need, and then set about trying to build the thing. I did not presume to enter the rotunda, or even to go near it. I went about my task and kept to myself.

At dusk the Emrys emerged and called me to him. 'Are

you hungry, Aneirin ap Caw?' the Emrys asked when I had climbed the gentle slope to the top of the hill. He pointed to his feet and I saw that a bundle lay before him upon the steps of the shrine. The Emrys sat down and unwrapped the rags made of dried and woven grass. Inside was new cheese and tough black bread, and a small joint of cold roast mutton. 'This is brought to me by the people hereabouts.'

'There are people?' Well I might ask. I had seen no sign of any holding or habitation since leaving the king's city. And except for the labourers' tents, I saw no place where men might dwell.

'Hill Folk,' he replied, and touched the tip of a finger to the faded blue *fhain* mark tattooed on his cheek. 'I once was one of them.'

The Emrys of Britain broke the bread in his hands and handed me half the loaf. 'Come, take it, eat. You will not taste better.'

Hill Folk food! I had heard all about the *bhean sidhe*, of course — as who would not, growing up in the northern hills? But I had never seen one of these mysterious creatures, nor did I know anyone who had. They might as well be Otherworld beings for all we knew of them. Many reasonable men doubted their existence altogether.

I stared at the dense, black loaf in my hand. It was bread, to be sure, but it smelled of fennel and other herbs I could not name. 'Eat, boy!' the Emrys told me. 'You cannot work if you do not eat — and I mean you to work.'

Lifting a corner of the loaf to my mouth, I bit off a chunk and chewed. The Emrys spoke truly; the bread was good; I had never tasted better and told him so.

The Emrys sat down on the step but, since he did not bid me join him, I stood to eat my meal. I fell at once to gazing out onto the sea to the west, and southward to the pale green hills across the bay. The breeze off the sea was cool. Lark song showered down from the clear blue sky, and I tilted my head back, shading my eyes with my hands and squinting into the airy void. I could scarce see the larks, so high did they fly.

'Fort of the Larks,' said the Emrys. 'That is what this place was called. Long have the larks enjoyed the use of it. Now it belongs to Arthur.'

It was his voice that fascinated me. Infinitely expressive, it served him in any manner he wished. When he lashed, it could have raised welts on a stone. When he soothed, it could have shamed nightingales into silence. And when he commanded, mountains and valleys exchanged places.

After we finished our meal, he took me inside the rotunda, which was even more remarkable than its exterior. For, rather than the cold, dark, cave-like appearance I expected, the interior was open, airy and light. The domed roof remained open to the sky, providing ample light to pour down gently curving sides of dressed white stone.

The Great Emrys spread his arms and turned slowly, indicating the perfect circularity of the shrine. 'This,' he said as he revolved, 'this is the Omphalos of Britain.'

As I remained silent, he asked, 'Have you never heard that word before?'

'No, Lord Emrys, I have not.'

'It is the sacred centre. All things have a centre — for the Kingdom of Summer, the centre is here.'

I pondered this for a moment. 'I thought — ' I began, 'that is, I heard that Ynys Avallach held that prominence.'

'The Glass Isle? No,' he shook his head, 'I know what men say of the Tor, but that belongs to another. . . '

Another *what*, he did not say. 'Besides,' he continued briskly, 'the Fisher King is not long there. There are too many people nearby — the south is becoming too crowded. I have prevailed upon Avallach and my mother to establish themselves in the north.'

I knew of the Fisher King, and Charis, the Lady of the Lake, next to Gwenhwyvar reputed to be the most beautiful woman in Britain. 'They are coming here?'

'Not here, but near. There is an island where Arthur has granted them lands,' he told me.

I slept that night in one of the workers' tents; the Emrys slept in the rotunda. In the morning I awoke, took my broom and went up to him. He greeted me and bade me enter.

Hesitantly, I stepped up to the entrance and glanced around the inside of the shrine. In the centre, beneath the all-seeing eye of the open dome, sat an immense stone chair, or throne, carved of a single slab of living rock and placed on its own raised table of stone. The curved inner walls were ledged with a series of ringed stones, hundreds of them, each one forming a small niche of its own. It seemed to me much like the bone-houses of elder times with their skull nooks — crevices carved out of stone to hold the severed heads of venerated ancestors.

All appeared finished, the white stone gleaming. 'What would you have me do, Lord Emrys?'

'Sweep,' he told me. The Emrys turned to a table, unwrapped a leather pouch that lay there, and withdrew tools: an iron hammer, a chisel, and a scribe for marking stone. He took up the hammer and turned once more to the nearest stone ledge and began inscribing letters on the smooth face.

'A name, Lord Emrys?'

'The names of those who have attained the Round Table will be recorded here,' he explained. 'Those who have distinguished themselves in the service of the Summer Realm will have their names cut in the stone. When death finds them, that will be recorded too, and their bodies buried within the sacred precinct, so that their renown will not pass out of this worlds-realm.'

Understanding came to me at last. The tabled rotunda was to be a place of spiritual refuge, a haven of tranquillity dedicated to the Prince of Peace, a reliquary of great holiness and honour, where the names and arms of great men could be venerated, a memorial to deeds of courage and valour.

Thus, I entered my servitude. I swept, carried water, gathered firewood, tended the camp and, when I was not otherwise occupied, washed the stone — time and again I washed it. When I finished, I swept the interior of the rotunda and washed it again. I scrubbed it till the stone gleamed.

Daily the food came. Sometimes in the morning, when we rose, I would go down to the stream below the hill and fetch it from the hollow bole of a willow. Other times we would emerge from the shrine, hungry from our work, to find the woven-grass bundle on the topmost step. Never did I see those who left it, nor could I guess whence they came.

Day by day, the names were chiselled into stone. Some of the names I recognized, most I did not. Sometimes the

Emrys would tell me about the man whose name he etched. More often, we worked in silence. But it was never a lonely silence. I knew the Emrys' thoughts were full, as were my own. Just being near him proved instructive and edifying. Still, I liked it best when he sang.

After a while, I little noted the passing of the days. My hands grew strong and tough. My life was a steady-beaten rhythm of work and rest. I desired nothing more. When one day I heard a call outside, I actually resented the interruption, although I had seen no other human being besides the Emrys since the day I arrived.

The Emrys laid aside his square and scribe. 'That is Tegyr with a message. Let us see what he brings us.'

It seemed an intrusion, but I reluctantly put down my broom and followed him out. Tegyr was there at the foot of the hill, and someone else with him: a warrior, I could tell by the size of him. One of Arthur's captains, I guessed. He was dark, with deep-set eyes and a high, handsome brow. There were scars on his arms and hands, and on his left cheek.

The battlechief regarded me placidly before turning his attention to the hill and the shrine, now cool blue-white in the westering sun. 'Hail, Myrddin Emrys!' he called, as we approached. 'What is this I am hearing about you? They say you have gone into your invisible fortress and will never more return.'

'Hail, Bedwyr!' cried the Emrys. 'It is that much like you to believe the idle gossip you hear.'

The two embraced like kinsmen and, linking arms, began walking up the hill. Tegyr, smiling silently, followed and I came on behind.

'It is beautiful,' breathed Bedwyr. 'Truly beautiful. Arthur will be honoured. And the queen will establish a perpetual choir to sing your praises!'

'Has Gwenhwyvar returned?'

'Yes. Tegyr said you asked him to bring word when she arrived, so I thought to come with him. I wanted to see what you had accomplished since I was last here. Do you object?'

'Never — besides, we are nearly finished as you can see. I will return with you to Caer Lial tomorrow.'

I listened to their talk and learned that the queen had been away in the south, helping with the Fair Folk migration from Ynys Avallach to the chosen island in the north. Arthur meantime held council at Caer Melyn and Caer Lundein. He was not expected to return before Lugnasadh. This would give the queen time to make her last inspection of the monument, and to arrange the ceremony and celebration of its completion.

Bedwyr and Tegyr spent the night with us and all of the next day, while the Emrys finished his work. All three left the following day, but I stayed at the rotunda to sweep out the last of the dust and stone-chips, and wash the floor and ledges. The Emrys was to return in two or three days with the queen.

As soon as the others left, I worked through the day without cease until finishing. It was dusk when I finally sat down to rest and eat. Though the sun had set long before, the sky at that time of year does not grow completely dark. Therefore did I enjoy a pleasant evening — sitting alone on my hill, monarch of all I surveyed, watching sea-gulls dive and glide in the clear evening air.

I had not made my fire. There was light enough yet, and the night chill had not settled on the hill. I ate my sweet dark bread and cold roast mutton, and then rose to find my water jar. I had left it inside the shrine, so went in to fetch it.

The interior of the rotunda was dark now, but I had little trouble finding the jar. I drank my fill and turned to go outside. As I turned, however, a figure appeared in the arched doorway — dark against the lighter sky beyond.

I froze, gripping the water jar tight in my hand lest I drop it.

The stranger stood full in the doorway, motionless, peering into the shrine. I do not believe he could see me in the darkness, but I imagined his eyes stripping away the shadow and revealing me. No, it was more than imagined, I think: I really felt something — the force of his presence, perhaps, groping, searching, penetrating the obscurity, and finally brushing against me. That fleeting touch chilled me and my heart lurched in my chest.

Blessed Jesu, Bright Protector, save me! I prayed — though I do not know why.

All at once, the figure turned and disappeared. I heard

only the swish of a cloak and nothing more. I waited for a moment — but only that — and then crept slowly to the entrance. Peering cautiously outside, I looked left and right before emerging. I made a quick circuit round the shrine. The stranger had gone, I decided; there was no one on the hill or below it.

Where had he gone? I heard no horse, and it did not seem possible that anyone could arrive and depart so quickly. Perhaps I had simply imagined seeing someone.

Nevertheless, I slept inside the rotunda and without a fire that night, lest I should attract any more intruders with my light. In the morning I found the bundle on the steps and suddenly felt very foolish.

My intruder was only one of the Hill Folk who brought the food each day. He had brought me this bundle and, not seeing anyone about, stopped to look inside the shrine. I had at long last chanced to see one of my providers and I had behaved like a child. I was only glad no one else was there to witness my shame.

Two days later, the party from Caer Lial arrived to inspect the monument. In the excitement, I forgot all about my mysterious visitor.

THREE

Queen Gwenhwyvar appeared at once more fierce than I could ever have imagined, and more lovely. She was a dark-smouldering flame clothed in the finely-formed body of a woman; an ardent, passionate soul, alive to everything around her. Because of the stories I had heard, I expected a towering, majestic figure like those famed Roman matriarchs of old.

Elegant she was, and graceful as the swan in flight, but she was not at all the forbidding matriarch. Her black hair gleamed; her eyes burned bright with delight as she beheld the wonder the Exalted Emrys had worked in the Fortress of Larks.

She stood before the steps and gazed at the marvellous shrine, beaming her pleasure. The others, including the Emrys and myself, waited a little away, watching her reaction. Gwenhwyvar remained a goodly time, merely looking up at the smooth curves of the monument. Then, lifting her soft-booted foot, she slowly mounted the steps and went in.

Gwenhwyvar had laboured long over her wedding gift to Arthur. And endured much in the way of contempt and derision. The ignorant said that Arthur had married a maid of the *bhean sidhe* and it was rumoured that she employed druid enchanters to summon Otherworld beings to move the sacred stone from Ierne, and had with spells and incantations raised the stone and rendered the site invisible lest anyone stumble upon it unawares.

Pure superstition, of course. Fiery Gwenhwyvar was not of the Hill Folk, nor was she a Pict. She was Irish, though proud as any Fair Folk maid; she could also command a warband with the skill of the best of Arthur's captains.

Some of the stone came from Ierne, it is true — but

from Gwenhwyvar's father, King Fergus mac Guillomar. The beautiful blue stone was cut from the mountains and floated across the sea in ships, then dragged by ox-drawn sledge to the site which, although hidden, was not invisible. She employed the best quarrymen, masons and carpenters to work the stone and raise it — not druid enchanters.

In all, the queen was simply following the practice of her race; women of her rank provided for the survival of their *fhain*, or family clan, in life and death and beyond. Gwenhwyvar, foremost of all queens of the Island of the Mighty, meant to give Arthur a monument that would endure for ever.

Thirteen years is a long time to wait for a wedding gift. It is also a long time to wait for an heir. More than a few of Arthur's lords had begun grumbling against Gwenhwyvar because the queen had given Arthur no sons. This, they thought, was more important than any monument.

Upon completing her inspection of the shrine, she emerged triumphant. 'Myrddin Emrys,' the queen said, taking his hands into her own, 'I am for ever beholden to you. No other in all the wide world could have accomplished this great work.' She turned and indicated the whole of the shrine with an arcing sweep of her hand. 'It is all I hoped it would be.'

'Thank you,' replied Myrddin simply. 'I am honoured.'

With the queen had come Tegyr and Bedwyr, and a few others of her retinue, and now they began to talk excitedly, praising the Emrys for his magnificent achievement. 'Arthur will be pleased,' Gwenhwyvar said. 'He will love this place as I do. It will be his sanctuary. There is peace here; nothing will disturb him here ever.'

The queen referred to Arthur's continued clashes with the lords and petty kings of the south, who worried at him constantly. If it was not one thing with them, it was another. Nothing ever made them happy — except baiting the Bear of Britain, which they considered good sport. Woe to them!

The northern kings knew better. The wars, only a minor vexation in the south, and now long forgotten, still lived in the memories of the people whose lands had been seized and families slaughtered by the barbarians. The tribes of the north revered their Pendragon, where the southern men merely tolerated him. More and more, Arthur looked upon the north as his home and he sojourned there whenever he could — but always at Eastertide and the Christ Mass.

Gradually, as the High King's sentiments had shifted, the heart of his realm had moved away from the south as well. Wherefore the lords of the south made greater cause against him. Petty dogs, all of them! The knew not when they were well off!

The queen did not stay at the rotunda. Having made her inspection, she was eager to return to the palace to begin ordering the celebration. Before the retinue left, the Emrys came to me. 'I am going to see my mother and Avallach settled in their new home. I want you to come with me.'

I had assumed that I would stay at the shrine. Indeed, I looked upon it as my duty. But I did as I was bade, and I went with him. We reached Caer Lial at twilight, slept in the palace, and departed again early the next morning. A ship waited in the harbour to take us to the Isle of the Fisher King, the island men of the north now call Avallon, or sometimes *Ynys Sheaynt*, Island of Blessed Peace.

I did not know where this island might be, nor how long our voyage would last. I did not care. For, with the sunrise on the sparkling water, my dread left me and all I could think was that I was on my way to meet the mysterious Fisher King and his renowned daughter. I had never seen Fair Folk — save the Emrys, if he was one — and anticipation flourished in me. The ship could not sail fast enough.

The island lies off the western coast midway between Ierne and Britain, a good day's sailing. It is the peculiar quality of this sea-girt land that it disappears from time to time. The Cymry say this is because Manannan ap Llyr, Lord of the Sea, grows jealous of this most fortunate isle and covers it with the *Lengel*, the Veil of Concealment, so that men will not covet it for themselves.

Avallon lies surrounded by deep blue waters, overarched by dazzling blue skies, caressed by gentle winds and weather. Fish of all types abound in its warm seas, and its broad plains bring forth grain in unmatched quantity, sheep and cattle grow fat on its hillsides. Indeed, it is a Fortunate Isle; fair in every way. Arthur had claimed this island and provided for a church and monastery to crown its unsung glory; these were to be overseen by Avallach.

Our pilot guided the ship into the cliff-bound bay, whereupon we made landfall at a stone-built dock and led our horses up the hill to the track. We then proceeded directly across the island to the western coast, passing by bright woods and dark-crested forests, and wide, green, flower-speckled meadows sown through with freshets and brooks, reaching the Fair Folk settlement as the last red-flamed rays of the sun dwindled into the sea.

I saw for the first time the two tall white towers, now glowing red-gold in the setting sun, which rose from a wall-enclosed mound overlooking the sea. Inside the wall, the high-pitched roof of a goodly hall glinted like silver scales, or glass, as the slate caught the light. Sheep grazed on the stronghold mound outside the walls, their white fleeces turned a rosy gold in the light, the grass shining like emerald. A clear stream sang its glistening way around the whole as it plunged to the sea-cliffs beyond. Horses roamed at will, noses sunk in the sweet-scented grass.

The Wise Emrys shouted with joy when he beheld the shining stronghold. He opened his mouth and sang out a hymn of holy praise, and lashed his horse to a gallop so that he might enter the gates all the sooner. I followed as fast as I could, marvelling at the blessed sight before me.

In all, the place seemed to me an Otherworldly paradise, a realm of gods on earth. I was confirmed in this observation when we rode through the narrow, high-arched gates and glimpsed the Fair Folk themselves moving about their tasks — much remained to be done before the fortress would be fully settled.

Tall and many-favoured, they are a handsome race. Fair to look upon, graceful, straight-limbed, firm of flesh, the elder race is greatly to be admired. The Creator's glory is much manifest in them. Yet for all their comeliness and favour they are a melancholy people; their time is not long in this worlds-realm and they regret it bitterly.

We were met by Fair Folk who recognized the Emrys and called him by name as they ran to hold our horses. 'Merlin! Summon the king! Merlin is here!'

Avallach greeted us as we dismounted. A dark mane of

curly hair, quick dark eyes, and a dark beard coiled in the manner of eastern kings gave him an ominous, threatening aspect, which his deep, thundering voice did not altogether dispel. The Bear of Britain is a big man, and Myrddin is not small, but the Fisher King stood head and shoulders above both. For all this, he was not awkward or slow in his movements as men of such size often are; the innate grace of his kind was in him. Nevertheless, as he strode towards us I marvelled that the earth did not shake beneath his feet.

The king's dark eyes glinted and white teeth flashed a smile in his dark beard. 'Merlin! I give you good greeting! Welcome home.'

The Emrys embraced the king and then stood off to view the stronghold. 'It is not the palace on the Tor,' he said. I thought I heard a note of sadness in his voice.

'No,' agreed Avallach, 'it is not. Ah, but I was growing weary with the Glass Isle. The good brothers were happy to have the palace and will make excellent use of it — a scriptorium, I believe, and a larger hospice. The sick make pilgrimage to Shrine Hill in ever-increasing numbers. They will find it a peaceful place.' He paused and lifted a hand to the gleaming palace. 'But come, Merlin. My hall has not yet been baptized with song — and now that you are here, that oversight can be corrected. Come, we will lift the guest cup.'

'I would enjoy nothing more,' the Emrys said, 'but I must greet my mother first.'

'Of course!' cried Avallach. 'She is in the grove, directing the planting. Go to her and bring her back. I will await you in the hall. Go!' The Fisher King waved us away.

We hurried from the yard, passed through the gates and made our way along the wall to the west side facing the sea. There, on the sunny slopes above the sheer cliffs, the Lady of the Lake had established her apple grove. The trees were sprigs and saplings brought from the Tor, and she knelt at one of them, pressing the earth around its roots with her hands.

At our approach she raised her head, saw her son and smiled. My heart soared. She seemed an earthly goddess such as the Learned Brotherhood revere in their ancient songs. But the *derwydd* speak in ignorance, for the flesh-and-bone reality far surpasses their bloodless ideal.

She rose to her feet and, brushing dirt from her mantle and her hands, walked quickly towards us. I could not move, or look away. All my life I had heard of the Lady of the Lake and, seeing her, knew the utter worthlessness of words justly to describe what lies beyond their scan. Hair like sunlight on flax, eyes green as forest glades, skin as soft and white as. . . it was hopeless.

'My mother, Charis,' the Emrys was saying. I came to myself with a start, realizing I had been transfixed by the Lady of the Lake's astonishing beauty.

'I — I am your servant,' I stammered, and blanched at my ineptitude.

Charis honoured me with a smile. She linked arms with her son and they began walking back to the yard together. I was happily, and gratefully, forgotten in their reunion. I was more than content to follow on behind. Fragments of their conversation drifted back to me, and I listened.

'. . . sorry to leave the Tor,' Charis said, 'but it is for the best. . . '

'. . . difficult, I know. . . much closer. . . be together more often now. . . '

'. . . a blessed place. We will be happy here. . . the Tor. . . too many. . . Avallach could not abide it. . . so much has changed. . . '

We reached the gates; Charis halted and embraced her son, holding him for a long moment. 'I am glad you have come; I could not be happier. Arthur has been so good to us. We will do all to repay his trust and generosity.'

'There is no need. I have told you, the High King views Avallach as an ally, and needs a strong hand to hold this island. It is an ancient and holy place — there should be a church here. With you and grandfather here, there will be a church and more: a monastery, a *llyfrwy* for your books, a hospice for the sick. Your work will flourish here.'

The Lady of the Lake kissed her son, and they walked through the gates. We crossed the yard and entered the king's hall to be greeted with rich cups of silver and horn filled with sweet golden mead. I was offered to drink as well, and did so, but it might have been muddy water in my cup for all I noticed. The hall of the Fisher King stole away my thirst.

High-vaulted the roof and many pillared, the structure could have held three hundred warriors at table with room for the bards, priests, stewards, serving boys, dogs, and all the retinue that went with them. At one end of the long room lay an enormous hearth, at the other a screen of gold-painted ox-hide, with the king's chambers beyond. The floor was of white cut stone, covered with fresh rushes; the pillars were timber, stripped, bound together and carved in upward spiralling grooves.

The king had ordered chairs to be set up, but we did not sit. Instead, we stood sipping the mead and talking — rather, *they* talked, I simply stared about me at the hall. Hearth and pillars, tessellated floor, and high-pitched roof — it was unlike any I had ever seen. What I saw, of course, was Fair Folk craft, blended with the lively artistry of the Celt.

Later, after our evening meal, the Great Emrys sang in the hall of the Fisher King for his mother and all gathered there. He sang *The Dream of Rhonabwy*, a tale I did not know and had never heard before. Both beautiful and disturbing, I believe it was a true tale but its truth had not yet taken place in the world of men; much of the song's meaning had to do with future things, I think. Though the High King was not directly mentioned, Arthur was several times implied.

This is what Myrddin sang. . .

In the first days of Ynys Prydein, when the dew of creation was still fresh on the earth, Manawyddan ap Llyr ruled in the Island of the Mighty, and this is the way of it.

Manawyddan, firstborn of Mighty Llyr, lived long and attained great renown through deeds of courage and valour. He had a kinsman, a man of lesser worth and rank, and this cousin, Medyr, became chafed and annoyed seeing the glory his kinsman enjoyed while he himself had nothing. So up he jumps one shining morning and calls to his tribesmen. 'Lleu knows I am sick of this,' he said. 'All day long I am distressed, but does Manawyddan take notice of my affliction? No, he does not. What shall we do about such a state of affairs?'

The tribesmen looked at one another, but could make no

answer. Medyr shook his fist at them. 'Well? I am listening, but hear nothing save the four winds blowing through your heads as through empty shells.'

One of the elder tribesmen spoke up and said, 'Lord Medyr, if it is advice you are wanting, we would be less than good men if we did not tell you to seek out the Black Hag of Annwfn, who knows all that passes everywhere and holds such powers of counsel as to make any man a king who heeds her.'

'At last!' cried Medyr. 'Lleu knows it took you long enough. But this advice seems good to me. I will do as you say.' At once he climbed upon his horse and rode off to seek the Black Hag.

This creature lived in a mound in a birchwood copse near a river. When Medyr found her he summoned her from her dank lair. Foul was her appearance; fouler still the smell which besmote poor Medyr's nostrils. But he had determined to see the thing through and he heeded her advice — which consisted of nothing more than that Medyr should go to Manawyddan and demand to be taken into his care.

This he did. Manawyddan, thinking no ill, received Medyr with good grace and honoured him far above his rank by offering to make him a battlechief and head of a fair warband. Medyr agreed and was satisfied for a little time. But in the end he tired of the work and considered that he might better himself more quickly by raiding. So he rode off and began a life of plunder and pillage, burning holdings, stealing cattle, killing any who made bold to oppose him.

Manawyddan was not the king to stand aside and see his people hurt in this way, so he called forth his best men and asked them to choose from among them the noblest and bravest who should go after Medyr and end his vile slaughter. These were the men who were chosen: Rhonabwy, Kynrig Red Freckles, and Cadwgan the Stout. Everyone agreed that if these men failed it would not be through fault of valour, or courage, wiles, or skill at sword, or through any other fault — for among them they possessed none — but through dark treachery alone.

'Very well,' said Manwyddan when they came before him,

'you know what to do. I bless you and send you on your way. Go in peace and return victorious.'

The three rode out at once and the trail was not difficult to raise, for they simply followed the scorched earth where Medyr had passed. For days and days they rode, and came at last to the holding of Heilyn Long Shanks. As twilight was coming on they decided to stay the night and approached the house.

When they came into the yard they saw an old black cave of a hall with smoke pouring out of it. Inside they saw a floor at once so pitted and bumpy, and so slimy with cow dung and urine, that a man could hardly stand upright without either slipping and falling down or sinking into the stinking mire. And over all was strewn holly branches and nettles which the cattle had been chewing.

Nothing daunted, they continued on and came to a chamber at the end of the hall where they found a sickly hag before a sputtering fire. When the fire guttered the hag threw a handful of chaff into the flames and the resulting belch of smoke brought tears to the eyes. The only other thing that was in this rude chamber was a hair-bare yellow ox-hide. Fortunate indeed was the man who slept on that!

The travellers sat down and asked the hag where the people of the holding were to be found, but she sneered at them, showing her foul teeth. Presently, a thin man, completely bald and withered, entered the hall. He was followed by a grey, stooped woman carrying a bundle of sticks. The woman threw down her bundle before the hag, who made up the fire. The grey woman then began to cook a meal, of which she gave a portion to the three strangers: hard bread and oat gruel and watery milk.

While the three ate this poor fare a fierce rainstorm arose; the wind blew so that trees bent nearly to the ground and the rain fell sideways. Since it was useless to travel on, and since they were tired from their long journey, they decided to stay in the hall, saying, 'After all, it is only for one night. Fortunate are we indeed if this is the worst thing that befalls us.'

Then they prepared to sleep. And their bed was nothing but a pile of flea-ridden straw with a tattered old greasy cloak thrown over it. Clamping their hands over their noses, they lay down. Rhonabwy's companions fell asleep to the torments of the fleas. But, after thrashing around on the filthy straw, Rhonabwy decided that neither rest nor sleep would come to him if he did not find a more comfortable place. He spied the yellow ox-hide and thought that if he did nothing else he might at least escape the fleas, so he got up and went to lie down on the ox-hide.

No sooner had his head touched the hair-bare old hide than did he fall asleep. At once a vision came to him. And this is what he saw:

He and his friends were riding along beside an oak grove when they heard a tumult the like of which they had never heard before. They halted and, looking fearfully behind them, saw a young man with curly hair and a new-trimmed beard riding a golden horse. This man was green from the hips down to his toes, and he wore a fine yellow mantle that shimmered in the sun. At his side was a golden-hilted sword in a sheath of fine leather, held by a belt with an enormous golden buckle. And the size of the man was all but twice that of any of the three companions!

The three companions knew themselves to be in the presence of a man of power and authority so they waited for him to draw near. 'Peace, friend,' called Rhonabwy as the man approached, and because the man was so big he added, 'and mercy, too.'

The young man in gold and green halted before them. 'You beg peace and mercy from me and you shall have that gladly. Do not be afraid.'

'Our thanks to you, and the thanks of our lord also. Since you grant us mercy, chieftain, tell us your name.'

At this the young man smiled and said, 'I am called Gwyn Ysgawd, and my father is the ruler of this realm.'

'Who might that be?' Rhonabwy asked.

'His name is not uttered except in praise,' Gwyn answered. 'He is Chief Dragon of the Island of the Mighty and its Seven Adjacent Isles, and much else besides, for he is Emperor of the West.'

The three friends peered at one another anxiously. 'We have never heard of this man, great though he undoubtedly is.'

'That surely is a wonder,' said Gwyn. 'But I will allow you

to judge for yourselves, for I will take you to him and you can pay him the homage you think he deserves.'

'Fair enough,' said Rhonabwy, and the huge man continued on his way. The three fell in behind him and kept up as best they could. Yet no matter how fast they rode, the yellow horse ahead of them galloped faster. When they breathed in, they seemed to gain a little, but when they breathed out the yellow horse was further away than before.

In this way, they passed over a great plain — wider and more vast than Argyngrog. And they crossed many rivers, each of them wider and more vast than Mor Hafren. And they rode through many forests, each of them wider, darker, and more vast than Celyddon. But at last they came to an immense shore at the very edge of the Island of the Mighty. And spread out along the shore as far as the eye could see in each direction were bright-coloured tents of all sizes — enough to hold the greatest host the world had yet seen.

They proceeded to the sea verge and came to a flat islet lying close to the shore. An enormous man sat on the small island on a throne of stone, and beside him Bishop Bedwini at his right hand, and Hafgan Chief Bard on his left. Before them stood a warrior dressed all in black. From the crown of his head to the soles of his feet, all black. His hands were covered with black gloves, and his cloak, tunic and mantle were black. All that could be seen of this warrior was only the span of wrist between sleeve and glove — and this skin was whiter than the white of a maid's eyes, whiter than lilies; and that wrist was thicker than the small of Cadwgan's leg. The strange warrior held in his hand a sheathed sword.

Gwyn led Rhonabwy and his companions across the water to stand before the mighty man on the throne. 'God be good to you, Father!' he called in greeting.

The man on the throne raised his hand in welcome. 'God be good to you, my son!' he said in a voice that surely shook the hills. He regarded the three travellers curiously, and said, 'Wherever did you find these little men?'

'Lord, I found them riding at the border of your realm,' Gwyn White Shield answered.

At this the great king shook his head and uttered a sharp, mocking laugh.

'Chief Dragon,' said Gwyn, 'what are you laughing at?'

'I am laughing out of the sadness I feel at this worlds-realm being held by such puny men as these, after the kind that held it before!'

Then Gwyn turned to Rhonabwy and asked, 'Do you see the ring on the emperor's hand?'

Rhonabwy looked and saw a golden ring with a purple gem. 'I see it,' he answered.

'It is the property of that ring that having seen it you will remember everything that passes while you sojourn with us. If you had not seen it, you would remember nothing at all.'

They were still talking like this when a great commotion arose on shore. Rhonabwy looked and saw a tremendous warband riding towards them. 'What warband is that?' asked Rhonabwy.

'The Flight of Dragons! And it is their pride and duty to ride before and after the emperor in every danger. For this they are granted the privilege of wooing the most noble daughters of Britain.'

Rhonabwy watched as the warband passed by, and he saw that there was not a warrior among them that was dressed in anything but the deepest red, like the reddest blood in the world. Together they appeared a column of fire springing from the earth and ascending to the sky. These exalted warriors hailed the emperor as they passed by, and rode to their tents on the shore.

With sweet golden mead and savoury roast pork the Pendragon feasted his Dragon Flight. Rhonabwy and his friends feasted with them and continually remarked to one another, and to Gwyn, that never had they tasted such a feast as the one set before them.

In the morning the warriors arose, donned their battle dress and saddled their fine horses. 'What is happening here?' asked Rhonabwy, rubbing sleep from his eyes.

'The war host is gathered,' explained Gwyn. 'It is time to join battle at Caer Baddon.'

So saying, they all climbed on their horses and began riding to the battle place. Now the emperor's war host rode so fast that they could not be seen — only the windrush of their passing could be felt. But Gwyn led the three along the track and eventually they reached a great vale where they saw the host gathered below Caer Baddon.

A warrior sped past them where they waited and proceeded at once into the vale without pausing. At the approach of this rider, all the war host scattered. 'What is this?' wondered Rhonabwy to Kynrig Red Freckles. 'Is the emperor's war host fleeing?'

Gwyn overheard them and replied, 'The emperor's host has never fled, but has ever been victorious. Lucky you are, for if that remark had been heard down there you would already be dead.'

'Who is that rider, then,' asked Rhonabwy, 'that he causes such tumult among the troops?'

'The rider you see speeding his way to the front of the battle line is none other than the foremost champion of the Pendragon's warband. The commotion you see at his arrival is that of men jostling one another to be near him in the fray.'

The tumult threatened to become a riot, so the emperor signalled his sword-bearer, the youth in black, who raised the Pendragon's weapon — a great sword with a golden hilt in the shape of twin serpents. He drew the sword and the brightness of the blade was like the brightness of the sun, so that it was not easy to look upon. The commotion quieted at once.

Gwyn, Rhonabwy, Kynrig and Cadwgan lifted their reins and rode down into the vale, where they found the emperor's tent. A huge, yellow-haired man approached with an enormous bundle on his back. He lowered the bundle and drew out a wonderful mantle of pure white wool with a golden apple at each corner. The giant man spread the fair mantle upon the ground before the tent. Next, he drew out a camp chair so large that three kings could sit in it at once; this he set up in the centre of the mantle. And then he withdrew a silver *gwyddbwyll* board and game-pieces of pure gold, which he set up in the centre of the chair.

Rhonabwy and the others dismounted and stood aside to see what would happen next, and what happened was that the emperor emerged from his tent and took his place in the chair beside the *gwyddbwyll* board. He raised his head, looked around him, and cried, 'Who will try their skill against me in a game of Chase and Capture?'

Immediately, a crowd gathered around the mantle. And such a crowd! For each man among them was nobly born, and not one was lower in rank than king, and some were kings with other kings in their retinue.

Up spoke a king with brown hair and a drooping brown moustache, who said, 'I will try my skill, Lord and Pendragon.'

'I recognize you, Vortiporix,' replied the Pendragon. 'Very well, I allow you the first move. Make it good.' And they began to play.

They were deep into the game when there arose a great din of such cawing and shouting and clashing of arms that it could only be a battle of unusual size and violence. This continued, growing ever louder, until from a nearby tent came a warrior. The tent was all of white, with a standard flying before it bearing the image of a jet-black serpent with poisonous eyes and a fiery tongue. The warrior was dressed all in yellow-green from neck to knee, and half of his face was painted yellow as well.

'Emperor and Pendragon,' said the warrior, 'is it with your permission that the Ravens of Annwfn tear at your brave warriors?'

'It is not,' replied the emperor. 'This I will not allow.'

'Then tell me what is to be done and I will do it,' said the warrior.

'Take my standard and raise it where the battle is fiercest,' said the emperor. 'Then stand back and let God's will be accomplished.'

The warrior rode directly to the place where the battle was going badly for the Dragon Flight, and there he raised the emperor's standard — a great red-gold dragon with teeth and claws bared. And when the Flight of Dragons saw the standard being raised in their midst they took courage and rose up with renewed vigour and began beating back the Ravens, smiting them and stabbing them so that they were wounded and killed.

Vortiporix went down in defeat to the emperor and his game ended. 'Who will play next?' asked the Pendragon in a loud, challenging voice.

'I will try my skill,' said a man, stepping out from the crowd which had gathered around the game board.

'Then sit you down,' said the emperor. 'I recognize you, Urien Reget, and grant you the first move. Do your best.'

They began to play the game, bending low over the board to study their moves. When they had played a short while they heard a great uproar of men and animals fighting and tearing one another to pieces. They raised their heads at this commotion, to see a rider on a pale horse galloping towards them. The rider wore a white cloak on his shoulder and a white tunic, but his legs and feet were covered in grey linen the colour of smoke or morning mist. In his hand he held a long, three-grooved sword; and on his head he wore a helm with a powerful sapphire gemstone on its brow, and on its crest the image of a white lion with poisonous blood-red eyes.

This warrior rode straight to where the game was being played on the mantle and, without dismounting, said, 'Lord and Pendragon, Emperor of the Island of the Mighty and all other lands of consequence, I beseech you.'

'Why do you beseech me?'

'I would have you know that the best warriors in the world, the nobles and kings of Britain and their vaunted retinues are being killed by wild beasts — so many, in fact, that it will not be easy to defend this worlds-realm henceforth.'

'This will never do,' replied the emperor when he had heard the sorry report.

'Tell me what is to be done and I will see that it is accomplished,' said the warrior.

'Take my sword in your hand and carry it before you by the blade, in the sign of the cross of Christ.'

The warrior rode directly to the place where the battle was going badly for the Dragon Flight, and there he raised the emperor's sword, holding it before him by the naked blade. When the wild beasts saw the flashing sword making the sign of the cross of Christ they fell to quaking with fear and lay down and became meek as newborn lambs.

Urien of Reget went down in sharp defeat at the emperor's hands. But the emperor still wanted a fair match at the game, so he called out, 'Who else is there to pit skill against me?'

'I will try my skill and cunning against you, O Mighty Pendragon,' said a king, stepping from the throng.

'I recognize you, Maglocunus,' replied the Pendragon. 'Very well, take your move and see that you make it your best.'

They bent low over the game-board, moving the golden pieces here and there as the game demanded. They had not played very long when there arose the greatest uproar yet heard anywhere in the world. Though the din was terrible, far worse was the silence that followed. Everyone trembled and looked around fearfully.

Out of the east came a warrior on a horse of dappled-grey with four red legs, as if the animal had swum through blood, yet its hooves were green. Both rider and horse were clothed in strange, heavy armour that gleamed like silver, with rivets and fastenings of russet. The warrior carried a long, heavy spear of grooved ashwood coloured half with white lime and half with blue woad, the leaf-shaped blade covered with fresh blood. On his head he wore a helm set about with shining crystals and crested with the image of a griffin holding a powerful gem in his mouth.

This warrior approached the emperor and cried out, 'Lord and Pendragon! Your warriors are slaughtered, your people killed, all who followed you are scattered and oppressed!'

Hearing this the Exalted Pendragon seized up a handful of pieces from the gwyddbwyll board and squeezed them in his hand until they were ground to fine gold dust. Then, looking around angrily, he demanded of the royal throng, 'What is to become of us? Why do you stand there empty-handed? Why do you stand idly by, watching a stupid game, while the enemy has laid waste to our lands and slaughtered our people? Are you even men at all?'

The emperor rose up and threw the game-board from him. He called for his sword and his horse. He took up his spear and his shield, and put on his dragon-crested helm. 'Whoever would follow me, take up your sword!' he cried.

At these words the crowd vanished — they simply faded from sight and blew away like mist. The tents faded from sight, and the horses and warriors and all that had gathered in the vale below Caer Baddon. Lastly the emperor and his son vanished, taken from sight by a shining cloud that covered them and bore them away.

Of the great host, not so much as a footprint remained. Everything disappeared, leaving only Rhonabwy and his two friends standing just where they were. 'Most wretched of men are we,' cried Rhonabwy miserably, 'for we have seen a wonder, but no one is here to tell us what it means! On top of that, we are lost and now must find our way home as best we can.'

No sooner had these words passed his lips than did a wind begin to blow and howl, and rain and hail begin to fall. Thunder thundered and lightning flashed, and in the chaos of the storm Rhonabwy awoke to find himself once more on the yellow ox-hide in the noisome black hall. His friends stood over him, their brows wrinkled with worry, for Rhonabwy had slept three days and three nights.

So ends the *Dream of Rhonabwy*.

The Emrys sang out of his bard's *awen*, and would not speak of his song or its meaning. The next day, however, I sensed this same unease in his conversation with Avallach. Clearly, something had begun preying on the Emrys' mind. I determined to discover what it was. Over the next days and nights I stayed alert to any word that might illumine me.

Our sojourn proceeded uneventfully. I spent several days wandering along the cliff-tops above the sea, watching the grey seals dive for fish and sun themselves on the rocks. I talked to the Fair Folk, when I could engage one of them, and struck an awkward friendship with one of the grooms in Avallach's stable. In this way, I learned some surprising things about the Fair Folk, but nothing about the matter I sought.

At night I stayed near the Emrys so that I might hear all that passed. My vigil availed me nothing, however, until the last night. We were to leave the next morning, to be in Caer Lial when the Pendragon arrived — which would be soon.

The Emrys sat between the Fisher King and his mother, and I served them so as to be near. They talked of crops and cattle, of fishing, and the winter weather on the island. . .

All at once, the Emrys grew serious. He dropped his knife onto the table, letting it fall from his hand as if he lacked the strength to grasp it. He turned to his mother and said, 'Where is Morgian?'

Charis' hand fluttered to her mouth. 'What do you mean?'

'Must I ask again?'

'Oh, Hawk, you cannot think she would — ' she did not say the words. 'Why do you ask?'

'Since coming here I have sensed her presence. If she has not been here, she is surely coming.'

Avallach, I noticed, stopped eating and swallowed hard, as if choking down the food in his mouth. He laid down his knife and gripped the edge of the board with his hands.

He knows something! I thought, and wondered whether the Emrys would see this. But he did not turn towards the Fisher King and continued to speak only to his mother. 'Do you think she would do this?' Charis asked. 'Why?'

The Emrys shook his head slowly. 'I cannot say. Her ways are beyond reckoning.' Then he reached out his hand and took one of his mother's and pressed it hard. 'Beware,' he cautioned. 'There is a matter here I do not know, and an end I cannot see. Please, beware.'

No more was said and, once it had passed, talk returned to more pleasant things. Still, I wondered. The Wise Emrys' words found a place within me and echoed like a hand-struck harp: *if she has not been here, she is surely coming*.

I did not find opportunity to speak to the Emrys about what I had seen at the Fisher King's table until we were aboard ship and well away from the island. The Emrys moved apart from the sailors to stand gazing at the waves scattering before the ship's sharp prow. I hurried to him and said, 'Lord Emrys, a word, please.'

He answered absently, without turning. 'Yes? What is it, Aneirin?'

Strangely, I did not say the thing I meant to say, but spoke something perhaps closer to my heart. 'Why did you wish me to come with you to Ynys Avallach?'

He considered this for a goodly time and then answered, 'I do not know, boy.' His eyes did not turn from the sea. 'Why do you ask?'

Now it was my turn to admit ignorance.

'Well,' observed the Emrys sagely, 'you see how it is.' He smiled and turned to look at me. I must have presented a sobering countenance, for he asked, 'Ah, there is a deeper thing that you have not said. Is this so?'

'Yes, Emrys.'

'Then speak it out, lad.'

I told him what I had witnessed of the Fisher King's behaviour. As I spoke, the Emrys' eyes narrowed. 'I did not think to ask him,' he murmured.

'Who is this Morgian?' I inquired, little knowing what I asked. Great the grief! I wish I had never heard the name, nor let it pass my lips.

Weary pain pinched the Emrys' features. 'She is. . . ' he began, and halted. Then shaking his head, he said, 'Have you never heard of the Queen of Air and Darkness?'

'No,' I told him with a shrug. 'The name means nothing to me.'

'Can it be?' the Emrys wondered. 'Men's memories are short, but evil endures long.' He turned back to his contemplation of the sea, but I knew that he did not see it. For his sight had turned inward and he no longer travelled the bright sea-path before us.

FOUR

Four days before Lugnasadh the Pendragon returned to Caer Lial. Three hundred of the Cymbrogi followed in his retinue. He rode at their head on a milk-white stallion, wearing a high helm of burnished steel set about with gold, the famed sword Caliburnus at his side. On his shoulder he wore Prydwen, the shield with the cross of the Christ painted in crimson upon its white washed surface. Caval, his enormous hound, trotted beside him, head up proud and high. Before him went the Red Dragon, the High King's standard wrought of fine red-gold and carried by Rhys, whose honour it was to go before all.

I stood on the rampart of the wall as the High King drew near. People from the city ran out from the gates below me and onto the road, waving bits of coloured cloth and calling out to him in greeting. All my life I had heard about Arthur, Wonderful Pendragon, High King of the Island of the Mighty, fairest monarch that is in the world — but nothing of all that I had heard prepared me for the glory of the man I saw riding towards me on the road.

The Bear of Britain was a mighty man, tall and strong, quick of eye and wit, steady of hand and purpose, keen as the sword at his side, and bright as the sun that shone upon him. Lord of Summer he was called and, God be praised, it was not a boast.

Gwalchavad and Bors rode at the king's left hand, and the exalted Llenlleawg at his right. I would have known those champions anywhere, though I had never clapped eyes on them before that moment. They rode high-stepping steeds, and carried spears with gleaming silver heads. Bold men, and brave; they wore their valour with authority, like the bright-coloured cloaks folded upon their shoulders.

The High King and the Cymbrogi — who, because of the Red Dragon standard, had become known as the Flight of Dragons — passed through the high timber gates and into the city. Caer Lial had been prepared for the Pendragon's return; the queen saw to it. The streets had been washed with water, and everywhere hung garlands of flowers gathered from the hills and woven into long strands. The people clamoured for their king, and shouted loud praises and welcome to him. To all, the Pendragon bestowed the estimable honour of his glad greeting. Clearly, Caer Lial had become the chief residence of his heart. Here was he loved and revered; here was he honoured above all.

Leaving the rampart, I ran to the palace, racing through the throng, its lusty acclaim loud in my ears. In the palace yard the crowd gathered, so tight-pressed that I could not move. The High King dismounted and climbed the steps, where he paused to deliver a message of greeting to the people. But I was so far removed, and the throng so noisy, I could not hear a word.

Only when the Pendragon had gone inside, and the crowds dispersed, could I make my way to the rear of the palace where I could enter. Everyone had gathered in the hall and Queen Gwenhwyvar had mead vats prepared and cups filled and ready. They were drinking the success of the High King's southern journey, for he had mediated and ended a long-running dispute between the Saecsens and Britons over farmland along the border between these two peoples.

In consequence, *Bretwalda* Aelle and his house carles had come to Caer Lial with Arthur to show his fealty to the High King, and to attend the ceremony of the Round Table. Other lords of southern Britain had also come, notably Idris and Cador, along with men of their warbands.

The sweet yellow mead circled around the hall in cups. Queen Gwenhwyvar stood proudly beside the king, who held her with his hand around her waist, and gazed out upon the glad company. The Emrys stood near, with Cai and Bedwyr beside him. So that I could remain with them, I took up a jar and filled it from a mead vat and began serving it out. Cai summoned me to him and offered his cup.

'Aneirin, bring your jar!' he called, and I was not slow to

obey. I poured his cup full, and Bedwyr's as well, where-upon the Seneschal said, 'Arthur's cup is empty, lad. Fill it!'

I turned to see the Pendragon's clear blue eyes upon me. He smiled and held out his gold-rimmed horn. Trembling, I lifted the jar, not daring to raise my head before him. I felt a touch on my hand. The High King placed his hand beneath mine to steady the jar, saying, 'Be easy, young friend.' He regarded me carefully. 'What is your name?'

'I am Aneirin ap Caw,' I replied. 'I am yours to command, Pendragon.'

'Bold lad!' laughed Cai.

'I remember you,' replied Bedwyr, 'though I confess I did not recognize you — covered in stone dust the last I saw you!'

'Indeed, Bedwyr!' chided the queen nicely. 'I remember seeing you with Myrddin,' Gwenhwyvar said. 'Forgive me, Aneirin, I did not know you were Caw's son.'

'He has been serving me at the shrine and at Ynys Avallach,' the Emrys said, stepping close. 'Already he has proven himself a worthy friend and ally.'

It pleased me overmuch to hear myself praised in this way, and I blushed crimson to hear it.

'Stay near, Aneirin ap Caw,' said the High King amiably. 'This looks to be a thirsty gathering. We may have need of your jar before long.'

'Oh, aye!' cried Cai. 'Do not wander far, lad, and keep your beaker filled.'

With such high-flown encouragement ringing in my ears, I slaved the night away, stopping only once, when the Emrys sang with his harp. The whole vast hall fell silent as a forest glade — indeed, the world itself seemed to hold breath to hear him! — and, with the True Bard's music filling my heart, I vowed that I would ever seek the noble path, and prayed I would be allowed to remain in Arthur's service for ever!

The next day the king and queen left Caer Lial and made their way to the Round Table. Only those whose names had been inscribed inside the monument were allowed to ride with them. I went, because the Emrys deemed my service valuable. Someone had to take care of the horses. And, since

I already knew the whereabouts of the shrine, better to take me than another.

Upon coming within view of the rotunda, King Arthur dismounted and walked the remaining distance, saying that, out of respect for the sacrifice of those who had given meaning to the monument, he would not draw near save humbly afoot. He mounted the hill and knelt before the shrine with great reverence.

Gwenhwyvar watched her husband intently, dark eyes filled with deep feeling for him and for this day, continually clasping and unclasping her hands in expectation.

The High King rose and, laying aside his sword, entered the Round Table. Whereupon, his captains followed him in solemn procession: Cai, Bedwyr, Bors, Gwalchavad, Llenlleawg — each putting off his weapons before entering. The Emrys, Gwenhwyvar and I remained outside for a little. Then the queen went in, and the Emrys last.

I settled myself at the picket with the horses near the stream, fully intending to stay there. The others had been inside the shrine only a short while when I heard the galloping hoofbeats of a rider approaching along the sea-strand below. I ran to the hillside and looked down to see a lone warrior pounding along the wave-washed sand.

I shrank back behind a bush, lest I attract his attention and he should be drawn to the shrine. But I might have saved myself the trouble. For, though he looked neither right nor left, as he drew even with the monument, he turned his horse and drove the animal straight up the hill track to the rotunda.

At first I thought to run and fetch the Emrys, or otherwise warn those within, but something stayed me, some familiarity of the rider. For though he was strange indeed to my eyes — dressed in bright red tunic and trousers, with a fine blue cloak edged in fur, and with a silver torc at his throat — I felt I knew him somehow.

He halted, swung from the saddle and jumped down. I had seen another do that just this morning. Gwalchavad had dismounted just that way.

But it *was* Gwalchavad! Impossible! I had seen him go into the rotunda only moments before. Another then, yet like enough. . .

Out of the corner of his eye he must have seen me lurking near the thicket, for he turned suddenly, his spear swinging level. 'Please, my lord,' I said. 'Put up your spear, this is holy ground.'

He grinned pleasantly. 'Startle a warrior and take your chances, boy,' he replied. 'I mean no one harm. Have they gone in already?'

I nodded. He dropped the reins to the ground and turned to gaze at the shrine. Then, without a word, he climbed the steps to go in. I rushed after him, thinking to prevent him, but he reached the doorway first and entered. Dreading the intrusion, I hurried after him and entered just in time to see the High King leap to his feet with a look of astonishment on his face.

The others appeared equally astounded, but no one seemed to mind the interruption. Gwalchavad recovered speech first. 'Gwalcmai!' he cried. 'Brother, where have you been?'

Gwalcmai ignored him and went straight to the High King and fell down on his face before him, stretching out his hands to either side. Arthur bent low and gripped him by the shoulder and raised him, saying, 'Rise, Gwalcmai, you are welcome in my company. Get up, brother, and let us look at you!'

Gwalcmai climbed to his feet and embraced his king, tears of joy streaming down his cheeks. Gwalchavad pounded him happily on the back and the two brothers fell into one another's arms. In all, it was a glad reunion. Bedwyr and Cai gathered near and clapped hands to him as well.

I saw the Emrys standing by and crept near. 'I tried to stop him,' I explained in a whisper.

'No need,' he said. 'He is one of our own returned from a long journey.'

'Very long?'

'Seventeen years.'

A far journey to take so long, I thought. 'Where did he go?'

'Oh,' replied the Wise Emrys, 'he went in search of himself and found God instead.'

This made no sense to me at all, but I did not pursue it further at the moment. I left the others to their ceremony, and returned to my place at the horse picket. The sudden appearance of the rider put me in mind of another intruder — the one who had come to the rotunda that night. The feeling made me uneasy, though I could not think why.

'I have been several years with Bishop Sepulcius, receiving holy instruction from that good man,' Gwalcmai said. 'And before that I wandered long in Llyonesse, Gorre, and Armorica.'

We were at meat in Caer Lial, having returned from the Round Table at dusk. Everywhere was Gwalcmai welcomed and greeted by one and all. He had been away so long, no one ever expected to see him again, thinking him dead and gone.

On the way back to the city, the Emrys explained to me how it was. 'He went in search of Pelleas,' he said.

'You said he went in search of himself,' I reminded him.

'So he did. He thought he was searching for Pelleas, but it was his own soul that stood in need of saving.'

'Who was this Pelleas?'

The Great Emrys sighed. 'Pelleas was my steward, and my dearest friend.'

'What happened to him?'

The Emrys fixed me with a stern glance from his golden eyes. 'You ask too many questions, boy.' He turned away and we journeyed on in silence.

As we sat in Arthur's hall, I listened closely, to hear any word that might explain the mystery of Pelleas. Gwalcmai spoke freely of his years away from his companions. I learned that he and Gwalchavad were sons of the rebel Lot, who I knew had once been one of the Pendragon's chief supporters.

That was news! Everyone knew that Lot of Orcady and Arthur had been uneasy allies at best. The rumour, never denied, was that Lot had failed to answer the hosting against the barbarians in the days of Cerdic's rebellion. For this was Lot ever outcast from Arthur's court.

But here were the sons of Lot, enemy to Arthur, sitting at his table, enjoying the favour of his presence, honoured among men with torcs of silver and rings of gold from the

High King's own hand — never languishing in a hostage pit for so much as a single day. It made no sense. Indeed, it served only to deepen the mystery.

'I was six years in Gaul,' said Gwalcmai, 'in the court of the Ffreinc king, Clovis. When he died, I returned to Ynys Prydein and once more took up my search for Morgian.'

At mention of Morgian's name, my interest quickened. I crept closer to the board, clutching my serving jar. What about Morgian?

Gwalcmai turned his gaze to the Emrys and said, 'Her trail led north.' Cai and Bedwyr exchanged worried glances and those at the table grew silent. Clearly, this Morgian was a person of some power — the mere mention of her name cast a shadow over the festivity of the gathering.

King Arthur slapped the table with his hand. 'God love you, Gwalcmai, but it is good to have you with me again! We have much to discuss in the days to come.' The High King pushed his chair back and rose. 'Please, take your ease and enjoy this night, my friends. I will join you again tomorrow.'

Talk continued around the table, but I followed Arthur with my eyes and saw that Gwenhwyvar had appeared in the hall. The High King went to her and embraced her. Together, arm in arm, they passed from the hall to the royal chambers beyond.

Nothing more was said of Gwalcmai's long absence. Gwalcmai wanted to hear about the wars, and the others were eager to tell him all. Bedwyr, who remembered well each and every array and ordering of each battle from the Glein to Baedun and before, spoke with great eloquence and at length. The others gradually conceded the field to him, encouraging him with remembrances of their own.

Gwalcmai listened to all in a rapture, now with half-closed eyes imagining the battle place, now with cries of amazement and praise for the courage of the combatants. Somewhere in the midst of the long recitation the Emrys left. I do not know when this happened, for I was absorbed in the tale myself. But when I looked up he was gone.

Since the Wise Emrys preferred his silence in the matter of Morgian, I thought that Gwalcmai would not mind speaking about it, so I determined to ask him at first opportunity.

Thus, the next morning when he came to the hall to break fast, I approached him boldly and told him what was in my mind.

'If you please, Lord Gwalcmai, I would have a word with you.'

I think he was taken aback by my presumption — a serving boy demanding council of a battlechief of the High King's retinue. But my boldness appealed to him, I think, or at least it brought him up short. For he stopped and stared at me. 'Do I know you, lad? Were you not at the board last night?'

'I was,' I told him, 'and before that I challenged you at the Shrine of the Round Table.'

The battlechief laughed easily. 'Yes! Yes, now I remember you. Plucky lad, you have a warrior's way about you. Tell me your name, boy, for I ween you were born to higher things than passing ale jars.'

'I am *filidh* to the Emrys,' I told him proudly. 'It is true that I was born to higher things. Yet I am content to serve the High King however I may — be it ale jars or sweeping floors. I am Aneirin ap Caw; my father is lord of Trath Gwryd.'

'I give you good greeting, Aneirin ap Caw. What word would you have of me?' The battlechief fixed me with a bemused and curious gaze.

'I would hear more of this person Morgian,' I said, little knowing what I asked.

Gwalcmai became suspicious. 'What have you to do with her, boy?'

'Nothing at all, my lord. But I am thinking that there is a mystery here, for no one will so much as speak her name aloud.'

'That is not difficult to believe,' replied Gwalcmai. He pulled on his chin and regarded me carefully. Then, turning quickly, he said, 'Come, I will tell you what you want to know. But not within these walls.'

We walked out from the hall to the training yard behind the palace. Gwalcmai remained silent for a while and we walked together, our eyes on our feet.

'May my Lord Jesu forgive me,' he began suddenly. 'Perhaps it is best for these things to remain hidden. It is beyond me to say. God alone knows what is best. But I think that it is time that Morgian's reign was ended, and I am pledged to bring about that end. Or, if I am not to succeed, it is for someone else. That is why I am telling you.' He stopped and gripped my shoulder. 'Do you understand, Aneirin ap Caw?'

I nodded solemnly. I, too, felt the dread weight of his words falling like lead into the clear pool of my heart. Clearly, this mystery was deeper than I knew.

'Seventeen years ago it began. We had been fighting in the north and returned to Caer Melyn to find that Myrddin was not there. Pelleas rode in search of Myrddin and, when neither one returned, Arthur sent Bedwyr and me to find them.'

He paused and shook his head. 'Pelleas — ah, it is long since his name has passed my lips.'

'Who was he, lord?'

'Pelleas was a matchless warrior; he was a Fair Folk prince who served the Emrys, and he was also one of Arthur's battlechiefs in those days. That both of them should go missing concerned Arthur in no small way. Bedwyr and I rode after them.' He paused, remembering that time years ago. When he spoke again his voice was heavy with sorrow. 'We found Myrddin sitting on a crag in Llyonesse, blistered and blind, and raving mad — or so I thought.'

'What of Pelleas?'

'There was no sign of him. We bore Myrddin to the Tor at Ynys Avallach, and then I went back to continue the search. . . I found never a trace of Pelleas.

'Still, I searched. From Llyonesse I travelled to Gorre — that diseased cluster of islands in the south. I found nothing there, but learned of a Fair Folk settlement in Armorica. I sailed to Less Britain and sojourned with Ban. The settlement I sought was near his realm, I was told, but if so it was no longer there. I travelled into Gaul and came into the court of Clovis, where I met Bishop Sepulcius and was baptised a Christian.

'My search has availed me nothing,' Gwalcmai concluded sadly.

'I would not say so,' I told him. 'The Emrys said that you left to find Pelleas and found God instead.'

Gwalcmai laughed. 'Oh, he is wise indeed. Yes, that is what happened in the end, I suppose. That is why I stayed so long with Sepulcius — I felt that my life had purpose when I was with him. And since King Clovis depended on that saintly man, I stayed to help him. The Ffreincs are even more contentious than the British — believe that, if you will.'

'You have spoken of Pelleas,' I said. 'But what of Morgian?'

'I was coming to that.' Gwalcmai grew sombre once more. 'She is the one who blinded Myrddin and left him to die in Llyonesse.'

'What!'

'It is God's truth I am telling you.'

'But how?' I could not imagine anyone besting the Exalted Emrys, Chief of Bards of the Island of the Mighty.

'She is a Fair Folk enchantress, a Fair Folk witch, most powerful and dire. She is evil itself, and potent as death.' He spoke with such vehemence I turned to him in wonder.

'You know her well?'

'Aye,' he said ruefully, 'I know her well enough to wish that I did not.'

'You said she had come here. We have not heard of it.'

'I said her trail led north,' he corrected. 'I do not think she would come here — at least not yet. I think she is in the north, in Ynysoedd Erch, perhaps.'

'Lot's realm — your father's'

'Perhaps,' he allowed warily. 'But there are other places she would be welcome. Wherever Arthur has an enemy, or someone wishes Myrddin ill — there will she find a friend.'

'She wishes Arthur harm?'

'She wishes *all* men harm, lad. Never forget it. And never let anyone tell you different. Listen well, I know whereof I speak: Morgian is poison; she is a viper, a demon in human form. And she is bent on destruction.'

We walked back to the palace, then. I went about my duties and could not help thinking of all that Gwalcmai had told me. Time and again I returned to his words, and the sense of evil foreboding grew in me through the day. I sensed doom in the sunbright air of Caer Lial, and I could nowise perform my duties satisfactorily. I had no one else to share my burden with to make it lighter. I laboured on in misery.

Yet we are not made to suffer long. We forget. In a few days the stifling sense of doom and suffocation left me, and I began to think of other things again. The sky did not fall, the earth did not swallow me, the sea did not rise up and whelm over Britain. I lost interest in Morgian and her schemes and turned to other concerns. Foremost among these, the fact that the Emrys chose me to go with him to the shrine.

Arthur wished to hold the first Council of the Round Table — those trusted companions whose names were carved in the walls of the rotunda — and we were to go ahead to make all ready.

The prospect of returning there, just the Emrys and me, filled me with pleasure. Fine as the palace was, I loved the bare rotunda more. Its solitude appealed to me. My spirit was at peace there. Peace, I have learned, is rare in this worlds-realm and highly to be prized.

FIVE

I know little of what passed at the Council of the Round Table. Those in attendance — Bedwyr and Cai, of course, Bors, Gwalchavad, Cador, Llenlleawg, Idris and the Emrys — were Arthur's truest companions. These were the first. Others would be added in time as good men were drawn to Arthur's court.

Each day for three days the lords held council with the High King. Each night for three nights they supped together and the Emrys sang. One of the songs he sang was *The Vision of Taliesin*, also called *The Song of the Summer Realm*.

I count myself for ever blessed to have heard it.

On the third day of the council, Gwalcmai arrived. Whether he had been summoned, or whether he came of his own volition, I still do not know. But he appeared at midday, greeted me, and made his way to the shrine. He knelt at its entrance, prayed, and then was allowed to enter. I picketed his horse with the others and waited to see what would happen.

In a little, he emerged, alone, and walked down the hill. He moved quickly, like a man with an important duty he must discharge. I learned later that Gwalcmai had been invited to become a member of the Round Table and have his name carven with those of the others. But since he had not fought in the wars against the barbarians, he must perform some other deed of great service to God, the Pendragon, and Britain.

This deed was to be of his own choosing. When it was finished, he could return and come before the Pendragon with proof of its completion. Then, if judged by the others as worthy, he would be admitted to their number.

That is why, when he rode away that day, I saw the steely glint of determination in his eye. I think he already knew what he would do to win his place in the Shrine of the Round Table.

On the morning of the council's fourth day, the High King and his companions departed. The Emrys and I stayed at the shrine, however, for the Emrys wanted some time alone to himself.

That night we sat together at the fire and ate our meal. I said, 'I wonder how the Hill Folk know when we are here?' For the food had begun appearing once more, as soon as Arthur and the others had gone.

'There is not much that happens in the land that they do not know.'

'Why do they bring it?'

'It is their way of honouring me. Ken-ti-gern, they call me. Do you know the word?'

I shook my head. 'No — should I?'

The Emrys regarded me sadly for a moment. 'There is so much passing away,' he said heavily. 'The Summer Realm blooms and the old world must make way.'

He was silent for a time. I watched his face in the light of the dancing fire. He was old, though he did not look it. Long had he gathered wisdom in this worlds-realm, and its weight was becoming a burden to him.

By way of lightening the mood, I said, 'I saw one of the Hill Folk last time.'

'Last time?' The Emrys glanced up, his golden eyes glinting in the firelight.

'When I was here — after you left with Tegyr and Bedwyr. I was alone and I saw one of them when he brought the food. He came up to the shrine and stood in the doorway for a moment, then left. He probably thought we had all departed and he wanted to see the shrine. He did not come inside though, and it was dark. He did not see me.'

Myrddin Emrys stared at me long and hard. 'You did not tell me this before — why?' he demanded at last.

Aghast, I said, 'It was of no importance. Nothing happened. He left the food and disappeared. I did not see him again. Why? Have I done wrong?'

'It is not your fault — you could not know.'

'Know what?' I said, my voice rising indignantly. 'What have I done?'

'Has it never occurred to you that the Hill Folk would not bring food if they thought you had gone?'

His question pricked me. I felt the hot blood rise to my face and was grateful for the ruddy glow of the firelight to hide my shame.

'Well?'

'I suppose not,' I answered sullenly; he spoke the truth and I knew it well.

'No, they would not. If they brought the food, they knew you were still here. Knowing that, they would not have allowed you to see them.' The Emrys paused, then softened. 'Well, it was probably nothing, as you say.'

My heart beat against my ribs, telling me that it was *not* nothing. There was a deeper matter here than I had yet been told. 'If it was not one of the Hill Folk,' I said, 'who was it?'

'I cannot say.' The Emrys turned his face away abruptly.

'Morgian?' I said, little knowing what I asked.

The Emrys whipped towards me. 'Why do you speak that name?'

I stared back at him, horrified. 'Forgive me! I do not know what made me say it.' That was God's own truth — the name just leapt from my tongue.

The Emrys' golden eyes narrowed. 'Perhaps,' he said slowly. 'Or it may be there is another reason.' His tone was deeply forbidding.

'What do you mean, Wise Emrys?' I asked, frightened of the answer.

He stared into the fire, gazing at the embers glowing cherry-red in its flaming heart. What he saw did not cheer him. 'I mean,' he said at last, 'that I fear you have guessed aright — if guess it was.'

Nothing more was said all night. We slept, and awoke the next morning to a thin rain. The rain lingered most of the day, clearing at last towards evening. The Emrys and I went about our work and emerged only at dusk, when the clouds parted and the sun began to gild the hills and sea with fine white gold.

'Aneirin!' Myrddin Emrys called to me from the hilltop. I stood below him at the stream, filling the water jars for the night. 'Do you want to see the *bhean sidhe*? Come here.'

I hurried with the jars and hastened up the hill. 'Go into the shrine and stay there until I summon you.'

I did as I was bade and the Emrys cupped his hands to his lips and made a whistling call that sounded like waves rolling stones on the shingle. He made it again and waited, standing perfectly still. In a moment I heard an answering call, identical to the one he gave. Myrddin Emrys replied to it in kind, and out from the thickets at the edge of the stream stepped two young boys, slender and brown as willow wands, carrying between them the bundle of food.

The two ran quick as shadows up the hill and approached the shrine. The foremost of the two crept close and placed the food bundle on the ground; he took the Emrys' right hand in both of his and kissed it. The other did likewise, and they began to talk. I understood nothing of their speech — it sounded to me less like human utterance than anything I had ever heard. It was all rushing wind and rustling leaves; the hissing of snakes and the buzzing of bees, and the gurgle of falling water.

After they had spoken for a time, the Emrys turned to the shrine and held his hand to it. The two Hill Folk glanced at one another and nodded. 'You can come out, Aneirin,' he called. 'They will allow you to see them.'

I stepped slowly from the doorway of the rotunda and proceeded down the steps. It was only when I came to stand beside the Emrys that I realized our visitors were not children, but mature men. Men full-grown, yet they were smaller than me!

They stood regarding me with bright curiosity, and I them. They wore short, sleeveless tunics made of leather and birds' wings. Their trousers were soft sheepskin; their boots were the same. They carried small wooden bows, and each had a quiver of short arrows at his belt. They wore necklaces of tiny yellow shells, and each had a thick ring of gold around his arm. Tiny blue slashes, three over each cheek — their *fhain* marks — distinguished them as Salmon Fhain. Their hair and eyes were deep and black as polished jet; their skins were brown and creased as their tunics.

The Emrys spoke a word to them and I heard my name, whereupon the two smiled. The foremost one thumped himself on the chest and said, 'Rei.' He repeated this until I said it, whereupon the second one presented himself, saying, 'Vranat.'

I said my name for them and they repeated it, only they said, 'Nee-rin,' and laughed as if this was a most splendid jest. Then they grew suddenly serious and began speaking to the Emrys once more, earnestly, one after the other with some urgency. This entreaty lasted only a moment. Myrddin made some answer to them and they departed, each kissing the Emrys' hand before turning and racing away. They were gone in an instant.

'There,' said Myrddin Emrys, 'now you have seen the Hill Folk. Is there any doubt?'

I knew what he was saying. 'None,' I replied. 'Even in the dark I would know the difference — the one I saw was not like these at all.'

The Emrys turned and began walking down the hill to the sea. I followed and we walked together a goodly while. It was cooler near the water, and the smell of seaweed and salt filled my nostrils. The sound of the waves washing back and forth over the sand soothed my troubled spirit. 'What are we going to do?' I asked.

'We will do what is required of us.'

'Will we know what that is?'

'All is given in its season. All that is needful is granted. We have but to ask, and if our hearts are in the asking it will be granted.'

'Always?'

'You are full of questions, boy,' the Wise Emrys chuckled. 'No, not always. We serve at the Gifting God's pleasure. In him we move and have our being; in him we live both here and in the world to come. If anything is withheld from us it is for the reason of a greater good to come.'

'Always?'

This time the Emrys became adamant. 'Oh aye! Always. Goodness is ever good, and the All-Wise God is a good god. From him goodness itself derives its meaning.'

'So, even if evil overtakes us, it is still for the greater good,' I said, trying to understand this philosophy.

The Emrys accepted my foolish answer, but corrected it gently. 'That is one way to say it, but perhaps not the best way. To see evil and call it good, mocks God. Worse, it makes goodness meaningless. A word without meaning is an abomination, for when the word passes beyond understanding the very thing the word stands for passes out of the world and cannot be recalled.

'This is a great and subtle truth, Aneirin. Think on it.'

I did, but could make no headway. 'But,' I said, returning to the former discussion, 'if the Holy God is good and yet evil overtakes me, what am I to say?'

'Only say, "Evil has overtaken me." God did not wish it, but being God he can use even that which is evil and meant for evil and turn it to good end. It is his labour in the world, and ours, to raise up the fallen and to turn the evil into good.' He raised a hand to his face. 'Even my blindness was turned to good in the end.'

This surprised me. 'Because your sight was restored?'

'No,' he replied. 'Because it was not.'

Now I *was* confused. The Emrys saw me struggling with this and said, 'It is because you do not believe that you do not understand.'

'But I want to understand.'

'Then hear me: God is good; his gifts are granted each in its own season, and according to his purpose. I endured blindness that I might discern the subtle ways of darkness, and treasure light the more. When I learned this truth, it pleased God to restore my sight — which he did in time.'

I knew that all this had something to do with Morgian, but I could not think how. The Emrys talked like a priest instructing his flock. I knew the words he spoke to be true, but the truths they revealed were too deep for me then. That, or else I was a vessel too shallow. I cannot say which.

That night, when we ate our meal before the fire, Myrddin Emrys told me of his time with the Hill Folk — how he had become separated from his people, lost, and found by the *bhean sidhe* of Hawk Fhain; how he had almost been sacrificed; how he had learned their ways, and the lore of their Gern-y-fhain, the clan's Wise Woman.

417

As he told me of his life, I began to understand the meaning of his words: *so much is passing away*. It was clear to me that the world I knew was much changed from the one he described — and was still changing rapidly in almost every way.

Behold! The Summer Realm blooms and the old world must make way. Peace! So be it!

We left the shrine a few days later and returned to Caer Lial. The Pendragon's court was busy with the affairs of Britain now that the High King was in residence. A steady stream of lords and landholders passed through the Pendragon's hall and chambers.

Priests and holy men came before him with petitions of need. The High King established churches, founded holy orders, and granted land to monasteries. Queen Gwenhwyvar aided this work with zeal. With her own resources and out of her own wealth she planted seeds of righteousness and nurtured good works of every kind. She was formidable in virtue, and fierce in piety. She was dauntless in love. No less a warrior than Arthur, she battled wickedness and ignorance, never granting quarter.

I watched all, heard all, and remembered all — hiding it away in my memory like treasure, as it seemed right to do. I talked long with Bedwyr, who became my friend. Bedwyr had the soul of a bard and the memory of a druid. Often we began to talk of an evening and rose to find dawn's ruby rays stealing into the hall.

Cai and I also became friends, and he aided me as he could. But Cai's unquestioning loyalty made it difficult to discover what actually happened in the battles. 'Well,' he would say, 'Arthur is Arthur, yes? He is the Bear. No one like him in battle — who can stand against him?' This would suffice for an entire campaign!

Two more councils were held at the Round Table shrine that year: one at the autumnal equinox, and the other at the winter solstice, just before the Christ Mass. I did not attend the former of these, but at the latter I served my customary function in caring for the horses.

I spent three cold, wet days at a crackling fire below the

rotunda hill with the wild wind blowing snow off the sea. When the others emerged from the council at last, I was near frozen. They came out singing into the winter squall, their voices loud and joyous. I knew something important had taken place. I spared no time finding out.

'What is the cause of this singing, Wise Emrys?' I asked, running to him.

King Arthur heard my inquiry and answered. 'It is a day for celebration!' he cried. 'A great work is to be accomplished. Greater than any seen in the Island of the Mighty since Bran the Blessed raised his golden throne.' By this he meant the legendary Judgement Seat — Bran's chair of gold on which he sat to dispense justice to his people. Bran's judgements, ingenious in fairness, became law for a thousand years. In elder times, Bran's law was the only law in the land and it was just.

'What is to happen, Pendragon?' I asked.

. 'The holiest object that is in the world is to become enshrined in the Round Table.' He smiled and clapped a hand to my shoulder, nearly knocking me off my feet. He and the Emrys moved on to the fire, leaving me no wiser than before.

Bedwyr came to my aid. 'What do they mean?' I asked. 'What is this holiest object?'

'Have you never heard of the Lord's Cup?' he said, moving on. I fell into step beside him. 'The Grail of Jesu at the last supper of his earthly life; the one he took and blessed with the sacrament of wine — where he said, 'This is my blood, shed for you, my faithful brothers. Drink of it often and remember me.'

'That cup,' I replied. 'Of course I know it. But what is it to do with us?'

'That *cup*, as you call it, is here in Britain. The Emrys has seen it, and so, I am told, has Avallach and others as well.'

'Where is it?'

Bedwyr laughed. 'That is for us to discover.'

'How?'

'How indeed!' He laughed at me for my curiosity — it is and always was my bane — and then explained. 'Not by force of arms, you may be certain. Nor by cunning or stealth or treachery. But,' he said thoughtfully, 'perhaps by constancy of faith and strength of rightdoing, by the true heart's firm devotion — these might win it, I think.'

'A man would have to be an angel,' I observed.

Bedwyr looked at me with his keen, dark eyes and nodded, the light hint of his smile touching his lips. 'Now are men called to be angels in this world, Aneirin, and to do the angels' work.'

What he meant by that, I only now have discovered and too late. It was so close I did not see it. May I be forgiven, I was young and there was so much I did not understand about the world.

The Christ Mass at Caer Lial. . . it is the closest thing to heaven that I know. That mass, above all others, was observed in my father's house, but it never called forth the celebration I witnessed in Arthur's court. Bishops and archbishops, priests and monks, kings and lords and their retinues, descended upon Arthur's city in numbers enough to do battle. Which, in a way, perhaps they were.

I was kept busy running from dawn's break to past time for bed, serving as groom and porter, cup bearer and steward. Now in the stables, now in the kitchens, now in the chamber — wherever another pair of hands was needed. I worked hard and went to sleep exhausted. But never was I happier.

For Arthur's palace, always a happy place, became filled with a spirit of ecstatic joy, of rapture sweet as honeyed mead, of kindly harmony and accord. Oh, it was a heady balm; I was dizzy and delirious with it! I still hear the laughter ringing in the furthest corners and echoing in the yards. Cups raised in friendship, voices raised in song.

The sainted Samson of Dol drew the honour of performing the mass itself, attended by Columcill, his pupil. He stood tall and gaunt, reading out the holy writ, his deep voice falling upon our ears like the tolling of a bell. He read the sacred text and lifted that extraordinary voice in prayer, and any of the Devil's ilk lurking near were surely put to flight, even as our own souls were lifted to rapturous heights of holiness.

After the mass there was feasting, and more singing, and the giving of gifts. I myself received a gold-handled knife from the High King and a fine blue gemstone from Bedwyr.

Cai poured me a cup of mulled wine, and bade me drink it all with his blessing.

At the height of this glad time appeared those who had come to pledge fealty to Arthur. Some were lords, and some were the sons of lords who wished to join the Cymbrogi. There were several young Pictish nobles among them who had come also, seeking Arthur's peace and allegiance. One of these was a youth named Medraut.

The petitioners came into the High King's council hall, where he sat to hear these requests. One by one they were given leave to plead their cause and, it being a day of holy celebration, each was granted the thing desired.

And then came Medraut.

He boldly approached the High King's seat and knelt down at once. With humble, downcast eyes he made his petition. 'Wonderful Pendragon, I seek fosterage in your noble house.' He spoke well, without the slightest hint of the thickness of the Picti tongue.

Some in the hall drew breath sharply on hearing this, for it was an affront to the High King's generosity. They thought the youth ill-advised in taking advantage of the holy celebration to ask such a thing. But Medraut was canny; he knew that he would in no wise be refused on this day above all others. And, once having given his word before all his nobles, Arthur would never take it back.

In this Medraut was right, but it won him no friends. No one liked to see the High King's generosity and fairness abused in this way. Many grumbled against him from that very moment.

'Fosterage is no small thing,' said Arthur cautiously, 'and not lightly to be entered. What is your name?'

'I am Medraut ap Urien, Lord of Monoth.' Where this might be I had no idea, and I had lived all my life in the north.

'Come to me when our celebration has ended, Medraut. Better still, bring your father and we will discuss this between us.'

The youth was not to be put off. 'For the sake of your celebration, Exalted Lord, I plead you not to refuse me.'

The Emrys looked on and observed what was taking place. 'Oh, that was well done. Do not play gwyddbwyll with this one,' he warned goodnaturedly, and added, 'and do not lend him your knife.' He flicked my new knife with his finger and moved off.

I studied the youth more carefully. His skin was pallid and wan, as if he never moved about in the sunlight; his hair was black and flowing, hanging down in his dark eyes, and curling over his shoulders like a woman's hair. He was slender and graceful of movement and manner; when he walked, he trod only on the balls of his feet, not the heel. He was fine-featured, delicate as a maid, but in the main not unpleasant to look upon. Some of the younger women of Arthur's court found him handsome enough, I believe.

Arthur the High King also observed the youth before him and, thinking no ill, acquiesced to his wish. 'I do not refuse you, man. In exchange for your fealty, I grant you fosterage until such time as I deem you ready to take your place in the world.'

On hearing this, Medraut fell upon his face before the High King. 'Lord and Pendragon,' he said, 'I offer you fealty and honour and loyalty. As long as my body holds breath, I am your man.'

Arthur accepted Medraut and bade him to join the celebration. 'A bed will be found for you and you will be made comfortable. Now then put aside this talk, come and feast with us and enjoy this glad and holy day.' Then he rose and declared the council at an end, whereupon all made way to the hall to continue the feast. It fell to me to find a place for Medraut to sleep — no simple task, for every chamber and bed was already well filled.

In the end, and at considerable trouble to myself, I arranged for him to sleep in the stable with some of the grooms. When I explained the arrangement he grew indignant. 'You think me beneath you, slave!' he demanded hotly.

'I did not say what I thought of you,' I replied, bristling. I confess I knew little of him, but that little I did not care for. I thought him arrogant and petty for binding Arthur with his word and manipulating the High King's generosity. 'I am a fosterling like as you are.'

He glared. 'I am a noble!'

'I take you at your word.' Indeed, we had only his word for any of it.

'Watch your tongue, serving boy! I am Arthur's man now, I could have you dismissed.'

He boasted to no avail, I did not fear him. 'You are the Pendragon's fosterling,' I corrected him coolly.

'Knowing this, you think to humble me — is that it?'

'I think only to obey my lord in completing the task he has given me.'

'You are instructed to taunt me and humiliate me.' He sneered suspiciously.

'I am instructed to find you a place to sleep,' I replied. 'If this humiliates you, then perhaps you have chosen the wrong house to honour with your presence.'

He was so conceited he did not even heed my scorn. 'I want *your* bed,' he said slyly.

'My bed, but — '

'There!' His laugh was short and sharp as a weasel's bark. 'I will have your bed and *you* will sleep in the stable.' His eyes glittered as if he had made a triumph.

'If that is what you wish — ' I began.

'It is.'

'Then so be it.' I walked away, leaving the young tyrant gloating and chortling to himself over his shrewdness.

Tyrant, yes. Breath-stealing, his audacity. I could not believe his impudence — nor how quickly he had insinuated himself into Arthur's intimacy. Of vanity he had no lack.

I did not see him again until after that night's feasting, when he came to me demanding to be shown to his chamber — he assumed I commanded such accommodation. The two Picti noblemen were with him. 'But this, my lord Medraut, *is* my chamber,' I told him, spreading my hands to the hall, now filled with smoke and the loud voices of those still making merry within. 'And there is my bed.' I pointed to one ash-dusted corner of the great hearth.

Two warriors were already wrapped in their cloaks and happily snoring in slumber. 'Look you,' I said, 'your companions are already abed. Best not to wake them when you tumble in.'

Medraut's face went rigid with fury. 'Liar!'

'It is the truth,' I replied flatly. 'My own bed was given over to another days ago. I have been sleeping in the hall since then.'

It was a fact. My sleeping-place had been occupied by a lord since the nobles began arriving for the Christ Mass. I had been sleeping in the hall on one of the benches, or wrapped in my cloak in a corner.

I do not know how much of this the two Picti with him understood, but one of them smiled and laughed and clapped Medraut on the back. 'Come, let us sleep in our cups!' he cried, and the Picti lost interest and wandered off.

'If you require nothing further, I am going to the stable.' I said when they had gone.

'You deceived me, slave!' He was livid.

'You invited the deception,' I snapped. 'If you thought me a slave, why assume I had better quarters than the stable?' He scowled but he could not answer.

I left him standing there and went out into the cold winter's night and made my way across the yard to the stable. The sky was clear, the moon well up and bright. Upon reaching the door I turned suddenly and thought I saw someone sliding along the palace wall across the yard. But it was late and my eyes were tired from the smoke and lack of sleep.

SIX

When spring came, the Emrys and I made another journey to Avallon in the western sea. This time we were accompanied by the queen and several of her women. The church and monastery being built there were close to Gwenhwyvar's heart, and she wanted to see the work for herself.

We sailed from the king's harbour one bright morning, with a fresh northwesterly wind filling the sails and sending us smartly over the white-crested waves. The queen and the Emrys spent the entire voyage head-to-head in earnest discussion. I do not know what they talked about, but at the end of it Gwenhwyvar embraced the Emrys and rested her head on his shoulder for a long moment, then kissed him on the cheek.

It appeared to me that something had been settled between them. Or perhaps they had become reconciled to one another in some way. Nothing was ever told me about this, so I cannot say. But I noticed that affairs between the Pendragon's queen and his Wise Counsellor were more warmhearted from that time on.

The rest of the journey passed with neither event nor incident, and we arrived at Avallon as the western sky faded from lapis blue to greenish gold. A party of monks came down to the water to greet us. They brought horses with them and sped us on our way. Still, it was well-nigh dark by the time we reached the Fisher King's abode.

We were expected and ardently hailed. The first boats to outer islands in spring carry with them the reminder that the world has not forgotten the island dwellers, and are greeted all the more zealously for that.

Once again I was awed by King Avallach's towering presence, and even more so by the beauty of his daughter Charis.

To behold Queen Gwenhwyvar and the Lady of the Lake together was to peer too long into the sun's brilliant dazzle, to feel the heart lurch in the breast for yearning, to have the words stolen from the tongue before the lips could speak them.

Charis and Gwenhwyvar embraced one another upon meeting and continued to cling together for some time after, as they spoke of other meetings and partings. Clearly, they were friends of the heart.

That night, harp-song echoed in the Fisher King's hall as the Exalted Emrys played and sang the songs of an elder time. These were songs I had never heard, whose melodies were older than anyone now alive, describing events that had taken place so long ago that men did not now remember them, save in song only. I listened and longed for some small portion of the gift that Myrddin Emrys possessed in such full measure.

Jesu love me, it seemed that time stood still in the Fisher King's hall when the Emrys sang. As in Bran the Blessed's court when Rhiannon's birds made song and eighty years became as a day, the ceaseless flow of time ebbed away to nothing and we all stood together in a single everlasting moment.

And in that eternal instant, all grief, all care, all pain and falsehood was extinguished, doused like shadows in the sun. Then were we each shown to be fairer and more noble than ever we were, more keen and quick, more alive than life itself.

These moments are rare enough, but they do exist. Happy is the man who knows at least one such time in his life, for he has tasted of Heaven.

I slept with the haunting harp-sound still lingering in my ears, and woke to find myself alone in the palace and the morning far spent. I rose and walked across the yard to the embankment, mounted the steps and walked along the walltop to see what I could see.

A little distance away to the south the white stone walls of the monastery shone in the sun. It came to me that there could be no finer thing than to live within that holy precinct and devote the whole of my life to the pursuit of the Most Holy God and his Saviour Son. I decided to go there and see for myself what kind of life was to be found.

In this I was disappointed, for although the walls stood, little else of the monastery had been completed. Heaps of stone lay scattered in the broad yard alongside stacks of cut timber. The foundations of several buildings had been laid and construction had resumed with the season. Everywhere men were at work, cutting and shaping and digging. The brothers laboured zealously, so it seemed, but there was still much to be done.

I watched for a while, little noticed by anyone there, before turning back to make my way across the soft green grass to the palace, the sea wind flinging my cloak away from my shoulders. Midway between the unfinished monastery and the Fisher King's palace I halted, unable to go on.

Strange to say — stranger still to feel — it suddenly seemed to me that this island became my life, the palace and the monastery the twin poles of my soul. And I was caught between them. I must, I thought, choose one or the other, and the choice must be soon.

I do not know why I thought this, or why it seemed so urgent to me at that moment. God knows.

I stood for a time, my heart heavy with the swing of emotion, first towards one choice and then towards the other. And then, as quickly as it had come, the feeling left me and I was able to continue on as before. But it was not as it was before. I did not know it then, but my life would never again be what it was before. Events were already moving swiftly to overtake us all.

A few days later we journeyed back to Caer Lial and reported to Arthur that the work on the church and monastery were proceeding apace. Gwenhwyvar especially seemed pleased that so much had been accomplished in so short a time. 'This time next year,' she declared, 'the church will be complete and the hospice will be ready.'

The Pendragon was glad to see us returned, for it was nearing the Eastertide when the next council of the Round Table would be held. He asked the Emrys to go ahead to the rotunda and make all ready for the council. I went with him, of course, and we readied the shrine — sweeping it out, washing the floors and steps, gathering firewood aplenty, and storing the food Arthur wanted served.

On the eve of the vernal equinox, the Emrys and I found ourselves once again together before the fire, as we ate our meal under the evening stars. 'Tomorrow the council will begin,' he said, breaking bread with his hands and offering me half the broken loaf. I knew this, of course, but something in his voice made me stop and consider what his meaning could be.

'Is this to be a special council, Emrys?' I asked.

He gazed at the heart of the fire, his eyes hooded and secretive. His answer was not what I hoped it would be. 'Mighty forces are at work in this worlds-realm, boy. Forces from which profound events are sprung. Where great good prevails, there great evil gathers.'

Then, as if to comfort me with a kindlier word, he said, 'Still I do not see the end; I see the beginning only.'

I know he did not mean to frighten me, but the truth is sometimes fearful. My heart sank within me and I felt weak and small. I felt the shadowed army of the Great Enemy drawing near, and I felt the light to be a feeble and pitiable, insignificant thing. That night I dreamed I saw a vast dark chasm yawning before me and a single broken trail leading down into it, as into a ravening beast's foul maw. In my dream I saw my feet treading that hopeless path and myself sinking into the darkness.

Yet the next day dawned fresh and fair. The imagined horrors of the night were once more slain by the power of the light. The Great God's faithfulness was once more manifest to the world. I took comfort in this.

At midday Bedwyr, Bors and Cai arrived leading pack horses bearing provisions and tents. To my dismay, Medraut was with them. Since that first night when I bested him in the matter of the beds, I had succeeded in avoiding him. It had not been difficult, for he had been given quarters outside the palace with the other warriors in the Pendragon's warband.

That he should appear now upset and angered me. He was the last person I wanted to see in this place. In my eyes, his presence profaned the sacred ground. How he had managed to worm his way into the company of men the like of Bedwyr, Bors and Cai, champions of Britain, I will never know. Unless, and this was close to the truth, Medraut hid his true nature from them.

'Hail, Myrddin Emrys!' called Cai. 'What remedy for a throat parched by the road?'

'Caius, God love you, I stand ready with the jar.' The Emrys stooped and retrieved the vessel at his feet and advanced to the three with cup in hand. He gave the cup to Cai and poured from the jar.

'Water!' shrieked Cai.

'Cold and clean from the spring below the hill,' replied the Emrys. 'Good for body and soul alike.'

Bedwyr savoured Cai's distress. 'Drain the cup, brother. We are thirsty, too.'

'Go on,' jeered Bors, 'it will not rust your belly.'

Medraut swaggered up, laughing. He slapped Cai on the back as if he were a true sword brother. 'Could it be the mighty Cai is affrighted of a little holy water?' he crowed.

Cai stiffened slightly and cast a baleful eye upon Medraut. The young tyrant laughed the merrier and leaned on Cai's arm. 'A jest, brother! A jest! Like Bedwyr here, I meant nothing by it.'

Cai muttered and stared at the cup. Then he lifted it and drained it in one motion, thrust the cup into Medraut's hands and stalked off. 'You went too far with that,' Bors told him flatly.

'Ha! It is but a small thing,' observed Medraut cheerily, 'he will soon forget it.'

'Perhaps,' said the Emrys sternly, 'but your jest is not welcome in this place. The hill is consecrated to a different god. Remember that.' He gave the jar to me and strode after Cai.

The smile never left Medraut's face, but as the cup was refilled and drained in turn his eyes watched as warily as any stalking wolf's. His fingers brushed my hand as I poured out his water and his touch made my flesh creep.

Later in the day, the High King and his retinue arrived, led by Gwalchavad and Llenlleawg. To my surprise Gwenhwyvar was with them, as she also would attend the council. 'I see that Gwalcmai has not come,' Arthur said. 'Well, we will begin the council and perhaps he will yet appear.'

They gathered straightway in the rotunda, and I began picketing the horses. Medraut was instructed to wait below the hill and help me with the tents and beasts, but this he would not do. I did all the work while he roamed around the hillside and along the stream. He appeared to be searching for something but, as I was glad not to have to speak to him, I let him go his way.

Dusk was gathering in the valleys and the hilltops flared as if a golden beacon fire kindled every one. Dark clouds gathered in the east, coming with the night; and I smelled rain on the wind as I finished watering the horses. The council had just emerged from the rotunda and were walking down the hill when I heard the drum of hoofbeats on the sand. I ran to the overlook and saw two horses approaching swiftly by way of the strand. I turned and ran up the hill to tell the others.

'Gwalcmai!' I cried, 'Gwalcmai is coming!'

Bors and Gwalchavad stood on the hillside and quickly turned to look where I pointed. 'That is Gwalcmai,' confirmed Gwalchavad. 'But who is with him?'

'I cannot tell from this distance,' Bors said. 'But he sits a light saddle.'

'It is a woman,' observed Gwenhwyvar.

'Trust Gwalcmai to bring a woman with him,' scoffed Cai.

'And what is wrong with that?' demanded the queen.

'Who can it be?' wondered Bedwyr. He glanced over his shoulder at Myrddin, who had just stepped from the rotunda. The Emrys halted. His limbs became rigid as stumps.

The riders came under the lea of the hill and passed briefly out of sight. A moment later they were pounding up the hillside and I could see them clearly. The rider with Gwalcmai was indeed a woman: dressed all in black and sable, her face covered by a veil.

Gwalcmai held the reins of her horse tightly in his hand. Something about the way he led her told me the woman was his prisoner.

A sensation of deep dread stole over me. The skin crawled on the back of my neck. I knew danger and death to be very

430

close. Glancing at Medraut, I saw a thin smile curl his full lips and the sight chilled me to the marrow.

The Emrys glanced at Arthur and flung out a hand to him, bidding him stay behind. His eyes on the pair before him, the Pendragon did not see the warning and moved closer. The others gathered before the horses as Gwalcmai reined up and dismounted.

'Greetings, brother!' called Gwalchavad. His welcome died in the still air and was not repeated.

Gwalcmai moved to his prisoner, pulled her roughly from the saddle, and stood her on her feet. Gripping her tight by the arm, he dragged his prisoner before the High King.

'Who is this woman and what has she done that she is treated so?' demanded the Pendragon.

'She is an enemy, Lord Arthur,' replied Gwalcmai. 'I have brought her to brave the justice she has so long eluded.' With that he raised his hand, lifted the veil and pulled the hood from her head. It was. . .

The Lady of the Lake!

But no. . . Even as I gazed in stunned surprise at the woman before me, I saw that it was not Charis, but someone very like her. Beautiful she was, undeniably beautiful, but hard as chiselled stone. Hate seethed within her and flowed out from her like venom from a serpent's bite.

I glanced to the Emrys, seeking his reassurance. But I saw him grim and distant. Like a wild animal caught in a snare, he seemed frightened and uncertain whether to flee or fight. The appearance was so unnatural to him that I turned my face away at once and did not look back.

'An enemy?' wondered Arthur.

'Even an enemy is allowed some dignity,' Gwenhwyvar said sharply. 'Release her, Gwalcmai. We are not barbarians.'

The warrior did as he was bade and loosed his hold. The woman drew herself up and stared boldly into the eyes of the king, who asked, 'Who are you, woman?'

'O, Great King,' she replied, in a voice as cold and hard as heartless steel, 'this *man*,' she spat the word, 'demeans me with slander. He calls me traitor. Where is my treason? I demand to know why I have been brought here.'

'You have been brought here to answer the accusations

against you,' Gwalcmai told her, 'and to confront the High King's justice.'

'Accusations?' the woman mocked. 'I have heard no accusations. You know nothing of me.'

'But I know you, Morgian,' replied Myrddin, his voice taut and low.

The Emrys stepped forward. Bedwyr laid hold of him, crying, 'No! Myrddin, for the love of Jesu, do not do it!'

'It is before me,' the Emrys told him, laying aside Bedwyr's hand. The High King made bold to stay him. 'Peace, Arthur. It is my time. Trust God.'

I heard his voice, strange and taut. I turned and gasped at what I saw, for the Emrys had visibly changed. The fear I had seen in him had vanished utterly and he seemed to have grown larger. He now loomed over us with great and terrible strength, golden eyes blazing with a fearful light.

He advanced to where Morgian stood and faced her. She lowered her head and parted her lips in a smile both beguiling and dire. My knees went weak to see it.

'Oh, I know you well, Morgian. You were ever a seducer with lies. Long have you fought against the True God and his servants, but I tell you this day your fight is ended.'

'Is this the crime you lay against me?' she scoffed. 'Where is the hurt? Where is the injury? Who have I wronged but your weak and fallible god? If he is so easily injured by the trivial actions of a mortal, let him come before me now and declare it!'

Oh, she was quick and subtle. She appeared at once so unjustly wronged that I believed her. The others wavered in their conviction. Myrddin alone remained steadfast.

'Stop, Morgian. Your wiles cannot avail you now.' He turned to the High King and said, 'The hurt this woman has done me, I readily forgive. It is for the harm that she has caused others that she is to be judged.'

'You are not my judge,' hissed the woman.

'The High King of Heaven is your judge,' the Emrys replied. 'And the Pendragon of Britain serves as the steward of his justice in this worlds-realm.'

'Well spoken,' said Arthur. 'Let us hear the accusations against her.'

The Emrys turned once more to Morgian and raised his

432

arm, forefinger extended. 'I charge you with the countless treasons great and small, practised against humanity and against Britain. I charge you with sedition, perfidy, wickedness and blasphemy. I charge you with evil most loathsome and foul. I charge you with the murder of Pelleas, my friend and loyal servant of King Arthur. I charge you with the death of Taliesin, my father.'

The Pendragon heard this gravely. 'What do you say to these charges?'

The Queen of Air and Darkness tilted back her head and laughed. A more ghastly sound I hope never to hear. 'Do you think I care about these trifles?'

'Murder is no trifle, woman,' Arthur said.

'No? How many men have you killed, Great King? How many have you slain without cause? How many did you cut down that you might have spared? How many died because you in your battle-rage would not heed their pleas for mercy?'

The High King opened his mouth to speak, but could make no answer.

'Do not listen to her, Bear!' cried Bedwyr. 'It is a trick!'

'Speak to me of trickery, Bedwyr the Brave!' Morgian whirled on him. 'You who have lain in ambush for unsuspecting prey, who have attacked and killed by stealth! How was it in Celyddon when you sneaked through the wood? Did not your heart beat fast with the thrill of your deception? Did it not leap for joy to see the fire spread at your enemies' backs? You are a master of trickery, it seems to me.'

Bedwyr glared at her and turned his face away. Cai rushed to his defence. 'It was war! We did only what we had to do.'

Like a cat with claws unsheathed, Morgian leapt on him. 'War! Does that absolve your guilt? You murdered men whose only crime was wanting to feed their children and see them grown. You made orphans of those same children and gave them up to the slow agony of starvation. You made widows of wives who knew nothing of realms or rulers. You stole the breath from their lungs and light from their eyes for ever. But how would you know — you, who have never shared bed with a wife?'

Cai, red-faced, was shamed into silence. But Morgian was

far from finished. 'Nothing more to say, bold Cai? Come, speak to me again of the cruel necessity of war.'

'Hold your tongue,' warned Gwalcmai ominously.

'Are you displeased, my son?' Morgian turned on him. 'You and your brother should be the last men alive to seek my death. We are blood kin, are we not? What would your father say if he learned his sons had caused his mother's death?'

'You are no blood kin of ours!' spat Gwalchavad.

'Ask Lot of Orcady about that,' she answered sweetly in reply. 'Or have you never wondered how he came by twin sons when his own wife was barren?'

It was an awesome display. She knew precisely the words to say to cow each and every one of them. I began to wonder if any man alive could stand against her. Surely, she was the Queen of Air and Darkness!

Gwenhwyvar stepped fearlessly forward, chin thrust out. 'You are shrewd, woman,' she said. 'I give you that. But sons are not responsible for their father's actions.'

'Oh, yes,' replied Morgian archly, 'speak to me of fathers and their sons. The Barren Queen — is that not what the people call you? Obviously, you know so much — you whose womb is sealed like a gravemound. And why is that? Could it be that you fear the ancient prophecy of your people, that your husband will be killed by his son?'

Gwenhwyvar was astounded. 'How do you know that!'

'I speak with the druids of Ierne, where it is a matter well known — and well known also what you do to prevent this prophecy from its fulfilment.'

Arthur glanced at his wife in shock. 'She is lying!' cried Gwenhwyvar. 'Arthur, my soul, believe me! It is a lie!'

'All our sins,' said the Emrys slowly, 'will be answerable before God. Yours are answerable to the High King now.'

'How can you even *think* to condemn me when you all have practised crimes far in excess of mine? Where is this justice you are so proud of? Answer me!'

Morgian raised her arm and flung the accusations back at us. I cringed before her wrath. 'You condemn yourselves! Your words are meaningless. Your accusations are the bleatings of dying sheep. Contemptible race, you fly headlong to your own destruction!'

She advanced towards Arthur. Her gloating smile sickened me. 'Did you think to better me? Your justice stinks of piss and vomit! You sicken me,' Morgian screamed. 'Fool!' she shrieked, drew herself up and spat full in the High King's face.

'No!' Gwalcmai leapt forward. He seized Morgian by the arms and spun her round. She spat at him, too, and, with a hiss like a devil cat, raked her fingernails across his eyes. He cried out and fell back, but she leapt on him, kicking and scratching. A long knife appeared in her hand and I watched in horror as she slashed it but a hair's breadth from his throat.

But Gwalcmai was quicker than she knew. Even as he rolled to the ground his hand found his sword, drew it, and raised it as she fell on him. The blade pierced Morgian in the side below the ribs, thrusting up into her black heart.

She shrieked once, stiffened, and stood upright, clutching the sword. The knife fell from her hand and clattered loud on the stones. Morgian stumbled backwards and collapsed upon the ground at Arthur's feet. Blood gushed from the wound and darkened the earth beneath her. Her eyes rolled up into her skull and her limbs convulsed.

It had all taken place so quickly that we stood looking on, stunned and confused, as if caught in a spell of enchantment. The Emrys moved first, kneeling over the still-trembling body.

Gwalcmai stood blinking in disbelief at what he had done. He got to his knees and raised his hands to Arthur. 'Mercy, lord! Forgive me, my king, I could not see her disgrace you!'

Arthur stared at him, and at first I thought he might reproach Gwalcmai. But the Emrys stood and said, 'Morgian is dead. In her bloodlust she has fallen on the sword Gwalcmai raised for his own defence. I see no fault here.'

Arthur turned to Gwalcmai who still knelt before him. 'Rise, Gwalcmai, you are forgiven. No doubt God has called her to answer her crimes as we will answer for our own.'

I heard a strangled sound and turned. Medraut stared at the body on the ground, his face contorted in a strange and unnatural expression: dark eyes wide with fear, lips curled in a ghastly leer of hatred, pale skin dark with rage. His fingers were curled like claws and he was scratching at his face in long raking welts. Ruby blood-drops oozed from the wounds and rolled down his cheeks.

Bedwyr was nearest and put out a hand to stay him. Medraut dodged aside. 'Stay back!' he cried in a shattered voice. 'Do not touch me!'

We looked in wonder at one another.

'Peace, Medraut. It is finished,' the Pendragon soothed.

'Murderer!' Medraut screamed, backing away. 'Murderer!'

Cai stepped close and made to grab him. Medraut's hand whipped up. The glint of a knife sparked in the fading light and Cai's arm spouted blood. He let out a cry, more in surprise than pain, and jumped back.

Medraut turned and fled to the horses. Llenlleawg unsheathed his sword and ran after him. Medraut slashed the reins free from the picket line with his knife and leapt into the saddle in one motion. He wheeled the horse and galloped away before the Irishman could reach him.

'Do you wish me to fetch him back?' called Llenlleawg.

'No,' said the High King, 'let him go. It is soon dark. He will not go far.'

Oh, Arthur, would that you had said anything but that!

I stared after the quickly retreating horse and rider, astonished at what I had just witnessed. When I turned back, the Emrys had already drawn the veil and hood over Morgian's face once more.

He stood slowly and put his hand on Gwalcmai's shoulder. 'This is not to your dishonour,' he said. 'Know you that Morgian earned the death she was given. You merely granted what she had purchased a thousand times over.'

'The things she said,' Gwalcmai murmured. 'They were all true. . .'

'Never believe it,' replied the Wise Emrys sternly, and turned to the rest of us standing together around the corpse. 'Hear me now, all of you! What Morgian has spoken before you were lies. Lies mingled with just enough truth to poison. She was lost and knew herself doomed; she hoped to inflame us with her corruption. My friends, do not let her succeed.'

I knew he spoke the truth, but it was difficult — still more difficult for the others who had been wounded by Morgian's words.

We buried Morgian in an unmarked grave in the sand on the shore above the high tide mark. The moon had risen when we finished and we were hungry. The talk around the fire as we ate was halting and listless. One by one the others crept off to their tents: Arthur and Gwenhwyvar first, and the others after, until only the Emrys and I remained.

'Do not fret about what happened today, boy,' he told me after a while. I glanced up to see him watching me over the fitful flames. 'It cannot be undone. We leave it to God.'

'I would be happy to do that,' I assured him, 'if I could. But I can still hear her voice screaming out those — those lies.'

'You believed her,' he observed, and I was ashamed to admit that I did. 'Well, that is all her craft. There is no fault in falling into a trap when it is set by a most cunning adversary. But you must not languish in it when you discover that it *is* a trap.

'Morgian was a champion of lies,' he said. 'Do not upbraid yourself for believing her. Only you must stop believing her. Do you understand what I am saying?'

I nodded, though I did not fully understand. The Wise Emrys knew this, so he said, 'You know Avallach, the Fisher King, and know that he suffers yet from a wound which he received many years ago. Do you know how he came by this wound?'

'No,' I answered. 'But what does Avallach's wound have to do with any of this?'

'I will tell you. Avallach was king of Sarras, a country far from the Island of the Mighty. There was a war and he fought bravely against his enemies. But one night, as he rushed to the aid of his son, he was ambushed and cut down.

'It was dark and he was not wearing his kingly armour, so he went unnoticed on the field. His enemies devised a torture for those they captured — they tied each living man to a dead one. Avallach, as it chanced, was bound wrist-to-wrist, ankle-to-ankle, and mouth-to-mouth to the corpse of his son.

'The enemy abandoned them to this insane torture, and

Avallach was left to die in the poisonous embrace of his once-beloved son.'

I had never heard such a hideous thing, and told Myrddin so.

'Yes,' he agreed, 'it is ghastly and terrible — Avallach bears the infirmity of it to this day.' He gazed steadily at me, so that I would understand him. 'And this is what Morgian hoped to do: bind us with half-truths to her corrupting lies. And like Avallach and his ambushed soldiers we are meant to flounder in their deadly embrace until we perish.'

'Is there no escape?'

'Trust God, Aneirin. Trust the Good God. We have sinned; yes, that is true. But we have the Christ's sure forgiveness. Only ask and it is granted. By this we will be loosed from Morgian's curse.'

I heard him and at last began to understand what he meant. 'What of Medraut?'

The Emrys shook his head slowly and dropped his eyes to the embers as if to glimpse the future there. 'Medraut is dark to me; his path lies in shadow and uncertainty. One thing is certain, however; we have not seen the last of Medraut.'

SEVEN

Seven bright summers passed, and seven mild winters. The Summer Realm enjoyed its fairest season. All things flourished which the High King blessed, and peace reigned in the Island of the Mighty and its Seven Favoured Isles. No more barbarians invaded, and the Saecsens kept faith with Arthur. Men began speaking of the battle of Mount Baedun as the greatest victory ever won in Britain, and holding Arthur Pendragon as the greatest king ever to rule in the world.

From across all seas — from Ierne, Daneland, Saecsland, Jutland, Norweigi, Gotland, Hoiland, Gaul, Ffeincland, Armorica and Ruten — kings and rulers came to pay homage to Arthur and learn his justice. In all it was a time unknown since Bran the Blessed banished war in Ynys Prydein. Jesu's holy church sank its roots deep into Britain's soil and spread its sheltering branches over the land.

Ships plied the wide, wave-tossed waters, bringing costly goods from every foreign port: fine wine in sealed amphora; the beautiful rainbow-hued cloth called samite; magnificent horses; worked leather; cups, bowls, and platters of gold, silver and precious glass. From out of Britain flowed other goods: strong steel, lead, silver, wool, beef and hunting hounds.

For a time the Fairest Island that is in the world flowered, filling this worlds-realm with a heavenly scent.

Through all trials did Britain triumph, and in all good things did it abound. The Island of the Mighty reached a height exceeding even that which it attained in elder times under the Roman Emperors. Britain was exalted then.

For this reason it was decided that Arthur should attain his highest honour. At Whitsuntide in the twenty-first year of the High King's reign he would receive another coronation: the Laurel Crown of the Roman Empire. *Yr Amherawdyr Arthyr*, he would become, *Imperator Artorius*; Exalted Arthur, Emperor of the West and Chief Dragon of the Island of the Mighty. The last remnants of the empire would be placed beneath his hand.

So widely renowned and revered was our Pendragon that as soon as word of this impending honour was spoken out, the four winds carried it far and wide throughout this worlds-realm to all foreign nations. And the best men in the world at that time began journeying to Britain to hail the new emperor. Kings, lords, noblemen, bishops and archbishops of the church — men whose worth was beyond measure in their own homelands. They came to honour Arthur, and to see him crowned in glory.

There were so many that Arthur was forced to leave his beloved Caer Lial and go to Caer Legionis in the south. For though it was not a fine city like Caer Lial, it was larger and could house all those streaming into Britain. Also, the deep River Uisc nearby gave safe harbourage to the innumerable ships arriving by twos and fives and tens as soon as the weather broke fair.

In this way, the old City of the Legions came once more under the authority of an emperor and knew again something of its former grandeur. Caerleon, as it was some-times called now, also boasted another benefit — the twin churches of Julius and Aaron, presided over by Arthur's friend Illtyd, lately archbishop.

Preparations for the coronation began directly after the Christ Mass. Braving winter seas, I sailed with the Emrys, Bedwyr and a hundred of the Cymbrogi to the south to help make ready. Most of my work consisted of reroofing and timbering the long-unused storehouses to receive the tribute of grain, lard, wine, ale and fodder which began flooding into the city as soon as the roads and mountain passes thawed in the spring.

Each of the others directed equally ambitious works of repair and reconstruction in the halls, the houses, the streets and walls. Indeed, the whole city resounded with so much uproar of carpenters and masons that it was called Caer Terfsyg — Fortress of Riot. I laboured from sunrise to long past twilight, tireless in my many tasks. My hands grew hard, and my muscles lean. I led men and commanded good works to be done. When the Emrys saw that I could accomplish much, more was given me to do. Thus I became one of Arthur's captains, though I had never led a battle.

From mid-winter to spring's end we laboured, and the ancient *vicus* was transformed. Walls were rebuilt, streets repaved, foundations shored up, roofs patched and leaded, gates repaired, aqueducts retiled; the marshland south of the city was drained to accommodate the myriad tents and bothies — thus even waste land began blooming with wild flowers again. The people of Caerleon threw themselves into the redeeming of their city, and nowhere did a labourer go without meat or drink, or a helping hand when he required it.

The Emrys oversaw the principal work of restoring the governor's palace. Actually, there had never been a governor in Caer Legionis. The fortress had been once been ruled by a *Vicarius* named Matinus, who lived well and was widely reputed to be a fair and honest man. His extensive house was later inhabited by a succession of legates and tribunes who added to its luxury and grounds, so that in after times it came to rival the governors' residences of Londinium and Eboracum.

This palace, the Emrys decided, should become the site of Arthur's triumphal reception. The coronation itself would take place in the twin churches: the Church of Aaron for Arthur, and the Church of Julius for Gwenhwyvar. The palace had long been abandoned and considered a prime source of good building-stone by the locals, who pulled down much of the dressed stone and plundered the furnishings. Only the tessellated mosaics on the floor escaped being carried off.

Yet the Emrys maintained that this house alone would serve. And when the citizens learned of the high honour to be paid them in hosting Arthur's coronation, and the work of restoration began in earnest, the pillaged furniture began to reappear. Even the dressed stone returned, liberated from whatever use it had served in the generations since the last tribune decamped for Rome.

When complete, the palace was a marvel. All who looked upon it came away inspired and cheered to see this revival of imperial splendour. But not only was the empire revived, Celtic nobility also roused from its sleep. Under Myrddin Emrys' guiding hand the inspired blending of both was accomplished: Roman in form and foundation, Celtic in execution and expression. No one who beheld the finished work failed to recognized that in the Pendragon's palace a new craft had come into being.

'It is magnificent!' cried Arthur, when he saw it at last. 'Myrddin, you are indeed a most magnificent enchanter!'

'Speak not of enchantment!' declared the Emrys. 'If this could have been accomplished by enchantment, I have wasted good men's sweat and sleepless nights for nothing!'

'Not for nothing,' soothed Gwenhwyvar, her dark eyes adazzle at all around her. 'Never say it. Your gift is the more precious to us because it wears your love in every line.'

'It is true, Exalted Emrys,' remarked Gwalcmai, who with his brother and the others of the Round Table, had come with the High King to inspect the work and order the final preparations. 'No king has ever had a palace so richly wrought. In this,' he spread his arms to the gilded hall around us, 'the Summer Realm finds its fairest flower.'

The Emrys smiled, but shook his head lightly. 'Its first, perhaps. Not its fairest. Higher, more noble works will be accomplished. What you see is a beginning only, there are greater things to be done.'

'Greater works *will* be done,' affirmed Arthur. 'But let us honour this one with the proper respect. Thank you, Myrddin. Your gift beggars me for words.'

The Emrys enjoyed the pleasure his gift gave the Pendragon, but he had little time to savour it. For, the next day but one, the first of the High King's guests began arriving. Some had wintered in Caer Lial, others at Caer Cam and Caer Melyn in the south. By ship and on horseback they came, and once the flood started it did not reach high water mark for many and many a day to come.

Thus, on the day of the coronation, a day of unrivalled glory in the Island of the Mighty since its beginning, were assembled lords, kings, princes, noblemen and dignitaries of great renown: Fergus and Aedd of Ierne, Cador of Cerniui, Meurig Hen of Dyfed, Ectorius of Caer Edyn, Caw of Alclyd, Maelgwn of Gwynedd, Maluasius of Hislandi,

Doldaf of Gotland, Gonval of Llychllyn, Acel of Druim, Cadwallo of the Venedoti, Holdin of Ruteni, Leodegarius of Hoiland, Gwilenhin of Ffreincland in Gaul, Ban of Armorica, and many, many others of various ranks and races entered the city to do the Pendragon homage.

Early on Whitsunday we gathered in the Church of Aaron and bowed the knee before the altar of Christ. When everyone was assembled, then did Arthur make entrance. He wore a pure white robe with a belt of braided gold. Before him walked four kings: Cador, Meurig Hen, Fergus and Ban, each wearing a red cloak of state and carrying a golden sword upraised in his hand. The church was filled with the music of a choir of monks singing praise-song and psalms of honour and glory in exquisite harmony, accompanied by the bishops and archbishops of Britain, robed and with their rods of office.

Another procession, like to the first, but made up of women, left the palace and made its separate way to the Church of Julius. This procession was led by the Archbishop Dubricius, who conducted Queen Gwenhwyvar to her own crown-taking. Before her walked the queens of Cador, Meurig Hen, Fergus and Ban, each wearing a red cloak and carrying a white dove. Following the queen came the ladies of Britain such as Gwenhwyvar deemed worthy to attend her, and the wives and daughters and female kindred of the Pendragon's subject lords.

Together this fair fellowship went forth from the palace, the radiance of their garments and the splendour of their joy so brilliant, so beautiful to behold, that the throngs lining the streets nearly prevented it from reaching the church at all; the press was so great, and the acclaim so loud, that Gwenhwyvar could hardly make her way through the city.

When all the royal guests and people were gathered in, the High Mass was celebrated in both churches. Never was a more joyous or more reverent rite observed in that city, before or since. At its conclusion, Archbishop Illtyd placed the laurel crown upon Arthur's brow and proclaimed him Emperor of the West.

Not to be eclipsed by her husband's glory, Gwenhwyvar likewise received a crown and became the Empress of the West. Then did such merrymaking ensue in both churches that the delighted congregations hastened back and forth from one church to the other to enjoy the festivity, and to fill their ears with the lovely singing of the churchmen and the beauty of the Emperor and his Empress.

Throughout all Britain that Whitsunday endured the most harmonious and glorious celebration, for the Light of Heaven shone full upon the Summer Lord that day.

Upon receiving the crowns, Arthur and Gwenhwyvar offered a feast to their guests. Whereupon the storehouses I laboured so long and hard to prepare were all plundered to provide the food for the feast. Of meat and mead, bread and ale, wine and sweet fruits there was no lack. When the tables were filled in the palace, the feast spilled out onto the yards and then into the streets, and from there outside the walls to the meadows and fields around the city.

At the height of the feast, the celebrants marched forth from the city into the tent-filled meadows and formed themselves into groups for games: riding and racing, throwing lances and stones, wrestling and sword-play, and feats of skill and daring. The day passed in a wealth of joy for everyone, and from this day men understood the meaning of happiness.

The feast continued three days, and on the fourth there appeared a small company of men from the east, white-bearded and round of shoulder, twelve in all and each with a ring of gold on his finger and an olive branch in his hand. These venerable princes came before the High King's throne and greeted him with great courtesy.

'Hail, Great King! And hail to all your people!' said the foremost visitor. 'We are come from the court of Lucius, Emperor of the East, to beseech you in his name, and to deliver his desire into your hands.'

With that, the man withdrew from his robe a sealed parchment which he passed to the Pendragon. The parchment was opened and Arthur ordered it to be read out before all those assembled. In a voice loud and clear, the Emrys stood beside the king and this is what he read:

'Lucius, Procurator of the Republic, to Arthur, High King and Pendragon of the Britons, according to his deservings. I marvel greatly at the unthinkable pride which has inflamed you. You hold all kingdoms in your hand and

444

deem yourself most fortunate, esteemed among men. Yet you do not spare a thought for Rome who taught you the law and justice you so rightly honour.

'Need I remind you that you are a Roman subject? Do you so lightly consider Rome? You think to set the Western Empire in your hand, and who is to prevent you?

'Yet I, Lucius, tell you that while one enemy draws breath beneath the blue sky of Rome, you are no true ruler! Barbarians beset the Seven Hills and roam at will through the empty Forum. Enemies kill our citizens and despoil the land. Free and loyal Romans are carried off in chains to serve foreign slave masters. The cries of the homeless and dying echo in the Senate, and jackals mutilate the corpses of children.

'We hear of the Mighty Pendragon, Exalted One of Britain, King of Champions. All day long the praise of Arthur fills our ears. Your renown has spread to the ends of the earth, Right Worthy Ruler. But do we see your armies rise to the defence of your birthright? Do we see you lift your hand to help those who granted you the benefits you now flaunt?

'Have you forgotten the debt you owe? If your courage is even half so great as the fame-singers tell, why do you delay? The barbarian dog tears at the throat of the Mother of Nations. Where is the Wonderful Pendragon?

'You call yourself Emperor! Call yourself a god! You know not who you are, nor from what dust you are sprung, if you do not offer protection to the Mother of your youth. You are but a faithless craven if you do not march at once to restore the *Pax Romana*.'

Silence reigned long in the hall when Myrddin Emrys finished reading. That such an acrimonious and belittling message should be delivered to the High King at the moment of his triumph shocked the assembled lords. Arthur withdrew at once to his council room to confer with his lords, sixty in all, and determine what answer he should make to the Emperor Lucius.

Once gathered at the board, Arthur spoke in a stern and solemn voice. 'You have been my closest companions, my Cymbrogi; in good times and bad you have supported me. Help me yet again. Give me benefit of your keen wisdom and tell me what we are to do in the face of such a message as this.'

Cador was first to speak. 'Until now, I have feared that the life of ease which we have won would make cowards of us, that we would grow soft during these years of peace. Worse, our renown as champions of battle would be forgotten, and the Flight of Dragons would cease in our young men's memories.' He smiled as he looked about at his sword brothers. 'Perhaps it is to save us from this indignity that God has allowed this rebuke to reach us. Can we really enjoy our peace when the Seat of the Empire is befouled by barbarians?'

Some readily agreed with Cador, but Gwalcmai was quick to speak up. 'Lord King,' he said, jumping up, 'we should not dread the folly of our young men. If they forget the sacrifice that we have made to bring about this holiest of realms, that is their loss not ours. Even if it were not so, peace is infinitely preferable to war.'

Gwalcmai's words greatly calmed the more quick-tempered among them, and many agreed with him. So the council was divided and began hotly debating the matter among themselves. Arthur listened to all that was said, a frown deepening on his face.

When this had gone on for a while, Ban of Benowyc in Armorica stood and silenced the argument with upraised hands. 'Lord King,' he declared loudly, 'long have I served you in goods and gold and men. I do not think it boast to say that no other lord has supported you more loyally or steadfastly.

'Now then, it is all the same to me whether we go to Rome, or whether we stay. What do I care for the opinions of the idle young men among us? Such renown as I have is sufficient for me; I do not need to raise my name still higher for my own sake.

'Yet I wonder if there might be some greater benefit to be won by marching to the defence of Rome. If, by doing so, we could extend the peace we have enjoyed to the rest of the world, even now suffering the vengeance of barbarians, would this not be a worthy thing? Further, would it not be accounted sin to us to ignore this plea for help, when we could so easily give it?

'I am an old man and no longer need the acclaim of others to think well of myself. But neither do I enjoy a private peace when others suffer injustice that I could prevent.'

At these words the council roared its approval. Who could disagree with such sane logic, they cried. This is surely what must be done. It is not for ourselves that we save Rome, they said, but for those who suffer the barbarians' oppression.

When all had spoken and order was once more regained, the High King stood slowly. 'Thank you, my brothers,' he said, 'for giving me your sound advice. I will withdraw now to consider which way I will go.'

Arthur turned and left the chamber and the lords returned to the feast — all except Bedwyr, Cai, the Emrys and myself, who followed him to his private chamber.

'I cannot believe you would even for a moment consider going to Rome,' Bedwyr said, wasting no time. 'You are power mad if you think to honour Lucius' letter with action.'

'Speak your mind, Bedwyr,' replied Arthur with a grin. 'Unbind your tongue and do not hold back.'

'I mean it, Bear,' said Bedwyr icily, 'nothing good can come of it. No Briton who marched to Rome ever returned. Macsen Wledig went to Rome and they beheaded him. Constantine became emperor and they poisoned him. It is a snake-pit. Stay far away from there.'

Cai disagreed. 'How can he call himself emperor if he abandons the Seat of the Empire to barbarians? Go to Rome, I say, free it, and carry the throne back to Britain. Then it will be saved for all time.'

I did not know what to think. Both arguments appealed to me. It was true that Britons who entertained dreams of empire tended to die upon reaching Rome. Equally true, it seemed to me, that to allow the heathen to defy justice tainted the peace we had laboured so long to achieve.

So it was that we, with Arthur, looked at last to the Wise Emrys. 'Why do you stare at me?' the Emrys said. 'You have already made up your minds. Go and do what you have decided to do.'

'But I have not decided,' objected Arthur. 'God knows I am adrift here.'

The Emrys gave his head a shake. 'Nothing I say will change the heart within you, Arthur. I marvel that you have not already given the order to sail.'

'What have I done to deserve this abuse?' asked Arthur in a wounded voice. 'Tell me and I will make it right.'

'I tell you this. If you uphold the council of men like Cador and Ban, then you deserve the abuse that comes to you!'

'But I do not uphold their council. I am asking for yours.'

'Then hear me well, for when I have finished I will speak no more about it.'

'As you will,' replied Arthur, sitting down in his chair.

'Listen then, O King, to the Soul of Wisdom!' The Emrys, in the manner of the druid bards of old, pulled his cloak tightly around him and stood before the king, head erect, eyes closed, voice raised in declamation. 'Through all things I have laboured, to this end only: that the Kingdom of Summer might be born in this worlds-realm. In you, Arthur Wledig, this has been accomplished. You are the Champion of Light that was foretold of old; you are the Bright Promise of Britain, you are the Chief Dragon of the Island of the Mighty, you are the Favoured One of God, who has so richly blessed you.

'Hear me, Arthur: Rome is dying — may even now be dead. We cannot revive it, nor is it right to do so. The old must pass away to make room for the new. That is the way of things. In the Kingdom of Summer, a new order has come to pass. It must not become allied to the old order, or it will surely perish.

'Do not allow the faded glory of the empire to dazzle your eyes, nor the words of men inflame your sense of honour. Be the Emperor of the West, if you like, but establish a new empire *here*, in Britain. Let the rest of the world look to the Island of the Mighty as once we looked to Rome.

'Be first in compassion! Be first in freedom! But let that freedom and compassion begin here. Let Britain shine like a beacon blaze into the dark corners of the world. Rome is a corpse, Arthur, let the barbarian hosts bury it. Let Roman justice fail; let the justice of God prevail. Let Britain become foremost in doing God's work in the world. Let Britain become the Seat of the New Empire of Light!'

So saying, the Emrys raised his cloak over his head and hooded himself. And he would speak no more.

Three days passed. Arthur kept his counsel to himself and held vigil in his chamber until the matter which so obsessed him could be resolved. In the end, he summoned his lords to council once more and delivered his decision.

'Long have I thought on this and weighed the various arguments in my mind. I have decided that it will be no bad thing to go to Rome, to do what may be done to relieve the suffering of the people there, and to receive the laurel wreath from their hands. When I have set Rome in my hand, I will return to Britain and rule the New Empire from the Island of the Mighty.

'Therefore, I order to be assembled the ships of my fleet and the ships of any who would sail with me, so that we may make all haste to Rome and end the barbarian oppression there. For I am persuaded that when injustice is allowed to reign unchecked, then no man is truly free.'

The High King's plan was greeted with wild enthusiasm by the assembly, especially among the younger men. But I noticed that Arthur kept his eyes upon his supporters while he spoke. Never once did he glance at the Emrys.

Immediately after, in his chambers, Bedwyr made bold to challenge the Pendragon to his face. Because they were closer than brothers, Arthur listened. 'This is insane, Artos. A more crack-brained idea you have never had. Defy me, if you will. But do not defy the Emrys.'

'I am not defying anyone,' maintained Arthur. 'Besides, what is so wrong with wanting to liberate the Mother Church from the persecution of the heathen?'

'Do not speak to me of churches, Bear. We both know why you are going. What if you get yourself killed over there, like Macsen Wledig? '

'It is only one campaign.'

'Is it? In any event, if the Seat of the Empire needs saving let Emperor Lucius save it! Did he offer to help? We will all grow grey-headed waiting for that! He expects you to do all the work. Just you see if you receive so much as a hot meal from him when you are finished. Somehow,

I do not see him extending his hands in friendship to you.'

'You are so suspicious, brother,' laughed Arthur.

'And you are so stubborn.'

'We make a fine pair, do we not?'

Bedwyr would not be appeased with light words. 'Hear me, Artorius! Do not go to Rome.' He folded his arms across his chest. 'I cannot say it more plainly than that.'

The Pendragon remained silent for a long moment. 'Does that mean you will not go with me?'

'Saints and angels!' sighed Bedwyr. 'Of course I will go with you. How else will I prevent you from foolishly getting your head carried off by a barbarian war axe?' Bedwyr paused, and added, 'But that brings to mind another matter: who will hold the realm while you are gone?'

'I have already thought of that,' replied Arthur happily. 'Gwenhwyvar is a reigning queen in her own right. She will rule in my place while I am gone.'

'Very well,' agreed Bedwyr. 'That is the first truly sensible choice you have made today. At least she will not be tempted to rush off saving any failing empires.'

In the end, the Emrys and I, and Gwenhwyvar, along with a small bodyguard of warriors, stayed behind to hold the realm in Arthur's absence. Gwenhwyvar was angry with Arthur for going — mostly because she thought that she should fight by his side, rather than languish alone in Britain. She raged and stormed for a fair time about this but, when the day of leaving dawned, she bore her duty with good grace.

Once in motion, Arthur's preparations gathered speed. By early summer, all was in readiness and the warriors of Britain assembled — like the legionaries three hundred years before — on the banks of the River Uisc to board ships bound for Rome.

We stayed in Caer Legionis for a few days after the ships sailed, then boarded our own ships and sailed up the western coast to the harbour at Caer Lial. I was not sorry to stay behind with the Emrys and the queen. Although I would have liked to have gone to Rome, just to see it, I was the least of Arthur's warriors and could serve him better by remaining behind and looking to his interests in Britain.

The journey to Caer Lial proved pleasant. We stopped at Avallon on the way and stayed a few days with Avallach and Charis, before going on to the city. Another day's sailing brought us safely to the harbour and at last we were returned to the north.

I was surprised to discover how much I had missed it. After the close-crowded city of the south, Caer Lial seemed spacious, the air fresher, the days brighter. I was glad to be at home once more and spent the next few days happily attending to affairs left untended since the winter before. Also, I made plans to ride to Caer Alclyd to visit my mother, whom I had not seen since Emperor Arthur's coronation — and then only for a moment.

The day I had planned to leave, I went to the stables for a mount. While the horse was being saddled, I hurried back to the palace to gather the gifts I was bringing to my family. Then I sought out the Emrys to bid him farewell, and to see if he wished to send any message with me.

It was as I hastened down the long corridor from my chamber to the hall that I heard a cry of alarm. It came from within the palace.

I raced to the hall, scattering all my bundles as I burst into the room and found myself face to face with Medraut.

EIGHT

Four warriors lay dead in pooled blood on the floor. The room was filled with Picti waving swords and clubs and spears. I was the only Briton alive to defend the queen and I was unarmed. Medraut's sword bit into my throat.

'What treachery is this?' I demanded.

'We have come to pay homage to the Emperor,' replied Medraut with a sneer. 'Imagine our disappointment when we discovered that he is not here to receive us.'

Two Picts thrust spears at me from either side. I know they would have killed me in that selfsame instant if Medraut had not prevented them. 'Cadw! Ymat!' he shouted in their coarse tongue. Then, to another swarthy Pict who looked to be a king, he said, 'This one is more valuable to us alive. Have him bound and put with the others.'

My wrists and knees were bound with thick leather thongs and I was dragged through the palace and hauled into the yard. There were signs of the briefest and most futile of struggles: here and there a cluster of dead bodies, some armed, most without weapons; men cut down where they stood.

No organized resistance had been possible. We were overcome before we could raise spear or draw sword. And those of us still alive were becoming Medraut's hostages. The humiliation was worse than death.

Shock and outrage coiled within me, twin serpents of revulsion. The evil of it! Vile disgrace! Vicious and wicked, Medraut had perpetrated the unthinkable.

More than thirty of the queen's warriors had been captured — attesting to the utter surprise with which the city had been attacked. No man, from the highest warrior to the lowest stablehand, would ever have allowed himself to be taken alive if he had weapon to hand, or, failing that, a chance to swing his fists.

The waiting warriors stood with their heads bowed in disgrace, hands bound, surrounded by Picti guards. Smoke rolled across the yard and coiled from numerous sites within the city. Shrieks and screams echoed in the distance. I was brought to stand with the other Britons and after only a few moments saw the Emrys and the Queen roughly dragged from the palace. The sight of Myrddin and Gwenhwyvar, bound and hooded, the hands of the enemy upon them, made the gorge rise in my throat. I retched and choked back bile. The tears welled up in my eyes.

Medraut, his expression wild and fantastic, strutted forth across the yard, a big Pict battlechief on either side of him. He was no true warrior himself, so moved only in the company of warriors. In truth, he was nothing more than a cunning coward.

Upon reaching the place where the captives waited he uttered a sharp command in the barbarian tongue. All at once, the Picti raised blade and spear and began stabbing the hostages. Brave men fell all around me. I saw more than one sword plunged into the belly of a defenceless man, and that man fall to his death without a sound, courageous to the end. One battle-scarred veteran even seized the sword as it swung towards him and with a defiant cry thrust it through his own heart rather than allow the enemy to kill him so shamefully.

I was struck to the ground and pinned there with the point of a spear. When the slaughter was finished, only eleven remained. Medraut saved the most important of his captives for the hostage pits: the queen, the Emrys, myself, and eight others whose lives he hoped to bargain with.

Let him do his worst. That day I watched good men die and pledged my life to seeing Medraut's headless corpse torn to pieces by the High King's hounds.

I was thrown into a loathsome pit beneath the roots of the fortress. There with some few of the other hostages I stayed. Whether day or night, I knew it not. Where the queen was held, or what had become of the Emrys, I could not say.

Occasionally, we were hauled from the pit and made

to parade in chains before our Picti captors who wished to boast of us before their chieftains. At one of these times I discovered that we were enjoying the hospitality of Keldrych, a powerful Pict king, who had succoured Medraut when the tyrant fled Arthur's fosterage.

Keldrych summoned the fierce tribes of the north to attend him in Caer Lial, there to see for themselves how he and Medraut had seized the Pendragon's city. Word of rebellion spread like plague among the Picti, who had never loved Arthur and needed little enough encouragement to break faith with him.

A blind man could have seen what was happening! Having stolen the queen, the traitor bargained with the lords and battlechiefs of other Picti tribes for support. And this he won.

Curiously, the Picti, among other primitive peoples, consider the kingship of a lord to rest in his queen. The king's wife is the living symbol of his reign. It is a belief ancient beyond reckoning, and more enduring than stone.

For this reason, the Picti were much impressed with Medraut's abduction of Gwenhwyvar: she was Arthur's *kingship*. As Medraut possessed her, so he possessed the throne of Britain. To the Picti this was self-evident. In seizing the queen, Medraut had made himself king, and in their eyes proud Gwenhwyvar became Medraut's wife. This treason moved the Picti as nothing else could. In treachery was Medraut the master.

Arthur, of course, was expected to return and fight for his throne. Medraut meant to be ready. With extravagant promises and subtle deceptions he wooed the rebel kings. As the summer waxed full, the forces of the Picti gathered for war. With each day that passed the enemy grew stronger, as more and more warbands arrived in Caer Lial, summoned by Keldrych and Medraut, and emboldened by the prospect of Arthur's defeat.

From the wild hills of the north they came — from Sci, from Druim and Gododdin, Athfotla and Cait. They came by the hundreds, gathering together in a mighty host, separate tribes united only by their quick-kindled hatred of Arthur, and the promise of enormous wealth through plunder.

At the riotous Lugnasadh celebration the hostages were once again dragged out to parade before the assembled battlechiefs. The sight of them nearly stole the breath from my lungs. Gathered in Arthur's hall was an immense host of blue-painted Picti lords, each and every one a chieftain with many hundreds of warriors in his keep. Never had such a host been assembled in Britain, I thought; surely the Pendragon cannot match such a force.

To our disgrace, we were made to serve our captors meat and drink and endure their crude sport as they viciously shoved us and choked us with our chains. When the riot reached its height, Medraut rose up and with much demonstration spoke to the assembled chieftains. I do not know what he said, but that night we were not returned to the hostage pits. We slept in our chains in a storeroom and the next morning were taken out into the yard.

The hostages were herded together and, to my joy and relief, I saw that the Emrys and the queen remained unharmed. I had not seen them since the fall of Caer Lial and had feared for their safety. Although the queen was held a little apart from the rest of us, I was encouraged to see that she appeared defiant and unbowed, full of fire. By stealth I managed to creep near to the Emrys.

'Emrys, are you well?' I asked.

'Well enough, Aneirin,' he answered, his voice low and raw. 'And you?'

'I have not been harmed — nor have the others,' I replied. 'Do you know what is happening?'

'Arthur is returning,' the Emrys told me. 'Word came to Medraut a few days ago that the High King's fleet had been sighted. Today the battle will be joined.'

These words heartened me, but I noticed they brought no cheer to the Wise Emrys. 'But surely this is good news,' I said. 'What is wrong?'

'We have endured so much and laboured so long to be undone like this,' he said, 'and you ask what is wrong?'

'Arthur will not fail.'

The Emrys regarded me long, his golden eyes deep-shadowed with sadness. 'Trust God, Aneirin. And pray that the sky does not fall upon us.'

I crept away, confused and dismayed. All I had suffered

till now was nothing compared to the despair I felt in the Emrys' few words. For the first time I began to sense something of the magnitude of Medraut's treason. My heart broke, and my soul cried for leaving. I was that unhappy.

After a time, we were marched through the city to the harbour, where some ships were arriving from Orcady. I little guessed that Lot was in league with Medraut but, to his everlasting shame, Lot did nothing to aid the queen. Instead, in the full view of all, he waded to shore with his chieftains and embraced the tyrant like a kinsman.

'How can he do this?' I wondered aloud to the Emrys as we squatted on the shingle. 'I thought Lot was Arthur's ally.'

'Do you not see it yet?'

Once again I was forced to admit that I did not. I had no idea what Myrddin was hinting at. 'You mean Lot has joined the treason?'

'Do you not know Medraut even now?'

'He said he was the son of a Picti lord — Urien of Monoth. That is what he said when he came before Arthur,' I answered.

'He is no Pict,' snapped the Emrys. 'Think! Did you not see how they treated with him, and how he wheedled and schemed with them?'

'I was in the hostage pit!' I reminded him. 'I saw nothing.'

'Medraut is Morgian's son!' The Emrys answered my disbelief with a further revelation. 'And the man greeting him on the shore is not Lot, it is his half-brother, Urien.'

'But Medraut said Urien was his father,' I remarked. 'Why should he lie about that?'

The Emrys shook his head slowly. 'That,' he said, 'is the one truth Medraut told — the same that killed Lot in the end.'

Slowly the grim meaning of the Emrys' strange words came to me. My stomach tightened with revulsion. 'Morgian married Urien, her own son,' I said, taking it in at last. The incest produced a child and that child was Medraut.

'My years of blindness were nothing to this,' the Emrys muttered bitterly. 'Alone among men, I should have known what we were fighting against. More than my sight was shattered, I think. But it comes to this: Morgian placed her devil spawn in Arthur's court, knowing that one way or another she would have her revenge.'

Revenge. The word stank of death. I heard in it the cry of ravens flocking to blood-spattered battlefields. Oh, the Enemy is tireless in hate and endlessly resourceful. I suddenly felt very small and ignorant. I knew nothing of the world's true nature. I knew nothing of the forces arrayed against us. I knew nothing. . .

'What is to be done?' I asked, hoping for some word of hope from the Ever Wise Emrys.

'That which is given to us to do we will do,' he said, and turned his face away. 'We are men and not angels after all.'

I drew neither hope nor comfort from these words, and once again was thrown back into the misery of despair as into the loathsome hostage pit. I beat my fists impotently against my leg. If I could have killed the traitor there and then I would have done it, even at the cost of my own soul! But I could do nothing — only stand aside and look on.

Urien's ships were drawn up and arranged to form a blockade of the harbour. When Arthur entered he would not be able to land directly, but would have to fight his way ashore. Shrewd Medraut gave himself every advantage.

But here I was mistaken, for after effecting the blockade, Medraut ordered the Picti host to withdraw into the hills. Gwenhwyvar, the Emrys and the other hostages were put onto horses and led away with Keldrych's warband.

Then did Medraut turn to me. 'Your Wonderful Pendragon is coming. When he arrives, tell him this: I am waiting for him in the hills. The Emrys and Gwenhwyvar are with me. He will come to me alone and I will receive him.'

'That he will never do!' I declared.

Medraut slapped me hard across the mouth. 'Tell him! If he brings his war host, I will kill the queen before he has set foot in the crooked glen. This is between us two alone. When we have settled the blood-debt for my mother, I will give up my hostages — not before.'

I glared at the tyrant with narrowed eyes. 'Say whatever you like, and know that I will tell him. But you are insane if you believe the Pendragon of Britain will meet you alone in a place of your choosing.'

Medraut stiffened. His hands began to shake, as if he were warring within himself to control his movements. His face twisted in a savage leer. 'Then let him bring his closest advisers. Yes, bring his best! But if I see so much as a single blade among them, the queen will die and the Emrys with her.'

My chain was then fastened to an iron ring used to tie up ships and I was left there alone on the shore. I watched and waited through the day, and endured a cold night on the strand without food or water.

As dawn faded the night to the colour of grey steel in the east, I awakened to the sight of thirty ships sailing into the harbour. The foremost ships bore the red dragon on their sails. Close behind followed fifteen sister ships, with twenty more just clearing the harbour mouth.

The Pendragon made his landing after threading his way through the blocked harbour. I stood in sea-water up to my shins, waiting for the landing party to make its way to me. Arthur himself was among the first to come ashore, and greeted me anxiously. 'Where are they? What is happening here?' Bedwyr, Cai, Cador and Gwalcmai quickly gathered around.

'We are hostages, lord,' I replied, indicating my chain — whereupon the High King drew Cut Steel and, with one mighty chop, freed me from the iron ring in the stone. 'Thank you, Pendragon. I knew you would come. I knew you would not leave us to suffer Medraut's treachery.'

'Where is that rat?' demanded Cai. 'I will see him hung upon the gates of Caer Lial.'

Bedwyr lifted my chain. 'What of the queen and the Emrys? Do they live?'

'They are alive,' I answered. 'But, aside from the hostages, all the rest are murdered.'

'He will pay with his life for this!' declared Cador. He smashed his fist against his chest.

Arthur turned his eyes to his ruined city, then back to me. 'Where have they gone?' he asked softly.

'Lord, I am instructed to deliver this message,' I said. 'But please, remember these are Medraut's words, not mine.'

'For the love of Jesu,' cried Cai, 'get on with it!'

I swallowed hard and began. 'I am to tell you that he is waiting for you in the hills. The Emrys and Gwenhwyvar are

458

with him. You are to go to him alone, but for your chosen advisers, and Medraut will receive you.'

Cai snorted and Bedwyr muttered under his breath. Cador opened his mouth to speak, but Arthur held up his hand for silence and bade me continue.

'Medraut says that if you bring your war host he will kill the queen and the Emrys before ever you set foot in the crooked glen. He says that when the blood-debt has been settled, he will give up his captives — not before.'

'Blood-debt?' wondered Bedwyr. 'What blood-debt could there be between you?' he asked Arthur.

'For his mother's death,' I answered.

All looked at one another uneasily. 'Who is his mother?' asked Cai.

'Morgian,' I answered. 'So the Emrys says.' And I told them what I had learned from Myrddin regarding Medraut's unnatural parentage. Gwalcmai listened in stunned silence.

'This answers much,' observed Arthur. He turned to Gwalcmai. 'You bear no fault.'

'I never *did* trust that schemer,' muttered Cai.

'What else can you tell us?' Bedwyr asked.

'Only this: that you must come to him unarmed. If he sees so much as a single blade among you, the queen will die and the Emrys with her. So Medraut says.'

'How many are with him?'

'Thousands — fifty thousand, at least. I cannot be certain, but there are more than I have ever seen before. All the Picti tribes are here.'

I thought for a moment that I saw defeat in the bold blue eyes. But I was mistaken. 'The crooked glen. . . ' he mused, searching the wave-washed pebbles at his feet. 'Camboglanna — Camlan?' He raised his head with a grim smile.

'Medraut is canny,' observed Bedwyr. 'If that is where he has taken them — a narrow valley with a fortress above. The place is a killing-ground.'

Indeed, I thought Bedwyr's appraisal only too accurate when later that day Arthur, Bedwyr and Cai surveyed the place from a nearby hilltop. I accompanied them and despaired to behold our ruinous position.

For Medraut had moved his army east to a sheltered valley

below the Wall. To the north rose a steep rocky ridge, and to the south an enormous hill, topped by one of the old Roman garrisons, the fortress Camboglanna, now called Camlan. The old word means crooked glen, and the place proved true to its name. Long and narrow, with a sharp-angled bend formed by the intrusion of the ridge, the desolate, rock-filled little valley appeared well suited to treachery.

The fortress, even in its ruined state, still commanded the region with its superior advantage. Medraut's forces could hold their positions with far less effort, while the Pendragon would be made to fight on two fronts from the beginning.

Cai observed the terrain and said, 'You cannot think of going down there to meet him unarmed.'

'I do not see that I have a choice,' replied Arthur.

'There is always a choice.' Bedwyr scanned the hillside and the fortress. 'They are waiting up there to ambush us — I can smell the treachery.'

'That I do not doubt, brother,' replied the Pendragon evenly.

Cai burst into laughter — a loud whoop of mirth. Bedwyr turned in his saddle to regard him. 'Fifty thousand Picti waiting for us — each with a thirst for our blood. You find this funny?'

'Na, na,' Cai replied, 'I was only thinking. Remember when Cerdic took Bors prisoner?'

Arthur smiled. 'Of course.'

'You crushed his hopes quick enough when you said: "Kill him if that is what you intend. . . " Cerdic never expected that.' Cai indicated the valley before them. 'Medraut would swallow his tongue if you told him that!'

He laughed again and Arthur laughed with him. I realized I had never heard the Pendragon laugh aloud before. 'That I would like to see!'

Bedwyr regarded them both with contempt. 'You cannot take this red-haired bull-roarer seriously, Artos. It is Gwenhwyvar's life we are talking about.'

'Never fear, brother,' Arthur replied lightly. 'I know my wife — she will appreciate the jest.' He cast his eyes to the surrounding hills. 'We will take the high ground — here and here — ' he said, indicating the twin hilltops above the valley. He had become the War Duke once more.

'Cador will lead the right flank, and Ban the left. . . ' The Pendragon turned and began walking back down the hill to where the war host waited hidden in the valley. Cai and Bedwyr joined him and I hurried after, as the three began making their battle plan.

Upon reaching the waiting army, the Pendragon's orders were conveyed to his battlechiefs, and the warriors began moving into position at once. Arthur donned his war shirt and high-crested helm; he strapped Caliburnus to his hip, and slung Prydwen, the white battle shield with the cross of Jesu, over his shoulder. He took up Rhon, his spear, stout veteran of many fierce and fiery combats.

Each of his great captains dressed themselves for battle as well: Bedwyr, Cai, Gwalcmai, Gwalchavad, Bors, Llenlleawg and Rhys. Champions all, helmed and armed for the fight. It made my heart soar to see them flaunt Medraut's challenge.

When the High King was ready he mounted to the saddle, and the others joined him. They rode together into the crooked glen — Camlan, valley of death.

I stood on the hilltop beside Cador and watched, my heart beating in my throat. I knew not what would happen — feared the worst, but prayed for the best.

At first, it appeared my prayers would be answered.

As the Pendragon and his men moved down into the glen, Medraut appeared from his hiding-place in the ruined fortress. With him came Keldrych and the hostages, together with at least thirty Picti warriors — naked and blue-stained with woad, their long hair stiffened with lime and pushed into white, spiked crests. They had also limed their shields and the heads of their spears.

Halfway to the stream coursing through the crooked valley, Medraut halted. He had seen that the Pendragon rode forth armed, in contempt of his command. Medraut whirled round, his arm went up and he pointed to the hostages.

But Keldrych stepped close, and after a quick consultation they advanced as before. No doubt, Keldrych had explained to the hot-headed Medraut that killing the captives removed any advantage they held over Arthur. However it was, the Pendragon's iron-hearted defiance had proven true again.

The two parties met a little apart, the stream between them. Arthur dismounted, but the others remained in the saddle. Arthur and Medraut advanced to meet one another alone. I would have given my right hand to hear what passed between them, but from my lofty vantage I saw its outcome right enough.

They talked for a time, whereupon Medraut returned to where the hostages waited, surrounded by the Picti warriors. Gwenhwyvar stepped out from among the others; the tyrant took her arm and pulled her with him back to where Arthur stood. Cai's hand went to his sword. Bedwyr put out a hand to steady him.

Upon reaching the stream where Arthur waited, Medraut seized the queen. He shouted something — I heard its echo, but could not make it out. He struck the queen cruelly on the face and she fell to her knees.

Arthur stood as one carved of stone. Not a muscle twitched.

Medraut stood over the queen and grabbed a handful of her dark hair. He jerked her head up, exposing her throat. Steel glinted in his hand. A knife!

Medraut shouted again. Arthur made an answer.

The knife flashed as it rose high in the air and struck swiftly down.

My heart stopped.

I opened my mouth to scream. Arthur's spear was in the air before the sound left my tongue.

Straight and true, like God's swift judgement, the spear streaked across the distance between them. I have never seen a spear thrown so swiftly, or with such force. It struck Medraut in the chest and pierced him through.

Arthur was on him in the same instant, driving the spear deeper. But Medraut, heedless of his wound, grasped the spear in his hands, and pulled himself up the shaft towards Arthur. He slashed wildly with the knife and caught Arthur a glancing blow.

Arthur dropped the spear and the traitor fell back writhing on the ground. The Pendragon drew Caliburnus and struck off Medraut's head.

I saw this clearly — and just as clearly saw Keldrych raise his spear and signal the attack. Instantly, the glen was alive with Picti! They came squirming out of the very ground it seemed — leaping up from behind rocks and bushes, and up out of shallow holes where they had hidden themselves.

'Ambush!' shouted Cador, and cursed, striking the ground with his sword.

Keldrych had hidden half of his warband in the glen and now they sprang to the attack — sixty in all, at least. The Pendragon was surrounded.

Gwenhwyvar ran to Medraut, plucked the spear from his chest and turned to stand beside her husband. They stood together to face the onslaught.

In the same instant, across the glen, a tremendous cry burst forth from fifty thousand throats as the hidden Picti rose up. Spears in hand, they stood on the hilltops, poised for attack, venting their hideous battle shriek. My skin pricked to hear it.

'Hurry!' I shouted at Cador. 'Sound the attack!'

Cador, his face grim and his jaw set, shook his head. 'I cannot. I am ordered to stand firm unless the Picti attack.'

'Look!' I flung my hand to the battle ground below. 'They attack!'

'I cannot!' Cador cried. 'I have my orders!'

'They will be killed!'

'God knows!' Cador screamed. 'But unless the war host commits to battle, I can do nothing!'

I understood then. However things went between Medraut and the High King, Arthur had made Ban and Cador vow not to interfere. So long as the main force of Picti held back, the British would not provoke them. If there was to be war, the Pendragon's host would not begin it. As the main force of the enemy had not yet joined battle, Cador could do nothing.

In a fever of horror and rage, I turned back to the crooked glen. Arthur had unslung Prydwen and Gwenhwyvar now held it. The Picti were upon them, but the warriors of the Round Table, the Flight of Dragons, charged into the fray.

The renowned Dragons met the Picti just as they reached Arthur. I stood amazed at how masterfully the Britons engaged the enemy, divided them, and began turning the attack aside.

Cai and Bedwyr, riding side by side, drove in towards

the centre of Keldrych's warband, their spears carrying the enemy before them. Gwalcmai and Gwalchavad struck in from the right, scattering the enemy as they thundered past. Bors, Llenlleawg and Rhys moved in from the left, hewing into the Picti, reapers at a bloody harvest.

In the churning mass of bodies, limbs and weapons, I saw the Pendragon's mighty sword Caliburnus rising and falling with relentless strokes, each blow a killing blow. The stream ran red; the water scarlet.

Any moment I expected to see the great Picti war host join Keldrych in the glen. But each time I stole a glance to the hills I saw them standing as before. What were they waiting for?

Sharp the battle clash that filled the air, a deafening din: shouting, screaming, shrieking, all dreadful to hear. The first frenzy passed and the combatants settled into the inexorable rhythm of the fight. Everywhere I looked, the enemy surged, struggling to join their ranks. Keldrych stood in the centre of the field, attempting to calm his frantic troops.

The Picti, however, dashed here and there to little purpose, striking out wildly and then running away. The Britons exploited this weakness and I marvelled at their dire efficiency. Fully half of Keldrych's warband lay dead on the ground before he succeeded in uniting his troops.

But once united, the rout slowed. The slaughter began to go the other way. The Picti advanced, stumbling over the bodies of their companions, forcing the Flight of Dragons back across the red-foaming stream.

God in heaven! Gwenhwyvar fell! Four big barbarians drove her down with spears. . . I could not look.

But the queen's fall did not go unnoticed. From out of nowhere faithful Llenlleawg appeared. He heaved his spear through the stomach of the largest Pict. The others fell back momentarily and the fearless Irishman threw himself from the saddle, snatched up Gwenhwyvar and lifted her to his horse.

The queen, the bloody shaft of a broken spear in her hand, threw the useless weapon aside and her champion pressed his sword into her hand. The enemy rushed in again. Llenlleawg turned to face them. He leapt onto the back of the foremost Pict, hacking with his knife and was carried down as the body fell. That was the last I saw of him.

Gwenhwyvar, saved from one death, now faced another. Three more Picti flew at her, even as she wheeled to Llenlleawg's aid. Two thrust at her with spears while the other jabbed at the legs of her mount. With one chop of her sword she neatly lopped the spearhead from the shaft, at the same time lifting the reins and bringing the horse's forelegs off the ground. One swift hoof caught the attacker just behind the ear. His skull cracked like an egg and he fell dead to the ground.

The two remaining Picti lunged desperately. The queen knocked their spears aside with the rim of Arthur's shield, and drew her sword across their throats in a single sweeping stroke. They dropped their spears and clutched at their bubbling wounds.

Gwenhwyvar rode over them as she flew to Arthur's side once more. Bors and Rhys had joined them and together the four pushed deeper into the tumult, where Gwalcmai and Gwalchavad had become surrounded. Those two fought like giants! But spears thrust and hands reached up and I saw Gwalcmai hauled from the saddle and overwhelmed.

Gwalchavad fought on alone. Could no one save him?

I scanned the battlefield and suddenly saw the Emrys leading the remaining hostages into position behind Keldrych. The Picti, so eager to attack Arthur, had left them on the hillside. They had swiftly succeeded in freeing themselves from their bonds and were now entering the fight at the enemy's back, using weapons retrieved from the dead on the ground.

Surely now, I thought, the Picti war host will attack. But they stayed on the hilltop, never moving forward so much as a step.

The hostages joined the battle with a shout. Keldrych turned to meet them, and this was his undoing. There were fewer than ten hostages and they were on foot. More dangerous by far were the Flight of Dragons still driving into the Picti ranks. But the barbarian warband was in disarray, lurching about in confusion, flailing uselessly with their weapons.

Perhaps he thought that subduing the Britons on foot

would hearten his remaining warband — numbering less than twenty now. Or perhaps he hoped to take the Emrys hostage once more and force Arthur to grant him quarter. I cannot say, but turning away from the Pendragon was a deadly mistake. Keldrych did not live to make another.

For the Pendragon saw the Pict chieftain turn and in the same instant struck. Caliburnus cut a terrible swath. No one could stand against that invincible blade in Arthur's hands. Too late Keldrych learned of Arthur's progress. He swung round, his sword sweeping in a deadly arc. Arthur deflected the blow with his shield and drove in with the point of his sword as Keldrych's arm swung wide.

The Picti chieftain gaped in astonishment as Caliburnus pierced him through the heart. Keldrych toppled backward to the ground; both heels drummed on the earth.

'The battle is won!' I cried. 'Did you see it? Arthur has won!'

The cheer died on my lips as Cador drew his sword and pointed to the hilltops across the glen: the great Picti war host was forming the battle line on the hilltop and the foremost ranks were already moving slowly down into Camlan to attack.

'Cymbrogi!' called Cador, drawing his sword. His call was relayed and I heard the ring of steel all down the line, as the Britons readied themselves to meet the foe. On the hilltop to our left, Ban's forces rose up in battle array, sunlight gleaming on their bright-burnished helms, spears clustered thick like a forest of young trees.

Fifteen thousand British stood to meet the foemen. Someone in one of the ranks somewhere began beating on his shield with the haft of his spear — the age-old challenge to combat. Another joined his sword brother, and another, and more and more, until the entire British war host was beating on their shields. The sound rolled across the narrow valley like thunder and echoed in the hills round about.

I felt the drumming pulse in my stomach and brain, and rise up through the soles of my feet. My heart beat wildly in my chest. I opened my mouth and combined my howl of jubilation with the din. It seemed to me that the sound poured up from my throat and spread out across the hills like the great and terrible voice of doom.

Though the Picti host greatly outnumbered the Pendragon's forces, we had six thousand horses with us. This, I think, and not our war cry — terrifying though it was — is what decided the Picti in the end. Nor do I fault them. Indeed, it would have been the height of folly lightly to disregard the horse-mounted warriors of the Pendragon's *ala*. It has been said that a warrior on horseback is worth ten men on foot, and there is wisdom in the saying.

Besides, it had been Medraut and Keldrych's rebellion, and both those traitors were dead. Any allegiance owed died with them. Even for the Picti, it took more than the lure of plunder to make death appealing.

So, as the battle of Camlan ground to its bloody end, the entire army of the rebel Picti simply turned and melted away, fading once more into the northern hills. When Arthur was at last able to raise his eyes from the slaughter before him, the enemy had vanished. The rebellion was over.

NINE

Rhys raised the victory call, and we answered it with the cry of triumph which shook the very hills. Clattering spear and sword on shield rims, and thrusting weapons in the air, we shouted for joy. Then all at once we were flying down the steep slope to join the Pendragon in the valley below. Men racing, horses galloping, the war host sweeping down to embrace the victors.

I shouted myself hoarse, running and running, relief and joy lifting me up. I cried my joy to the dazzling sky above, to the Great Giver, the All-Wise Redeemer who had not abandoned us to our enemies. I raced down the rocky slope, the tears flowing from my eyes.

All around me were glad Britons raising the victory cry. The rebellion had been crushed. Medraut was dead. The Picti had fled and would trouble us no more.

Breathless, I reached the glen and splashed across the stream where I immediately came upon a group of Britons gathered tight around someone lying on the ground. A horse stood by, the saddle empty. I wormed into the crowd, now grown suddenly silent, and heard a familiar voice complaining.

'It is nothing — a scratch! Let me up, God love you. I can stand. . . '

I pressed closer and glimpsed a shock of red hair. Cai.

The Boar of Battle was lying against a stone, his legs splayed out before him. He seemed to be struggling to rise, but no one would help him. I wondered at this and then saw the wicked gash in the battlechief's thigh.

'Rest you a moment,' one of the men said. 'The Emrys should attend you.'

'Then let me up!' Cai said. 'I will not have him find me

flat on my back. I can stand.'

'Your leg. . . '

'Tie it up with something. Quickly! I must go to Arthur.'

One of the men was already working to bind the wound with a bit of cloth. I backed from the throng and ran stumbling over the corpse-strewn battle ground to the Emrys, whom I found at last, binding a warrior's broken arm. 'Wise Emrys!' I called. 'Hurry! Cai is wounded! Please!'

He turned aside at once. 'Take me to him!'

I led him to the stream where the group waited with Cai. The Emrys hastened to the place; upon reaching it, the crowd parted to admit him and closed again. I pushed in after him and thrust myself to the front in time to see Myrddin stooping over Cai, whose face was now pale as a winter moon.

'I can stand, God love you!'

'Cai,' the Emrys soothed, 'it is bad.'

'It is but a scratch,' he protested, but his protest was weaker now. 'The heathen slashed wild. He barely touched me.' The great warrior made to push himself up, he grabbed at the Emrys, who held him. Blood pooled on the ground.

'Easy, my friend,' said the Emrys in a low, commanding tone. He tightened the strip of cloth around Cai's leg just above the knee.

'Are you telling me I am hurt?'

'The wound is deeper than you know, Cai.'

'Well, bind it then. I must go to Arthur.'

The Emrys glanced up quickly, saw me and said, 'Bring Arthur at once.' Distracted by the change in Cai's appearance, I hesitated, but only for an instant. 'Go!' Myrddin urged. 'For God's sake, hurry!'

I turned and ran without thinking, saw the gleam of the red-gold dragon standard, and made for it, dodging among the crowds of jubilant warriors thronging the glen. 'Please, my lord,' I gasped, pushing my way through the press around Arthur. 'Cai is wounded,' I blurted. 'The Emrys said to come at once.'

Arthur turned. 'Where is he?'

I pointed across the glen. 'Over there by the stream. The Emrys is with him.'

The king mounted the nearest horse, slapped the reins,

469

and raced over the field. By the time I returned to the place, Cai was unable to lift his head. He lay cradled in the crook of Arthur's arm, and the Pendragon of Britain smoothed his brow. 'I am too old for this, Bear.'

'Never say it, brother,' said Arthur in a choked voice.

'Na, do not take on so. We walked the land as kings, did we not?'

'That we did, Cai.'

'What man needs more?'

Tears glinted in the High King's eyes. 'Farewell, Caius ap Ectorius,' he said softly.

'Farewell,' whispered Cai. He raised a trembling hand and Arthur clasped it to him. 'God be good to you, Bear.' His voice was little more than a breath on the wind, and then that, too, was gone.

Arthur Pendragon knelt long beside the body of his friend, their hands clasped in a last pledge of loyalty. Cai stared upward into the face of his king, the colour already fading from his deep green eyes. A small, satisfied smile still lingered on his lips.

'Farewell, my brother,' Arthur murmured. 'May it go well with you on your journey hence.'

Then the High King laid the body gently down and stood. 'Bring a wagon. We will take him to the shrine. I will not see him buried in this place.'

The Pendragon ordered Cai's body to be sewn in deer-skins and placed on the wagon. As this was being done, Bedwyr appeared, ashen-faced, leading his horse. A body was slumped across the saddle. I took one look and sank to my knees on the ground.

Arthur met him and without a word gathered Gwalcmai's broken body from the saddle and lifted it down. The bloody stub of a broken arrow protruded from his chest just above the protecting mail shirt. His face was smeared with blood, as were his hands where he had tugged in vain at the arrow, succeeding only in snapping it off.

'Where is Gwalchavad?' asked Bedwyr gently. 'I will tell him.' Then he saw the wagon, and the men arranging the body there. 'Blessed Jesu! Cai!'

Bedwyr walked stiffly to the wagon and stood with eyes closed before it. Then he took Cai's cold hand in his and held it to his heart. After a long moment he turned and walked away.

I stayed to help with the wagon, and a little while later Bedwyr returned with Gwalchavad's body across his saddle. Gently, Bedwyr lifted the body of his sword brother and placed it beside that of Gwalcmai. Bitter were the deaths of these champions, whose lives the hateful Medraut had claimed as his blood-debt.

Arthur stood looking on in sorrow as we wrapped the corpses in deerskin. Myrddin returned, noticed the blood on the Pendragon's war shirt, and told him, 'Sit down, Arthur. You have been wounded. Let me see to it.'

'Peace,' replied Arthur, 'it is nothing. Care for the others.' He turned his gaze to the battle ground once more. 'Where is Gwenhwyvar?'

Arthur found the queen clinging to the body of her kinsman, Llenlleawg. She raised tearful eyes at her husband's approach. 'He is dead,' she said softly. 'Protecting me.'

Arthur knelt down beside her on the ground and put his arm around her shoulders. 'Cai is dead,' he told her. 'And Gwalcmai and Gwalchavad.' He regarded the queen's champion with sorrow. 'And Llenlleawg.'

At these doleful tidings Gwenhwyvar lowered her face into her hands and wept. After a time, she drew breath and composed herself, saying, 'As dark as this day is to me, it would be a thousand times darker still if you had been killed.' She paused, put a hand to Arthur's face and kissed him. 'I knew you would come for me, my soul.'

'I should not have gone away,' the High King said in a voice full of regret. 'My pride and vanity have caused the death of my most noble friends. I will bear their deaths as a weight upon my heart for ever.'

'You must not speak so,' Gwenhwyvar scolded lightly. 'Medraut is to blame and he will answer to God for his crimes.'

Arthur nodded. 'As I will answer for mine.'

'Where is Cai? And the others — where are they?'

'I have ordered a wagon to be made ready. They will be taken to the rotunda and buried there as is fitting,' he answered. 'I cannot bear to leave them here.'

'It is right,' agreed Gwenhwyvar, and then noticed

Arthur's wound for the first time. 'Artos — my love, you are bleeding!'

'But a scratch,' he said. 'Come, we must look after our dead.'

Of Medraut's hostages, only myself, the Emrys and Gwenhwyvar remained; the others died in the fight when they attacked Keldrych. These were brought to a place on the hillside below the fortress. A single massive grave was dug and the bodies of our sword brothers carefully placed in it. The Emrys prayed and sang holy psalms as we raised the *gorsedd*, the burial cairn, over them.

The corpses of the enemy we left to the wolves and ravens. Their bones would be scattered by the beasts, with never so much as a single rock to mark the place where they fell.

A little past midday, the Pendragon assembled the war host. Rhys sounded the march and we began making our slow way back to Caer Lial, moving westward along the Wall, each step heavy with grief and slow.

The bodies of the renowned battlechiefs were carried to Caer Lial where they were placed on torchlit biers in what remained of the hall of the Pendragon's palace. Much of Arthur's beloved city lay in ruins: the Picti did not restrain themselves in any way, but freely destroyed all they touched.

The next morning we departed for the Round Table. Out of respect for the holiness of the shrine, and the secret of its location, only the lords of Britain and Arthur's subject kings — the Nine Worthies — were allowed to attend the funeral at the shrine. The Emrys bade me accompany him, through no merit of my own. He required someone to serve him, and since I knew well the location of the rotunda it would save entrusting another with the secret.

The day dawned fair, the sun a dazzling white disk as we passed through the gates and out upon the road. The lords rode two by two; the four wagons followed, each one covered with a crimson cloak for a pall, and drawn by a black horse with a single raven's feather set in a golden war cap.

I did not continue with the funeral procession, but once through the gates travelled on ahead, driving one of the big supply wains. Upon reaching the shrine, I unloaded the tents and set about raising them, so that when the others arrived the camp would be ready. I went about my work quickly and with the sense that I was giving a good gift to my friends, that my labour was a devotion.

When I finished, the tents encircled the shrine and the camp was established. As I began unloading the provisions, the procession arrived. At once I fell to preparing food for them. Some of the lords helped me with this task, while the others saw to arranging the rotunda where the bodies of our beloved sword brothers would lie in state until their burial the next morning.

When the meal was ready, I carried a portion to the Pendragon's tent where the High King and Queen had withdrawn to rest. Then I sat down myself to eat. But as I glanced around I noticed that Myrddin was not among us, and remembered that I had not seen him emerge from the shrine. I put down my bowl and quickly walked up to the rotunda.

I entered the cool, dim interior. A small fire burned in the centre of the rotunda and a torch at the head of each bier. I saw that the bodies had been placed, each on its bier beneath the ledge bearing their names, and their weapons — sword, spear and shield — arranged on the ledge. The Emrys knelt beside Cai's cloak-covered body, unwrapping the leather bundle which contained the stone-carving tools.

'I have prepared food, Emrys,' I said.

'I am not hungry, Aneirin.' He picked up the scribe, turned to the ledge at hand and began with practised strokes to incise the death date below Cai's name. It broke my heart to see the iron bite into the stone, for once in stone it could never be otherwise.

'Shall I bring something to you here?'

'I will eat nothing until I have finished this work,' he answered. 'Leave me now.'

Throughout the rest of the day we held vigil in prayer. As the first twilight stars appeared in the sky, the Emrys emerged from the rotunda. Arthur and Gwenhwyvar joined us, and I saw that the death of his friends had visibly weakened the Pendragon. He appeared haggard and ill-rested, despite keeping to his tent.

Nor was I the only one to observe this, for I saw Bedwyr lead the Emrys aside to exchange a private word. And Bedwyr's eyes did not leave Arthur the whole time.

We ate a simple meal before the fire, and listened to the lark song in the darkling sky above us. Night stole over the camp and Arthur ordered the fire to be built up and called for a song. 'A song, Myrddin,' he said. 'Let us hear something of the valour of brave men — in memory of the friends we bury tomorrow.'

The Emrys consented and took up his harp to play an elegy for the departed. He sang *The Valiant of Britain*, which he had first sung following the victory at Mount Baedun, and to which he added the life-songs of Cāi, Gwalcmai, Gwalchavad and Llenlleawg. If there was ever a more beautiful or heartfelt lament, I never heard it.

That night I slept outside the Pendragon's tent on a red calfskin — I wanted to begin my duties before anyone else awakened. Accordingly, I rose before dawn and hurried down to the stream to drink and wash myself. Passing along the sea-face of the hill, I happened to glimpse a ship gliding out of the mist on the water, sailing towards the shore.

I stopped. Who could it be? Few among those left behind in Caer Lial knew the location of the Round Table.

I watched as the ship drew closer — yes, it was definitely making for the shrine — and then turned and ran back to camp. Not wishing to disturb the Pendragon, I ran to the Emrys' tent. 'Emrys,' I whispered at the tent flap. He awakened at once and came out to me.

'What is it, Aneirin?'

'A ship is approaching. Come, I will show you.'

Together we hurried back to the place where I had seen the ship — just in time to see six more emerge from the mist. The first ship was already drawing towards shore. 'It is the Pendragon's fleet,' I said, observing the red dragon painted on the sails.

'I was afraid of this,' remarked the Emrys.

'What are they doing?'

'They have come for the burial ceremony.'

It was true. Thinking only to honour their dead companions, the Cymbrogi, and the assembled war hosts of Britain, had embarked in the Pendragon's ships to discover the shrine. And discover it they did. The Emrys and I watched as ship after ship came into the bay and the warriors waded to shore.

They came dressed as for battle, each with helm burnished and shield freshly painted. Their swords were newly honed, and their spearheads gleamed. They gathered on the beach and then moved silently up the hill towards us.

'What shall we do, Wise Emrys?'

'Nothing,' he replied. 'There is nothing to be done. These men have risked the Pendragon's wrath to come here. They will not be turned away, nor should they be.'

'But the shrine. . . '

'Well,' observed Myrddin Emrys, 'the Round Table will no more remain secret. After this day, the world will know of it. Easier to hold back the tide with one your brooms, Aneirin, than to call back a word once it has been spoken.'

As they assembled on the shore, the Emrys sent me to fetch the Pendragon. I did so and returned with Arthur, Gwenhwyvar and Bedwyr to see ten thousand warriors — all the Cymbrogi, of course, and a good few others had come to observe the funeral rites of their battlechiefs.

'God love them,' said Arthur, gazing out upon the strand, now populated with warriors drawn up in ranks and divisions, and arrayed in bright battle dress. 'Their disobedience is greater tribute than we can boast. Let them join us.'

'Very well,' replied Bedwyr, and started down the hill track to the shore.

'How did they find this place?' wondered Gwenhwyvar.

'Tegyr, I suppose,' said Myrddin, and I remembered the steward.

'Or Barinthus,' offered Arthur.

'Your pilot? He would never do such a thing,' the queen insisted. She looked upon the ordered ranks of warriors and smiled. 'I hope that I receive such homage when I go to my grave.'

'For me,' the Pendragon said, 'let there be a perpetual choir established in a church built over my tomb. I will have need of such prayers, I think.'

At these words the Emrys looked round and observed the High King closely. 'Are you ill, Arthur?'

'I am tired this morning,' he admitted. 'The battle has left its mark. It will pass.'

'Let me tend your wound.'

'A scratch,' said Arthur, making a dismissive gesture with his hands. 'There is nothing to see.'

But the Wise Emrys was not to be put off. 'Then I will see that as well. Open your mantle and have done with it.'

The Pendragon hesitated, but no man alive is able to resist the Emrys for long. At last Arthur gave in and drew back his cloak and pulled aside his mantle. The wound was, truly, nothing more than a long, ragged scratch, running around the base of the throat where Medraut had caught him with a wild slash of the knife.

But that scratch had festered and was now an angry red welt, visibly raised and, I imagine, very painful. The edges of the wound were tinged with green and a watery pus oozed from several places where movement had opened the gash afresh.

Gwenhwyvar gasped. 'No wonder you cried out when I touched you — it is a nasty thing.'

'It is slow healing,' Arthur allowed, pulling his cloak over his shoulder once more. 'But I have had worse.'

The Emrys shook his head. 'We will go back to camp and I will bind it properly.'

'The burial rite,' said Arthur, lifting his hand to the warriors gathered on the shore. 'We must not keep the Cymbrogi waiting.'

'After the rites then,' Myrddin told him flatly. 'I have neglected it too long already.'

Four graves were dug on the side of the hill facing west. They were dug deep and lined with white stone which the Cymbrogi gathered from the nearby hills. When the graves were ready and everyone had performed homage in the shrine, the Nine Worthies, led by the Emrys, ascended the hill and entered the tabled rotunda. After a few moments they emerged with the body of Cai, which they proceeded to carry on its bier to the grave site.

But the Cymbrogi saw this and, rushing to them, pressed close, halting the bier. Then, forming a long double line — somewhat like the battle line, the Companions passed the bier one to another, hand to hand, down the hill from the shrine to the grave. The bodies of Gwalcmai, Gwalchavad and Llenlleawg were cared for in this way as well, so that they were borne to the graves by their friends and gently laid to rest on the hillside.

Arthur and Gwenhwyvar stood at the foot of the graves and, as each body was lowered in, the queen laid a small stone cross upon the chest. The cross was of smooth, black stone on which was inscribed the dead man's name and lifeday in Latin. Beside each cross, Arthur placed a fine gold cup — from which to drink one another's health in the palace of the King of Kings in Heaven, he said.

When each body was thus laid down, the Emrys raised the lament which we all joined until the hills and valleys round about rang with the dirge-song, growing and growing to the very last when it was cut off short. This symbolized the growth through life and the sudden sharp death of those we mourned.

After the lament, the Emrys sang the psalm and prayed Jesu, Son of the Living God, to welcome the souls of the brave into his fair company. After this we each took up stones and laid them on the graves, raising the *gorsedd* over them. All this was done under Arthur's gaze and, when at last the burial cairns were complete, the Pendragon turned to his Wise Emrys and said, 'Emrys and Wledig, I would hear again the prayer which you have so often sung.'

Myrddin assented, raising his hands in the way of the bards of elder days when they declaimed before their kings. But instead of a eulogy, he sang this prayer:

'Great Light, Mover of all that is moving and at rest, be my Journey and my far Destination, be my Want and my Fulfilling, be my Sowing and my Reaping, be my glad Song and my stark Silence. Be my Sword and my strong Shield, be my Lantern and my dark Night, be my everlasting Strength and my piteous Weakness. Be my Greeting and my parting Prayer, be my bright Vision and my Blindness, be my Joy and my sharp Grief, be my sad Death and my sure Resurrection!'

'So be it!' we all cried. So be it!

TEN

That night we built the fires high and lifted our voices in songs and stories of remembrance. Although no wine or mead or even ale was given out in drink, the Cymbrogi gathered in amiable throngs around the fires and filled the star-dazzled night with a richness of laughter. If the spirits of the dead know anything of the world they leave behind, I believe they would have been pleased to see how well they were loved and honoured by their friends. I went to my bed earnestly wishing that the day of my own death would be so revered.

As before, I slept that night under the stars, wrapped in a red calfskin on the ground before the Pendragon's tent. I did not rest well; something kept sleep from me. During the night I heard a stirring and woke to see the Emrys standing at the embers of the nearest fire, scowling into the dying light. I rose and went to him. 'You are troubled, Wise Emrys. What is the matter?'

He regarded me for a long moment, his face in deep shadow. I saw his eyes glinting sharp in the fireglow, as if weighing out the value of his words. At last he said, 'Dare I trust you, Aneirin?'

'Please, Emrys, if I have ever shown myself false in any way, strike me down at once.'

'Well said,' the Emrys replied, turning his eyes back to the glowing embers. 'You have earned the trust I will place in you — though perhaps you will soon wish otherwise.'

'If the burden be lightened for sharing, I will bear it, Lord.'

The Emrys drew a deep breath. 'I like not the look of Arthur's wound. It should be healing, but instead it is getting worse. I fear poison.'

The Picti sometimes smeared poison on their blades before going into battle. That would appeal to Medraut, of course.

'What is to be done, Emrys?'

Just then the flap of the Pendragon's tent opened and Gwenhwyvar stepped forth. She came quickly to stand beside the Emrys. Standing there, wrapped in her bold cloak, eyes bright, dark hair glinting, features soft in the deep fireglow, I thought that I would never see another woman so proud, so beautiful. Or so worried.

'He is fevered,' she said. 'He sleeps, but it is not a healing sleep. Myrddin, I am afraid. You must do something.'

The Emrys frowned. 'I will open the wound and bind it with herbs to draw out the poison.'

'And then?'

'And then we shall see.'

Gwenhwyvar returned to the tent, and the Emrys and I wrapped our cloaks around us and walked down to the stream in the valley. By the moon's bright light we gathered certain leaves and stems of plants he knew to have healing properties. Then we made our way along the stream to the shore, where the receding tide had left fresh sea-plants on the strand. Some of these we harvested as well, and then returned to the camp where the Emrys built up the fire once more.

I fetched clean water in a good iron pot and put it on the fire. When the water boiled, the Emrys carefully added some of the leaves we had obtained and in this way brewed a healing draught. We tended the cauldron through the night and, at dawn's first light, poured the healing liquid into a bowl and carried it to the Pendragon's tent.

I confess I was shaken by the sight that met my eyes. So changed was the High King that I would not have recognized him: skin grey and damp, hair matted on his head, lips cracked and dry, the cords of his neck straining as he shivered and moaned. . . Even by the uncertain light of the smouldering rushlamps, I would have sworn he was not the man I knew.

Gwenhwyvar sat beside her husband, clasping his hand in hers. She stirred as we entered and I saw that her eyes were red from weeping. But I saw no tears.

'Arthur,' the Emrys said softly, kneeling beside the

bedplace. 'Hear me, Arthur, I have brought you a draught.'

At these words the Pendragon opened his eyes. Those eyes! Hard and bright with fever, piercing, pain-filled. I could not endure the sight and had to look away.

The Emrys bent over Arthur and raised him up. He held the bowl to the cracked lips and gave the Pendragon to drink. Glory of glories, the potent elixir's effect was remarkable and immediate. Colour returned to the High King's face, the shivering stopped, and he relaxed as strength returned.

'Myrddin,' he said, seeing him for the first time. 'I had a dream.'

'I do not wonder,' Myrddin replied. 'You are sick, Arthur. Your wound is poisoned; it must be opened at once and the poison drained.'

'It was a strange and marvellous dream.'

'Tell it to me, Arthur, while I tend your wound.' So saying, the Emrys brought out his knife, which had been honed with sandstone and sea-water. He loosened the Pendragon's mantle and drew it away from the wound.

Bitter bile rose in my mouth. The gash was swollen and purple, the edges black and suppurating. It seemed a hideous serpent winding around the High King's neck, venomous and deadly. 'Take the bowl, Aneirin,' the Emrys said sternly.

But, as I reached out my hand to take the empty bowl, Gwenhwyvar interceded gently, 'Allow me. I will hold the bowl.'

'Very well then,' replied the Emrys. 'Aneirin, bring good new rushes for the lamp. I must see what I am doing.'

I ran to the supply wain and fetched new rushes for the lamp. Bedwyr appeared at the tent, just as I returned. 'How is he?' His voice was low and secretive.

'Not well,' I replied. 'The Emrys is about to open the wound to draw off the poison.'

Bedwyr nodded and followed me into the tent. Once the new lamp was lit and burning brightly, the Emrys set to work. With small, quick strokes of the knife Myrddin laid open the festering wound. Blood and pus spurted from the swollen flesh, and trickled into the bowl.

Arthur neither winced nor cried out, enduring the agony in silence. Gwenhwyvar bit her lip and her brow beaded sweat, but she held the bowl firmly between steady hands. While Myrddin gently kneaded the long, jagged incision, Bedwyr knelt opposite the Emrys holding Arthur's right shoulder up to allow the vile ooze drain more freely. I held the rushlamp at the Pendragon's head, so that the Emry's would have the light he required. The stench of the seeping matter rising up from the bowl sickened me.

'There,' said the Emrys at last. 'You can take the bowl away.' Gwenhwyvar removed the bowl and set it aside. Myrddin took up the remaining leaves we had gathered and began applying them, one by one, along the line of the cut. 'These will draw out the poison,' he explained. 'I will replace them in a little while. We will leave the wound uncovered until then.'

'It feels better,' Arthur said. 'I am hungry.'

Bedwyr's relief spread over his face in a grin. 'You are always hungry, Bear. It is your one unfailing virtue.'

Gwenhwyvar placed a hand lightly on Arthur's forehead and stroked his brow — a gesture of such delicacy and intimacy that it filled me with longing. 'I will bring you food and wine.'

'A little bread, but no meat,' replied the Emrys. 'And mead — it will help him sleep.'

'I will bring it,' I said, and hurried away at once.

The sun was full on the horizon, tinting the low grey clouds with the imperial purple. A cool breeze blew out of the east, and the camp had begun to stir. On the hillside across the stream, where the Cymbrogi slept, the camp fires had been revived and the warriors were roused to their warmth. As I passed the tents of the kings Cador stepped out, saw me, and called me to him. 'I give you good day, Aneirin,' he said. 'Is the Pendragon well?'

His question caught me unawares. I could not guess how much he knew, and knew not how much to say. 'He spent an uneasy night, lord.' I answered. Cador nodded. 'I am bringing him food.'

'Hurry on, then. I will not delay you.' He yawned and returned to his tent.

From the provisions in the supply wain, I took two good

loaves and filled a small jar from the mead skin. These I tucked in my cloak and hurried back to the Pendragon's tent.

Gwenhwyvar and the Emrys stood together outside the tent talking in low tones. They stopped at my approach, and the queen received the food and went back to Arthur's side. 'Emrys,' I said, 'Cador asked after the Pendragon — '

'What did you tell him?'

'I did not know what to tell him,' I admitted. 'I said only that the Pendragon spent an uneasy night. I thought it best not to say much.' The Emrys pursed his lips. 'Did I do right?'

'Yes,' he said finally. 'But say no more to anyone who asks — at least until we see how this will go.'

I hovered near the Pendragon's tent through the day. The kings and Cymbrogi sported in the valley during the long, sun-filled day. Once, I wandered half-way down the hillside for a better view. I sat on a rock and watched their lively contests.

The sound of their laughter and cheering drifted up the hillside to the Pendragon, who awakened and called out. I hurried back to the tent to see if I was needed. No one was about, so I opened the tent flap and peered in.

The Pendragon stood in the centre of the tent, clutching the tent pole. 'Forgive me, Pendragon,' I said, 'I did not mean to intrude.'

He released the tent pole at once. 'Ah, Aneirin,' he said, his voice husky and low. 'I am thirsty.'

'I will bring the Emrys.'

'Let him rest. Bedwyr, Gwenhwyvar — let them rest. Just bring water.'

'Yes, lord,' I said, and ducked out at once. A water jar sat beside the entrance, so I grabbed it and ran down to the stream to fill it with fresh water. I plunged the mouth of the jar into the swift-running stream, then turned and raced back up the hill.

Arthur stood outside the tent, shielding his eyes against the bright sunlight as he gazed around the camp. I brought the jar and gave it to him. He lifted it to his lips and drank at once, without waiting for a cup. 'Thank you, Aneirin,' he said, 'I am much refreshed.' He straightened his cloak over his shoulder and, taking up his spear, Rhon, which was standing in the ground before the tent, he began to walk down the hill towards the valley where the Cymbrogi sported.

I followed, and fell in beside him. We came to the stream and started across it. One of the warriors at the edge of the field saw our approach and called out. 'The Pendragon!' he cried. 'The Pendragon comes! Hail, Pendragon!'

Immediately, a throng gathered and pressed close around him. 'We heard you were wounded, Pendragon!' someone shouted, and a dozen other voices chorused their concern in voices sharp with apprehension.

'Do I look wounded?' the High King asked. 'A touch of fever troubled my sleep. I am better now.'

Arthur began to move among his beloved Cymbrogi then, speaking to them, calling them by name, asking after their wives and families. This one he knew had a new son, that one had just married a woman from the south, another trained hounds, still others were sons of former soldiers — Arthur knew them all. Remarkable, I thought, that he should know the small concerns of each man. But this he appeared to do. And I heard in their replies to Arthur, and in the banter that accompanied their talk, enormous relief. Clearly, they had been worried for their king and were now reassured.

The Pendragon moved off in the company of his men, and soon the sport began once more. I watched for a time, then returned to my duties. I gathered firewood and refilled all the water jars, then took a horse from the picket and rode to a nearby hilltop to cut fresh heather for the Pendragon's bedplace. As the sun touched the western hills, I returned to camp with my bundle of heather.

The Emrys was waiting for me outside the Pendragon's tent. He had the pouch of stone-carving tools in his hand, for he had been at work in the Round Table. 'Where is he?'

I pointed to the valley. 'With the Cymbrogi. He awoke and went down to them.'

The Emrys turned, walked across the camp, and started down to the valley. Suddenly alarmed, I threw myself from the saddle and hastened after him.

Sunlight the colour of the golden honey mead filled the valley. The sky shone like molten brass, the field like emerald. We came upon Arthur sitting on stone as on a throne, his spear across his lap, eyes half-closed, a smile upon his lips. Gwenhwyvar stood beside him, her hand on his right shoulder, watching the contest before them: two riders speeding at full gallop to snatch an arm-ring from the grass with the point of a spear. She turned her head towards us and smiled, but her smile was tight and unnatural.

'Arthur,' said the Emrys softly.

The Pendragon opened his eyes and turned to greet his Wise Counsellor. 'It is a fine day, is it not?'

'Yes. How do you feel?'

'I am well.'

'When the sun sets it will grow cold. We should return to camp now.'

'But the sun is not gone yet,' said Arthur. 'Sit with me a little while.'

'Gladly,' replied the Emrys, kneeling next to him.

The three of them watched the riders for some small time. The sun dipped lower and the shadows crept long. The sky paled; the brilliant colours faded. Sea-birds circled overhead, keening their mournful call to the dying day. I heard the waves tumbling on the nearby shore. The light in the valley dimmed.

The Emrys stood and touched Arthur on the arm. The Pendragon stirred — he had fallen asleep. However, he stood at Myrddin's touch, straightened himself, and called the victors of the contest to him. With good words he praised their prowess, while Gwenhwyvar presented them gifts of gemstones. When this custom had been served, Arthur bade farewell to his men and returned to camp.

At supper, we ate roast venison which some of the warriors had stalked in the nearby wood earlier in the day, and drank ale from the stocks aboard the ships. The night came on cold and damp, as the Emrys said it would, so the fires were banked high. Gwenhwyvar and Bedwyr tried on several occasions to persuade Arthur to withdraw to his tent to rest, but the Pendragon would not.

Instead, he insisted that he should remain with his lords and battlechiefs and called for a song. Myrddin Emrys at first resisted the summons, but at length consented and ordered his harp to be brought to him. 'Which of the tales of Britain would you hear, Pendragon?'

Arthur's brow wrinkled in thought as he paused, then answered, 'It is not of Britain that I would hear tonight, but of the Otherworld. A cold night, with a fresh wind blowing — on storm-tossed nights like this such tales should be told.'

'Very well,' agreed Myrddin Wledig, 'hear then, if you will, the song of Bladydd, the Blemished King.'

I wondered at this choice, for it is an obscure tale and very strange — concerning a prince with a voracious hunger for wisdom, who falls foul of an Otherworld king and is blighted and eventually destroyed by the very knowledge he sought. But the company of lords and battlechiefs loved this tale and, indeed, it was beautifully sung by the Exalted Emrys, last of the True Bards of the Island of the Mighty.

The tale grew long in its telling and when it was over Arthur bade his companions sleep well and with Gwenhwyvar on his arm, went to his tent. I stretched myself on the red calfskin next to the fire, wrapped my cloak tightly around me, and went to sleep.

In the night I heard urgent voices. I arose and saw torchlight flickering inside the Pendragon's tent. Something was wrong. My stomach tightened in alarm.

The camp was dark and no one else was about. I crept to the tent and peered inside.

Bedwyr and the Emrys were with him. Gwenhwyvar stood a little apart, her hands at her side, twisting her silken mantle in tight fists. Blood smeared her face and the front of her mantle.

'Lie still, Bear,' Bedwyr was saying. 'Let the Emrys care for you.'

'Be easy, brother,' said Arthur in a rasping voice. 'I am going to get up now. I cannot let the Cymbrogi see me here like this.'

The Emrys toiled at the wound; his hands were dripping with Arthur's blood.

'The Cymbrogi have seen you lie about before,' Bedwyr told him. 'They are well used to the sight. Be quiet, now.'

'I will not! Help me stand.' He snatched at Bedwyr's cloak

and made to pull himself up. The covering slipped from around his neck. I saw the wound and gasped.

It was a ghastly green-grey, with violet thread-like fingers stretching across the Pendragon's shoulder. The flesh along the original cut was withered, black and rotting. Arthur's neck was red and inflamed from his throat to his armpit. The wound had apparently burst in the night — the pain must have been unbearable! — and the Emrys had been called to stop the bleeding.

'I am finished,' said Myrddin at last. 'I can do nothing more here.' Bedwyr and the Emrys put their arms around Arthur's wide shoulders and raised him up.

'We have made an end of Medraut at last,' Arthur said carelessly. 'It will be a cold day in hell before anyone dares attack the Emperor of Britain again. Where is Gwenhwyvar?'

'She waits over there a little,' Myrddin Emrys told him.

'I hope she is not hurt. . . '

'No, she is well. Arthur,' said the Emrys, speaking in low, urgent tones, 'your wound is swollen and has broken open. I am at the end of my skill, Arthur — do you understand? I can do nothing more for you, but I know where help can be found.'

Bedwyr glanced up and saw me. He motioned me closer and gripped my shoulder hard. 'Quickly!' he said in a voice tight with dread. 'Go find Barinthus and tell him to make ready a boat.' I stepped to the tent flap and Bedwyr added, 'Aneirin — take care. No one else must know.'

Alarm and dread warring in me, I dashed away to rouse Arthur's pilot and charge him with this secret task. Barinthus was never difficult to find, for he always stayed near the ships. I hastened down the hill track, a stiff wind whipping my cloak against my legs. Rags of cloud streamed across the moon; the white-crested wavetops glinted darkly in the shifting and uncertain light.

I made directly for the lone camp fire, flickering on the shore before the dark hump of a small skin-covered tent just above the high tide mark. 'Barinthus!' I hissed amid the sough and moan of wind and waves.

He stirred and thrust his head out through the hide-covered opening, and I charged him with Bedwyr's command. He ducked back into his shelter for his lamp, and emerged wearing his bearskin. He marched into the tideflow to where his coracle was moored.

I hurried back across the beach and saw the glimmer of a guttering torch on the hill-track above me. Bedwyr and Myrddin, with Arthur sagging between them, met me as I reached the foot of the hill. Gwenhwyvar, holding a torch in one hand, and the High King's sword in the other, went before them.

'The boat is being readied,' I told Bedwyr.

'Was anyone with Barinthus?'

'He was alone. No one else knows.'

'Good.' The Emrys gazed out onto the sea. Though the wind still blew and the sea ran strong, the waves were not driven overmuch. 'It will be a rough voyage, but swift. All the better. We have a little time yet.'

'I am going to sit you down now, Arthur.' Bedwyr shifted the High King's weight.

'No — I will stand. Please, Bedwyr. Only a little longer.'

'Very well.'

'Bedwyr, my brother. . . '

'What is it, Bear?'

'Look to Gwenhwyvar. See that she is cared for.'

Bedwyr swallowed hard. 'Do that yourself, Bear.'

'If anything happens to me.'

'Very well. . . if you wish it,' Bedwyr told him, pulling the red cloak more closely around Arthur's shoulders.

The Pendragon could scarcely lift his head. His speech had grown soft, almost a whisper. 'Myrddin,' he said softly, 'I am sorry I could not be the king you wanted me to be — the Summer King.'

'You were the king God wanted. Nothing else matters.'

'I did all you ever asked of me, did I not, my father?'

'No man could have done more.'

'It was enough, was it not?'

'Arthur, my soul, it *was* enough,' Myrddin said softly. 'Rest you now.'

The queen stepped close and handed me the torch. She embraced her husband and held him. 'Rest your head on my shoulder,' she said, and placed her cheek against his. They stood like this for a long moment and Gwenhwyvar spoke soothing words into his ear. I did not hear what she said.

After a moment we heard a whistle. Bedwyr turned. 'It is Barinthus. The boat is ready.'

I walked ahead, holding the torch high to light the way across the stone-strewn beach to the water's edge, where Barinthus had brought the boat. He had chosen a small, stout vessel with a single mast and a heavy rudder. There was a tented covering in the centre of the craft where Arthur could rest.

I waded into the water and stood beside the boat, with the torch lifted high. The wave-chop slapped the boat and rocked it from side to side; I gripped the rail with my free hand to help steady it. Bedwyr and Myrddin made to carry Arthur to the boat, but he refused. The Pendragon of Britain strode into the water in his own strength and boarded the pitching craft.

While Barinthus busied himself with the sail, the queen fussed over Arthur, to make him comfortable beneath the canopy. At last the Emrys said, 'We must go. It will be dawn soon, and we must be well away before we are seen.'

'Let me go with you,' Gwenhwyvar pleaded.

'You are needed here, Gwenhwyvar. You and Bedwyr must buy Arthur time to heal,' Myrddin explained. 'I tell you the truth, I fear for the world if knowledge of Arthur's weakness reaches Britain's enemies. No one must know,' the Emrys said earnestly. 'See you keep the secret well.

'Tomorrow, send the lords back to their realms and the Cymbrogi back to Caer Lial. I will return here in three days and bring Arthur with me, or take you to be with him.'

Gwenhwyvar clutched at Arthur's hand. 'Have no fear,' Arthur whispered. 'I go to Avallon for my healing. I will return when I am strong once more. Wait for me but a little.'

Gwenhwyvar nodded and said no more. She knelt and kissed Arthur with a lingering kiss. 'Farewell, my soul,' she whispered, and pressed the sword Caliburnus into her husband's hand.

'Bedwyr — he should have it,' Arthur protested weakly.

'Keep it,' Bedwyr replied, 'you will need it when you return.'

Gwenhwyvar kissed Arthur and laid her head against his chest. She whispered something, and he smiled — I do not know what she said. She climbed from the boat and watched as Bedwyr and I pushed it into deeper water. Once it was free of the sand, the pilot turned the bow towards the open sea and raised the sail.

The Emrys stood and called to us, 'Have no fear! Arthur will return. Keep faith, my friends. The final danger has not come. Watch for us!'

We three stood on the strand and watched the boat draw away. We watched until the small, bright point of light that was Barinthus' lamp disappeared into the cloud-wracked darkness of the sea and night. Grief, sharp as a spear-thrust, pierced my heart. For, in the mournful sigh of wind and wave, I heard the lament for the lost.

A sea-bird disturbed from his night's rest took wing above us and raised a solitary keen. Seeking some word of consolation, I said, 'If there is healing for him anywhere in this worlds-realm, he will find it in Avallon.'

Gwenhwyvar, dark eyes gleaming with unshed tears, pulled her cloak high around her shoulders, then turned away, straightened her back, and began ascending the hill track. Bedwyr stood long, gazing into the void, the restless wave-wash around his feet. I stood with him, my heart near to breaking. At last he reached out to me, took the torch from my hand, and with a mighty heave, threw it into the sea. I watched its flaming arc plunge like a star falling earthward and heard it hiss as it struck the sea and died.

ELEVEN

'Myrddin should have returned before now. Something is wrong!' Bedwyr threw down his bowl and stood up.

'He said to wait. What else can we do?' Gwenhwyvar asked, her voice raw with torment.

'He said he would come back in three days. Well, the third day has passed and he has not returned!'

Indeed, since dawn, when I arose and took up my place of vigil, we had watched and waited, gazing out over the western sea whence the Emrys' boat would come. I stood my watch all day, relieved by Bedwyr from time to time, or Gwenhwyvar, or sometimes both at once. We talked of this and that, small things, matters of no consequence. The one thing we did not mention was the boat, though our thoughts were full of nothing else.

The day had faded into a dull and sullen sunset. Still none of us saw so much as a thread of sail or a sliver of mast. But one day before, the bay had been alive with ships. The queen had let it be known that the Pendragon and his Wise Counsellor were communing together and did not wish to be disturbed. She bade the lords and kings of Britain return each one to his own realm and await the High King's pleasure. The Cymbrogi she ordered back to Caer Lial.

Fergus and Ban grew anxious and approached the queen in private. Yet, through all her assurances Gwenhwyvar protected the secret and gave nothing away, though her heart was breaking all the while.

Bors, Cador and Rhys had been the last to leave. They insisted that they would wait and ride to the palace with the king, but Gwenhwyvar urged them to hasten back and see to readying the Pendragon's palace for his return — much had been ruined by the Picti. In the end, they reluctantly agreed and rode away, so that by evening of the second day we three were alone on Round Table hill.

Then we had waited and watched, as the sun climbed to its full height and started its long slow slide to the west. But the sea remained empty; no boat appeared. Nor did we see any sign of it at dusk, when Bedwyr set a beacon fire on the beach below the hill.

Now we sat in silence before the Pendragon's tent. The red-gold dragon standard rippled in the evening breeze. As if in answer to Bedwyr's outburst, a flight of gulls wheeling overhead began screaming. Their complaint echoed up from the valley below. Bedwyr gazed at the bowl he had thrown down and kicked it aside. 'We should not have let him go,' he muttered, his voice full of reproach and pain.

'Then we will go to him,' Gwenhwyvar said softly. She turned to me, and placed her hand on my arm. 'You have been to the island, Aneirin.'

'Several times, yes. As you have been, my lady.'

'You will pilot,' declared Bedwyr.

'But we have no boat!' I pointed out.

'Arthur the Shipbuilder is our lord,' sniffed Bedwyr, 'and this fellow says we have no boat. I will get one.'

'Then I will be your pilot — may God go with us,' I answered.

Bedwyr saddled one of the horses and left at once. Gwenhwyvar and I spent a fretful dusk before the fire, neither one of us speaking. She withdrew to her tent when the moon rose and I spread my red calfskin before the entrance and lay down with a spear next to me — no fire to warm or cheer me, no roof above me but the stars of heaven, bright with holy fire.

I lay down but I did not sleep. All night long I twisted and turned on my calfskin, watching the long, slow progression of the moon across the sky and praying to Jesu to protect us — which he did. At last, just before dawn, I slipped into a strange sleep: deep, yet alert. I knew myself asleep, yet I heard the sea moan on the shore below the hill and the wind sigh through the grass around me.

It was the time between times, neither day nor night, darkness nor light, when the gates of this world and the next

491

stand open. The restless wash of the sea below the cliffs sounded like the troubled murmurings of distant crowds in my ears. The wind-sigh became the whisper of Otherworld beings bidding me rise and follow.

I lay in that Otherworldly place and dreamed a dream.

In my dream I awoke and opened my eyes and I saw green Avallon, Isle of Apples, fairest island that is in this world, next to the Island of the Mighty. I heard the strange, enchanting music of Rhiannon's birds, and I smelled the sweet fragrance of apple blossoms. On my lips I tasted the warmth of honey mead, and I arose.

I walked along the way-worn path from the sea cliff to the Fisher King's palace. Where the palace should have been I saw nothing but a cross of Jesu wrought of stone and lying on the ground — and, beside it, a leather pouch containing Myrddin's stone-carving tools. I bent down to trace the words inscribed upon it, but a cloud passed over the sun and the light grew dim, and I could not read what had been written there.

I looked to the east and saw stars glimmering in the sky, though still the sun shone in the west. Storm clouds gathered above me. Lightning flashed, and thunder quaked. The whole earth began to tremble with the sound.

Across the green land the thunder became a roar, and the tremble the footfall of a terrible beast. I turned to the east, whence came the storm, and saw a great golden lion bounding towards me over the weald. The lion seized me, and snatched me up in its jaws. And then it began to run. The enormous beast carried me over the island to the sea, where it plunged into the white-foamed waves and began to swim.

The waves surged around me and the lion changed into a fish that bore me on its back to a rock in the middle of the sea, and there it left me. The storm which had pursued me now broke with fury upon the rock. The gale screamed and raised the sea; water crashed and waves beat upon me, but I gripped the rock with all my strength, lest I be torn away to drown in the whelming flood.

I clung to the rock, cold and wet, and sick with sorrow — for all my good companions had gone from me and my death drew near. I trembled and began to shake, so that

I thought my very bones would break. My body began to burn as with the flames of fire.

A shining mist came down over my rock, and out of the mist I heard a voice that called me by name. 'Aneirin,' the voice commanded, 'leave off your trembling, neither be afraid. I have seen your miserable plight and will help you. Stand up! I will show you what is to be done.'

I stood on my rock and it became a mountain, strong and high. And though the storm-flood raged, the angry water could not overwhelm it. An ancient oak grew atop the mountain. I took one of its branches and struck the earth, and out from among the roots a spring appeared and began flowing down the mountainside.

The spring poured forth, cold and clean. And wherever the water flowed forests and meadows appeared to clothe the barren slopes, giving food and shelter to the beasts of the field and to the eagles that soared in the heights.

The old oak fell down, but the spring flowed on and became a stream, and the stream a mighty river. I picked up my branch and began to walk. Grass grew up in the places where my feet touched the earth, so that my tread was easy and the path clear. I came eventually to a green meadow — the same meadow that I had known before. And I saw that the mountain was in Avallon.

The stone cross was there, and the leather pouch of tools. But now I saw what I did not see before. Inscribed on the cross was a name: ARTORIVS REX QVONDAM REXQVE FVRTVRVS.

Arthur, king once and king to be. . . Though well begun, the carving was unfinished.

The voice which had spoken to me from the cloud hailed me again. 'Arise, Gildas. Finish that which has been set before you.'

'My name is Aneirin,' I replied. 'And I know nothing of stonecraft.'

The voice answered me, saying, 'Aneirin you were, Gildas you shall be, True Bard to the High King of Heaven.'

The dream ended and I awoke at once. It was dawn, the time between times had given way to daylight and I was back in the world of men. I rose and hurried to look out upon the sea. And behold! As the sun rose above the eastern hills I saw a ship coming towards us. I ran and told the queen and we went down to the shore to await its arrival.

'He must have ridden through the night,' I remarked, as the ship put out a coracle to meet us. The queen nodded, but said nothing. Her eyes were red-rimmed from lack of sleep or weeping, I know not which.

Closer, I saw that it was Bedwyr come to fetch us. 'I am sorry,' said Bedwyr as he helped the queen into the small boat, 'I would have returned sooner, but the horse foundered and I had to walk some of the way.'

Gwenhwyvar opened her mouth to make a reply, but her gaze slid past Bedwyr to the others standing behind him: Rhys, Bors and Cador, looking repentant and stubborn at the same time, with their arms folded defiantly over their chests.

'I could not get the ship without them knowing,' Bedwyr explained, 'so I brought them with me.'

'All respect to the Emrys' wishes,' put in Cador, 'but we would in nowise be left behind.'

'I see,' replied Gwenhwyvar. 'Since that is the way of it, I grant you leave to accompany me — in pledge for your silence.'

'That you shall have,' said Bors, 'and gladly.'

'Swear it on your fealty to Arthur,' the queen said.

'Lady,' protested Cador, 'have we lived so long in Arthur's service that we must be treated this way?'

'Swear it!' the queen demanded. 'Or I will put you over the side myself.'

The three swore as the queen directed, and she gave the order to sail. Bors, who had spent fully as much time aboard the heaving deck of a ship as astride a galloping horse, acted as pilot. But since he had never been to Ynys Avallon, I stood with him to guide him as best I could from my memory of previous voyages.

The day was clear, the sea-wind strong. We fairly flew over the water like the gulls that soared above our mast. And it seemed that the dun-coloured cliffs of Rheged had just fallen away behind us when I saw the faint blue smudge of the island on the horizon away to the south-west. 'There it is!' I cried. 'That is Ynys Avallon.'

Bors adjusted his course and steered for it. I settled in the bow and fell asleep listening to the slap of the waves against the hull. I awoke some time later, thinking to see the isle directly ahead. Instead, I saw nothing but a grey sky and grey sea all around.

My shipmates were all asleep, save for Bors, so I crept back to sit with him at the tiller. 'Where is it?' I asked, sliding onto the bench beside him.

He pointed ahead. 'Rain is blowing in from the east and it has come over misty. But the island is just before us, never fear.'

It was true. The island was before us, though I could not see it. That is the peculiar nature of the isle — which is why the men of Ierne consider it an Otherworldly island: it appears and disappears, seemingly at will.

But Bors proved a good pilot and we reached Avallon after midday. 'Where is the best place to put to shore?' he asked, scanning what we could see of the coastline through the mist.

'We must go round the southern point to the western side,' I told him. 'The harbour is not so good there, but Avallach's palace is on that side. That is where Myrddin has taken Arthur to be healed.'

So we made our way round the southern end of the island and round to the western side. It was difficult in the mist, but the queen helped, for she had visited the island and remembered where to look for rocks below the surface, and where to find harbourage.

Nevertheless, it was late when we finally came into the harbour and drew in beside the boat Barinthus had used. We made landfall and tied our boat beside Barinthus' vessel, and gathered on the red rock shingle below Avallach's towered stronghold. We looked up at the cliffs rising before us, their soaring tops lost in the mist above. 'They will not have seen us coming,' Bedwyr said. 'You had better lead us, Aneirin.'

I turned to the queen, but Gwenhwyvar said, 'Go ahead, Aneirin. You know the way better than anyone here.'

I did as I was bade, and found the winding, rock-cut steps that led to the palace. They were wet with mist and slippery, which made the going slow.

By the time I reached the top, I could scarce make out the

contour of the ground before me as it rose slightly before fading into the grey obscurity of shifting cloud. I walked a few paces forward over the curled, wet grass to the path leading to Avallach's fortress, feeling all the while as if I had crossed one of those invisible boundaries and entered the Otherworld. For, even as my foot touched the path, the mist grew luminous and bright, all gold and glittering, shining with the westering sunlight through it.

The sudden brilliance dazzled my eyes for a moment, I admit. But only that. Even so, mist or no mist, I know we would have seen the Fisher King's palace if it had been there.

But it was gone. Neither tower, nor wall, nor gate, nor hall remained. There was nothing left at all.

TWELVE

A grave for Constantine; a grave for Aurelius; a grave for Uther. All the world's wonder, no grave for Arthur!

I know neither the how, nor the where, nor the why. I only know what is: the palace of the Fisher King was gone and Arthur with it. The mist parted and we saw only the flat expanse of grass and the trees beyond. The smooth white towers, the high-peaked hall, the stout gate and wall — not a stone or straw remained. I had slept beneath that roof! I had eaten food from that board! Like a dream passing from memory upon waking, all had vanished out of the world of men.

We stood blinking in strong sunlight as the mist dissolved and knew ourselves to be witness to a miracle. Loath to believe it, we said foolish things.

'A sea wave has carried them off!' said Cador. Yet there was no storm, and Barinthus' boat was still tied in the bay.

'Sea Wolves!' cried Bors. 'Barbarians have attacked them!' Even the barbarians have not so mastered the art of destruction as to leave neither smoke nor ash where they have plundered.

We said other things and began at once laying plans to search the island and surrounding sea for any sign of them. Even as we began our search, we knew — each of us, in our deepest hearts, *knew* — the sharp spear-thrust of despair: all our effort would avail nothing.

Still, we searched. A fire is not more consuming than our scouring of Avallon. The rain is not more penetrating than our plying of the sea round about the island. For many days, and yet more days, we searched both land and sea. Gwenhwyvar sent Bors to bring the Cymbrogi to ride from one end of the isle to the other, and assembled most of

Arthur's fleet to sweep the sea from Caer Lial to Ierne, and from Môn to Rheged.

While we searched, we prayed. Gwenhwyvar sent for the renowned Illtyd and many of his followers to join with the brothers there on Avallon and pray unceasingly. And ever while there was a boat or rider yet searching for Arthur and the Emrys, the holy men besieged the throne of the Most High God with their prayers.

In the end, we found what we knew we would find all along.

Winter gales rising in the sea-paths, snow and rain blowing in, the sky a darkling slate, the world growing colder — the queen had but little choice. Sadly, Gwenhwyvar commanded the searching to end. With tears in her eyes, she ordered the ships and Cymbrogi back to Caer Lial, where she attempted to begin her rule alone. But word of Arthur's disappearance had spread far and wide throughout Britain, and the people cowered in fear.

'Arthur is gone!' they wailed to one another. 'What is to become of us?'

'We will be attacked by our enemies! We will be killed!' they cried.

'Woe! Woe and grief! Our life is done!' they said, and lifted their sharp lament.

And the more they said these things the more fear blighted their souls. Gwenhwyvar could do nothing against this. Despite her skill and courage, it was not an enemy she could fight. And the small kings, without Arthur's strong hand upon them to keep them in their places, began raising all the old complaints against her. 'She is Irish! She is not of our kind! She is a barbarian!'

In truth, it came to this: they would in no wise hold a woman sovereign over them.

Oh, she fought valiantly. She was ever more than a match for any adversary. But a monarch cannot rule where there is no faith. The petty kings and lords of Britain set their hearts against Gwenhwyvar and would not be appeased. Of Arthur's subject lords only Bors, Ector, Meurig, Cador and Bedwyr held faith with Gwenhwyvar.

At Eastertide the following spring, Gwenhwyvar gave command of the Cymbrogi to Cador, and returned to the home of her father and kinsmen in Ierne, where she founded a monastery on the coast within sight of Avallon, there to devote her life to prayer and good works among her own people.

Bors, Bedwyr and Rhys, who had served so long with the Pendragon, could not be happy with any lesser lord — even the honourable Cador. They determined among themselves to answer the long neglected challenge of the Grail. They rode off in quest of this most holy vessel, to find it and establish it in the Round Table.

They hoped by this to honour Arthur's dearest wish and, I believe, to restore the quickly fading glory of his exalted reign. For the darkness that Myrddin and Arthur had so long held at bay was, like flood water spilling over an earthen dike, already rushing in to extinguish the feeble glow that yet lingered upon Britain. The last of the renowned Flight of Dragons hoped yet to turn men's hearts from fear, and to crown the passing age with its highest honour.

Alas, they did not succeed. I learned later that of the three only Bedwyr came back alive. Bors and Rhys ended their days in the Holy Land, where it was rumoured that Rhys' head adorned a spear atop the gates of Damascus. Bors, it was said, lived long and died in his bed, surrounded by a wife and five brown children. Bedwyr alone returned to Britain. He became a hermit and took the rotunda for his hermitage. I never saw him again, for he died in that holy precinct soon after.

Cador asked me to join him, but I had had my fill of fighting and longed to lose myself in prayer and study. I travelled with the Cymbrogi as far as Dyfed and found a place at the Abertaff monastery, under the wing of the revered Teilo and his superior, the venerable Illtyd. I sojourned there and learned much to my advantage of holy matters.

In time, a call came to me from the Britons in Armorica. Hopeless in the face of increasing strife among the small kings, good men were abandoning the Island of the Mighty in ever increasing numbers. The exiles asked me to come to them, so I left my cell and took up my work in the church at Rhuys. I stayed there long; married, raised my children in peace and saw them grown. But ever I yearned to see the green hills of Britain once more. I returned and joined the good brothers at the Shrine of the Saviour God at Ynys Avallach, where I endure to this day.

I am an old man, and my heart grows heavy with the weight of grief. Most unhappy of men am I, most untimely born: to have witnessed both the dazzling radiance of the True Light, and the blinding darkness of evil, black and rampant. More fortunate by far are those who lived and died with Arthur, knowing nothing but the world made bright by his presence. Would that I had gone with him in his boat to Avallon!

To serve him in whatever court he now resides is all I wish. My voice would not be silent in his hall, nor would he lack the pleasing sound of heartfelt praise in his ears. I would make of his name a song, of his life a tale fit for the instruction of kings.

I look back on my life from a prominence of some years, and see shining still that golden time when I was young — shining all the more brightly for the gloom. It glows like a polished gem picked out by a single ray of the sun's dying light and fired to wonderful brightness, so that all around it is illumined and charged with splendour.

But the sun passes, as it must. And the gem, still a gem, grows dark once more.

I waited — all my life long I have waited — for some word or sign of Arthur and the Emrys, whether they were dead or living still. In all my journeying I have asked and sought and listened for what I longed to hear. I have grown old in listening!

Of Arthur and his Wise Counsellor never any word or sign came to men. Of Avallach and his daughter Charis, Lady of the Lake, and their people, never more was heard. The Fair Folk and their kind were no more to be found in this worlds-realm; their passing went unmarked and unlamented.

I have laboured long over this through the many years since that first unhappy day. Alas, I am no wiser for all my ardent contemplation!

Perhaps God in his infinite wisdom and mercy simply reached down and gathered that bright company to his loving heart. Perhaps the Lord Jesu in his unceasing compassion looked upon Arthur's suffering and spared him the indignity of death and, like Elijah of old, carried our king bodily into paradise in a golden chariot with wheels of fire.

Or perhaps the last True Bard of Britain hid the beloved Pendragon from mortal eyes with a powerful enchantment, until such time as need calls him forth to battle Britain's enemies once more.

So it is told, and so many believe. I do not say that this shall be so. I will say only that here in this worlds-realm Arthur's life was changed. For Myrddin Emrys was a prophet, and like his father, Taliesin, was a bard aflame with God's own virtue. From his holy *awen* he spoke forth many things, but ever he spoke the truth. And the Wise Emrys said that Arthur would yet come again to lead his own.

EPILOGUE

False Kings! Power-mad dogs dressed in purple robes! Bloody-minded barbarians to a man! We are not sunk so low as to revere your names in song. When you die, as soon you must, there will be no lament, no grave-song, no weeping of heartfelt tears. The eyes of your people will be dry as the dust in your tombs, and your names will decay more swiftly than your disgusting bones!

Would that you had never lived! With both hands, like ignorant children scattering good grain from a sack, you threw away Arthur's peace. You exchanged hard-won freedom for slavery to vice and every corruption. In your greed you have wasted all the land. And what you did not destroy, you gave to the enemy to despoil!

Look at you! You sit with your fat-bellied warbands in your fetid mead halls, drunk in your cups, inflamed with your small treasons. Cattle thieves! Raiding your neighbour lords and men of your own race and blood, worrying one another with unworthy conflicts, warring on your kinsmen and brothers while heathens burn and plunder!

Your legacy is death! The disgust of good men is your renown! The lowly languish; humble make curses of your names. Does this please you? Does it swell your hearts with pride?

Speak to me no longer of great lords. I will hear no more of kings and their lofty affairs. Their concerns are the concerns of the maggot in the dung-heap. I, who have soared with eagles, will not wallow with pigs!

To our everlasting shame, the very barbarians who everywhere supplant us are proving better Christians than the Britons who first taught them the Faith! Their zeal is as sharp as the spears they once raised against us, while that of our kings has grown dull, their hearts cold. Are they to show themselves better men?

Once there was a time, now all but forgotten, when the world knew what it was to be ruled by a righteous lord, when one man of faith held all realms in his strong hand, when the High King of Heaven blessed his High King on Earth.

Britain was exalted then.

Not for the tongues of mortal men is the elegy of the Pendragon. Oh, Arthur, your Matchless Creator alone chants your funeral song, the echo resounding in men's souls to the world's end. In the meantime, the knife of great longing pierces the heart. The High King of Heaven has left the nation without a roof.

Woe and grief! The ruin of Britain! For the wickedness of men endures to the end of the age! To the day of doom and judgement the plagues of iniquity and cruelty and strife beat us down! Evil thrives, good is forgotten. The usurper sits on the righteous lord's throne. The unjust man becomes judge. The liar dispenses truth. That is the way of the world. So be it!

My black book is ended. I, Gildas, write this, and I will write no more.

Other novels by Stephen Lawhead
published as Lion paperbacks

THE DRAGON KING TRILOGY
1984 C.S Lewis Medal Honor Books

Book 1: In the Hall of the Dragon King

Quentin, a young acolyte serving in the temple of Ariel, is thrust into the centre of a conflict in which the life of the king and the future of the realm of Mensandor hang in the balance. Drawn into the web of intrigue spawned by the Necromancer Nimrood, Quentin, with the aid of friends loyal to the Dragon King, embarks on a dangerous quest.

ISBN 0 85648 859 3

Book 2: The Warlords of Nin

Mensandor is once more in desperate straits. The Wolf Star grows nightly greater and more threatening as the power of Nin increases and black terror reigns. It is Quentin, once again, who holds the kingdom's destiny in his hands. Hope lies in the forging of a sword – Zhaligkeer, the Shining One. But the secret source of lanathil, the living metal from which it must be made, is long since lost.

ISBN 0 85648 874 7

Book 3: The Sword and the Flame

Quentin now reigns as the Dragon King, and is faced with the bitterest onslaught of all – the insidious attack of evil from within himself. As a young acolyte in the temple of Ariel he set out gladly on a journey which was to take him away from the old gods to a life-giving encounter with the Most High. Now it is not simply his own life, or the kingdom, which hangs in the balance. Nimrood holds Quentin's son hostage. The Dragon King has lost his sword – Zhaligkeer, the Shining One – and he has lost his way. Will he also betray his vow to the Most High?

ISBN 0 85648 875 5

THE PENDRAGON CYCLE
Book 1: Taliesin

'I will weep no more for the lost, asleep in their water graves. The voices of the departed speak: Tell our story, they say. It is worthy to be told. And so I take my pen and write . . .'

So begins the tragedy of lost Atlantis, extinguished for ever in a hideous paroxysm of earth and sea. Out of the holocaust, three crippled ships emerge to bear King Avallach and his daughter to the cloud-bound isle of Ynys Prydein.

Here is another world, where Celtic chieftains struggle for survival in the twilight of Rome's power. One heroic figure towers over all, the Prince Taliesin, in whom is the sum of human greatness — grandeur and grace, meekness and majesty, beauty and truth.

This is a tale that spans two worlds, a vision that sings in the heart, and a love that creates the miracle of Merlin . . . Arthur . . . and a destiny that is more than a kingdom.

ISBN 0 7459 1309 1

THE PENDRAGON CYCLE
Book 2: Merlin

'Was there ever a time such as this? Never! And that is both the glory and the terror of it. If men knew what it was that loomed before them . . . they would stop their mouths with their cloaks for screaming. It is their blessing and their curse that they do not know. But I know; I, Merlin, have always known . . .'
This is Merlin's story, the story of the Island of the Mighty — of warring battlechiefs and bloody Saecsen invaders, of the hidden Hill Folk and the waning power of Rome.

It is Merlin's story as none but he could tell it — a tale of love and savagery and madness. An all-consuming vision — of the glorious Kingdom of Summer . . . of treachery and death . . . of the saving of a babe new-born, and a sword in a stone . . .

ISBN 0 7459 1310 5

EMPYRION
An epic SF fantasy

Stephen Lawhead

Sent on special assignment to the new colony of
Empyrion, ten light-years from Earth, Orion Treet
and his two companions find themselves enmeshed in
deadly conflict between two civilizations dramatically
opposed.

Can the free and perfect world of Fierra escape
annihilation? Treet, with a handful of rebels, stands
alone against the evil might of Dome, as events move
inexorably towards a world-shaking climax.

ISBN 0 7459 1872 7

SONG OF ALBION
Stephen Lawhead

A new cycle, mining the rich vein of Celtic mythology

Book 1: The Paradise War

Wolves prowling the streets of Oxford, a Green Man haunting the Highlands ... Lewis Gillies is face to face with an ancient mystery. The road north leads to a mystical crossroads, and he finds himself in a place where two worlds meet, in the time-between-times. This world and the Otherworld are delicately interwoven, each dependent on the other. But a breach has opened between the worlds—and cosmic catastrophe threatens.

ISBN 0 7459 2242 2 ('C' format)
ISBN 0 7459 2466 2 ('A' format)

Book 2: The Silver Hand

The great king, Meldryn Mawr, is dead and his kingdom lies in ruins. Treachery and brutality stalk the Otherworld kingdom of Prydain. Prince Meldron, prompted by the cunning and grasping Siawn Hy, now claims the throne. But the bard Tegid Tathal chooses another—and the Day of Strife begins. Kingship and sovereignty, passion and power, heartbreak and hope lie at the heart of this story. The fate of Albion and the destiny of the long-awaited Champion, Silver Hand, are inextricably interwoven.

ISBN 0 7459 2245 7 ('C' format)
ISBN 0 7459 2510 3 ('A' format)

Book 3: The Endless Knot

Fire rages in Albion: a strange, hidden fire, dark-flamed, invisible to the eye. Seething and churning, it burns, gathering flames of darkness into its hot black heart. Unseen and unknown, it burns ...

Llew Silver Hand is High King of Albion and the Brazen Man has defied his sovereignty. Llew must journey into the Foul Land to redeem his greatest treasure. The last battle begins.

ISBN 0 7459 2240 6 ('C' format)
ISBN 0 7459 2783 1 ('A' format)